Praise for [barcode: T0029021]

'Unsettling and thought-provoking.
Fflur Dafydd has a unique voice'
Clare Mackintosh, *Sunday Times* bestselling author of
The Last Party

'A testament to the power of the written word'
The Times

'An entrancing literary thriller; elegant and compelling. At the heart
of a society that is spinning disturbingly off course, Dafydd's grand
library guards the darkest of secrets. Step inside if you dare'
Emma Rous, author of *The Au Pair*

'A gruesome revenge comedy set in the National Library of
Wales [with a] final wonderful denouement'
The Tablet

'A fantastic thriller. The premise, the characters, the writing
style – all absolutely perfect! A book I wished I had yet to read
upon completion'
Yrsa Sigurdardottir, author of *The Fallout*

'One of the most original plots I have read ...
So beautifully written'
Belfast Telegraph

'Sassy, smart and suitably bookish ... A novel which excels in the
tension-ramping department'
Nation Cymru

Fflur Dafydd is an award-winning novelist, singer-songwriter and screenwriter who writes in Welsh and English. She is a graduate of UEA's Creative Writing MA, a former Hay Festival International Fellow and an alumna of Iowa University's prestigious International Writing Program. She has also been nominated for several BAFTA Cymru awards for her screenwriting work. She lives in West Wales with her husband and two daughters.

Fflur Dafydd

The Library Suicides

HODDER

First published in Great Britain in 2023 by Hodder & Stoughton
An Hachette UK company

This paperback edition published in 2023

1

Copyright © Fflur Dafydd 2023

The right of Fflur Dafydd to be identified as the Author of the Work has
been asserted by her in accordance with the Copyright, Designs and
Patents Act 1988.

Extract on p. vii from Joseph Brodsky, 'In a Room and a Half', *Less Than One*
(Farrar, Straus & Giroux, 1986)

Extract on p. vii from Waldo Williams 'Cofio', *Dail Pren* (Gwasg Aberystwyth,
1956). Translation by Menna Elfyn, 2022.

All rights reserved. No part of this publication may be reproduced, stored in a
retrieval system, or transmitted, in any form or by any means without the prior
written permission of the publisher, nor be otherwise circulated in any form of
binding or cover other than that in which it is published and without a similar
condition being imposed on the subsequent purchaser.

All characters in this publication are fictitious and any resemblance to real
persons, living or dead, is purely coincidental.

A CIP catalogue record for this title is available from the British Library

Paperback ISBN 978 1 399 71110 4

Typeset in Sabon MT by Manipal Technologies Limited

Printed and bound in Great Britain by Clays Ltd, Elcograf S.p.A.

Hodder & Stoughton policy is to use papers that are natural, renewable
and recyclable products and made from wood grown in sustainable forests.
The logging and manufacturing processes are expected to conform to the
environmental regulations of the country of origin.

Hodder & Stoughton Ltd
Carmelite House
50 Victoria Embankment
London EC4Y 0DZ

www.hodder.co.uk

In loving memory of Siân Elfyn Jones

Just like the foam that breaks on lonely beaches
And the wind's aria with no one there to hear,
I know they call in vain on us to listen,
The old forgotten things we loved so dear.

Waldo Williams, trans. Menna Elfyn

More than anything, memory resembles a library in alphabetical disorder, and with no collected works by anyone.

Joseph Brodsky

Ana and Nan

9PM

The twins always saw themselves in the seagulls, even as children. Their feathered doppelgängers would come and sit on the bathroom ledge every evening and stare in at them as they had their bath, watching them with their curious pink-rimmed eyes. There would be a flash of recognition between both parties. Something vermin-like, something poisonous, would pass between them. Rats with wings, their mother would shout, before shooing them away. But the birds always came back; unlike their mother, who – six months ago – wasn't able to navigate her own drop from the ledge with quite the same ease.

There was a strange comfort in it now for Ana and Nan; to have the seagulls there during their bathing ritual, those webbed feet padding confidently across the cramped space where their mother had once stood. The twins watched these rolling resurrections with fascination, gazing at their feathered aggressors jostling each other, pushing each other off, with each ousted bird returning seconds later as though the fall meant nothing.

Ana and Nan could see the gulls trying to decipher – with every twist of their ugly, slanting heads – why two identical women would sit opposite each other in the bath every evening, conjuring stiff white peaks from their fingers until the suds obscured each one's view of the other. The shape afloat on the water was a replica of that building on the hill where the twins worked. They saw themselves as architects of foam, carving out from the amorphous mass the contours of a library in miniature – weaving windows from the fine white webs, moulding scented stacks and stairwells, their fists firming up each angle, their fingernails scraping away space for reading rooms and archives, all the while ensuring the egg-white roof was sturdy enough not to collapse on top of it all, and wash away their efforts.

What the gulls could not see was that this was more than mere bath play. Tonight, Ana and Nan were preparing themselves for the day that was nearly upon them, a day when they would take charge of the library, and expose its delusions of grandeur, of safety, for the soap-mirage it always was.

'When do you think we'll next have a bath?' Nan asked, as she straightened her right palm in order to forge a lower level into the structure, a squeaking subterranean corridor, the concrete version of which they would soon enter.

Ana knew what Nan was really saying was: *There will be no baths in prison. None of this intimacy, none of this togetherness. No more of each other.*

'Could be years, I suppose,' said Ana, wiping sweat from her cheek. 'A small sacrifice,' she added, taking her fingers for a leisurely stroll around the back of the building, imagining herself entering there as they had planned, Nan around the front. She used her left thumb to smooth out another step, then her right pinkie to make an outline of the doorframe.

'I know you're thinking about Mum,' Ana said, moving a little too suddenly so that her left breast bulldozed away half the North Reading Room. 'Wondering what she'd make of all this, aren't you?'

Nan sunk lower into the foam, kicking the library basement away with her toes, her hair morphing into a dark overgrowth on the library's roof. The structure was crumbling now; the suds having become limp and shapeless, even the gulls no longer interested. Nan hated the way Ana insisted she could read her mind, as if Nan's brain were a vacant room through which Ana was free to roam as she liked, opening and shutting doors, ransacking through cupboards, running her fingers over everything. Nan could never read Ana's mind; the doors were always shut, the windows dark.

'Yes, I suppose I am,' Nan lied, relieved that if nothing else, she owned her own mind.

'I think she'd approve, you know. Of all this. It's what she would have wanted. I don't think we need to be scared.'

Nan was not scared. If anything she was excited. Whatever happened, however things eventually played out, it would be the end of something. The start of another.

'If we just stick to the plan,' Ana continued, 'we'll be fine. Nothing's going to go wrong.'

Everything would go wrong, Nan thought. And this is how she knew her sister couldn't really read her mind. Because her sister still believed that Nan would carry things out in exactly the way they'd planned, when Nan had no intention of doing so – she was going to do things her way, even if it meant a longer sentence; and forgoing her right to a bath forever more. She had long imagined herself with that gun in her hand, taking control of it all; desperate to know how it would feel when she finally got to pull the trigger.

'Whatever we do, we do together,' Ana continued. 'After all we're the same person, you and I, aren't we?'

Ana's foot swam towards her. Nan lifted her own foot and pressed against it. She knew Ana saw this as a moment of unity, but for Nan it was the opposite: a real, physical sign of the boundary between them. Where one thing broke away and became another.

'Ana and Nan. One person. One soul. Palindromes.'

Nan hid her smile in the froth. Ana was obsessed with the fact that their names could be read forward, and backward, that they could formulate no other possible sounds. Ana was convinced that their mother had chosen them so that no one could interfere with

3

their names; that their identities remained strong, unshakeable. Nan didn't see it like that. She saw their names as dull and uninspiring in their plainness; neutral as anything. As a young child she'd always dreamed of having a longer, greater title, something complex, multisyllabic. Something that spoke of revolt. Something like Arianne – a silvery wheel of a name; or Gwenivere – a girl glowing in the dark. Something that enticed yet terrified you.

'Palindrome,' Nan echoed quietly, as she opened her mouth to ingest the rest of the soap ruins.

*

As she tapped on the bath plug to drain the water, Ana saw that the doppelgänger gulls had flown away, leaving in their place a strange, black-headed seagull. She'd seen him several times before, parading the promenade near the flat, squawking at day-trippers, boasting his tar-tipped head. He'd never dared to come and stare at them like this before, either. Ana thought he must know what they were up to, wanted to be a part of it.

'Just ignore him,' Nan said. 'He's desperate for your attention; don't give it to him.'

Ana couldn't resist, somehow. She found herself sneaking a look at him every now and then as Nan finished rinsing the soap out of her hair. It felt like he was mocking them; the way he'd scared off the gentler gulls, just to assert his individualism, his singularity. It was as if he was saying that the sisters' doubleness wasn't right in some way – for there to be no birthmark, no scar, no blemish that set them apart, it was as if he was making out they were the freaks, rather than him. She stood up suddenly, hoping her nakedness would scare him off, but he wouldn't budge.

'Shoo!' she shouted, like her mother had once done. 'Shoo!'

'You've still got a bit of conditioner in there,' Nan said. 'Sit back down.'

'Shoo!' she said again, now determined to get rid of him, her breasts squished up against the window.

Still the black-headed gull refused to budge. He cocked his head; again Ana felt that he was waiting for something, waiting to be consulted about their plans, perhaps.

'OK, well you can sort your own hair out, then,' Nan said, standing up suddenly, hoisting one leg out of the water.

'Help me get rid of him,' Ana pleaded with her, grabbing on to her sister's slick, wet arm.

Nan reached over to open the window wide, knocking the seagull off his perch. It should have been the end of it. But the gull saw the open window as an invitation and glided smoothly past them and into the bathroom. They both went into a blind panic then, the bird flapping and squawking in the air above them as they grappled with him, entangled in one another's nakedness, their fingers sticky with feather and soap, both shrieking, the gull breaking away, fleeing this way and that before suddenly coming to a halt at the bathroom mirror.

It was perhaps the first time the black-headed seagull had seen his own reflection. Perhaps he thought this was the way of things; that in entering the twins' world, this is what happened – everything, everyone doubled. Became a perfect, clear, luminous reflection of each other. He perched there on the side of the sink a while, staring, trying to work things out.

'Grab him,' Nan said quietly, as though the bird might hear their intent. 'Do it now.'

Ana was frozen to the spot. She couldn't take her eyes off him, as he began to peck away at the reflection, disturbed by how easy it was to replicate himself. Nan eventually pushed her out of the way and grabbed him herself, but instead of hurling him back out of the window, she pulled him towards her and forced him down into the diminishing bath water. Ana backed away, watching as he thrashed relentlessly against Nan's hand, knowing somehow that if he held fast the water would soon be gone. But Nan had other plans, swiftly wringing his neck as the last of their soap structure died in the plughole.

'I didn't know you knew how to do that,' Ana said. Her sister was, for this one moment, no longer a twin; suddenly merely herself, just like the black-headed seagull.

'Neither did I,' Nan replied, with a curious calm.

There was a strange smell in the room now, the stench of pavement and death mingled with the perfumed steam coming off their bodies. Nan handed the bird to Ana.

'You can get rid of it,' she said, wrapping herself in a towel and marching out of the room, leaving Ana alone with the executed bird hanging limply from her hand.

Ana almost couldn't bear to touch it, and so she hurled it back out through the open window as fast as she could. She shut the window firmly and leaned her head against it. She tried not to think of the dead bird's ungraceful descent through the air, the final, dirty slap. How it had come in alive, and gone back out dead, all because of them.

A few minutes later, after checking the doors and the lights, Ana returned to their bedroom to find Nan already fast asleep, her back turned away from her. She was disappointed that the evening had ended so abruptly, but she supposed that the incident had exhausted them both, and they would need to conserve their energy to carry out all they had planned, for they had not slept well these last few months. She clambered in next to Nan, shuffling around to see if she could rouse her; but no, she was a dead weight across the mattress. Ana lay down next to her and tried to clear her mind and assume the inertia of a normal person, a person for whom tomorrow was just another working day. But those people were all fools, she thought; because their lives would never be the same. And there would be one fool in particular walking among them along that red carpet. The fool who had brought all this upon them in the first place; the fool who was finally going to get what he deserved.

Before long, she found herself entering the deadening dark that was both her friend and co-conspirator, the only place she could really be alone. Where only one vision awaited her, a vision that recurred all night, just beyond the thin veil of her eyelids; that of the library of soap and feathers evolving, sud by sud, feather by feather, brick by brick, into the National Library up on that hill; a building shining brightly into the darkness, bold and fearless in the face of night, without the faintest idea of what the morning would bring.

Eben

7AM

Eben had decided that today would be the day he would make a start on those daily affirmations his therapist was so keen on. He had attempted, and tried countless times before, of course, but because she had insisted that these affirmations needed to be carried out first thing, he had not been able to face it. The mere thought of having to heave his early morning, blotchy, bloated self over to the mirror in his pants and T-shirt was too much for him. No one in their right mind, he imagined, would consider it an image worth affirming.

Today, however, he knew he had to put those anxieties to one side. It was absolutely paramount that he walked into the National Library with his head held high, convinced of the fact that he belonged there and that he was not doing anything wrong. And in the absence of anyone else around him to affirm his decision – apart from his disinterested cat – it was simply up to him to tell himself that there was nothing sinister in his request to access these materials in the National Library. And that it was a means of atoning for something he knew he hadn't done. A kind of belt-and-braces response to the accusation.

He had been awake for hours, just staring at the Artex swirls on the ceiling, trying to avoid the moment when he would come face to face with his own awfulness. What the therapist simply didn't consider in all this was how much it actually took to get him functioning in the morning in the first place. He had a crick in his neck that needed rectifying before he could do anything else, and so he hauled himself to the bottom of the bed to grab

8

his trusty rolled-up towel, placing it behind his neck and hoisting it up until he felt the familiar clunk of his head sliding back into place. Then he reached for his nasal spray to relieve some of the congestion that had built up overnight, but somehow managed to squirt most of it into his eye, leaving him squealing in pain as he tried to redirect it into his nostrils. The final undertaking in his self-assembly was to choose between his contact lenses and his glasses, a decision made easy by his watering eyes, but he paused before putting them on, as the thought struck him that the therapist hadn't actually specified that he had to take 'a good look at himself' with twenty-twenty vision.

He approached the mirror with caution. In front of him was a blurred image. For all his therapist's smugness, she obviously hadn't foreseen this particular loophole in her self-affirmation nonsense. He now realised he could cope with talking and looking at himself if all he was dealing with was a haze of colours and contours, which could very well have been anyone. Even someone worth affirming. He kicked himself he had not thought of it before, this half-acknowledgement of himself, half-blindly accepting he was enough. 'Perhaps I'm simply a person who *does* do things by halves,' he said to himself, quietly congratulating himself on coming up with this rather original affirmation.

'I feel,' he said out loud now to the blob in the mirror, trying to get used to the sound of his own nasal voice in the dry air of the flat. 'I feel confident in every situation.'

He was suddenly aware of the cat staring at him from the corner of the bathroom, unconvinced.

Eben lowered his shoulders, trying to assume a more authoritative poise.

'I like who I am,' he said, with more conviction this time, although he considered it to be the least true of the many affirmations on his therapist's list.

And finally, at the therapist's request – because he needed to utter a minimum of four, she said – he forced his parched, reticent mouth to deliver the words:

'I am not responsible for the death of Elena Oodig.'

He felt the heat of shame prickling up his neck, imagining a cacophony of other voices echoing across the town, all uttering the affirmations they'd been prescribed by the town's one and only therapist. What power she held, from that battered-looking leather chair of hers, knowing everything about the people in this town, hoarding every little secret they had. Who else did she have telling their reflection that they had not killed anyone? He imagined he was not alone in this; yet at the same time he had felt hopelessly alone in the whole debacle for months. It brought to mind another affirmation he had been asked to try, but quickly disregarded: *Nobody else has my unique skill set*. That, at least, was true. Nobody else had been accused of snuffing out an author on the basis of several scathing attacks in the press; no one else's words had been hailed as a 'hate crime', said to have driven a woman out of a window, out of her mind, and then over a ledge.

Today, however, he hoped to put all that behind him. Or at least to put his unique skill set to good use. It was his interest in her, the therapist had eventually convinced him, that had led to what others erroneously considered to be his *annihilation* of her. He had come around to the idea that he had been simply doing his job; was it not a critic's job to dissect a writer's work, draw those weaknesses to the surface, bring them to the attention of the less observant reader so that they could demand more of their writers in future? Was he not also trying to get Elena's attention by doing so; highlighting that he expected more from her; that, in fact, he knew she was capable of something deeper, better? Had his intent not been to push her to the brink of her own genius, rather than off the ledge of her bathroom window?

He shuddered again at the image, recalling the details of the fall he had read online. How some of her brain had been exposed on the pavement. The frontal cortex – that brilliant place where all her plots had been concocted – rolling right out of her skull, before being descended upon by seagulls.

Stop it, Eben, he told himself, trying to breathe through it and erase those images from his own, still-intact brain. All that mattered right now was that he was, at last, going to be able to read Elena Oodig's diaries. The very first person to get access to them.

He'd sent several requests of course; all of which had initially been denied. Eben eventually realised he needed a project in order to justify his research, and had written a lengthy letter to her daughters to ask for their permission to write Elena's biography; a task he insisted would be near impossible without access to private materials. After a long silence, he'd received confirmation via the library that they were happy to grant permission – and that he alone would be given the exclusive right to undergo the research, with a view to publishing her biography, if her girls approved of his angle. He saw this as an absolution of sorts: it perhaps indicated that her daughters were sensible enough not to hold him responsible for her death, the way others did, and that they, perhaps, saw better than most that there was no one better positioned to write about her than her most involved (not obsessed, as others said) critic.

He took a shower, deciding against a shave for fear of mishaps – under the circumstances it was hardly appropriate to arrive at the library dripping with blood – and then set about putting on his suit. The formal outfit was a departure for him, as he never usually gave any thought to his library attire, but he felt like the occasion demanded it. You had to dress properly if you wanted to be taken seriously as a biographer. A crisp, navy-blue blazer and a mustard-coloured tie to show that you had a modicum of personality, but not too much. No one wanted a biographer to have too much personality, for such a thing could eclipse their subject. But you wanted something for onlookers to latch on to. Your subject was dead after all; you were the only visible link. That's why he chose the mustard colour. And it wasn't the colour of the strong, brash mustard like you'd get in the bigger countries, the kind that would get up your nostrils and make you cry – but a gentler, taste-bud-teasing thing like they still made here in his own country – mixed in with honey.

It was exactly the sort of endorsement he hoped the book would get. *A honey-mustard offering of a biography, sweet and sharp.* He would ask a friend of his, Frankton, to write it. Frankton had made himself an expert on all things literary in this country, despite having no literary credentials of his own. He had fashioned himself into a critic, using the internet to create just the right persona, while he sat in his pants at his laptop eating jam tarts, typing away with little care or consideration for others. He was always open to offers; writers could actually pay him to write a good review and to rubbish their rivals – a great system that a certain group of male writers had benefited from for decades, boosting sales of the most mediocre books. But everyone knew you had to keep him onside. Having someone like Frankton offside simply was not an option. He was a word-filled grenade waiting to go off in your face and his castigations would fly your way like shrapnel, to lodge in your literary reputation forever.

Eben had met Frankton at one of Elena's book launches around a decade ago, where Frankton – his teeth blackened with red wine stains – had grilled him on his thoughts on Elena's work. Having seemingly passed some sort of test he hadn't been aware of, Eben was then invited by Frankton to be part of an underground collective called 'The Smotherhood', a group of reviewers who could snuff out the writers who annoyed them, making sure they were too insecure to write anything ever again. It didn't work with all writers of course. It made the odd one more determined, drove their success even; but there had been some small triumphs. And one great big colossal victory, depending on which way you looked at it.

'I am not responsible for the death of Elena Oodig,' he told himself again in the mirror.

Dan

7.30AM

His first task, every morning, was to complete a circuit of the empty library before the visitors arrived. For Dan, this was one of the rare perks of an otherwise shit job; the thrill of superiority as he took ownership of the vast, valuable emptiness around him. He would parade through the newly polished, deathly silent North and South reading rooms, relishing that they were not yet sullied by their readers' sweat and whisperings; before padding up the luxurious red-carpeted stairs into the main gallery, where he could fool himself, momentarily, that this was his own property, and that all the artworks there had been purposefully chosen by him, to enjoy at his leisure.

But his roleplay only lasted a few minutes before a beep on his security device told him to move on, through the door that linked him to the archives and storage areas, and then on to the basement of the library; the darker side of the institution no one wanted the public to see. From there on, the building that had been so plush and cavernous closed in on you, became a haunting labyrinth, where there was seemingly no order to anything, dead writers' memorabilia stacked in boxes, awaiting to be allocated a place, yellowing manuscripts lying like corpses on top of each other on dusty shelves, and the paintings no one knew what to do with scattered haphazardly behind filing cabinets, the eerie eyes of historical figures looking accusingly at you as you sauntered through in the dark. This part of the library, Dan thought, seemed to resemble the bowels of a ship; and those on its spacious, clean, orderly deck had no idea of the mechanics of it, of what it took for a place like this to function.

And that's where he came in. It still surprised him that they trusted him to be the only one alone in the building first thing in the morning like this, just as they trusted Glyn, the rather paunchy porter who was so partial to a kebab delivery, to complete the night shift alone before him. There had been a time when they'd needed two porters to be on duty at all times in order to make sure the other one didn't simply doze through a night's duties; but with the recent cuts, and the advancement of the new wireless porter-cams – which tracked each porter's movement throughout his shift – the building was now deemed safer than it had ever been. The porter-cams, clipped to each porter's belt, meant that others could stream their live actions, seeing what each porter saw in front of them as they went about their rounds. As well as watching them, the management team could also listen and hear everything they said through the microphone located in the device, making sure each porter had to watch his mouth, even when he was alone. Even if Dan managed to slip out of view of the CCTV for a while, that noose around his waist meant he was never truly free, and might as well still be in prison. It was perhaps the arch-porter's smugness about this new foolproof wireless security that had driven Dan to start exploring the configurations in the programme, determined to find some loophole in the technology, to see if there was a way he could somehow reconfigure the dismal present he found himself in.

Before embarking on the circuit around the building and taking over from another porter, the security handbook noted – rule 45 – that all porters should be briefed on the events of the previous shift, even if there was little to report.

'All right, Glyn?' Dan said, plonking himself down next to him in front of the CCTV screens. 'Busy night last night?'

'Seagull impaled itself on the flagstaff,' Glyn replied, pointing to the screen on the far right, showing footage of the library's roof. 'Hell of a mess up there – I didn't notice it until around seven thirty, so I thought I'd leave it to you to clean up, otherwise I'd be doing overtime.'

'Oh, and we couldn't have that, could we, Glyn?' Dan replied, trying to make out how much of the mess in question could be seen on the grainy footage, zooming in on a burst of feathers and blood clinging stubbornly to the metal pole. It was probably a two-minute job, Dan thought, if that.

'Anything else I should know?'

'Don't think so, no,' Glyn said, heaving himself up off the chair, belly flopping over the rim of his trousers. He then flung the security contraption at Dan, whipped up his coat and left without saying goodbye, leaving a waft of body odour in his wake.

Dan got up and scanned the security device against the strip of metal to clock in for his shift, activating the locking and unlocking function on the device via his staff ID. It was one thing Dan still couldn't get his head around, how there were no more keys, now, because they were seen as hoarders of bacteria, a complete health hazard. Dan missed the jangling of a good set of keys in his hand, the cold coupling of steel and skin. He had liked the sound as you hoisted them out of your pocket when you approached a door; the way the jangle of keys announced an arrival. Certainly in prison it had been a symphony of sorts; it signalled your warden was coming to release you, to give you some much-needed time outside; it signalled movement, change, anything but the awful humdrum of his cell. This silent contraption made from antibacterial plastic that the porters were asked to hand over to each other just didn't have the same effect. It reminded Dan, with its single white stripe across its black plastic head, of those nuns who'd visited the prisoners when no one else would – and of that one sister in particular who had advised him that the best way to secure an early prison release was to volunteer for the library's security training while he was still inside.

'People who show an interest in libraries are usually good people,' she'd said, looking up at him with her kind, unassuming eyes. Dan had turned away, then, suddenly emotional with the idea that someone could think him capable of being a good person. She knew what he'd done; and he was grateful that she had kept coming to visit him in spite of it, so much so that he'd agreed to apply for the library scheme.

Not that he'd ever seen her again, either, after that day, but he honoured the memory of her by referring to his security device as *the nun* or *the sister*, though the term had not particularly caught on with the other porters, who mainly referred to it as 'the whatsit'. Then again, he supposed that none of the other porters equated nuns with freedom, or even knew what it was to lose your freedom in the first place. Most of them, he'd deduced, came to work here because it seemed the most piss-easy of jobs in this dead-end seaside town; so much easier than being a bouncer in one of the seafront casinos or amusement arcades. All it was, they said, was parading back and forth in empty rooms checking the old books were still where you'd left them and that paintings were still fixed to the wall. What could be easier than that?

He attached his porter-cam to his belt, and started on his hour-long journey round the building, gliding through the stacks, the basement, the gallery, on autopilot, aligning the nun contraption with each metallic strip as he moved through. He wondered whether that nun in prison had in fact known exactly what she was doing by suggesting he should come and work at the library. It was freedom, and yet it was not, because so much of what happened here reminded him of his time inside. He was fed at regular intervals. He was instructed to walk up and down the same old strip of corridor. He was generally treated coldly and apathetically by those around him, spending his days staring up at windows that were too high to see out of, wishing he could be somewhere else.

Perhaps it had indeed been a joke of sorts, on her part, perhaps she had even foreseen that the nun in his hand would be a constant reminder of what she had tricked him into. Which was that a library was in fact a different kind of incarceration, and it meant being locked into a building with people who were more irritating than your cellmates.

His least favourite part of the circuit was the library's attic. Not only did the floor feel a little unsteady, like it was ready to collapse underneath him at any moment, but there was no light in there, and a certain row of portrait busts always freaked him out as he illuminated them with his torch, a grotesque cast of four heads – a former prime minister with a commanding moustache, a playwright with a smile like a scrunched-up balloon, a dismal-looking historian and a smug-faced female poet – they all seemed to form a certain opinion on him as he shuffled quickly past their ghastly beheaded selves.

He never stopped to look at any of their names, but he did stop now to notice an absence where one of the heads had been, where a record card noted that the head had been moved to an archive in the basement, the archive of a novelist by the name of Elena Oodig. He only remembered her name because the arch-porter had asked him to move it a few months ago, after the writer's death, in order to start compiling an archive for her in the basement. He had found the whole thing rather eerie as he'd placed her portrait bust on his trolley, and felt a huge responsibility as he trundled along with it, afraid that he would somehow end up smashing it to pieces and kill the poor writer all over again.

Having finished his rounds, he returned to the porter station and sat down at the CCTV screens in front of him. Some of the early-bird staff were arriving in the car park: the cleaners, the kitchen staff, those archivists who worked on God-knows-what in the corners of the archives, their heads obscured by stacks of fragile-looking manuscripts no one else was allowed to touch. He spotted the arch-porter, with a couple of minion porters trailing behind him, heading towards the car park. Today, the arch-porter was taking a group of porters down to the city, for some specialist security training. As all the porters were now being trained to double up as security guards, they needed to be vetted by government officials and the arch-porter had deemed it a good opportunity to give a presentation to the government on the superiority of their security protocols, and their first-of-its-kind porter-cam, which captured much more detail than your average CCTV footage, which he claimed made the library the most secure building in the whole country.

There was talk of a terrorist attack on the smaller countries, the arch-porter said, now that all the big ones had been hit over and over. But Dan couldn't actually believe it would be coming their way. Not in this end-of-the-line seaside town, with its one remaining national institution on top of a hill. A library wasn't a target, no matter how much they went on about it. Nothing exciting or dangerous ever happened here. It was a dull void, in which he was condemned to guarding nothing but space, in truth.

Luckily, the arch-porter had cherry-picked the ones he wanted to be vetted first, which did not include Dan. The excuse for leaving him behind was that, being a decade younger than most of them, he was *au fait* with the technology; and he could be responsible for linking them up to the central system and his own porter-cam, and making sure their presentation went off without a hitch. Dan knew that the real reason he wasn't being selected for the training was because of his criminal background, with the arch-porter constantly reminding him how lucky he was to be here in the first place. He hadn't given a shit about it either way. For him, the city was just the place he had spent most of his life up until now, and he could do without having to drive past that prison wall and be reminded of all the time he had spent on the other side of it.

The arch-porter's plan was to present the library's new security features via CCTV from the government buildings as part of the presentation. He wanted to zoom into an ordinary day in the library's existence in order to show the running of the place, but also to boast about the careful, watchful eye of the porter-cam – and to be able to access the audio so they could hear every word Dan said that day. Despite the fact he was being left behind, the arch-porter emphasised that Dan's role would be crucial, and that it was his opportunity to star in his own show as the exemplary porter, who would be shown to be doing his rounds, helping library goers, assisting with the day-to-day function of the library. It could even lead to an increase in duties; a reduction in probation, both criminal and professional.

'You'll be your best self,' the arch-porter had said. 'It'll be a good opportunity for you. Make sure you take advantage of it, prove yourself.'

Dan had smiled back at him, knowing full well how he'd take advantage of it and how he would prove himself.

He moved now towards the CCTV screens in front of him and zoomed in on the poor sucker porters heading one by one into the white van that featured both the library and the government's logos. Dan noticed the self-important way in which the arch-porter carried himself: his head thrown back to emphasise his lack of tie; his new, crisp corporate shirt and blazer ruffling uncomfortably around his blubber. He remembered overhearing a student saying that this is what happened when a country like this finally formed its own government (or at least when the neighbouring country pretended to let them do so without quite cutting the apron strings); the funniest people were put in positions of power. People the neighbouring country's government had approved; because they knew they would probably mess it up. It wouldn't be long, Dan thought, before the likes of Glyn started walking around in that way, those who had sleepwalked into an easy job only to be given a tie and turn into megalomaniacs overnight.

Next came the head librarian – a woman rarely seen in the library's public areas. He didn't think he had ever even seen her in the flesh; he had only perused her from the CCTV, her mass of hair swept beautifully into a chignon at the nape of her neck, resting on her posture-perfect shoulders, above a red blazer.

The arch-porter shuffled out of the van to open the door for her, and soon she was obscured from view behind the van doors.

'We'll be watching you, Matthews!' he shouted at the camera. 'Don't you forget that, OK? Now link those cameras the second we leave, do you hear me? The rest of them will be watching your every move in the back of the van on their tablets.'

Dan smirked at the thought of what the porters in question would be watching and hearing on their tablets. It would not be him. Not really.

He waited for the van to leave and then reset the CCTV screens, linking up his porter-cam to the pre-recorded footage he'd manipulated into the system. What they would be watching would indeed be the best version of himself that he could be – a version he'd had such fun assembling over the last few weeks, a version that actually cared about doing the right thing.

The arch-porter had wanted him to be his best self, after all, for the camera. He'd said nothing about following that principle through in real life.

Ana and Nan

8.30AM

As they got dressed, Ana noticed a mark on Nan's back: a bruise, past the best of its purple, on the verge of being reabsorbed into her skin. Still, it was there. It demanded to be seen. She wanted to ask her sister what it was, but it would be too much like admitting that she couldn't actually feel every single thing her sister did. All too soon, the mark was shrouded by Nan's red blouse, making Ana wonder if she'd really seen anything at all.

Ana faced the mirror. Nan stood beside her. She knew it was impossible for either one of them to look in the large bedroom mirror without recalling the countless times their mother had done the same, twirling her flamboyant dresses in the mirror's depths, admiring herself before a reading. 'Giving birth to twins was inevitable,' she'd said in one of her last lucid interviews. 'There isn't a part of me that hasn't, at some point, split in two, wanting to become more than one thing.'

They had agreed to wear exactly the same outfit. It would make everything easier. Red blouse, grey pencil skirt, black shoes. It was something they often did anyway, apart from that one time when Nan went rogue last winter – her green-coat phase – when she had dared to be different. Ana knew it wasn't in them to be different. She had shoved that green coat into the back of one of the tour buses visiting the library, then returned to the office to find Nan frantically searching for it. As her sister rummaged around, Ana had calmly watched from the office window, as the bus zigzagged through the streets of the town, on its way back to the capital city, taking with it every notion of separation, of difference. From that day on, Nan was once more consigned to her black raincoat, and balance was restored: they were once again impossible to distinguish from one another.

Ana was surprised that she, too, had felt the urge to stand out surfacing in herself recently – from the first day she'd started speaking to Dan, a purposeful manoeuvre in the reading room that had been carefully timed to come straight after Nan's first meeting with him in the basement stacks the previous day. They took it in turns, every other day after that, to build on the relationship and continue to engage his interest. They had chosen him specifically because he was the newest recruit – only a month into his placement – and he didn't yet know that there were two of them; yet every now and then, when Ana was in his company, she was tempted to say something to make him understand that she was not the same girl he had spoken to yesterday. But she knew that doing so would derail all their hard work.

They had studied him closely for weeks since his arrival: he had no confidants, spoke to no one except the odd student here and there, and was stoned most of the time. He was the only one, they surmised, out of around two hundred staff members, who took absolutely no interest in the institution whatsoever and was biding his time (around six more weeks), before his probation period was over; after which, they'd imagined he would probably reoffend.

He was the perfect ally for their plan, primarily because he wouldn't even realise he was one. And he would make today, which was already a quiet day with most of the security staff away, and only limited access granted to most parts of the library, so much easier for them.

They were ready. Ready for the very thing they'd been planning for months. The red blouses buttoned up, the grey pencil skirts just tight enough around their waists, their ginger, poker-straight bobs placed like armour above their angular chins. They had purchased two silk white, designer scarves for the occasion too, remembering that their mother's villains always had a lavish, signature accessory. The garment felt outlandish against their pale skin, but both agreed that, if nothing else, the material would serve to hide the throb of panic in their thin necks.

Ana caught their reflection again in the mirror. She was hoping to see worldly, professional criminals but, instead, the mirror captured two plain, twenty-seven-year-old women who had never even been touched by a man – not properly, anyway. She had been so close with Dan – so, so close to experiencing all those things she'd heard her colleagues whispering about over the years. But she had to push the thought away, just as she'd done with his hand when he dared to go there. Dan was part of the plan, and their dalliance with him came with its own set of rules. They were not meant to go too far. 'If he gets what he wants, too soon,' Nan had told her, 'he's not going to be willing to help us. And you remember what Mum always said: "No good will come from the love of a man." She was never that weak, was she?'

Ana had believed those words when she'd first heard them, but things had changed since then. Dan expected something from her now – he expected it soon – and Ana had been terrifyingly close to letting it happen. Perhaps it was a good thing, she thought, that whatever frisson had been stirred up between them was punctuated by his run-ins with Nan, who would be far more capable of cooling the whole thing down.

An image flashed across her mind, of Dan's hands roaming her body. Images like these occurred to her more than she would like, far more than they should. Even thinking such things seemed like a betrayal, and so she closed her eyes and willed it all away. She was the eldest, by a mere twelve minutes, and was meant to lead by example. They had come so far now; they had prepared so thoroughly. They could not afford to be distracted. But she could not shake the image, which soon became more potent in her mind and sent uncomfortable sensations zinging through her body.

She opened her eyes and met her sister's gaze at the far end of the mirror. For a fleeting moment, she imagined her sister saw the image of Dan there, playing on a loop on the screen of Ana's mind. There he was, pummelling away at her, ripping her blouse open, using her scarf to tie her hands above her head. And yet there didn't seem to be condemnation in Nan's eyes. Almost a softness, a concession of sorts, a feeling that Ana was permitted to think these things. To entertain notions of other lives they could live, other futures that could open up ahead of them.

As long as she knew that it was fruitless; that they would never happen.

As they opened the front door and stepped out, Ana half expected to see crowds thronging outside, shouting abuse at them for what they were about to do. But outside the world was completely still and ordinary, like any other day. No one seemed to be watching them – no one except for the seagulls on the seafront, their caws and squalls sounding above. A small congregation of gulls were encircling something on the pavement as they walked past. Ana assumed they were competing over yet another breakfast bagel they'd managed to wrestle from a tourist's hands but saw that the morning's offering was in fact the body of the black-headed seagull, which was being dismembered expertly by its feathered comrades.

'We can't let them do that . . .' Ana said.

'Yes we can,' her sister said. 'Just leave them to it.'

'But they shouldn't be eating each other, surely,' Ana said, not able to take her eyes off the spectacle of the black-headed seagull's right wing being devoured by another gull, its jutting contours passing down its bulbous, feathered neck.

'Shoo!' Ana screamed at them, but to no avail. They would not be distracted. She was no longer a threat to them. 'Nan, stop them . . . They can't do that, it's . . .'

'It's just how things are now,' Nan said. 'The seawater's too hot for them, the plankton and the fish they used to feed on are mostly gone. What choice have they got?'

'I should at least move it . . .' Ana began.

'We haven't got time,' Nan said, more firmly now, grabbing her sister's hand and pulling her away from the carnage.

*

Nan had always been made to feel like the lesser twin. Ana had twelve minutes on her – twelve minutes she'd clung on to desperately throughout her life, as though those twelve minutes entitled her to some kind of superior power. It was nonsense, of course. Nan had seen the footage of their birth. All Ana had done in those extra twelve minutes, streaked in a viscous white substance and blood, was wail inconsolably in the arms of a midwife. It was a wail of devastation; the sudden realisation that there was more in existence than merely herself and her sister, that they would have to let other people be a part of all this. Still, Ana upheld the dictum that it was necessary for her to be twelve minutes ahead in everything.

Birthdays were a long, drawn-out affair; partygoers had to wait twelve exact minutes between the first round of happy birthdays and the second. For a brief time, Ana had insisted Nan needed to go to bed twelve minutes ahead of her. Nan would set the alarm clock twelve minutes past the hour and sit there at the top of the stairs like an effigy of her sister, hair pulled over her face, fists clenched in her pyjama sleeves, the alarm sounding as Ana came up the stairs.

It was time to leave now. Everything was ready. All as it should be. But despite the fact they'd gone over everything countless times, and that every mistake or possible fallout had been accounted for, rehearsed, dealt with, Nan knew she could never account for what tricks her mind would play on her as they went about their business. Things had been getting worse recently. Occasionally, when Ana talked about the plan she'd think: *What plan?* And it was as simple as that: the whole reason for doing what they were doing would be erased from her mind, only to return slowly, minutes later. But she never let on. She couldn't.

Ana referred to it as 'the twelve-minute delay', laughing it off, considering it to be nothing more than the lesser twin's absent-mindedness. But for Nan, it was frightening. It was like being absent from her entire body momentarily, and then re-entering, finding someone had been there while she'd been gone, and they had moved everything around. Not that she could ever admit this to her sister. Not now. Not ever. It would be like agreeing to the fact that those twelve minutes had made a difference after all.

There had been lengthy discussions about whether they would walk to the library that morning. In the end, they had decided there was little point in driving there in the little red Mini, without knowing what would happen to it afterwards. The hassle they'd had with their own mother's car when she died had been ridiculous enough. It had been parked on double yellows (entirely deliberately, according to one heartless journalist) minutes before she'd taken her own life. And the letters from the council kept coming; a white avalanche of insult, piling up by the front door.

By the time they'd managed to reply, they were heavily in debt. 'But she's dead,' they told the town clerk.

'So?' the clerk had replied. 'The dead are the worst offenders. And in this case, a case of suicide, well we have to take it into account that the perpetrator intended for this to happen. She knew she wouldn't be here to pay the fine, and in our view, that makes the offence all the more . . . well, offensive. Tap when you're ready, please.'

Nan left the council offices thinking the woman had a point. What had been the purpose of parking on double yellows – one tyre turned outwards into the middle of the road – throwing the keys into the sea only for them to wash up days later, entwined in seaweed? Ana, who saw the significance in everything, considered it an entirely deliberate act: 'She was telling us not to accept the world as it is. It was a reminder of the absurdity of rules, systems, obligations. She wanted us to form our own rules, our own system.' Nan thought she'd probably just forgotten where she'd parked her car, and that throwing away her keys was a means of washing the whole sorry business away.

Their mother had remembered one crucial thing, however. She had remembered to leave a letter. When Nan had arrived back at the flat that day – twelve minutes or so ahead of her sister – a folded note addressed to Nan was on the table, written on the back of a ripped out title page of one of Elena's novels. She'd been so stunned, not only by seeing paper being left out so brazenly like this (for paper was gradually becoming prohibited for domestic use) but also at the notion of being addressed individually by her mother (for even their birthday cards spelled out their name as one – ANAN), that she'd read it straightaway, forgetting, for once, to call out her mother's name to let her know she was home. At the end of the note, her mother had left instructions that it should be destroyed immediately, not only because of what it said, but for fear of her daughter being caught with contraband during what would already, undoubtedly be such a difficult time for her.

Her mother, she realised later, was actually still alive while she was reading those words, when it actually sunk in that what Elena meant by this 'difficult time' was the grief of losing her mother, the thing that could still have been stopped, because at that point she was merely edging one leg out of the bathroom window, a toe's breadth from death. But in pausing to read the note, Nan missed the opportunity to stop the whole thing from happening. She'd heard the scream, just as she'd hurled the paper from her hand, refusing to accept what it said. But then again, when she'd peered down over the balcony and seen Ana running towards the scene, clueless as to why it had happened, and almost claiming the tragedy as hers alone, at least Nan felt she understood the act in a way Ana never would, and some kind of pride surfaced from the depths of her grief, that her mother had confided in her. The lesser, twelve-minute-delay twin would be the one to carry out her wishes, and bring forth justice. There would be another statement emailed to the press, already crafted on Elena's laptop, for Ana and the rest of the world to read, explaining her death in a slightly edited version.

By the time the ambulance arrived that day, it was too late. Elena was gone. Ana had to be prised off her, streaked with her mother's pulped remains. People were already speculating about the political intent of the act, as though it were her greatest fiction yet. If anyone had known she was up there, had caught her in the act, then it would have been a different story; there would have been an intervention of some kind, and she would forever be consigned to history as a woman on the brink of madness, hovering above death. Nan knew that was never her mother's intention. She wanted to do it quickly, for no one to see it happening, for it to be a clear-cut narrative. One that would shock the world, if she was lucky.

The statement pinging into every inbox, minutes after her death, said that she could no longer write. Someone had made sure of that. And without her writing, she was nothing. Less than nothing. Although she had not mentioned his name, his name was there, on everyone's lips: Eben Prytherch. A kind of literary stalker who never let any publication of hers pass by without reviewing the hell out of it; a man obsessed with finding fault with everything she had written and publishing lengthy, scathing reviews in every journal in the country. Although Elena had not explicitly said in her press release that it was his fault, she had made enough references to the Smotherhood's abuse of female writers that many came to believe that Eben Prytherch had written her out of the country's history and that he should now be held accountable for the Elena-shaped hole where great fiction had once flourished.

The twins had waited for the fallout, for Eben Prytherch to leave town, cloaked in regret and shame. But he had not. Worse than that, he seemed to have changed his tune in the immediate aftermath of her death. He'd written several tributes to her, had declared her novels – those he had tarnished repeatedly – to be great works of genius that he had misunderstood on first reading. And live on television one evening, while the twins sat eating pizza on their laps, he'd announced his intention to write her biography. He only had one obstacle, he'd said, which was that he couldn't get access to her private materials in the National Library.

It was a brazen move on his part. The twins knew he was appealing to them directly, invading their space, as if he might reach through the screen and into their living room to grab a slice of their pizza before retreating back into the safety of his TV-sofa.

That's when Nan had looked at Ana and said that something needed to be done.

It's what their mother would have wanted.

Eben

9AM

He felt different this morning as he approached the library. Legitimised. He'd been given a specific time slot, and had been told that on arrival he'd be provided with a dedicated archivist to assist him with sorting through Elena's diaries and materials. Dedicated. The notion that it was someone's job today to dedicate their time to him made him feel like he was shedding his skin as an ordinary, run-of-the-mill library goer, and entering the higher echelons of literary research. And so by the time he ascended the stairwell and saw his usual cast waiting outside, he had already decided to forgo his role in the daily pantomime.

The usual opening scene would go something like this: Professor Nicholas Griffiths, his library-step confidant, would be waiting for him. The super keen library goers always got there at nine, despite the fact that the door wouldn't be opening until nine thirty, because if you weren't there early enough to get the right desk, a whole day's work could be ruined. Nicholas's first greeting would be, without a doubt, some sort of joke about Eben's name.

'Fortunate really, that Ebenezer is a name you can crack in half like a monkey nut, because you wouldn't want to be carrying a heavy name like Ebenezer with you for the rest of your life would you?' The professor would then laugh, before starting to digress about the poet whom Eben had been named after – 'Eben the Poet', one of the long-forgotten poets of their small country.

Today, Eben refused to even look up at the professor as he hurried onwards towards the step; pretending not to know him, even. He kept his eyes firmly on the concrete.

'Are you all right, Ebbie? Eben? Ebenezer? Ebenezer the gee-zer guy? My – have I accidentally spouted some poetry there?' he sang. 'Are you OK? You seem . . . distracted.'

'I'm fine thanks, Nick,' he said, abbreviating the professor's name in a way he was sure no one had ever done before. He saw the surprise in his eyes – a great man reduced to one syllable.

Once they were inside the building, the waif-like Professor Nicholas was somehow able to slip past the porter undetected, without being subjected to any of the usual security checks, whereas Eben was met head-on by the porter who always liked to frisk him for no apparent reason, just to alleviate his own bore-dom it seemed. He'd once confiscated a pencil Eben had forgotten he had in one of his blazer pockets, insisting it could have been used as a weapon; and he'd denied him entry for the rest of the day. This morning, the porter simply wanted to annoy him by asking for his library card and vaccination status. By the time Eben arrived at the issue desk in the reading room, Colleen the so-called dedicated archivist reprimanded him for his lateness.

'I've never been late in my life,' he told her. 'It's only nine thirty-five.'

'Exactly,' Colleen replied, lowering her eyes over the precipice of her glasses. 'I had you down for nine thirty. A dedicated archi-vist would expect a dedicated researcher.'

'But I was . . . detained by the porter!' he cried.

'Five whole minutes chatting with that good-for-nothing porter?' she said, seemingly missing the point intentionally. 'What on earth did you have to talk to him about?'

'Sanitisation protocols,' Eben said, cringing at the way he'd walked into that one. The porter had tried to convince him that his glasses looked like they could have been carrying bacteria, and Eben spent three minutes vigorously scrubbing them with anti-bacterial wipes.

'I would kindly suggest, Mr Prytherch, that you sort out any sanitation issues before you enter. That way, you won't be wasting anyone's time. Now, let me see, what have we got you in for this time? Oh—' She paused, reading the information on the screen in front of her. 'You're going *down there*?'

Colleen looked up at him curiously. He felt like apologising, the way he'd felt like apologising for everything this past year.

'Surprised the twins have agreed to it,' she continued. 'But it definitely does say here that permission has been granted. You do know that they work here? Shall I get them for you?'

He shook his head. 'That won't be necessary.' He planned to avoid the twins until the book was written, until they saw what a good job he'd made of it; until he could claim, in some way, to have resurrected Elena, making their loss a little easier to bear. The truth of the matter was that he, like all members of the Smotherhood, was much happier hiding behind his keyboard, bold as brass as he made his repeated requests to the twins (at least once a month for the past six months) but knowing that his capacity for speech or thought would leave his body if he ran into them in person.

He followed the archivist down into the depths of the library; places he'd never known existed – winding, darkened corridors that led into a whole new, exciting underworld. The archivist had a fine layer of hair covering her face; she reminded him of his cat, leading him somewhere yet appearing wholly indifferent whether he followed her or not.

The dark shadows of mahogany and pine suddenly gave way to a brightly lit corridor with a row of blue doors. There was something morgue-like about it, as if he'd stumbled on a clinical part of the library – the place where books came to die. As they moved slowly down the seemingly endless corridor, Eben noticed the foreboding yellow hazard signs of the fire suppression system on the heavy-looking doors. He felt the panic rising in his chest.

'These archives are safe, are they?' he asked.

'Safest place on earth, as far as the books are concerned. I mean, since the fire, you know, we have to be extra careful.'

'But the system couldn't be triggered with a person inside, could it?' Eben started. He could hear his therapist scolding him now. *No need to voice your catastrophising out loud, Eben. Keep it as a conversation with yourself.*

'Not unless that person is actively starting a fire, no . . .'

'But if it were to go off, accidentally, I mean, doesn't it suck all the oxygen out of a room . . .'

'Planning an arson attack are we, Mr Prytherch?' Colleen stopped in her tracks. She was less of a cat now, more a primate, waiting to jump on his head and pull his hair, rummage in his pockets for nuts. 'Perhaps we should rethink this visit?'

'That won't be necessary,' he replied hurriedly, bringing himself back into the moment, like his therapist told him. The important thing was that he was actually here. At last, he was going to access Elena's diaries and, by default, access her mind. By the end of the summer, he could be done with the project. Considering how quickly the turnaround was in this country, he could have her biography published by the end of the year.

Not that any actual publishing really happened anymore. Following the clamp down on paper use at home, the government had recently instigated a policy for all new books to be released only electronically. It was deemed safer; paper bred germs, they claimed, and their country had been particularly hit by the recent Great Sickness. Many blamed all the books that had been passed back and forth between people, carrying a sly little variant of the disease in their print. It was fine for any existing publications to remain, as long as they were only perused under supervision, in institutions like libraries and universities, but the use of any new paper was now strictly prohibited. The neighbouring country, despite having seen the same levels of sickness, were still allowed their paper; which made no sense, but the head of government argued that other countries would soon follow suit, and that eradicating paper was a means of forging a new future in the country. Cutting out another source of disease, along with the carbon footprint. And the government argued that the old people who were still resistant to online reading, those were all dependent on their parish newsletters and local magazine, were all gone, anyway, because of the Great Sickness.

It had turned into a kind of self-fulfilling prophecy. People had become accustomed to the loss of paper; they had deemed it a good thing, and there was less disease; and the people in this country thought themselves to be superior, because they were healthier. The 'health is wealth' banner seemed to be plastered on every national institution, in order to make sure that their small country did not somehow notice that it had less of everything everyone else had.

He followed Colleen sheepishly towards the end of the corridor. Eben couldn't bear the thought that his book, now that he was ready to actually write one, would exist in electronic form *only*. Why did the system have to fall apart like this, when he was finally ready to make his entrance into the literary world? What kind of writer did that make him? He wasn't even sure what it was, or how it worked – that virtual space that constituted the page. A virtual page meant you had written a virtual text, did it not? It was only space and shapes. Black and white. A real page had scent. It had odours. It kept the smudges of your biscuit-buttery fingers, sometimes forever, until they became so embedded in the page, they were part of the narrative.

Again he was jealous of his subject: of Elena. Hers had been the heyday. Each and every one of her novels had been a solid, real thing. There had been a picture of her on every glossy back cover. She had given people paper cuts; she had left purple imprints on people's hands. A well-known critic had tripped over one of her novels at the top of the stairs and broken his neck. True, some had been riddled with disease and ended up on ventilators from reading her second-hand paperbacks; but that, too, made her powerful, did it not?

She had owned her books in a way Eben would not own his own academic articles and reviews. In a way he would not even own his own biography of her. She had been blessed with quotes on her front covers that urged you to read, all the superlatives one could wish for: *The most dazzling. The most mesmerising.* They tried to insert quotes inside e-books, of course, but what was the point if the reader was only going to scroll past, racing towards page one, where the actual text started? Who considered anything worthy before page one? Anything that preceded one was minus your attention.

Elena's books had demanded attention in shops, airports, on kitchen counters, beautifully produced as they always were (she was sleeping with the illustrator, he was sure of it) and they had been deemed a thing of beauty, a must-have on your shelf, whether you wanted to read her or not.

Elena had trumped him in so many ways, no matter how things had played out in the end.

Colleen finally stopped and reached for her security pass. Elena's archive was the very last blue door at the end of the corridor. Outside the archive a glittering plaque read: *Elena Oodig, novelist.*

'You'll find everything you need in here,' she said, as she guided him into the tiny, cramped space and began unscrewing the stacks inside them.

He stood back and waited. This was always a moment Eben revelled in: the moment when the stacks suddenly exposed their hoard: a whole other life between them. And seeing real-life books, real-life diaries – sweated over, written in – was thrilling in itself. As they slowly came into view, he saw that they were colourful, Elena's diaries. It was like looking at a row of jars in a sweet shop; each tiny diary had an embroidered, multicoloured design, a pattern. And again, he felt something deep inside, some annoyance towards her, even in this moment. What was wrong with a hardback, black diary like the ones he used to have? Why did she have to be different?

But there was some deeper annoyance too; it was too much of a reminder of all that had been lost in this country. Now everyone was ordered to keep an online journal, if they wanted to keep one at all. An online journal: who in their right mind did that? It could be accessed by anyone. Sections could be copied, pasted, sent out into the world. Eben felt like running towards these real-life diaries and pressing them to his face. They were begging to be devoured. He wanted to lick them, ingest them, so that they were part of him forever. These books seemed to him alive in the way others were not; because the scrawls of handwriting would show the moods of the author, the crossings-out, the smudges, the slippages of a writer's mind and personality. Elena would come dancing out of these pages and stand beside him.

'How will I make notes?' Eben asked.

The porter had confiscated his laptop and his phone. 'You could be setting a bomb off with either one of those,' he'd said.

'Oh,' Colleen replied, 'you can use the library's computer over there. It auto-saves any files, and then, at the end of the day, we can send them to you.'

Auto-save, Eben thought, suspiciously. *Not before reading through them and taking the piss.* The library obviously felt they were entitled to access his private thoughts on Elena. Any discoveries he made, they would see them. He wondered if, for today, he'd refrain from writing anything at all, wondering how much his own memory's hard drive could store.

'You'll find most of the diaries here, and the juvenilia, of course,' Colleen continued. 'Her letters are over here, and some notes on her novels. From childhood to adolescence over here, then from adulthood to motherhood here, and then anything after the switch-over, the more recent ones, well you can read them off the screen over there.'

And there it was: the mention of the dreaded switch-over; the cusp on which Elena had lived, in her final years. When the concept of paper had evaporated along with Elena.

'And then obviously, they come to an end . . .' she said, without looking at him.

'What happened to her final year?' he asked.

'She didn't write anything that year. Not a single word,' she said. 'We all know why, of course.'

The librarian looked at him accusingly. Eben looked away. He regretted asking the question. Of course she hadn't written anything down that year. He had made sure of that. Or at least his friend Frankton had, pulling at Eben's puppet strings, getting him to silence her, the best he could. And Frankton's modus operandi was never to be held accountable for anything, leaving other people to take the blame. Despite being a hefty nineteen stone, he could escape from uncomfortable situations like a nimble-footed sprite.

'Thanks for your assistance,' Eben said, waiting for Colleen to leave, hoping that her dedication didn't, in fact, extend to the duration of his time in the archive. He felt claustrophobic enough without having her in his orbit as well. 'I'll come and get you if I need anything else.'

'No you most certainly won't,' she said. 'You'll need to press the emergency button, so we can get one of the porters to let you out.'

'You're locking me in?'

'New security policy,' she said. 'I'm sure you'll be aware how precious this material is, especially considering the paper ban. We're not going to take the risk of letting you walk out of here with them, are we? We've lost quite enough already, don't you think?'

'But I'm her biographer,' he said.

'Exactly,' she replied. 'You've already stolen someone else's life because you haven't got a life of your own to write about.'

'But . . .' Eben continued, 'what if I need to sanitise my hands?'

'There's plenty of sanitiser there,' she said pointing to a dispenser in the corner of the room.

'But what if I need the toilet . . .'

'The same rule applies. Press the red button. A porter will bring you a bucket.'

'A bucket?'

'A joke,' she said, mirthlessly. 'The gents' is down the corridor on the left, but you'll still need to press the button to be let out. Now then, the only other thing I would request is that you wear these gloves.'

She handed him a pair of white gloves; their cotton fingers poised in condemnation. Even the gloves, he thought. Even the gloves know what I did.

'Not to go to the toilet, obviously,' she added. 'To handle the resources, the materials. You see, you won't even need the sanitiser; they already have a special antibacterial coating . . .'

Resources. Materials. Eben took note of the purposefully chosen terms. He'd heard that the government was trying to discourage people from using words like *diaries*, *books*, and *pages*. There was little point in eroding paper itself if the vocabulary was going to remain. He wasn't sure the word librarian was even in use now. He had heard terms like 'resource-handler' being used. Everything in your hand was considered *material*. Books were considered a writer's *output*. 'We don't want our vocabulary to hold us back as a nation,' he'd heard the head of government say in an interview. 'One of our many problems as a nation is our archaic vocabulary, our obsession with moving backwards instead of forwards.'

But you can't get rid of the word library! Eben thought to himself. But even as he considered the word, it became nonsensical on his tongue. Li-brar-y. Libraria. Librarius. Liber. Libr. The word got smaller and smaller until it folded back into its own origins. He could imagine what would happen. The National Library would become The National Archive. And then it would become a Material Archive; just a place to store materials. And then it would become nothing; maybe a five-star hotel with a spa.

He could only hope he'd be dead by then.

Colleen left the room, closing the door with a thud. He heard a little electronic clunk, which signalled that he was now locked in, and he pressed his hands onto the handleless door, breathing in deeply, trying to tell himself it was OK; it was simply a security measure. He was still a free man. He had not killed anyone, and he was free to do what he wanted.

It was only then that he noticed the glint of dark, marble eyes staring at him from a shelf above his head. He was not entirely alone, for Elena's portrait bust was in here with him, and her disembodied, celebrated head would be watching his every move.

Dan

9.30AM

Opening up a library was a thankless task. However much he had fooled himself, walking along the red carpet towards those huge double doors, that the audience outside were hungry for his arrival, that they considered him the hoarder of all treasures, there was no superiority attached to his job whatsoever. All they wanted to do was get past him. To bagsy the best desks. For these people, a porter was never going to be anything more than a guy who opened and closed a door. The one who let them in and let them out again.

He could never truly get his head around what would make anyone want to spend a clear, beautiful day inside a library; to queue up in sunshine for a place in the dark. He saw the same old faces, every single day; he was on first-name terms with the *lifers*: those in it for the long haul, and he also recognised most of the *part-timers*, those who only visited intermittently but really committed when they did – coming every single day for weeks on end until, that article, that PhD, or a family tree, whatever it was, was complete. Others he eyed with suspicion; those who came and went like the wind and seemed to have no specific intent; who came because a library was free, because it judged no one, and seemed like a better option than hanging out by yourself at home.

He did, however, feel a particular affection for the *mappers*: a special breed in wax jackets and thick spectacles who came to pore over yet another map of a terrain long gone, as though trying to navigate their way back into the past. He found them fascinating and sad at the same time, but in his mind they were all ultimately losers, because it was their choice to be here, when they could very well be somewhere else. A choice that was no longer an option for him.

After that door creaked open they would trample ungraciously over one another in order to get to their chosen desks. They bickered every morning about a corner of a table, competing over certain patches of mahogany, complaining about the angle of a seat, the crookedness of a chair leg. They bemoaned the way the sun poured in through the tall windows and obscured their screens; some said that an angle of sunlight was detrimental to their thought process, that too much sun – or too little – impacted upon their creativity, that a great theory could shrivel up in sunshine.

This was why Dan liked to have a bit of fun with them; especially those who came to stand outside at nine so that they could be ready to charge when the doors opened at half past. His first victim today was a girl who'd bored him to death a few weeks back telling him all about her research project – she was compiling a study of the nation's firsts, she said: the country's first known poet; the first language activist; the first registered transman. Primacy was simply a way of life for her, she told him, looking him in the eye for a fraction too long. He'd assumed she was flirting with him and asked her to go for a drink with him. She'd laughed in his face and walked off.

Looking back at the porter-cam footage later, Dan realised that this little dalliance was just a ploy to make her boyfriend, who was watching them from the next desk in the reading room, jealous. He supposed that there could be nothing more threatening to the second-rate lover of a prima donna to think she might engage the interest of a third-rate porter. Since then he'd been biding his time to get back at her.

Dan noticed how her voice was the first to be heard every morning; the first face he saw when he opened the door, her foot raised in anticipation, ready to pirouette past him. Her boyfriend, a rather dopey-looking creature with a lock of hair that closed like a curtain over his left eye, was usually dragged along behind her, his hand firmly in hers.

'No physical contact please,' Dan told them.

'It's fine. He's part of my household, if you know what I mean,' the girl said with a wink, manoeuvring her way around him.

'Can I see your library card?' he asked her, stopping her in her tracks.

'But I was here yesterday,' she said, visibly annoyed now, the boyfriend's hand trying to extract itself from hers, which seemed an insurmountable task. The other library goers whooshed past her, a first, second, third and fourth contender for the largest desk in the reading room.

'It's for security purposes,' he said. She fumbled in her bag for the card. 'We need to be careful these days. Are your vaccinations up to date?'

'Yes of course they are! Look at me, picture of health! I don't see what the fuss is about – I didn't bring my card today, because no one asked to see it yesterday, or the day before. Or the day before that, for that matter. Don't you remember me? I've been coming here for six months! You know me!'

'No, sorry, I don't,' he said, satisfied now that he was trampling all over her delusions of primacy in his own substandard way. 'You'll need to make a request for a day ticket. Over there.'

He tried to direct her towards the library reception but ended up touching her elbow, the tip of his finger catching the sleeve of her cotton print dress. Her skin swelled indignantly beneath it.

'Did you just *touch* me? Without gloves or anything?'

Dan tried to move away, but it was too late.

'I think he just touched me!' The girl turned to her boyfriend for support. 'You saw that, didn't you? He touched me.'

'I suppose he did,' said the subordinate boyfriend. 'He could have contaminated you.'

By now the library goers had stopped in their tracks, congregating around the drama.

'Just collect a day ticket at reception,' he said, not wanting to let her win. 'Then you can go in.'

'This is about me turning you down, isn't it? How up to date are your vaccinations, eh? That's what I'd like to know?' she continued. 'Going around touching everyone and everything.'

She glared at him. Dan recalled the four horrendous weeks when the Great Sickness had hit the prison, where it had been rife among the inmates. He'd been placed in a cell on his own, where he'd been hallucinating about the royal family of the neighbouring country, who'd paced around his bedside and told him all about their plans to rule his country forever.

'Just fuck off will you,' he whispered, defeated.

She flounced off, not concerned with him or his errant germs anymore, cantering up the red carpet towards her table. Her boyfriend slowed down and lowered his voice.

'You got any . . . you know?' His words dried up in the air.

'Not today,' Dan answered, moving him on before the next library goer came too close. 'Keep your distance please, sir . . .'

'But you said . . .' the boyfriend continued, hovering around him like a fly.

'Come and see me later, OK? At lunchtime.'

The boyfriend walked off. Dan sighed. He supposed it hadn't been the best idea in the world to start dealing drugs to students. Or at least, to this one, when his girlfriend was in the business of recording anything that made anyone a maverick, a first-timer. He was pretty sure that a library porter had never been caught drug dealing, and it was the first time the library lockers had ever been used to stash spice.

He also liked to taunt a few of the academics in the queue. You could spot them a mile off; so engrossed in their own thoughts that they wouldn't even notice him. They were hilariously rude, because they couldn't imagine anything coming between them and their work, which made them the most fun to hassle. He decided to pick on one creepy-looking guy with glasses who seemed in a rush. He asked him about his vaccination status, asked him for his library card, without needing or wishing to see either one of them. Told him he could see the germs on his glasses, until he had the poor sod scrubbing them with wipes, and did it all for the hell of it, even though in actual fact nothing was required of Dan but to stand, and scan, and stare as they all whooshed past him, as though he were invisible.

After the initial flood of visitors came the lull. By nine forty-five, there was hardly a soul to be seen. He returned to his porter station to check on the whereabouts of the van on the app. It was now protocol for anyone going on a work trip outside the library to be trackable, which suited Dan just fine, because he'd be able to make sure he'd got himself back into his rightful position by the time they all rocked up at the car park again. According to the map, the porters were still stuck in traffic just outside the city centre right now, on a link road, right in front of the prison wall. He checked the CCTV footage on his own home screen to see what the rest of them were seeing when they connected to the system. In this particular version, the library was a bit busier than usual, and there Dan was, happily greeting all of the library goers, scanning their passes and cards, not unduly hassling anyone on their way in, but merely being a pleasant, exemplary doorman. You could hear his pleasantries loud and clear on the audio, captured via porter-cam, being the best self that the arch-porter asked for. Then, he saw himself moving away from the entrance on the CCTV and entering the space he was in now, sitting upright at his desk, where he was simultaneously keeping an eye on the screens and diligently reading the security handbook, a porter completely committed to climbing the ranks of the porter world.

He sat back smugly, looking at the concentration on his face in the CCTV footage he'd captured a few weeks back. He remembered why he had that expression on his face in the first place, and it was simply because he'd discovered that rule 34 in the security handbook stated that security guards were not to enter into an emotional or sexual relationship with any person or persons for whose safety they were responsible, a rule he had already broken, much to his own surprise.

When he first arrived here, fresh from prison, the 'ex-con' label all but tattooed to his forehead, he was lucky if anyone even smiled at him. The female librarians did not even appear to be sexual creatures; or at least, they did not want to acknowledge the slightest sliver of their sexuality, which was their right, and their privilege, the arch-porter had said. 'This place is about books, not people,' he'd said. 'They *want* to be considered secondary to the material.'

But then, around a week into the job, he had met her, down in the basement. He knew, from the moment he saw her walking towards him, that she wasn't a woman who needed saving from anything. And in his own personal handbook, that meant he was free to do as he wished.

She was later than usual this morning. And when she finally arrived, she had this white scarf round her neck, tight as anything, as if it were keeping her head in place. She glanced in his direction, briefly, just enough to acknowledge him, before looking away again and disappearing to wherever she went every day.

He'd never thought to ask her where in this huge building she worked. It wasn't like that between them. He didn't even know her name. He liked the neutrality of the whole thing: the fact that he had never breathed a word of it to anyone. There was something tantalising about the secrecy of it; it was like a fiction of his own making; a narrative huddled along with all the others on the shelves.

He walked as far as the North Reading Room to see if she was in there. The archivist at the issue desk glared at him, as his pacing was making the automatic doors open and close, open and close, open and close.

'What the hell is wrong with you?' she whispered. 'Go and find something to do, will you?'

He turned his back on the North Reading Room and followed the river of red carpet in the direction of the librarian offices. It wasn't time to start on another circuit, at least not until lunchtime. But today, his key fob, the little nun-contraption, was his alone, and he was free to roam the building as he liked – open any door, roam any corridor, without being seen elsewhere. His superiors would be watching the CCTV footage of several days ago, compiled with footage from a few other uneventful days to create an exemplary day in Dan's history. That's all anyone needed, he thought. One perfect, blemish-free day, cobbled together from your best moments, to play over and over while you went on your merry, imperfect way.

He buzzed himself into the darker corridors, moving silently past the public offices; the places no one knew about. He looked in and saw each head bent diligently over a desk in concentration; no one seemingly daydreaming or procrastinating. Totally focused. From here, they could well be mannequins, held in static poise. The solitary nun-device felt light in his pocket, but he knew how powerful she was. He only needed to hold her up against the security sensors and he would lock everyone into their offices.

Locking people in was now more effective than letting them out, according to the arch-porter. The new cladding that had been installed was now fire-proof, bomb-proof, even tsunami-proof, if it came to that (which it could, the arch-porter said, in a coastal town, even on top of a hill). And they were all a little bit more cautious now, of course, after the fire; when half the roof had been consumed in pungent, black flames, and a large number of the rare books and handwritten diaries of the country's best-loved authors had gone up in smoke; remembrances turning into an impressive display of pyrotechnics above the town.

Nothing would bring the building down now, the arch-porter said. Not even a nuclear disaster. Not even the Apocalypse itself.

Dan sometimes wondered whether anyone in these offices would notice if he locked them in. He'd spent so long being enraged about his incarceration – so long spent unmoving in the one cell – and yet here, people seemed fine with confinement. It was a daily ritual to sit, and exist, and not move; to be so engrossed in something the outside world didn't really matter. Even when he sounded the last bell of the day he saw some of them were reluctant to pack up and leave; as though he was spoiling their fun by bringing their working day to a close.

He walked back in the direction of the main part of the building, following the red carpet back towards his own desk, feeling the nun grow strong in the hollow of his pocket.

Suddenly she came running at him, up the stairs, a black bag on her shoulders.

'There you are,' he said, excitedly, reaching out for her. He hadn't expected her to come find him so early on, but he supposed that now that the CCTV was sorted like she wanted, they could go ahead and have sex anywhere they wanted to. Even right here, right now, he thought, if they were quick.

'Not now,' she said, pulling back and looking at him strangely. She did this a lot. As if he were some unknown creature that had just walked out of the sea, speaking a language no one had ever heard before. And yet, a few nights ago, it had been a completely different story. He'd helped her carry the last of her mother's materials down into the archive. That was the first time he'd realised that her mother was Elena Oodig, that spare head he'd been wheeling about not so long ago, but it didn't feel right to ask her about it somehow. He'd found her a trolley, and they'd wheeled it together, fingers almost touching, down to the blue corridor of the archive, the wheels squeaking and squealing, a sound he hadn't wanted to end, because it meant the whole thing would be over. This was the kind of girl she was. She could make a rusty wheel, a linoleum floor – storage itself – sexy.

He'd locked the doors of the archive with his nun-device – two taps for a double lock, and extra security. When he turned around, she was sitting on the trolley, lifting her skirt, pulling her knickers down. He almost wanted to laugh; it was so direct, so immediate. It had completely thrown him, and there had been a lot of inexpert fumbling with his trousers before he finally got inside her. He knew that everything they did would be caught on tape, and so he'd gone straight to the control room afterwards to destroy the evidence, and to put another in its place. He'd kept the original, of course, for his own private use, but when he sat down to watch it later on, unbuckling his belt in anticipation, he'd been disappointed to see how hard and cold her eyes were as he pummelled away. She was making all the right sounds, but her face betrayed her. And so his penis shrivelled in shame inside his boxers, and he fastened his belt back up again.

Although it had happened again since then, he'd been careful to make sure they were out of the reach of the cameras, primarily because he did not want to see his own failure staring back at him from those cold eyes. He wanted to hang on to the fiction of her wanting him, rather than the reality.

She was staring at him now, with that white scarf around her neck, as if expecting him to do something. Again he was confused by her signals. Why was she making it so difficult for him to initiate this? He leaned in, trying to go for a kiss now, which, oddly, hadn't been part of the deal so far. He leaned in; she leaned back, pointing at the camera poised directly above them.

'It's sorted,' he said, winking at her. 'I've sorted it. Like you wanted.'

She'd been getting increasingly paranoid about the CCTV footage. She hadn't trusted him to get rid of it. Last time they'd spoken she said she would only have sex with him again if he made sure there would be no record of it, anywhere in the world.

'Things that are erased can still be retrieved,' she'd told him. 'Some things don't need to be recorded, anywhere, for anyone. We should record them when we experience them – in memory alone.'

That's when he had come up with the idea of replacing the footage instead of destroying it.

She seemed to give in finally, and moved towards him now, shoving her hand in his pocket, rummaging around for his penis in the dark fabric. As her hand had closed around it, he'd let out a moan, swallowing it away as Colleen from the enquiries desk passed by and gave them a funny look.

'Save it for later,' she'd said, releasing her hand.

'Oh come on,' he said, 'come with me now, down to the archives. Or we could go to one of the empty offices. Or the storage unit. Anywhere. I'm here all alone; no one gives a shit where I am . . . No one can see us. And I've fixed the porter-cam too, they're hearing something completely different . . .'

'No, Dan,' she replied firmly. 'I've got work to do. You'll have to wait.' He noticed something then, as she turned away from him, as her red blouse rose up, a mark on the small of her back. A memento, he realised, of their rather hurried coupling against the stacks last week. She hadn't complained at the time, but it looked nasty. It struck him then that maybe he was too rough with her, too greedy; that maybe he needed to ask her if she'd like to take it slower sometimes; maybe even find somewhere they could make love properly. He sensed that perhaps he'd taken his own fiction too far; that for all his enjoyment, he was merely an experience for her. Something to distract her from the ennui of her day. And it didn't help matters that when she turned to look at him now as she rounded the corner, she seemed to look through him, as if looking for someone else, someone better, to appear in his place.

It wasn't until he arrived back at the porters' station that he realised what the true purpose of the exchange had been: she had stolen the nun-device from his pocket.

Ana and Nan

10AM

Nan walked into the office she and Ana shared with three others. She was still trembling from the encounter with Dan, having shocked herself at the boldness with which she'd navigated her way around that bulge in his trousers, skilfully hooking the top of the security device with her ring finger as if she was the kind of woman who fished around in men's trousers all the time. She tried her best to hide the tremor in her hands now by keeping them firmly rooted in her pocket, feeling around for the security device in the dark lining, this tangible proof of this new person she'd become.

But it was also proof of how she'd messed up the timings, because she had taken it from him much sooner than planned, and he would know that something was amiss. If they were going to secure the next part of their plan, they needed to do it now, urgently; there was no time to waste. Dan, being the only security guard on duty today, would be unlikely to alert the security team that his device was missing right away, because such negligence would likely result in his immediate removal from the premises. But when he finally did alert the rest of the team – assuming he'd be able to get hold of them in the middle of their security presentation down in the capital – it would then instigate an instant, complete shutdown of the library. Everybody locked inside, until the security forces had located the missing device.

That would surely be Dan's last resort, she thought, considering it meant they would soon discover his own wrongdoing. And if so, then they still had an hour maybe; while he tried to work out his options.

Ana did not look up when she entered the office. Nan steadied herself and booted up the computer, firing a quick email over to her sister, using their code.

The fourteenth-century pamphlet needs amending, the email read.

Ana looked up at her then, rather startled, before turning back to her own keypad and firing back an answer.

When do you need it? the reply flew back at her.

Asap? Nan typed, trying to avoid her sister's gaze as she heard the familiar chime of the message landing in her inbox.

Ana got up, quickly, put on her protective mask and gloves, and made her way to a trolley of books in the corner, turning it around in order to wheel it past Nan's desk. Nan reached into the black bag underneath the desk and hoisted out a large, heavy book from its depths. All the while, their colleagues in the room – three female archivists, Summer, Lily, and Pale – continued with their work, heads bowed over their desks. They hadn't even acknowledged their presence in the room yet. It was the way of things in this place – the twins were more or less invisible to them. Their doubleness, rather than making them more visible, often had the opposite effect on people. It made them less than one whole person somehow, as though they cancelled each other out. Nan thought that her colleagues paid so little attention to them both that she could have easily pulled out the gun from under her desk there and then and handed it over to Ana. Their idea of placing it inside a hollowed-out copy of one of the earliest editions of the Bible, when no one, not even the CCTV screen was watching them, seemed superfluous somehow.

Nan also swiftly deposited the security device into Ana's hands in the exchange. Ana pocketed it, placed the Bible on her book trolley and began wheeling it out of the room, but not before pinging one last email over to her sister. With her face partly obscured by her mask, Ana was difficult to read, but Nan noticed the sweat gathering at her sister's brow; her once nimble fingers appearing clunky and heavy as they clattered along the keyboard, sighing as she typed the wrong letters, deleting them, starting again, over and over.

As Ana left the room, Nan read the email.

We need to refer back to the original copy.

The original copy. Nan tried to recall what the code meant now, because her mind was starting to scramble itself again, those white spots appearing in front of her. Had Ana said something about Nan keeping Summer, Lily and Pale at their desks once she had left the room, and to stop them from roaming? Was that it? The original copy, the original plan, or was there something else she was meant to be doing? Did she have time to go and double-check with Ana, running the risk of letting these three leave the room? She decided that it was probably best that she kept things simple for now; and let her sister take care of the rest, hoping that Ana would somehow be able to manoeuvre the whole thing back on track. It was something, after all, Ana prided herself on being able to do, her twelve-minute superiority making her more than capable of clearing up any carnage the lesser twin left in her wake.

Not that there was any real danger of their colleagues going anywhere. Summer, Lily and Pale – at the far end of the archive – were like figures in a weather clock, only leaving the room when it chimed eleven fifteen, one and three. All had names that didn't really suit them. Summer was like a thunderstorm, her dark eyes clouding beneath her too-thick glasses; Lily let off a noxious body odour whenever she shifted in her chair; and Pale was flushed with colour, her skin betraying the dark, heavy blood that lay beneath. Nan tended to be on the periphery of their conversations, a spectator to their bond, but she knew their movements, inside out. Which was helpful on a day like today.

There was a slight variation to the routine these days, however. Pale was eight months pregnant, her belly ballooning over the rim

of her trousers. She kept running back and forth to the toilet, paranoid that her waters had broken. She *knew* the baby would be early,
she said, to no one in particular, as if asserting her maternal super-
powers. She had been showing off about the pregnancy from the
very beginning, as if implying that the other women in the room
would never manage such a feat. Summer and Lily seemed to have
created a breakaway group of their own as a result, and were often
flitting back and forth to each other's desks, sharing the latest gossip
about their various sexual exploits, flaunting their childless, carefree
status in Pale's face. Nan and Ana as ever were left to their own
devices, everyone assuming they had formed their own alliance long
ago and didn't wish to be in anyone else's orbit.

Pale suddenly announced to the room that she felt a trickle
down the side of her thigh. She got up and started to move
towards the doors. There was nothing for it but for Nan to follow
her, however strange it looked.

'I don't need you to come with me,' Pale barked, as Nan followed her down the spiral staircase from their office and towards
the staff toilets. 'I'm only checking. It could be anything. It might
be my mucous plug, rather than the waters breaking. Or I could
have just pissed myself.'

'You read about babies being born in toilets when mothers
least expect it. You might need my help,' Nan said, trying to
feign concern, yet somehow unable to imagine what kind of help
she'd really be in a situation like that. The thought of something
emerging between Pale's legs, herself being the one responsible
for its safe entry into the world, terrified her.

'And what would you be able to do, seriously?' Pale called out,
echoing Nan's thoughts from inside the cubicle. 'We're OK. It
was just some discharge. False alarm.'

Pale waddled out towards the large mirror, and Nan was struck
again by the bulbous life that hung there casually behind the
thin wool of her jumper. How on earth had their own mother

accommodated two of them inside her? And what had they considered themselves to be, her and Ana, during their formation, as they held on to each other in that cramped, dark space? Had they been conscious of anything? Capable of thought? Sometimes she wished she could return to that state of ignorance, that oblivion of the life that was yet to come. That baby inside Pale knew nothing of anything beyond its mother's womb, or of the thing called life that lay just on the other side of it.

'There's no closer bond than the one between the three of us, is there?' their mother had always said, holding them tight, trying to recreate the feeling of them being one whole thing again. 'And thank God that there isn't some annoying man to come between us and take all the credit.'

She was always so proud of the fact she'd been able to raise them alone; that she'd never had to let a man touch her – not like that. Their father was no more than a nice little introductory letter in a file.

Nan suddenly felt compelled to put her hand on her own flat, smooth stomach. Pale caught her doing it.

'It might happen one day – you never know,' Pale said, smearing some mauve lipstick across her lips. This was another one of Pale's pointless rituals. Nan couldn't work out who the lipstick was meant to be for; but it rarely survived the morning. It snaked its way up polystyrene cups, onto Pale's teeth, her fingers. The colour itself seemed to have an aversion to Pale's lips.

'I'm not sure I'd really want one . . . but then, never say never,' she replied. 'Can I touch it?'

Pale nodded and Nan moved her hands across to the fleshy dome. She was surprised by how solid it felt. Not like a baby, more like a bomb.

'At the beginning, it just felt like a flutter,' Pale said. 'And now it's sort of violent, like it's fighting to get out. You can see it doing it. Wait for a moment – you'll see.'

Pale lifted her jumper. The whole belly now glared at Nan like an accusing eye.

Suddenly the oval stomach moved sideways, as a tremor flitted through.

'Did you see that?' she said. 'I think that was a fist. This baby is ready to come out, I'm telling you!'

'But how do you cope?' Nan said. 'With something inside you? Something living, that's going to be your responsibility . . . forever?'

Pale looked up at her then, either with disgust or pity, Nan couldn't tell.

'Well when you're this far gone, you just have to, I suppose,' she said. She looked away then, as if seriously considering Nan's words for the first time. The burden of it. The horror.

'I mean, it's going to ruin everything, of course. But we've been conditioned to believe that that's our function in life, haven't we? And it's not as bad as it was . . . At least they make the dad take leave now, so I won't miss out too much.'

Elena, of course, had not had this, back in her day, but had welcomed the fact that government policy now honoured single mothers by giving them a free-of-charge nanny when there wasn't a partner in place to do the work. These days the mother, any mother, was entitled to work as much as she wanted, and the baby was brought into the mother's workplace by the sleep-deprived husband or partner, and placed on the breast as needed.

The head of government had made the radical change three years ago when she herself had had a baby: the official line was that as head of government it was her duty to set an example to other working, breastfeeding mothers out there; to show them that motherhood did not hinder their careers, but in fact, could accelerate it. They would be freed from their domestic roles for a whole two years during this pre-school period, while their other halves stayed at home. The unofficial story, Nan had heard the head librarian say, was that she had not wanted a baby, but that she had drunk too much at a party and forgotten to take her contraceptive pill. And when the baby was born and she realised that her husband, a diplomat, expected her to stay home for at least six months she had said: *fuck that shit*, and swiftly made obligatory paternity leave national policy so as not to make herself an anomaly.

There was a sudden swell in Pale's eyes. She looked like she was about to cry. Nan heard a sneeze now – three sharp sneezes, one after the other. That meant the coast was clear, and also that Ana had been aware of the change in Pale's location. Yet the sneezes were a little too loud, and presented Nan with a different predicament.

'Who the hell was that, sneezing that way?' Pale said indignantly, marching towards the toilet doors. 'Have they been tested? They shouldn't be allowed to come to work with those germs . . .'

Pale entered the corridor, searching for the perpetrator of the disease-riddled sternutation. She started walking down the corridor, where Nan suddenly caught a glimpse of Ana's reflection in a display cabinet, hovering on the other side of the white pillar.

'OK then, back to work,' she said, grabbing Pale's arm and tugging her away, towards the doors that led back to the office.

'Aw!' Pale shouted. 'You're meant to take things slowly in my condition . . .'

'Yes and you shouldn't be traipsing round the building either. You need rest now – come on, back we go,' Nan said.

By the time they returned, it was almost ten thirty, which was usually the time that Summer hauled up one of those intense long sighs from the depths of her soul, having found her piece of work impossible and insurmountable. Seven seconds later, Lily would begin getting restless in her seat, and say she wanted a career change. Pale would make some sort of comment about how uncomfortable her seat was; how no one had any idea what compromises a pelvis had to make to accommodate new life.

Such were the rhythms of Nan's working day. It comforted her, the knowledge that at least something, somewhere, was fixed, unchanged. That she could remember these details, and that they presented themselves to her time and time again, making her feel she was in control of every single passing minute, every single day. Yet her sister always hated the predictability. She said it stifled her. Right now Nan felt a strange alchemy of both emotions – she almost wanted to get up from her seat and encourage them to do something different; warning them that predictability could be a dangerous thing. Predictability meant you were known and seen. That you were vulnerable.

*

Ana felt the old sibling annoyance surface like bile in her throat as she clattered down the corridor with her book trolley. She wondered whether Nan's mismanagement of the first part of their plan was deliberate. Something to wind her up, at the worst possible time. Her heart was thumping in her chest, her mind racing to cover all eventualities if she saw Dan coming towards her now along the corridor, asking her where the security device was. There was a good reason they'd decided not to steal Dan's device until after his sneaky spliff at eleven thirty; after everyone's coffee break was done and dusted. Then, they were planning to inform him that a theft had taken place inside, which meant he needed to get all the library goers out of the public areas of the building at once to conduct a search, telling him they would round up any remaining researchers left in the archive. They anticipated that at that point in his day, his mind would be so fragmented and slow that he'd lap up any eventuality they presented to him, and in the ensuing chaos, once everyone was out, they would get him to hand over his device to them before swiftly locking him and everyone else out, so that they could head to the archive in peace.

Nan had argued against this, of course, saying they didn't need the whole building to themselves in order to confront Eben, but Ana had studied the new security handbook carefully, and knew that if any kind of terrorist threat was identified by the new sensors, then staff was permitted to trigger a silent alarm, which would pump a kind of sleeping gas into the public areas, a powerful opioid that were meant to incapacitate everyone – both terrorists and bystanders – until help could arrive. The more people there were in the building, the more risk there was that someone might sense something was up, and trigger the gas, stopping them in their tracks before they even got to Eben. But worse still, Ana had read about a recent malfunction with this system recently during a terrorist attack on the neighbouring country's main concert hall, where a large number of both victims and perpetrators had fatal allergic reactions to the gas and died during the rescue operation. Ana felt she couldn't justify endangering anyone else, but Nan didn't seem overly concerned about this and felt it was a risk worth taking – if anything, she told her sister, surely it would be better to die than be awakened from a slumber utterly humiliated. 'But what if he gets away, and he runs,' Ana had whispered to her sister in bed one night, 'if he gets out into the main building, and someone sees him or us, then all hell breaks loose. Surely it's better that there isn't anyone around to help him.' Ana had wondered whether there was a part of her that wanted to make way for this interlude, perhaps wanted a plan so complicated that it would eventually prove unmanageable. Perhaps she liked the idea of scaring Eben more than the thought of killing him; and she worried that for Nan, it was the opposite.

'I'll make sure he doesn't get away,' Nan had said, before turning on her back in the half-light, looking off into one of those faraway places that Ana could never access. Sometimes she waved her hand in front of Nan's eyes to bring her back to reality, only to find that she simply couldn't penetrate the thin, invisible film between her sister and the world. But then her sister, unlike her, had been born cocooned in the amniotic sac, a *mermaid birth* her mother had called it, and she often wondered, when Nan went into one of her dazes like this, whether her veiled entrance into the world still influenced the way she saw things now; whether she felt things differently because she'd entered the world encased in something that was designed to protect her from harm. Ana, on the other hand, had apparently kicked and screamed her way out of that bag way before she was born, the sudden gush of water testament to the fact that Ana didn't need protecting from anything, or anyone.

Ana imagined now how it would all play out, and saw it as a plot their mother could have written, one she would perhaps be proud of. However it unfolded, she felt instinctively that it was better that it would not be witnessed by anyone but them, and that none of it would be captured on CCTV; which meant that there was always a possibility that they could, eventually, twist the story into implying that he had been a threat to them, especially if – and she shuddered at the thought – if he were no longer around to give his side of the story.

Ana approached the corridor of the management team, wheeling her trolley along, pausing silently at each office door to lock them discreetly with the security device. It was safer, for now, to keep the management team suspended, and disable the Wi-Fi and phone networks inside their offices. Her thumb hesitated above the button disabling the phone networks of the whole building, but she thought better of it for now; the last thing they wanted was a disgruntled Colleen from the enquiries desk marching up to IT in the management offices wanting to know why her desk phone wasn't working.

The device showed a red light, indicating that the management team's phone networks were now down. No one roused within the offices. No one had noticed a thing. In Ana's experience, most of their mornings were taken up with meetings anyway, and – having their own coffee machines – they didn't usually bother mixing with other staff in the canteen.

And yet despite these little luxuries, they didn't possess their own keys to their offices, and the porters alone were able to lock and unlock these doors. She remembered Dan saying: 'If anything truly bad did happen, you can always depend on some bloody idiot to try and be a hero about it, making everything worse for everyone. It's best to lock them in, shut them down, if you can't trust them to stick to the plan.' With every single click, Ana recalled Dan's words. She felt close to him now, performing these actions, just in the way he would.

She then made her way towards the main entrance. If she could locate Dan, it was more than possible that they would still be on target. She could perhaps even reason with Dan that she had taken the security device *because* she had spotted a missing manuscript, and needed to vacate the North and South reading rooms quickly. She wasn't sure how much time she had before the first member of the management team would try to exit to use the lavatory and realise there was a problem. He or she wouldn't panic immediately – it happened every now and then with these electronic doors of course – but if the problem wasn't resolved within those standard five minutes, then panic would spread, and though they wouldn't be able to get out, it was more than possible that a wandering reader, walking past the corridor to go to the toilet, might pick up on something and raise the alarm.

She arrived at the porter station to find it completely empty. She felt the prickle of panic zinging along her fingers and down her back. What if he'd already alerted the authorities? Would he do that before confronting her? She hurried along the strip of red carpet towards the main entrance. There was of course the option of closing those doors now, and finding some other way to vacate the reading rooms; but if Dan was still roaming the building, looking for them, he'd be a liability. She remembered that vacant stare in Nan's eyes, the way she'd looked when they'd practised holding the gun. Would she shoot Dan? Kill him there and then? Ana wasn't sure it was a risk she was willing to take.

As she moved closer to the front door, she finally saw him. He stood a few feet away from the entrance, smoking a spliff. She stopped dead in her tracks, knowing that any movement right now would betray her, and she wouldn't have any idea what to say to him when he noticed her. She tried to imagine herself telling him about the theft in that panicked voice she'd rehearsed, and yet her mouth now felt dry and sticky, like no words could ever be forced out of it. *A missing manuscript,* they had decided was their best bet, for according to rule 532 in the handbook this specified that all visitors needed to be removed from the building, kept in the car park under the watchful eye of the porter, and that a thorough search of their possessions should happen outside, while the rest of the security staff scoured the building for evidence. Dan could only do one of those things, being the only porter on duty, and she and Nan could offer to do the rest. Stoned as he was, he probably wouldn't realise until he'd finished searching everyone that he was locked out of his own building.

A missing manuscript, she rehearsed again. She had not decided which one – she was pretty sure he wouldn't ask. She stepped forward, trembling, and told herself this was it now; this would be the moment everything would start hurtling into action, and there would be no turning back.

Yet she found that she couldn't move an inch. Her body would not carry out her mind's intentions. Something about the fact that Dan had gone ahead with his spliff break anyway, despite not knowing where his keys were, made Ana feel desperately sorry for him somehow. She recalled how he'd opened up to her, that one time when they'd nearly kissed, about how he felt he was destined to repeat the same old patterns time and time again. 'When everyone assumed you'll reoffend anyway,' he'd said, 'it's just too easy to slip into that role, whether you want to or not.' She had never been as attracted to him as she was in that moment, his vulnerability almost palpable in the sadness of his dark blue eyes, and it was this – more than anything – she thought of now, at this most opportune moment, as she stood looking at him in the open door. How involving him any further in this would be dragging him down with them, writing the rest of his story for him, the one everyone expected of him, when she had told him, with conviction, that he alone was the author of his own history. That he was free to change the story at any time.

As Dan lifted his head and saw her – looking right at her with a smile of relief forming on his face, perhaps thinking she had come to give him his security device back – she shoved the heavy door shut. As she engaged the lock and walked away, she only hoped that, when he realised what she had done for him, he would appreciate this small detail of hers that had kept him on the right side of the law for once.

Perhaps this door, she told herself, had always been destined to be shut between them.

Eben

10.15 AM

Eben's gloved fingers had found their way into a year with a soft, candy-cane cover. Elena was eleven and her handwriting an abomination, each syllable leaving tiny ink whorls in its wake, and it thrilled him as well as annoying him, seeing tangible evidence of her existence on the page. He had just finished reading an extremely dull account of a cricket match at Fox Spring Primary School, where Elena randomly noted members of the team (Eddie, Lissa, Gwennie and John). Following this was a cryptic recollection of another game played with Lissa in the cloakroom – where Lissa had to pretend to be Elena's husband – and where, according to the diary, they 'did what mummies and daddies do'.

He paused for a second. What was this? A kiss? He wondered whether it was worth noting this as the start of Elena's revolt against men. Then again, the link was pretty tenuous. He decided to take note of it anyway. If he found nothing else, then he would simply have to make the most of this anecdote – perhaps devote a whole chapter to it: *The Sexual Awakening in the Fox Spring Cloakrooms.*

He tossed the diary back onto the pile. He couldn't help but feel uncomfortable about wading through the reminiscences of a little girl, at his age. He knew that deep down he was not interested in the early recollections, he was only interested in reading about his own – supposedly devastating – impact upon her state of mind, but, looking up at the CCTV, he wondered how it would look to them if he disregarded these early entries. Like a person who only reads the most horrific, heart-wrenching sections of a misery memoir, somehow to make himself feel better about his own life. No, he had to do this properly if he was to redeem himself. Then again he knew he could only truly be redeemed if she came back from the dead. 'And trust me, that's the last thing this country needs,' he muttered in the direction of Elena's portrait bust.

Since the world had learned about the motivation for Elena's suicide, and since Eben had been held accountable as the straw that *literally* broke the camel's back (back, neck, and the femoral shaft), it was as if their lives were destined to be intertwined. It was another suggestion of Frankton's (in a bid to undo the unhelpful suggestion that had led to the fiasco in the first place) that instead of railing against this uncomfortable connection with a dead author, Eben could somehow 'lean in' and accept that if the whole thing was his responsibility, then it could also be the making of him. But Eben was also hoping, secretly, to discover that he would be featured in her diaries in some way, that he would be able to finally see, in truth, what kind of impact he'd had on her. Perhaps even find a way of exonerating himself through interpreting the way she had seen him differently.

'It might mean that I get the last word on why you killed yourself,' he said, getting up now to walk towards her portrait bust. 'What was it, Elena? The idea that you could live forever if only you died before your time?' He ran his fingers along the side of her face, down the ridge of her nose, trying to resist the temptation to poke her in those glinting eyes, then he remembered the CCTV cameras in all four corners of the room, watching his every move. He imagined the porter and the archivist, sitting there, watching him conversing with a chunk of bronze.

Recalling those people who had access to the room made his bladder throb. Not that he really needed the toilet – not yet – but he knew he was prone to needing the loo very suddenly, and if he didn't start making preparations for the eventuality now, then things might get messy. He tried his best to think it through. Should he press the red emergency button slightly ahead of time? How long would it take for them to come and open the doors? What if they arrived straightaway? If he went too soon it was possible he'd have trouble urinating and then he'd have to make the same request again almost immediately, making them think he had some sort of problem. He considered, paced, waited, and tried to distract himself with a few more diary entries in the interim.

Then he thought: *Bugger it, better play it safe than piss your pants in the National Library*, and pressed the emergency button. He returned to his seat, knowing he had a bit of a buffer still, ten minutes or so before he really needed to go, by which time he assumed someone would definitely be here to let him out. But it was hard to concentrate with all this uncertainty. He managed to flick through a few more entries, distracting himself as he read about Elena's scandalously under-marked essay in Fox Spring primary, her first real crush on a girl (not Lissa, it turned out after all, but Gwennie, her other cricket-team pal), her first period and all its confusion, and then her father's sudden death on the last day of a perfect summer.

He took his time with this particular entry. The death of a parent was surely the most significant event in the life of any writer; an event he would need to delve deeply into in the biography. As he read on, he discovered it had been a boating accident while they were on the holiday of a lifetime in a tropical country. The eleven-year-old Elena had witnessed it all as she cartwheeled along the shore. Two speedboats had been travelling towards another, one boatman understanding the rules of the sea, which was to alter course to the right, but the other boatman had not known this, hitting the speedboat side-on, with the anchor of the second boat hurtling through the air, hitting her father with brute force in the head, taking away half his skull in an instant.

Elena described the unreality of the scene, being suspended topsy-turvy as she was when the boats approached each other, trying to perfect her cartwheel with only the one hand along the yellow ridge, the blood rushing to her head, making her giddy; the colours of her world intermingling. She could not stop laughing, she said, when she had finally become upright again, when the world in front of her slid back into its vertical position, the kaleidoscope of sea and sand solidifying. And she had still been laughing when she witnessed a faraway stick man who she had not known was her father, go flying backwards into the sea, to change its hue forever.

That's when the beach had seemed to fall away from her, making her lose her balance; the moment she realised that she could no longer depend on the co-ordination that she prided herself on. *It was as if my time of happiness, of sunshine, of ease had drained like sand in the hourglass timer,* the young Elena had written. *Like I had cartwheeled into another existence. That as I landed, I found that entire beach and myself inside the glass, just falling away down to the bottom, never to return to the top.*

Eben looked up and thought about his own father's death, five years ago now, the gradual stiffening of him in that chair in the sun room, whilst he and his mother had been washing and drying the dishes in the kitchen. There had been nothing poetic in that. They had been avoiding him; because he was in one of his foul moods. *Let him sleep it off,* his mother had said, as they both moved into the lounge to watch some television. They had drifted off themselves then, perhaps for an hour or more. By the time they'd resurfaced from their own naps it had gone dark in the house, and they had known, somehow, upon waking, that something terrible had happened. Something that could have been avoided, had they known.

He couldn't ascribe any particular significance to the way his father had died, not in the way Elena could. It had not been poetic like her loss; her mainstay literally uprooted from the very depths, leaving her unmoored in life. He was feeling jealous of her even now, because she had done family tragedy better than he had. He tried to distract himself from the ugly feeling by making a note to explore the significance of her father's death in her works.

But it was hard to think clearly now with his bladder preoccupying him; taking up too much space in his brain. He closed the diary and pressed the red button again, frantically this time, not once but twice, three times, and on the third attempt he looked pleadingly into the eye of the security camera in the corner of the room.

Then, in desperation, he did it the old-fashioned way: he went towards the door and he knocked. He knocked and knocked and knocked.

He waited by the door. With every passing minute of nothingness came hope, and then it scurried away again. Still, he clung on to it, that hope, because it was still there; the opening of that door was still possible, and believing in it kept him calm, kept him focused. He knew he needed to focus now, because otherwise it could tip into a fully fledged panic attack.

He recalled the last one he'd had, the week Elena died. He'd been walking down the high street in town feeling absolutely fine, after a reassuring phone call with his mother, and then he'd noticed – or imagined he'd noticed – every single pair of eyes on the street turn to look at him. There were so many of them, bobbing and glistening until they formed into a tide that came crashing towards him, pulling him down, down, down into their depths. He couldn't move. He could barely breathe. He slid down the side of a lamppost and willed himself to drown. By then, everyone on the high street really *was* staring at him, and the seagulls seemed to have encircled him, blocking his way out.

After he'd been checked over by paramedics, Professor Nicholas appeared from somewhere like an apparition, trying to heal him with a quote from two centuries ago.

'What was it that Eben the Poet said?' he'd said. 'A writer has no comment or judgement to make on the ways of the world, or something like that.'

Eben had merely closed his eyes and willed Nicholas to go away.

'Too modest, you see, old Eben the Poet,' Nicholas had continued, trailing Eben's unsteady footsteps back towards the seafront. 'He saw through the sham of literature even as he was writing it. He knew it couldn't really change anything, just a random collection of words on a page. Elena Oodig, on the other hand, well I don't think she was capable of that particular insight. You only pointed out what everyone was thinking, that her novels were not as important as she thought they were.'

Eben paused. Had he said such a thing? It seemed so ridiculous now, that he – who had never written a word of fiction in his life – had felt himself entitled to express such opinions, as if on behalf of the masses. The fact that Nicholas agreed with him was not reassuring in any way; for Eben saw now he had been speaking on behalf of a contingent of people he did not particularly like.

'I mean, did she ever really work a day in her life, that woman? She should have tried getting a real job, like Eben the Poet. None of this full-time writing business. Who can devote a whole day to writing? It's madness. Ebenezer had several jobs, he was a schoolmaster, but more importantly, he was also a bookbinder. He bound some of the greatest books of our great nation. Actually used his hands for the good of others. And you'd do well to remember that my boy – we've all got a duty to live up to the semantics of our names.'

It was some small comfort for Eben to think that his name had some historical significance, even if he was yet to make his own historical impact. He had been named after a long-dead ancestor his mother had heard her grandmother talking about; the only one in their family to make a mark on this world, until now, she had said, gazing down hopefully at him as a five-year-old child.

Not that there was any evidence, either, of this Eben the Poet's existence; less still of the so-called poetry with which he had made his mark. And yet Nicholas talked of him as if everyone should know who he was. Eben more than once had run the name through the library's search engines, to find nothing. He had tried many variations on the name – Eben the Great, Eben the poet, Ebenezer Thomas, Thomas, Ebenezer: nothing. He'd requested to peruse the special collections recently, only to be told that they were in no condition to be manhandled, but even scanning the digitised copies he couldn't find any trace of him.

If he had ever existed (which all the specialist archivists seemed very much to doubt) then perhaps, they told him, his work had been lost in the recent fire. Eben had walked away feeling despondent, thinking that perhaps his grandmother had greatly inflated the importance of their long-lost relative, a man who existed only in the brains of octogenarians like Professor Nicholas, taking up stubborn residence there like a tumour.

By now, Eben's panic level was rising along with the urine in his bladder. He visualised the humble salvation the library toilets would give him, and vowed never to take them for granted again – those wondrous, heavenly urinals that were always there for you to pour yourself into, and those other useful things around them that one could hold on to in the advent of a panic attack – sinks, rails, even hand dryers – all wonderful testimony to the solid texture of the world, its practicality, its usefulness. Feeling his breathing becoming more laboured now, he also felt as though he needed the reassurance of the bathroom mirror to convince himself that against all odds, and unlike his poetic predecessor, he still existed.

'I am a valid, real thing. A real person,' he said out loud. Then, in a hopeful whimper, 'I can hold. I can hold. I can hold.'

It was crunch time now for his prostate. The tragedy surrounding Elena's dad, as unfortunate as it was, had simply been an unfortunate reminder of an uncontrollable mass of water. He scoured the archive quickly for an alternative lavatory. He tried to think of his body in clinical terms as a container that needed emptying, and convinced himself that every container everywhere could be emptied into something else. Wasn't life all about moving things from one space into another? Hadn't all these books been elsewhere once? He merely needed to transfer the urine from his body into something that would absorb it, or make it disappear. He was in an underground archive so there were no windows, nothing to pour oneself out of. No bins. No baskets. The hand sanitiser bottle was already brimful, and even if he emptied it, it was transparent. His utter shame could be dispensed in handfuls for all to see.

Every other thing in his eyeline seemed impossibly horizontal and flat; a shelf was a place one simply could not piss. And besides, any flash of genitalia would be caught on the security camera and he would more than likely be barred from the building for the rest of his life.

And so Eben did the only thing he could. He sat down perfectly still at the desk and pretended to be reading about Elena's dad's funeral, while the hot urine poured shamefully out of him and into his dark corduroy trousers.

Dan

10.30AM

He was locked out of his own building and stoned out of his mind. The curlicues in the wood now seemed to be forming a million monster faces, all mocking him.

He couldn't think straight. Not that it was a requirement, at this point in his day, to think straight: it would usually suffice to simply *walk* straight, zombie-like, towards his checkpoints, punching the nun-device into the sensors, working his way methodically through his rounds, while his mind roamed in nonsensical circles. But now this – a locked door, having hollow, nun-less pockets – had made him *focus*. He no longer had his checklist. Again and again he recalled the image of her, standing in the doorway with that strange look on her face, shoving the door shut.

Had he agreed to let her do this? Had they discussed it, only for him to forget? He was getting a bit annoyed with her now. He'd thought that once she knew the CCTV had been switched that she'd be up for it, that they'd have sex anywhere and everywhere, but for some reason she was making him wait longer than usual. Then again, perhaps this was some twisted sex game on her behalf, some kind of strange challenge, something to make sure he'd go looking for her, beg her to give the device back. The thought aroused him instantly, though the heaviness in his body from the spice made him slightly anxious that he wouldn't be able to perform, when it came to it.

He kicked himself now for having his morning spliff earlier than usual, and for not giving the theft of the device much thought. He had assumed she was going to come and find him sooner or later. Smoking so openly in that little alcove just outside the library entrance had given him a particular kind of thrill, especially when he checked his double on the porter-cam and heard on the audio the voice of the Dan of a few weeks back scolding postgraduate students for doing the exact same thing he was doing now and sending them on their way. He listened to the audio file he'd replaced the live stream with, and felt impressed with himself as he puffed out the blue smoke all around him.

The arch-porter and his cronies would probably be erecting the screen in the conference room right now. He imagined them pointing at the version of himself he'd created for them, smugly demonstrating how their advanced porter-cam meant that a porter could be left alone in the building for a whole day without anything going awry. Not only could you see him on CCTV, but you could see what he could see and hear his every move via the porter-cam. The arch-porter would click away to each and every corner of the alcove, and the fake, perfect day in a national institution would shine back at those who financed it; a sham of the past masquerading as the near-perfect future.

The spliff was a good one; perhaps a bit too good. He'd tried mixing in a bit of old-school skunk into the spice – a combination he hadn't tried before. He'd felt that familiar burn in the back of his neck, before the explosion of sweet, mellow smoke. He tried not to think about what was going on in his body when he inhaled, what protests surely came from inside an otherwise healthy body. So many of the other inmates had come out and hadn't touched a drug since. But the only thing that got Dan through prison was knowing he'd be able to smoke again. Who in their right mind would choose to live without *this*?

Once he realised that she wasn't coming back to open the door, the paranoia kicked in, sending his stoned mind into overdrive. The library itself seemed to double in size in front of him, and he looked down at himself, wondering if the reality of the situation was not that the library was bigger, but that he was shrunken to half his size somehow. Had she put something in his coffee that morning, to make him smaller? Would he eventually become so small that he would be trampled by her, squished into the fibres of the red carpet like an insect?

He rubbed his eyes and tried to push the thought away. Being no longer in possession of the nun-device meant he didn't know what to do with his hands, and they seemed like a distinctly alien prospect to him, these five-finger-digit splays at the ends of his arms. What were they for, exactly? He ended up moving them around his body to check that he was still clothed, because a gust of wind had come from somewhere and its chill had convinced him for a second that he had completely neglected to get dressed that morning.

He sat down on the library steps and turned his face outward, towards the sea, which seemed a more forgiving space than the impenetrable building behind him. The sun came out from behind the clouds, silvering the waves, turning them, it seemed, into sheets of aluminium. *I could walk away on those waves,* he told himself, *leave all this behind.* Closing his eyes, he became completely at ease with the notion that there was a way out of the mess he had created. He simply had to get away from here, down to the beach, and walk away on those rigid sheets to whatever was on the other side. It seemed, for a brief moment, like this was an entirely plausible thing to do. And she'd be waiting for him on the other side, he fantasised, splayed out naked on a rock like a siren, congratulating him for working out the puzzle, for realising that their relationship did not belong in there, in the confines of the building, but out here, in the open air, where they could finally be together properly.

But on opening his eyes again, the feeling slipped away. And just like that, he returned to being the broken thing he knew he was, and suddenly the sea's vastness wasn't comforting, but menacing

– ready to devour him whole. A cry rose up in his throat, a lump the size of a golf ball, and he tried desperately to push away the bad thoughts that plagued him; faces and voices from another time in his life, those that had led to his incarceration. Voices screaming accusations at him outside a court.

'No, no, no,' he said aloud. 'Think of something funny.'

The problem was that being on his own on this step outside a towering building he hated was not funny. The fact he was there because he'd rigged the CCTV, for a nameless woman he'd only known for a month, because he thought himself safe to do whatever he wanted, was not funny. The notion of himself as a real porter and himself as an unreal porter, walking along corridors in the past-that-had-become-the-future was also not funny. All the fun had been sucked out of him. He realised how much of a fraud he had been, what a bad person he continued to be. Pacing back in forth in his library uniform, as if it meant something. As if it could right the wrongs of the past. Outwardly displaying the version of Dan that the world wanted him to be; inwardly knowing he could never be that person, even if he wanted to. It was too late for all that. The real Dan had been formulated a very long time ago, the second he'd forgotten that there were real people out there who could be damaged, or even erased entirely from life, by his thoughtless decisions.

Suddenly, nothing was more urgent than opening the door back into his life, his job, his routine – despite how much he hated it. Because after months of guarding nothing, of following a checklist, now suddenly something was happening. Something that he had to formulate a plan for. He was being called upon to act. Doors were shutting in his face in a way they never had before; and even if there was a predetermined direction in which the Dan on the porter-cam would travel, the narrative of the Dan of the present had not yet been written. In that one hopeful, potent, stoned moment of euphoria, this seemed to give him hope that he could still be someone else; that perhaps all his life he had been waiting for this moment, for two versions of himself to run concurrently, so he could have the option of which one he wanted to be; that he didn't have to be the one who had been so swayed by a woman's passing affection that he had abandoned all sense of duty and decency.

And for the first time since starting his job at the library, he realised that he perhaps wanted to be the Dan who had not yet taken his usual route, one who wanted to ensure the safety of everything, and everyone, inside.

Ana and Nan

10.50AM

'This is a security announcement. Will all staff please make their way to the North Reading Room. A security drill will now take place. Will all staff please leave their desks immediately.'

Nan looked up, surprised to hear her sister's voice over the tannoy system. She had expected to hear a rather stoned, breathless Dan making an announcement, tripping over his words, trying his best to sound stone-cold sober. *All staff and visitors to leave the building immediately and to gather in the library car park,* was the announcement she had expected to hear, imagining Ana placing the handbook right in front of him to see the wording he needed to use, in the unlikely event of a manuscript going missing.

Summer, Lily and Pale sighed in unison; a chorus of stale breath. Without the officiousness of a porter's voice they weren't taking it seriously. They barely registered an announcement had been made. Summer, the exhibitions officer, was arguing on the phone with someone from the neighbouring country about being loaned a medieval manuscript that was actually theirs in the first place; Lily, the photography officer, was hunched over a black and white photograph that she had been scanning repeatedly all morning; and Pale, the equality and diversity officer, was wading through job applications disinterestedly, trying to filter out all the male candidates, at the head librarian's request.

'Come on. We need to go,' said Nan, trying to control the quiver in her voice.

'It'll be a waste of time,' Summer said, muting her call, gesticulating wildly at the phone. 'God, this guy is such a dick! He thinks I should be grateful that they're loaning us our own bloody manuscript.'

Summer went back to the call, getting up now to pace in the corner of the room as she continued her negotiations. Nan turned to the other two women.

'You heard what Ana said. We need to go now. It sounded urgent.'

'They only get the staff to do them to train them up,' Pale replied, eyes squinting at her screen. 'It would be the head librarian if it was important. It wasn't even one of the porters.'

Nan's mind was breaking apart again. Perhaps they had in fact agreed on this, and she'd already forgotten? Looking down and seeing Ana's phone left on her desk (another thing they had agreed upon: no phones, no selfies, no unnecessary text trail that could be used to further incriminate them), she had no way of knowing or confirming that this was how they were to proceed from now on. If Dan was not making the announcement, then something had gone terribly wrong. Either that or he was too stoned to care.

'Head librarian isn't in today,' Summer added, now back at her desk looking irate. 'She's down in the capital with the security team.'

'Exactly,' Pale said, reading her screen, rubbing her bump in response to another painful twinge. 'What kind of security drill is it going to be without the security team?'

'It's more than likely part of the security presentation,' Nan added. 'They're probably demonstrating to the head of state how effective each drill is, how up to date our security training is.'

'Well yes it's so bloody up to date that's all we ever do! Look, I don't hear anybody else stirring, in any case,' Lily added, without taking her eyes off her photograph, which she was now perusing through a large magnifying glass.

Nan stared blankly ahead of her. Like them she had noticed the silence in the corridors; the obvious lack of movement. She wondered what had become of the rest of them, those standing in Ana's way.

'Well I'm not shifting,' Pale added. 'Not in my condition. Surely a pregnant woman has some kind of get-out clause in this situation.'

'We could take the lift,' Nan said, her voice venturing out timidly into the air. The three women turned to look at her. She saw the surprise in their eyes. She never usually said a thing. She certainly never volunteered an opinion; and now here she was suggesting a plan, bordering on issuing a command.

After the shock had been absorbed, Summer spoke. 'Lifts are prohibited in emergencies. Haven't you been listening to anything they've told us?'

'But it's not an emergency,' Nan replied. 'It's a drill. There's a difference. The purpose of the drill is to pre empt an emergency.'

'Well one minute you say it's urgent, the next it isn't. Which one is it?' Pale challenged her.

'It's not actually because they want every institution to be safe,' Lily said, 'it's so they can tick the box and say that every institution is now "technically" safe.'

'There have been a lot of attacks recently,' Nan continued, feeling time slipping through her hands, their mission floating further and further away. 'You never know when we might be hit.'

'We're not the kind of institution the terrorists are interested in,' Summer said. 'It'll just be a demonstration of the porter-cams. The security guards are probably watching the whole thing from the capital, to see how we'll cope, just to see if we've been listening to what they've been telling us. That's all this is, I tell you.'

'You can't presume that terrorists won't attack us,' Pale said. 'Terrorism isn't elitist anymore. They've terrorised the shit out of the neighbouring country already; they might be getting a bit bored of that . . .'

'But that's where the power is,' Lily replied. 'It's pointless targeting us, when we've got no power anyway. Most people in the neighbouring country won't even have heard of this place, let alone care about it being attacked . . .'

'Yes, but the terrorists might get some random person to per-
petrate the crime here, so that our country gets annoyed with
the neighbouring country because they think it's all their fault,
and we turn against them too, and perhaps even join the fight
against them . . .' Pale continued. Nan remembered how obsessed
Pale had always been about these arbitrary attacks, being afraid
to go anywhere further than a two-mile radius because she was
convinced that even their capital city was a place of danger. It
had all changed since she'd become pregnant, of course. She was
strangely fearless now, as though she thought that the baby made
her exempt from threats. Either that or she couldn't process the
knowledge that an unborn baby could be vulnerable to anything.

'Wait, you think we need some terrorists here in order for us to
get annoyed with the neighbouring country?' Summer was pacing again now, phone in hand. 'Just try talking to one of their
management team, that'll annoy you plenty. There's the small
matter of five hundred years of colonisation, stealing all our
resources . . . but oh no, we were all still bending over backwards
until the terrorists came. Oh hi, Neil . . . how are you doing? Sorry
about that . . . So, any movement with processing that loan?'

Nan circled their desks now like a vulture as they continued
their conversations. They didn't seem to even notice her doing
it. Five to eleven, on each of their screens, on every single watch
and clock in the room. Two elevens lying on top of each other,
obscuring each other, becoming one: perfect twins for one whole
minute, despite their differences. All clocks seemed to her now
a devastating reminder of the unstoppability of time, how their
throngs and gongs and chimes, which pretended to be signalling forward movement, were all just eerie ends. Another hour,
another minute gone, never to return.

She sometimes wondered whether she was actually ready to bid
farewell to the last few months, a time when she and her sister had
united for a common cause, agreeing for once as they conspired

together. Giving all that up, and entering a dangerous new time zone of things yet to achieve, yet to be done, yet to be agreed on, wasn't easy to do.

'If we were going to get killed by terrorists, do you really think a security drill would make that much difference?' Summer said. 'Because surely we know that we're going to die in that situation. There's nothing much we can do to get out of it. Because who's to say, even if we followed their bloody instructions, did everything they asked of us in an emergency, that we would actually be able to follow their advice when it came down to it. I mean it's like if you encountered a lion in the wild . . .'

'Oh don't be going on about the lion,' said Lily. Nan had heard this argument countless times before from Summer. She looked at the clock. Time was leaving them behind.

'Lion? What lion?' asked Pale.

'If you were out in the wild and you suddenly happened upon a lion, apparently the only way to survive is to stand your ground. To show the lion you aren't afraid of it. You have to continue facing it, even if it comes at you. They tell you to clap your hands, to call out, wave your arms around, do stuff that makes you look bigger, so it'll think twice about attacking you. But I mean, in all seriousness. How could anyone be calm enough to do that? I mean, who'd actually *wave* at a lion? You'd shit your pants and run, wouldn't you?' Summer said.

'Yep,' Lily replied. 'Let's face it, ninety per cent of people would just go on instinct in that moment and make a run for it – not that *you* could with that stomach.' She laughed, gently caressing Pale's pregnant belly.

Nan felt the sweat pooling in her blouse. Time was now a hungry, approaching lion: ready to charge at her. She needed to do something; to make herself bigger. Distract them with a wave. Ana would probably be arriving at the North Reading Room now, the readers impatient to get on with their work, wondering where the rest of the staff were. She hoped her sister would know what to do, how to improvise, how to stall things, confidently.

'Look, we've been summoned so I really think we should go,' Nan said, standing up. She was going to give them one last chance before she had to do something drastic. 'Can we go, please?'

'I'm not going anywhere,' Pale said defiantly, one hand on her swollen belly. 'These applicants won't choose themselves.'

'And I've really got to sort out this shitshow with the medievalists,' Summer said.

'I'm not missing out on my coffee break for it,' Pale said. 'They've got almond croissants today.'

And that was it; the three women turned their backs and went click-clacking their way towards coffee time.

Nan had no option. She had tried her best. She reached for her bag underneath her desk. She opened it and stared into its black insides, reaching for the thing that she had felt digging into her ankles all morning. She lifted it, shivering slightly, then she stood up. Held it aloft. And then Summer turned, just to flick a chewed nail into the waste basket, and turned and saw what Nan was holding.

Summer tapped Lily on the shoulder, who in turn lowered her hand onto Pale's back. Pale finally understood that coffee time wasn't happening anytime soon.

The lion had walked brazenly right into their office.

*

Nan was late. Ana assumed it would be by twelve minutes. That she was making a point.

She'd had no choice but to press ahead with the security announcement – and ditch the missing manuscript scenario. She had decided that a simple drill was the best way to get them out – cleanly, efficiently, quickly. Once she'd disabled the audio in the management team's rooms so that they wouldn't hear the announcement, there was no time now to go back to the office and try to explain to Nan that she had decided to leave Dan out of it. But because Nan was nowhere to be seen, she'd had no choice but to address the small congregation in the North Reading Room while she waited for her sister. It seemed like a sensible enough thing to do while she counted down the minutes; she didn't want them getting bored, or restless, or – even worse – for them to leave the room only to find that all the doors to the reading room were locked. As long as everyone considered themselves free, everything would be fine, and no one would panic. Which is exactly how she wanted them: a calm, obliviously incarcerated crowd. When she saw some of them reaching for their phones in pure boredom she quickly reached for the security device and disabled the internal phones and the mobile phone signal, ensuring it was now cut off across the building. She saw some attempt to refresh their screens, others turning them on and off to try to bring them back to life, but to no avail.

'Right then, people, can we settle down please,' she shouted, finding some new confidence in her self-appointed authority.

Some were still talking amongst themselves, consulting with each other about the loss of signal. Mainly the younger members of the crowd. The older male historians were engrossed in conversation, leaning against the sculpture of the library's founder – Sir John – finding solace in his marbled masculinity. In his day Sir John had been a respected historian, book collector and obstetrician, apothecary to the queen. After his day, he had been nothing but an ignored piece of marble to lean against, and accused by one of his descendants of being Jack the Ripper. Some had since called for his removal, despite the fact that without his donation of some twenty-five thousand books from his personal collection, heaved up here by horse and cart in an age long ago, the place would never have been built.

'If I could have your attention now please,' she shouted, louder this time, getting up onto a chair so that she was level with Sir John. Everyone stopped talking. A little bit of height was all it took.

They turned to look at her. Some of them – a blonde-haired student and her spectacled lover in particular – clearly considered this as a bit of entertainment. They never seemed to be very hard at work, those two, gazing soporifically at the screens in front of them, playing footsie with each other under the tables. Those who genuinely came here to work – the odd lecturer on a sabbatical who was trying to finish a book, who knew that term time was yet again approaching – were not so pleased with the disruption. Who knew what her intrusion had cost them? Perhaps they were on the verge of a great discovery that could, in time, earn them another sabbatical, another term of library time.

'Now then, this is just a drill, but I want you to imagine that the whole building is in lockdown, like we were during the Great Sickness,' she said, still hoping that Nan would emerge any second, with their three colleagues in tow, so that she could discreetly release the doors, making them look like they had not been locked the whole time, and get them all out of the building through the emergency exit at the back, which was at the opposite side of the building to where she had left Dan. Possibly the sound of the hostages emerging would attract his attention, but by the time he'd reached them, they'd be shutting the door on the hostages and Dan, and would be able to get on with things, leaving Dan to deal with the chaos that ensued outside. She could imagine that most of the visitors would be angry, annoyed at having their day so rudely disrupted; but that Dan would also have his own back-tracking to do in his dealings with them. He was not going to admit to a crowd of people for whom he was responsible for their safety, that he had done anything untoward. He would find a suitable story, she was sure of it, and send them on their way. She felt a pang of affection for him again, thinking of how he'd been so willing to change the CCTV screens with the simple promise of sex, and hoped he would be able to rationalise her decision in time. That through stopping him from going any further, committing any other crime, she was showing him how she felt. That, in any other universe, she would have been more than willing to do what he wanted to do with her.

'The phone signal's gone,' said the blonde girl. 'Fat lot of use that would be if we were in danger, eh?'

'No one's in danger, OK? If you'll just bear with me,' Ana continued, as the murmurs began to spread across the reading room. 'I just want you to imagine that we're all under siege so that we can carry out a recce of the best routes to—'

Someone, somewhere laughed.

'A library, under siege?' It was the spectacled second-rate boyfriend Dan had told her about.

'Don't think of it as a library,' she continued. 'It's a national institution. A symbol of a nation, of the culture that makes the nation what it is.' She was riffing now, but curiously impressed with herself for what was coming out of her mouth, a rehashing of the stuff she remembered her mother saying. 'What makes us unique, what makes us different, it's all here. It's what makes this building so much of a threat. If they want us to conform, better get rid of the place that makes us bold enough to think for ourselves.'

A thought struck her then, that if those in front of her knew the specifics of her job at the library, how outraged they would be with her actions. It was a job neither her sister nor her mother knew anything about; a job that threatened to eradicate the very principles she was pretending to uphold now: *what makes us unique, what makes us different*. She pushed the shameful thought from her mind. It was just a job; and ultimately it would not matter now – whatever tasks she had carried out in here – for surely she was about to do something far worse.

'But wouldn't the Government Office be a better place to start?' said the lady in charge of archives. 'I'm thinking of the media coverage here. An attack is nothing if nobody notices . . .'

'I accept your point,' Ana continued, slightly annoyed at the intrusion, 'but that's rather predictable, don't you think? OK, so . . . the exit areas are what I'd like to concentrate on . . .'

'Where's the porter?' queried Colleen, the archivist behind the enquiries desk, munching on an apple. 'Isn't he meant to be the one doing this . . . ?'

'He's um . . .' Ana thought of Dan now, roaming outside. Free as a bird. 'The head librarian is delegating some of the porter's duties to the library staff . . .'

'Of course they are,' Colleen replied, rolling her eyes. 'Before you know it, they will have done away with porters altogether and it'll be us unblocking the toilets and doing the night shift. Well he won't have opened up the archive in that case. There's a researcher down there . . . that Eben Prytherch . . . I should go and get him . . .'

'Oh you can leave him where he is for now,' Ana said, trying to sound nonchalant.

'I don't see why he should get away with it when everyone else is being dragged away from their work. I thought you of all people wouldn't want to make life easier for him . . .'

A numbness descended upon her, her whole body fighting against the panic that wanted to claim her now. Colleen was raising the internal phone behind her desk in order to call the porter's office, and would soon find it defunct. She needed to distract her.

'Colleen, look,' she said brusquely, with a force she'd never used before to confront the archivist everyone was terrified of, 'if we were being attacked now, you couldn't just wait for everyone to join us. That isn't how it works. We have to do this in a realistic way.'

Colleen looked up at her, lowering the phone. She seemed curious, if not a little impressed, by Ana's boldness.

'So, who's attacking us in this hypothetical scenario? Who's interested in attacking a country without power, honestly?' Colleen asked.

Ana could feel herself getting bogged down with the discussion; investing too much in it, when all she needed to do was to get them out of the building.

'That doesn't matter now, OK. Let's just say there *is* an attack, from an unknown source, for an unknown reason. And the front doors are locked, for your own protection, because it's been foreseen. You have five minutes to file out of the building safely, to the back of the building, where you will find police vans at the ready to escort you from the building. If such a thing happens, we need to ensure that you know exactly where you're going. I'm just waiting for a few colleagues to arrive and then after that I'll show you exactly how you should proceed if and when this happens for real.'

'What about the gases?' Colleen said, deadpan. 'Aren't we meant to trigger the sleeping gases in the event of a terrorist attack? There's a button down here somewhere isn't there?' Colleen's head disappeared momentarily underneath her desk.

'Lord, no, please!' said the elderly professor. 'Don't you remember what a mess our dear neighbours made of that? The opioid was too much for most of them, especially those of a certain age. Well, my age. . .'

'I think the sleeping gases would be a last resort in this kind of situation,' Ana added hurriedly. She recalled those dreams that had plagued her these last few weeks; bodies strewn everywhere in the reading room, convulsing, fighting for breath. 'Colleen, if you could please come over here now. . .'

Suddenly it seemed that the imaginary gasp from deep in Ana's subconscious was actually coming from inside the room somewhere. The elderly professor was staring in the direction of the doors, looking as though he might pass out.

'It's OK,' she added, thinking that perhaps she needed to adjust her tone slightly. 'There isn't any actual threat. The gases won't be necessary. As I've said repeatedly, this is just a drill, no one is going to come to any harm.'

The professor pointed in the direction of the double doors. On the other side stood Nan, Lily, Summer and Pale. It appeared momentarily that he was simply drawing Ana's attention to the fact that the automated doors weren't opening as they should to let them in, but on closer inspection she saw what the problem was. She saw what he'd seen through the glass. Soon the others would notice it too. She still had the option of not releasing the doors; to keep the whole fiasco that Nan had created for herself on the other side of the bomb-proof glass, but it was too late in the day now. They had to synchronise, and act together. As one. They had to erase those twelve minutes forever if they were ever going to try to become the same person, as their mother had always wanted.

And so she released the doors, so that Nan could enter the room holding a gun up to the heads of their three colleagues; and so that at last, those in the North Reading Room could finally acknowledge that a threat was a threat, no matter who presented it to them.

Eben

11.15AM

'I am resilient,' Eben whispered to himself for the second time in three minutes, the discomfort of the wet, urine-soaked trousers seeping into his bones, and into the very core of him, making it difficult to concentrate. He tried to distract himself by fantasising about getting into a warm bath, washing himself clean of the whole sordid business, but then he became overly aware that focusing on water again was too risky, for fear of aggravating his bladder again. Where the hell was the porter who was supposed to let him out? Was he himself on the toilet, Eben wondered, enjoying the simple freedom that Eben had been denied? The thought that he was not only incarcerated now, but stripped of a basic function that even an actual prisoner was permitted, wasn't helping his anxiety one bit, and so he turned back to the task at hand, forcing out one last affirmation through gritted teeth:

'I take full responsibility for making the most of my life,' he croaked into the stuffy air. 'Even if it means sitting here in soiled underpants.'

Eben sped on towards another decade of Elena's life, wanting to see for himself the unravelling that had led to her suicide. He wasn't willing to accept that it had been as simple as being ground down by one reviewer. No one was that fragile, and there were sure to be others who could be made accountable for what had happened to her. He wanted, if nothing else, to assess her thoughts and processes for himself, to see what else could be deduced from them. He came across a curious entry, which read:

In my inbox today was the latest issue of the magazine Small World. *I scrolled down, as usual, to the reviews. They tend to be a little on the light side, not even all that long, but this time there was just one, an extremely long rant (poorly disguised as a review) by Eben Prytherch about my novel* The Sperm Suicides. *My publisher had warned me that something was coming. I've seen him in readings. He sits in the front, rubs his nose incessantly, paranoid there must be something dangling there, with his stomach flopping out over the rim of his trousers. He socialises, awkwardly with people who obviously don't have time for him; tries to give the impression of being happy, but if you look closely, you can see it, in the crevices of his moon-bland face, that he's a late-night drinker (cheap supermarket wine, more than likely, for there is nothing classy about him), torn apart by loneliness, struggling to find meaning in life.*

He'll be waiting impatiently, throughout the reading, for the question and answer session at the end (for this is why he attends, not to listen to my thoughts but to voice his own). It's what he lives for. He's one of those who – when he starts speaking – you can hear the passive-aggressiveness knocking around in his windpipe, and the audience will give each other a look. He often asks me about my characters (he's the type who will start with: 'not a question, more of an observation really'), and will start to edge towards blaming me for their motivations, as if I live and breathe by my characters' actions. Even when I try to answer him calmly, I find it hard to hide my condemnation. Surely we know, as everyone around us does, that what is passing between us is pure vitriol. He gets up and leaves. Usually leaves something behind – a scarf, a pair of gloves – as though unwilling to remove himself completely. Always too embarrassed to return to retrieve them. My editor has great satisfaction in putting them in the bin afterwards.

Eben was stunned by this entry. He didn't remember asking any particular questions or making any comments. It was possible enough that he had rubbed his nose – he had allergic rhinitis for God's sake! He did remember being so flustered that he would leave things behind, yes, and she was right, too, that he was too embarrassed to return to gather them, because he imagined the whole auditorium would be talking about him by then. He had lost countless hats, scarves, and pairs of glasses in this way. But as for her other assumptions: he never touched wine, because it did not agree with him; the sulphites made him sneeze. He could only tolerate cognac, and an expensive brand too. He wanted to scribble all over the entry right there and then.

Suddenly he felt devastated by the fact that a pen – a real piece of paper – weren't even a possibility in this moment. Such things were now contraband, disease-riddled as the government claimed them to be.

'You can't rewrite the story,' he said, turning back to scold the portrait bust. 'You can't claim to know the truth of other people's lives, Elena.'

With his fingers over his eyes, he dared to move on to read Elena's review of *his* review:

Eben Prytherch had decided from the outset that he was not going to enjoy The Sperm Suicides. *I'm sure the title alone is enough to rile him and the Smotherhood. He already had an agenda, before he'd even turned the first page. For one thing, anyone who calls himself a friend to Frankton Emlyn, that idiotic non-writer-cum-critic, cannot be trusted. But here's another thing – Eben P is himself a wannabe writer, or so some say. So he will not be viewing the novel objectively, like a reader, but more like someone who could do better himself (or so he thinks).*

Some highlights of the review include him saying that my novel is 'unreadable' and that the idea of a society in which women are immortal is a preposterous concept in the first place, as though fiction were not a place for imagined worlds. He also wonders whether the recent addition to the family – the twins – conceived by a sperm donor, may have unduly influenced the writing – as though it is somehow wrong for a woman to be influenced by a sudden colossal change in her circumstances. I will admit that it sometimes pains me that I know nothing about the identity of the twins' father, and that so many men in this town are known to have contributed their sperm to the local sperm bank: imagine if I found out that he or Frankton Emlyn was their father! Such a thing could well be possible!

Eben didn't find that funny in the slightest. In fact, he'd been absolutely horrified when he'd heard Elena was pregnant by a sperm donor, only a few months after he'd made his own (obligatory) donation to the local sperm clinic. They had just passed the legislation that any man over thirty years of age without a partner had to donate, in order to get the population numbers back up after the Great Sickness, which had cruelly wiped out a number of young boys.

He remembered his mother being pleased about the new legislation, especially as she saw no other real prospect of becoming a grandmother. As most donors were less than enthusiastic about having to give up their sperm, it was, thankfully, up to each donor to choose whether they wanted their identities to be known to their children once they turned eighteen, and Eben, much to his mother's disapproval, had checked the box saying 'no'. Absolutely not. He couldn't think of anything worse. Not that this dampened his mother's enthusiasm for the whole thing. 'You give it a couple of years, and they'll have the right to find out, you mark my words,' she'd said, rubbing her hands gleefully at the thought of her own flesh and blood multiplying once, twice, three times – hundreds of times – across the small nation. 'I'll have hundreds of grandchildren!'

Eben shuddered at the memory as he read on:

Then he goes on to note every single inconsistency in TSS in a completely unintelligent and brusque fashion – he refutes that there can be any scientific basis for the concept of sperm annihilation, even though he can see in my acknowledgements that I have consulted with a scientist who has proven that sperm, indeed, do commit suicide in order to prevent harmful muta-tions being passed to offspring, and that my novel is just a playful expansion of this idea; what if men were to start dying to make way for the women of this world? It's obviously too much for some men to handle. I think what's bothering him the most, of course, is what an impact this novel has made. How much it has influenced society today. That it proves that fiction is powerful. That it can change the way people think.

Eben banged his head against the desk. He remembered all too well the avalanche of responses he'd received to the review, noting his shallow reading of the book, pointing out how ridic-ulous it was that a dystopian book like this had damaged his fragile ego to such an extent. He hadn't read it properly of course. He'd skimmed it, under duress, with Frankton telling him it was the worst thing he'd ever read; a ludicrous book, he had called it, and it was during a time where he never thought to question Frankton's authority.

Elena obviously displayed nothing but cold indifference to what he had written; she had given it no real consideration whatsoever. The review had bounced off her like a ping-pong ball.

He picked up the copy of *The Sperm Suicides*. A hardcover, with an image of a sperm with a noose around its neck, which had been very controversial at the time. More controversial, in Eben's opinion, was the fact that hardly any authors in the coun-try were permitted such an expensive delicacy as a hardcover, even before the paper ban. And now, they weren't even given the luxury of a physical copy. It was only if you went into the neighbour-ing country you could buy an actual book, and flaunt it around poolsides and parks and trains as a thing to be enjoyed. Try bring-ing it back into this country and it was a different story. You'd be reported to the police, the book would be taken off you and destroyed, in case it was hoarding harmful germs, and that would be the end of that.

Elena's books were some of the very last ones to appear in print. *The Sperm Suicides* had become vital reading for every teenage girl in the country, and had gone to reprint several times, right up until the paper ban. It was the likes of Elena, Eben often thought, who had used up all the paper before the Great Sickness, with this book being read time and time again, prohibiting the publication of other stories, other ways of thinking about the world. Elena had brainwashed an entire nation.

No doubt Elena had known, once the government started to issue warnings that excessive reading could lead to disease, what was to come with paper legislation. Perhaps she had pushed for these reprints, perhaps she had been buying up the copies herself. Considering how vocal Elena was about any kind of social injustice or inequality, she had remained curiously silent on the paper ban, and had not joined the chorus of literary voices who had objected to it. *Now if you had killed yourself over that,* he told her, *it would have been something.* Her suicide seemed a wasted opportunity. Making everyone hate him instead of loathing a system that enforced such random policies, which didn't seem to affect the neighbouring country one bit.

He reread the first paragraph of the novel, *The Sperm Suicides.*

It was the saint's day in the small country – the very first one that the government had approved as a public national holiday – and all the men in one small town died overnight, which was just the beginning. Many of the older wives did not notice until late into the morning; most assumed that their spouses were making use of the fact that they did not have to go to work and were merely having a lie-in. These wives sat at their windows looking out at the clear blue skies and the perfectly calm sea and called their husbands lazy so-and-sos under their breath, annoyed at how the best part of the day was gone now, never to return. They stomped and banged their way around their kitchens, hoping to rouse them, and when there was no further stirring, started ringing each other, making alternative plans for the day. Many of them did not notice anything was amiss until they were up on the hill overlooking the seaside town, when one of them saw, through the camera obscura, a fleet of black vehicles moving silently through the town like cockroaches, spreading out it seemed, to every street in the town, at least two or three black cars on every block. It was the younger men's bodies, of course, who had been discovered first, for their young wives had been up since the crack of the dawn with the children, and were not willing to accept the notion of the entitled lie-in their husbands seemed to have taken without asking, and so many of them kicked the bedroom doors open around eight am, baby on one hip, toddler trailing after them, all hurtling unsuspecting into a room heavy with death.

He cringed remembering how he'd called the concept 'reductive' because it only mentioned heterosexual couples, but this was the problem with skim-reading, because he'd missed another whole section of the book where it explained her reasoning for this. Again Elena had been influenced by her research, through which she'd discovered that several species, especially males, only lived long enough to reproduce, and then simply died, with the elevated stress levels from the mating causing their immune systems to collapse. She was playing with this concept, she said, applying it to mammals, who felt a certain pressure to reproduce in order to keep their small country populated enough so that it would not be overtaken by the neighbouring country. *We are just animals in the wild, trying to survive,* she'd written.

But even though Elena protested in every single interview that this novel was not some kind of warped fantasy on her behalf, but an expansion of a scientific concept, Eben remembered being haunted by the seemingly jubilant tone this opening presented, as though she were delighting in eradicating all the men who annoyed her. Although the novel never specified where the town was, it did not take a genius to work out that she had modelled the town on their own seaside town, where everyone knew everyone, and one rubbed shoulders uncomfortably with one's fans, one's critics, and one's haters. He could not shake the feeling that Elena gleefully condemned them all to death in their beds in one paragraph; that she was imagining himself and Frankton and other members of the Smotherhood lying there, grey and lifeless, all their purpose and intent drained from them. It was a thrilling, but unsettling read. One you couldn't stop thinking about. Again, he cursed her. For being who she was, conjuring up these vivid optical illusions from thin air.

He moved towards the monitor in the far end of the archive. He'd already tried accessing the internet, wondering if he could email his way out of here, but found that it was offline. Thankfully, there were still a few logs of writing forums one could read through the library's internal records system. He was not in the mood for any more reading about Elena now; he wanted a distraction. Something vacuous. And the best one for literary schadenfreude was the periodical *Bast(b)ard*; where disenfranchised poets got to be absolute monsters, safely veiled under the cloak of anonymity. Nearly every morning there would be some rant or other about Elena, which would be commented on by around a hundred of her supporters. He hadn't checked the forum in a while, but looking at the log now, he saw that even after her death nothing had stopped the posts.

Someone had recently claimed that Elena's death was her biggest publicity stunt ever. And then Eben's name had somehow come into the discussion, with another (he presumed, prose) writer stating that: *Eben Prytherch's announcement that he is to write the biography of a woman he so clearly despised has got to be the final nail in Elena's coffin. Send forth your viruses to his computer, let us bring him down, stop any such thing from ever happening.*

Another had written: *Forget about Eben Prytherch, the nobody that he is. It would be far more valuable to go in search of his fellow persona non grata, his so called long-lost relative, Eben the Poet, who seems no longer to exist in the library's archives. I am researching the poets of the nineteenth century and I cannot find a single resource that confirms his existence! Does anyone know what's going on?*

Underneath this someone had written: *Who? The only Eben I know of is that tosspot who wrote those bad reviews about Elena Oodig.*

He read past the unhelpful scourge and rested his eyes on the *Who?* that seemed to him to quiver perilously on his screen, as though that, too, might disappear. No one seemed to have taken any notice of the comment, and the thread had been abandoned for around ten weeks now. His fingers hovered above the keyboard. He wanted to add his own comment, but then remembered that it was a read-only forum. Instead he clicked back onto the library's search engine.

He typed Eben the Poet into the search box. It was the same response every time: no results found. It told him – or so he imagined – in a patronising voice to check the spelling of his search item and try again, or to use similar terms. He tried Ebenezer Thomas. Nothing.

For some reason there was added urgency now in conducting the search in Elena's archive. He was doing it in spite of her, as if Eben the Poet could somehow take prominence in this moment. It was as though Ebenezer, too, like the men in Elena's novel, was lying dead in his bed, his death ignored by all those around him. Someone, somewhere, must have taken enough notice of him to recognise his existence. Eben knew full well that a catalogue search on Elena revealed no less than twelve thousand results. It felt imperative now to find one reference to Eben the Poet, even as a footnote in someone else's history. Something to show he had existed.

He typed again, furiously, trying all sorts of combinations. Eben the Poet, Thomas Ebenezer, Ebenezer Thomas scholar, Eben the Great, Eben – winner – writer – historical figure. As his hands moved quicker and quicker, the words scrambled in front of him to the point where he wasn't even sure what he was typing at all. All the while, the faster he typed, the bigger Elena's portrait bust seemed to become right next to him, as though she were mocking him for trying so desperately to validate his own existence, whereas even in death, she didn't even have to try.

Something suddenly changed. There was a result – a single red line beneath the search engine. Finally, the search had taken him to an officious-looking page with the government's logo on it, which asked for a username and password. Underneath, in tiny lettering, it asked: *Do you have authority to access this page? This action must be validated by a government official.*

He couldn't quite understand it. Years of searching, years of nothing. Now this curious page that looked as though it may well hold classified information if only he were able to get through to the next level, like those computer games he had loved as a kid. He then stood back to stare at what he'd actually typed in. It wasn't Eben at all – he'd actually typed in 'Ebb end poet'. And this coupling of the *Ebb* and the *end* somehow made more sense to the machine than the name of someone who'd once, or so Nicholas and his mother claimed, been a literary figure in this country. *Ebb-end* meant something. Eben meant nothing.

He attempted a password. A random coupling of numbers, then a few letters and symbols. After a few attempts, an alarm sounded on the computer. Then an automated voice, the recorded voice of the head librarian herself: *You are trying to gain access to confidential files. This is a crime. You are not authorised to carry out this operation. You are trying to gain access to confidential files. This is a crime. You are not authorised to carry out this operation.* Eben was overcome by waves of nausea. He lay down on the floor while the automated voice kept on going. The computer plug was inches away from him. He ripped it out, hoping to silence the machine, but it kept on and on at him. Then, finally, after what felt like two hundred years, the battery died, the voice dissipated, and all was silent.

That's when Eben realised he'd silenced the very thing that was keeping him company. The only thing that could alert the authorities to the fact that there was someone in here.

Ebb-end. The word echoed like a faraway tide.

Dan

11AM

Dan hurried around the side of the building to peer inside the windows of the canteen, determined now to resume his duties and sort out whatever strange business was taking place inside. It was eleven o'clock. Break time. He was surprised to see it completely deserted. That was never a good sign, for it must have taken something colossal to keep the librarians from their morning coffee. Rows of pastries shone back at him, untouched. He felt a pang of hunger then; a desire to grab the whole row of them and stuff them in his mouth.

He pressed his face harder into the glass, trying to get a better angle. Still, he saw no one. Only the smug, mottled smiles of freshly baked almond croissants: a once-in-a-week delicacy he often saw the librarians competing over, leaving nothing behind for the porters. He knew who they were – the greedy croissant grabbers. You could not hide that kind of secret in your body: it bulged out, beneath your chin, above your belt, as the frangipane congealed, sunk into you like concrete. But then, what else was there, in a library, to appease yourself with? To make it all worthwhile?

He spotted movement. Dora, the chef, was leaning over the croissants, arranging them in a row with her latex-gloved fingers. Behind her stood Kenvin, her sous chef (or shit chef as Dan referred to him), a short man with peroxide blond hair. Dan knocked on the window. The effects of the spice were lessening now, and he could see a logical way out of this. He needed to get back in, find out where she'd taken his security device, and – presuming she

100

hadn't undone any of his complex programming – he could surely reason with her to get things back on track before the arch-porter reappeared.

He knocked again, and waited for them to release the crash bar to let him in. It wasn't linked to the rest of the security system because of the highly flammable nature of the kitchens; nobody wanted to be locked into an inferno, the arch-porter said. Although sometimes Dan had thought he might, if his life continued like this.

He caught Kenvin's eye. Kenvin simply ignored him and went on with his business, actively trying to distract Dora so she wouldn't turn around and look at him. He banged the door again; knowing how deaf Dora was, hoping the vibrations would grab her attention, Kenvin continued steering Dora away, pointing at random things in the opposite direction, manoeuvring her expertly like a chess piece. Dan began kicking at the glass door then, looking around for something to smash it with. Dora was swiftly deposited back into the kitchen, and Kenvin finally came towards him.

'What the fuck do you think you're doing?' Kenvin said, opening the door.

'I've been locked out, OK?' Dan said, moving forward. He was surprised with the strength of those tiny hands, pushing him back. 'Just let me in!'

'I don't fucking think so, mister,' Kenvin said, looking suddenly to Dan like some maniacal devil at the gates of hell. 'This is a staff entrance.'

'I am staff,' he replied.

'*Kitchen* staff.'

'Don't pretend you're somehow above me,' Dan said, again pushing his way forward. 'We're the same . . .'

'No we're not. I'm an honest, hard-working guy. I haven't just landed here because of some cock-and-bull probation programme. Do you think all the other crims have it this easy?'

Easy? Clocking into another institution day after day? The only freedom Dan enjoyed was walking along the strip of pavement between the library and his flat. A flat situated above an arcade: the place of gambling that he wasn't permitted to enter, because gambling was strictly prohibited as a condition of his probation. He was not even allowed a dabble on the coin pusher. Those machines jangled and whirred and beeped at him every evening through the thin ceiling; taunting him.

'I know how people feel about me,' Dan answered, softening now, taking a different approach. 'But I'm trying to follow the regulations, to do what I'm meant to do, to make an honest go of things.'

He held fast and tried not to think about her; about the rigged CCTV, the nun-device she'd stolen, the massive spliff he'd just ingested. Again he saw those faces screaming at him outside court two years ago, about how he'd *ruined their lives*.

Kenvin took a long pause and finally said, 'I'll consider it if you put on the hygiene gloves.'

'Jesus, Kenvin, I'm not here to touch the food,' he said.

'Health and Safety Handbook, rule 668,' Kenvin said, holding out the blue latex offering. 'No one is to enter the kitchen without wearing hygiene gloves. You wouldn't let anyone handle the books without gloves on, would you?'

Begrudgingly, he pulled them on. He raised a palm and looked curiously at the phenomenon of his new blue fingers, as everything slowed down around him.

'Wait. Are you high?' Kenvin suddenly said. 'Were you . . .'

'Good to proceed,' he said firmly, looking up just as Kenvin seemed to change his mind and tried to close the door on him again. He manoeuvred his foot in, at the last second, wincing as the door closed in on his right leg. It was the tipping point, the justification he needed to put Kenvin in his place. He was once again an angry inmate – no longer a sensible security guard – and he wanted to punish the little fucker. He jumped on top of him, knocking him backwards onto the canteen floor. He raised a hand to punch him; a reflex, muscle memory from prison days when you were always lifting a fist to defend yourself. He almost couldn't stop the force of that fist coming down, though he knew it to be a bad thing, even as he was doing it. But then strangely, it seemed as though his fist wouldn't land as it was meant to in the middle of Kenvin's brow. It was as if it floated to some other, better place, of its own accord. It wasn't until he heard another voice that he realised the reason for this: Dora, the chef, was holding him aloft by his shirt.

'You leave him alone,' she said. 'You porters are bloody riff-raff.'

He turned around to face her. She looked so much like his own grandmother that he wanted to cry: she had died when he was in prison. He'd never had a chance to explain to her why he'd done what he'd done. He knew it was probably the weed, but he wanted Dora to curl herself around him then: to become his grandmother, just for that one moment.

'Look, Dora,' he said, 'there's a problem with the front entrance. With the security system. I need to get back into the building and this is my only option, OK?'

'OK, but I don't see why you have to make such a song and dance about it,' Dora said, with Kenvin now glaring at him over her shoulder. 'Assaulting staff! Can't you enter the building like any other decent person. Honestly, Dan, you're determined to end up back in jail, aren't you?'

Again he wanted to cry, remembering his own grandmother uttering another version of those words: 'You don't have to be who they think you are, my love.' He did not want to go back the way he'd come; what he wanted was another life. Something simple. Good, even. But how could that ever be achieved now, after the mess he'd made of things?

'Listen, I really need to . . .'

'Everyone's at this security majiggy, are they?' Dora said, spinning around to view the empty cafeteria. 'Never seen it this empty! And something funny's going on with the electricity – it's been off for the last half hour, after that announcement. I mean, those pies are only half-cooked – any longer and I'll have to throw them away . . .'

'What do you mean, it's off? What security thing?'

'Well I don't know . . . I didn't hear it, did I? The hearing aid clashes with it, it just buzzes in my ears. What was it, Ken?'

Kenvin spoke through gritted teeth; obviously annoyed with Dan for still being in the room.

'There was an announcement calling staff to the North Reading Room for a security drill.'

Security drill? Dan racked his brain for answers. Had it slipped his mind that he was meant to do a drill? Had someone been in touch from the city, trying to instigate one? Did they wonder why he wasn't instigating it? Shit, he thought. His cover might already be blown.

'What are you two still doing here, then?' he asked.

'Well they don't mean *us*, do they, surely? It's only for the people they'd want to save, if anything happened. And let's face it, we're not going to be very high up on that list, are we? Neither are you, come to that.'

'But the security staff aren't here!' Dan said, struggling to find any logic in this in his spice-addled brain.

'No, I know. Whoever heard of a security drill without security?'

Something in Dora's words chimed with him, but his brain still struggled to function rationally, thoughts half-forming, then halting, disappearing back into darkness. The lack of security. The fact she knew he'd been alone here today. That perhaps the security drill was a fake one, designed to do what, he wasn't sure. But it would probably be the very opposite of security.

'I think we need to go up and see what's happening,' he said, gesturing for them to follow him. 'You need to stick with me, OK? It's my duty to protect you both, so if you'd just . . .'

'No thank you,' Dora said defiantly. 'Like I said. We don't really matter. And I really need to be here when that oven gets turned back on, for the sake of those pies. I'm responsible for *their* lives.'

'Dora,' he said, moving forward now towards her. 'Something bad might be happening here. And you've got a right, as a civilian, to be saved like anyone else. As a security guard,' he continued, thinking of ways to win her over, 'I wouldn't really consider you any lesser than anyone else I was trying to save. The security guards view all lives as equal. Rule 865 in the security handbook.'

Her eyes softened. She considered his little speech, to be fair, before dismissing it.

'Oh God, no. You can't put all lives on a par. Some of us are designed to serve, even in emergencies. I mean, if something happened. If lives were at risk, if there was a siege, if the apocalypse was coming – and it is, you know, my grandsons say, coming soon – then you know what they say, or was it, some writer or other said it. I remember hearing them talking about it in the canteen – his name was something to do with food as well . . . but anyway . . . the line was something like – food is a "small good thing" at a time like this. People would still need a cheese roll, probably wouldn't they, while they were waiting to die?'

Oh, a cheese roll! Dan felt his stomach contract in anticipation. But now was not the time.

'Dora, you are not going to hell in a hand basket for the sake of a cheese roll,' he said, and manoeuvred his proxy-grandmother and his miniature blond devil out of the canteen and back into the heart of the National Library.

Ana and Nan

11.30AM

A hush had descended on the North Reading Room. Its quality, Ana thought, was somehow different to the usual, comfortable quietude of the reading room. It was almost palpable, a densely woven web that had descended upon them all. She remembered how she had once stood in admiration on one of those balconies above the vast, open-plan reading room, looking down upon those working away diligently under the stone-gaze of the commanding Sir John. She had been transfixed, utterly captivated with the notion that every single bowed head was going through a different thought process. She imagined those thoughts floating up from the readers' skulls; fused with the thoughts of those writers and critics who had prompted them to think differently. All those words, quotes, musings rising up into the air, like a swarm of bees leaving a hive, scattering off in little black dots in different directions. Not one single mind, she had thought to herself with wonder, worked in quite the same way.

Yet what her sister had done, by bringing the gun into the room like that, was to somehow unite those wildly divergent minds. This, perhaps, was the very reason for the change in the texture of the silence. It was the silence of unity. Of synchronicity. Every single person in here was surely focused on the exact same thing for once. They were all thinking how on earth they were going to get out of this.

She caught their eyes sliding towards openings and windows; eyelashes fluttering at bookshelves and balconies. The swarm of thoughts scattering in the air. She tried to think as they did, wondering what a layperson would consider an escape route in such a place. A dash up some of those spiral staircases perhaps, those they had never been permitted to climb, towards those balconies on which she'd once stood looking down on them. Up those ladders that led to the highest bookshelves, on which some of the rarest manuscripts were purported to be kept, though Ana knew full well that the shelves only contained expertly crafted cardboard replicas of manuscript spines. The general public knew that they had to obey the paper ban on a day-to-day basis, but a national institution like theirs had to give the illusion that it was above such legislation, that part of its prowess was to preserve what was rightfully theirs, regardless. It was a sham of course, one which haunted Ana daily, but she tried to forget about it as much as was possible, deliberately squinting when she looked up at those manuscripts, imagining that their gold lettering actually glinted in the sun like the originals did rather than sitting there dully, emanating nothing remarkable at all, as fake manuscripts were wont to do.

But then, even if the hostages managed to get that far and used the shelves to propel them upwards, they would only then come up against the impossibly huge arch windows, which were painted shut, and as much as they clung to them like geckos, they would be noticed by no one but the sea, mocking them in the far distance. And then even if they climbed down and tried again, they would find that the doors on that upper level of the reading room could only be accessed via a staff card. The archivist on the main desk, Colleen, seemed to be the only staff member with the card still around her neck, Nan presumably having forbidden their other colleagues from bringing theirs. Ana knew that Colleen didn't have the best co-ordination in the world, especially when her eyewear retainer was lost in her lanyard like it was right now, her hand becoming completely entangled as she tried desperately to free her glasses to see what was really going on.

Ana had no choice but to bring her own gun out, lifting it off the trolley and out of the Bible. She made sure to do it swiftly, to make it appear as though that had always been her intention. It was surprisingly effective in terms of quelling the restlessness among the readers, the appearance of the second gun focusing their thoughts on how best to stay alive, rather than how to escape. But keeping these two guns pointing directly at such a number of hostages entailed a focus they had not been entirely prepared for. How could they now converse with each other, without losing their concentration, and also without the hostages hearing their every word? As expertly and proudly as they had woven the silence around them, it was now a burden, leaving them completely exposed. Any second now Ana imagined that the hostages would see through them, would understand that, though they had reached this point together well enough, they did not necessarily know where to go from here.

The guns had not been meant to be seen by anyone but Eben, but now that the weapons were here, held aloft – a real, tangible, threatening thing – Ana hoped that Nan could see their usefulness in getting the whole thing back on course, and back to Eben.

'Please,' came a voice from the back of the room. An elderly man in a blazer, with tufts of white hair strewn across his scalp in a desperate attempt to hide his baldness, stepped forward. 'Whatever this is, whatever you plan to do . . . please . . . don't kill us . . .'

Whatever this is, Ana thought, her hand remaining tightly gripped around the gun, *is a colossal cock-up. A waste of everyone's time.* She wished, now, she had not cared so much for their welfare, for it was the *what if* of the gases being released that had led her here.

'There's nothing to worry about. We just need you to vacate the building,' Ana suddenly ventured, glancing over towards her sister, hoping for some kind of signal of understanding. But Nan would not look at her. She was going into one of her strange trances again. 'However this might seem, there is a good reason for it,' she continued, buying herself time to think what that good reason could possibly be. That's when the idea struck her. Something to calm them down. To make them see her and Nan's actions as rational; or as rational as they could possibly be under the circumstances. To bring the focus back to something they would understand; and something she imagined most of the academics in the room would consider a more serious threat to their nation than a pathetic little terrorist attack.

'There's a missing manuscript,' she continued, hoping to see some relief in their eyes. It was an excuse that would have sounded thin and insubstantial if she had relayed this information to Dan, but she was sure it would help the library goers understand the seriousness of the situation. 'We couldn't tell you right away because we didn't want anyone trying to make a run for it. We need to . . . check your bags . . . conduct a thorough search. Everybody out, please. And please don't panic. No one's going to get hurt, OK?'

'We can't promise that, though, can we?' said her sister, suddenly looking at her. 'I mean, it all depends on how well they behave, doesn't it?' Nan moved forward a little, pushing the gun into Pale's pregnant belly. Someone in the crowd gasped.

Ana couldn't quite fathom what was happening. She saw how perplexed the crowd looked now, trying to keep up with all the conflicting information that was being thrown at them. *A drill. A terrorist threat. A missing manuscript. It depends on how well they behave.* A million misunderstandings rising from the chasm that was opening up between her and her sister. It was as though twenty-seven years of unity, of understanding, had broken apart in seconds. A thousand bees were dancing out of Nan's head but she couldn't see them leaving the hive at all; the air was empty. On the other hand she had a much clearer understanding of what was going on in the hostages' heads. Most of them had not bought the supposedly reassuring addition of the missing manuscript into the scenario – for them, the twins had simply turned into terrorists, right in front of their eyes. She wondered if they could see the faint trembling in her hand as she held the gun, mistaking it perhaps for adrenalin, even though she wasn't even sure if she could fire it at all, certainly not in the way she had when they'd practised it at the shooting range.

They'd been clay-pigeon shooting every weekend these last few months, just to get used to the thundering in their hands when it went off. Ana recalled the way her sister had rejoiced at each shower of clay in the air; whereas she had failed to hit the target every time. The guns they'd actually sourced for the occasion, from a local farmer who was known to have links with an underground organisation, Ana had barely touched. She'd only brought hers out from under the bed every now and then, placing it on the bed next to her outfit, trying it out for size against their headless outlines. Nan, on the other hand, had walked around the house with hers several times, casually slinging it at her side, trying to get used to it, she said, though it had made Ana uneasy.

Ana now regretted, to some extent, that she had not listened. Nan seemed perfectly at ease holding her own gun, whereas she knew how unconvincing she looked to them all, sweating profusely, her white manuscript-handling gloves making the gun slip from her grasp. She finally took the gloves off and was momentarily pleased by how solid and real the object felt in her hand, how the tremor seemed to subside now that she was more in control; until it struck her again, with alarming clarity that what she was holding was a gun, and that those in front of her thought she intended to kill them with it.

They had planned for other eventualities, of course, for they had been planning this for months, but when they imagined being in charge of a crowd at gunpoint – it was always, somehow, after they had dealt with Eben, where they had nothing left to lose, when their victory had been claimed and there was nothing else for it but to appear as guilty as they undoubtedly were.

She'd had no intention of threatening anyone but Eben. The security cameras were not recording any of this, and she felt a sudden pang of guilt for Dan, for the way his own misconduct mirrored theirs, how he'd made everything so much easier for them; but had also forged another dangerous pathway. Now that nothing would be seen or recorded, somehow things had the possibility of becoming worse than anyone could ever imagine.

There would be no way anyone would think he wasn't in on it. She had not saved him, after all. She had thrown him to the wolves.

*

Every now and then, Nan struggled to remember a word. It was normal, so everyone said. A small word, like *shoe* or *chair.* Their letters just fell away, like letters from a keypad becoming unstuck under her fingers. They left behind absences that disturbed her, a feeling of incompleteness inside her skull. And it took her ages to try and rearrange the letters, to make the keypad appear normal again. She saw those objects and thought: *that is a small leather boat-shaped thing where a foot lives* or *that is a solid wooden thing where a bum goes,* but that was not enough to make sense of things. When she forced her foot into the little boat, without a word to attach to it, the very act somehow seemed wrong.

The consultant had advised her to 'find a path back to the word. Look at the other objects around it. Put it in context.' She had thought his use of the word 'path' was insensitive at the time, considering you needed a *shoe* to tread most paths. But she had now developed an art for it. Next to the *door* were the *stairs*, and down the stairs she went in her mind, looking for the word, knowing it was somehow linked to what she was doing. Then on she sped, in her imagination, out of the door, down to the beach, where she could see a whole cluster of the object in question on the beach, being discarded from feet, toes joyously touching water; and that was it, the word washed up right next to her naked feet – *shoe! Shoes, shoes, shoes!* she rejoiced. And then almost, as a by-product of this, she remembered the other thing, seeing a long row of them on the sand – *chairs! The thing where the bum goes. Deckchairs!* Her mind was revived by the flapping of candy-striped canvas.

But things would get worse, so the consultant had said, without being able to tell her how much worse – 'because in rare cases like yours, more research needs to be done.' Rare. She still recalled how the word rang out then, a word she would not forget. She was a rarity; unique even. Not one of a pair, half of something, but a whole, individual thing of which there was not a copy. Her illness, finally, brought her an identity.

'Some days,' the consultant had said, 'you'll feel like everything is normal. And then it won't be. But then you'll go back to normal again. But the gaps between the normal and abnormal will get less and less, until they're all bound up together and very little will make sense to you, I'm afraid. You'll need to tell those closest to you, so they can be prepared.'

She had not, of course, breathed a word to anyone. And today hadn't gone too badly, all things considered. She had remembered most parts of the plan. It was only the occasional flicker that bothered her now, her mind becoming sporadically awash with whiteness, like a blank screen. It was part of the reason she pre-empted things, before their logic could be snatched away from her. Taking the security device; reaching for the gun. It had made sense to keep achieving those things, though perhaps her sister's visible annoyance was because she had not done them in the right order.

But although she now remembered, just as suddenly as she had forgotten, that the plan had never entailed pointing the gun at her colleagues like that, there was something about the very action that somehow felt right. Was there not a valid reason she and Ana had discussed, why they had to be out of the building, for their own safety? Being a threat to them felt crucial, therefore, a means to a good end.

She could see from the corner of her eye that Ana was urging her to move on, to get the hostages out, but for reasons she didn't even understand herself, she started barking orders at the crowd in front of her, organising them into pairs in front of her (because she didn't like the mess of them as they were, scattered haphazardly across the room). She put Lily next to Summer. A man she knew as Professor Nicholas next to another academic, the name of whom she couldn't recall. She told the blonde girl who was always here to stay with the shifty boyfriend who followed her around like a shadow. She put Pale next to the archivist, Colleen. Once she had rearranged this chaotic, disorganised space into a neat line she was happy. There was a clear pattern to it now; and patterns were things she understood. A pattern kept her reality secure.

But the fact that Ana had promised them their freedom upfront sent the room into a spiral of chaos. The old academics kept asking which manuscript it was that was causing all this bother; the young couple were emptying their bags on the floor in protest, showing they had nothing to hide; and Colleen had started to scream once she'd got her glasses back on – a delayed reaction, it transpired, to realising the twins were not in fact holding staple guns. Someone from the back of the room was bold enough to ask why they were being paired up, with someone else unhelpfully suggesting that perhaps they were going to be executed two by two, which sent Colleen's wails rocketing up towards the balconies.

'No one's being executed here, OK? Can we all just stop?' said Ana. 'We need to be sure we have everyone before we move on . . .

don't we, Nan? It's only protocol, isn't it. Colleen, please . . . can you be quiet? No need to frighten everyone.'

Colleen's scream tipped over into a sob. 'Me? I'm not the one doing . . . You're the . . . Oh God . . . Oh God . . .'

Nan wanted the sound to stop. She felt she had no choice but to push the barrel of the gun into Colleen's face, right as she seemed to be gathering up enough air for one final scream. Her breath seemed to leave her body entirely then, making it pliant and help-less. She closed in on herself like a clam, shivering next to Pale, who seemed entirely indifferent to it all, with even the flicker of a smile forming in the corner of her mouth.

'Fucking hell, this is the most fun I've had in ages,' Pale whis-pered to Nan. 'What a brilliant idea. So is this it, is this how we get our security rating up? Fair play to them, I knew they were planning something big. But choosing you two, to do this, it's genius isn't it?'

Choosing you two. The words haunted her, suddenly seeing herself and Ana as Pale did. How innocuous they seemed, how unthreatening; so much so that none of this could be real. None of it even registered.

Ana had caught the tail end of Pale's words. She was now star-ing at Nan, the gun dangling limply from her palms. Her sister no doubt considered this a lifeline for them, the realisation that those who knew them well – or at least thought they did – were constructing their own truth about the matter. All they had to do was lean into it now, use this to quieten the panic, make them think they were part of some security scheme, where the most ridiculous people had been posited as threats, simply to make a point.

But Nan didn't want to buy into that reality. Even as she marched them outside, she wanted them all to take her seriously, and so, as she saw Ana losing her grip on her own gun, she rushed over to retrieve it.

'Nan,' her sister pleaded with her, quietly. 'Please, we just need to get them out. We're wasting time.'

Nan turned to face the crowd once more, poised, ready to speak, but became aware that the blankness was returning, names and letters and logic falling away into the abyss. She quickly checked that she could name everything in her eyeline: gun, library, people. Casting her eyes further she even remembered the name of the statue at the far end of the library: Sir John Williams, the library's founder. She remembered why they were in this room to begin with, but then remembered that there were things she'd done recently that Ana knew nothing about.

She remembered all this and yet, as Ana looked up at her, Nan could not for her life remember what was meant to happen next.

Eben

11.45AM

After another fruitless flurry of knocks, Eben leaned his head against the heavy, handleless door, unable to face the mockery of the empty room behind him. It was now as if Elena's portrait bust had sprouted hands and legs, as though she was creeping up on him like a pantomime villain.

He had been musing about the *Ebb-end*, wondering if there was any real significance to it. Eventually he'd concluded that it was more than likely some unreadable, bureaucratic nonsense that had been disguised as something vaguely literary. That's the way things were going, in any case, in this country. Frankton had said that soon there would be no books at all, even in the archives, that gradually they would all stop having access to them. That people would soon be provided with only summaries of novels, to save them time in reading the actual book. Acronyms, he'd said, would be used far more frequently to denote all sorts of things, shortening the life expectancy of actual sentences. 'Literature as we know it,' he'd claimed, rather dramatically, 'will wither and die, and it will be such a subtle death, we won't even notice it happening.'

Eben shook the thought from his mind. He could not think about literature's death now, any more than he could think of his own grey, decaying corpse lying in a bed in Elena's book. He turned his attention back to her sculpture. Despite his resentment, he relished the fact that she still existed, through her novels, through her letters and diaries; that there was tactile evidence of her on paper, every thought, every musing she'd ever had. She was still alive, as long as she was there on the page, and it was hard to imagine how she could ever be erased. A life written down was a life remembered. Unlike Eben the Poet, who had simply not tried hard enough to leave any real evidence of his existence behind.

But the sudden need for the toilet again made his anxiety resurface. It had made him realise it wasn't normal, actually, to be stuck in here for this length of time. He remembered seeing the head librarian on the news a few weeks back boasting about the superior lockdown capacity of the library, how it would safeguard itself from any kind of attack or invasion. What if his captivity was something to do with security? What if there was a fire in the building, even? He looked up at the fire suppression system warning above his head. He imagined seeing a thin, grey river of smoke filtering into the room, watching it drift up towards the sensors, knowing there was nothing he could do. A long, torturous end, deprived of oxygen in Elena's chamber. *But the books were saved; that's the main thing,* he imagined the head librarian saying, as they interviewed her about the tragedy.

'Now you'd love that, wouldn't you?' he said, turning his head to face Elena once more.

She seemed to laugh at him then, really laugh. *Nothing stands between us but death,* she seemed to be saying. *We'll be together again soon.*

What if there were terrorists in the building? Terrorist. The term scurried around in his brain like an insect. The term that came into existence every couple of months or so and then disappeared again, with people forgetting such things existed until the next building or the next person or the next massive crowd got blown up. He remembered Frankton going on about this once: 'It's actually the obvious target, because it's the last place you'd expect it to happen, but the best place if you wanted to wipe out a nation's legacy. Think about it. Full to the brim of civil servants who wouldn't say boo to a ghost. Porters who are sleepwalking half the time. You'd find it easy to get access. All those secret underground tunnels. Easy to get into the heart of the building and blow it up. But I wouldn't be surprised if the government would be behind it all. I mean, they're already trying to eradicate it, from the inside.'

Eben didn't know what Frankton meant by this, but he was afraid of looking stupid so he'd just nodded and agreed. But now the thought hovered at the fringes of his consciousness. *Trying to eradicate it, from the inside.*

'It's your anxiety talking, Eben,' he mumbled to himself. 'There is no conspiracy. No bomb. No fire. No terrorist. The archivist's probably been waylaid by someone asking her about a missing sixteenth-century pamphlet and that porter is probably ignoring you to wind you up.'

They wouldn't be able to ignore him indefinitely. They would get to him eventually. Perhaps the library was a bit like all the hospitals in the country were now; you had to be actually dying before they tended to you. They didn't consider it an emergency unless your head was hanging off your body.

There was nothing for it but to return to his research, and to face Elena's final year of life. It was simply an empty, page-less book; and a note in the file explained that the empty manuscript had been discarded and the pages sent off to a laboratory to be tested for parasites.

But she had written plenty the year before that. It was a struggle to read her musings the closer she moved towards her own death – it was the writing of a woman losing herself with each syllable. But he ploughed on, knowing deep down that it was the main reason he had come, to see if there was any truth in her published suicide letter, where she claimed that he, and The Smotherhood, had forcibly driven her to her death.

The first day of the new year. It feels like the last day in many ways; because I think this is possibly my last full year of life. The last few years have been gliding by, almost as if I've been watching them pass by the window like clouds, with myself trapped on the other side. My days are this strange process of trying to get beyond the glass, to witness something real. It seems impossible. And then even when I manage it – getting outside – it's like I take the glass with me, like it's permanently fixed to my eyeballs. Like it has crystallised over my eyes. It is the most unsettling feeling. Each day feels like the one just gone, until I'm not sure myself if I am actually moving forward at all. Have I been; am I gone? Will I ever be here again? Am I just observing life, not being a real part of it?

He skimmed January. He saw that she had managed to get over her January blues; that she seemed to be doing better, living and feeling things again. But then, on January 23:

Hateful, horrible words have kept me inside again. They've confined me behind the glass; indefinitely it seems. It's enough to make me not want to exist.

The words sent a shiver down his spine. He knew these words all too well. They'd been quoted on various sites; in various news articles, following her suicide; her family having released choice extracts from her diary to the press.

Hearing those words, knowing I no longer have the power I once had – it makes me feel that living is pointless. That if he so wants to get rid of me, maybe I should give him his triumph.

Eben cringed. True; the review he'd written at the beginning of that year had been his most scathing yet. Her collected short stories had just been issued digitally; and he'd taken the time to go through every single story with a fine-toothed comb, looking for any weaknesses, any anomalies he could. There were a few stories there that were an obvious attack on the Smotherhood, one where all the attendees of an all-male literary conference perished in an explosion, or where a group of fishermen who knew nothing of the ways of the sea, sunk without a trace trying to catch an exotic fish they had heard about, which did not actually exist.

Frankton's words had spurred Eben on as he typed out his review; how he'd ranted and raved that there was no real honesty in any of the reviews of Elena's work in this small country, that everyone was scared of offending the great Elena, because they worried about becoming subjects of her novels, how stupidly misguided all the praise of her was, elevating her to God-like status, as someone who could do no wrong. How absurd it was that her dystopian musings – not meant to be taken seriously, surely – were now forming the basis for changes within the small country's society, how her works were seen as influential on a political level, and how she had orchestrated the whole thing, almost like a politician herself, in order to be able to influence the society in which she lived. It was no secret that the head of government and Elena were old friends, that they were often seen drinking together on the balcony of the head of government's plush capital-city waterfront flat.

He was exhausted by the time he'd finished the review, utterly spent; as though he had run a marathon. Not that he knew what that felt like; but he imagined the mental exertion he'd endured could very well correspond to that of a long-distance runner, for his mind had been stretched in all sorts of directions as he typed – he had forged onwards through the uphill climb of ambition, he had paced himself across the uneven terrain of self-doubt, and he had raced his way to the finish line of recognition, even as the crowds on either side of his brain shouted objections and insults. He did not pause to reread, or even to think. He was proud of himself that he had been able to be objective, to be honest. To be brutal; when it was needed. He had been entirely convinced that he'd voiced the opinion of hundreds, if not thousands.

Off it went. One click. Gone. He hadn't given it a second thought, for some reason, despite it being the most damning thing he'd ever written. Less damning reviews had been agonised over for weeks. But not this one. This review, somehow, was his voice coming to the fore. His identity surfacing for the first time in his life. This was *the one*.

His very final review of Elena, as it turned out.

But he had not expected it to have the impact that it did. To silence her indefinitely. In the worst way possible. And when it had happened, and when it started being reported by readers as a hate crime, even Frankton told him he'd gone too far, even though he'd been the one to give it the sign-off in his online periodical. Like him, Frankton was also questioned after Elena's death, but he had wriggled out of it on the basis of being bed-bound with the Great Sickness at the time of publication, blaming an inexperienced assistant editor for the blunder. Subsequently the case against Eben was also dropped. Dropped in legal terms, but not in literary terms. He was still known as the author-killer, as far as the rest of the town was concerned. He looked back down at the entry in front of him, where Elena continued:

When I read those words in black and white, they dragged me down. Down into the depths. There is nothing to do now but to admit that he has undone me. That I will never be whole again.

It brought him to tears in a way it hadn't done when he'd read these comments online. The angry Eben, full of bravado, the one panting at the finish line after finishing his review, was gone. In his place was this one: a gibbering wreck, in urine-soaked trousers, locked in a room from which there was seemingly no escape. A prison cell, wallpapered with images of a woman he'd destroyed. A literary purgatory of his own making. He closed his eyes, bracing himself before reading the rest of the quote, because he knew how it would end: *Eben Prytherch brought me down. Brought me to this.*

He was yet to see those words in her handwriting; to witness the emotion in the angles and slopes of her letters. He was both terrified and curious to see his name set down, forever condemned in ink, the year before her death. He tried to remember what his therapist had said. He had to face what he had done before he could accept it. Only through acceptance was it possible to stop the panic, the remorse, the intrusive thoughts.

I accept what others think I have done, he thought to himself. *But I did not do it.*

He finally opened his eyes and looked down, expecting to see his name scrawled accusingly in Elena's trademark dark-purple ink, the name she claimed that had brought her down. If nothing else, he thought, his name would be immortalised, no matter what he did from now on.

Except it wasn't his name written down in the original document from which she'd been quoted, supposedly, in the online articles. Not his name at all.

Dan

12PM

Dan had never been so pleased to see the porter station. There it was, shining at him like some Messianic vision at the end of the red carpet. Dora and Kenvin were close behind, urging him to slow down as Dora struggled with the stairwell ('everyone knows you don't take the lift in an emergency!' Kenvin had barked at them, and so here they were).

Dora and Kenvin followed him around to the front of his desk and took in the myriad CCTV screens in front of them.

'How can you be there, if you're here?' Dora asked, pointing at a screen that showed him patrolling a busy reading room.

'And now you're over here!' Kenvin screamed, his eyeball scrutinising another virtual Dan walking around the canteen. Everyone knew you couldn't get from the reading room to the canteen in seconds. Dan spotted the anomaly now, and hoped no one in the capital city was paying close attention.

He watched as a version of himself left the canteen, and in a miraculous beat, was then seen stationed again behind his desk, where the three of them were now, staring back at the fictional Dan who had his head buried in the security handbook. Dora actually looked behind her to try and find the errant, other Dan.

'How come I'm invisible?' she asked, waving her arm at the camera. 'Have I died?'

'Well Dan is definitely going to be dead when the arch-porter finds out about this,' Kenvin said. 'How long have you been doing this?' he asked, almost impressed.

'I haven't done anything!' Dan protested. 'Sometimes we just show old footage. It's perfectly legit,' he said, fiddling with the controls, trying desperately to switch back to the current day so he could see what was happening now. But it wasn't possible. He'd been too clever for his own good. He'd imagined, of course, that someone in the capital city would try to refresh the screen just to double-check; in which case he'd programmed the system to respond so that the screen would move to a slightly altered version of the footage. The only thing he couldn't account for was that he himself would be the one doing it, trying to see what was really going on, and in doing so he'd completely messed up the programming, so that all twenty-four screens now showed twenty-four different Dans, and you knew full well they couldn't all be in the same place at once, while the porter-cam, whose live feed was being streamed on the office monitor, showed him doing his usual rounds, seeing his nun-device go up and down across each security strip, whilst the audio played him whistling merrily away as though nothing were amiss.

'Well there's no getting out of this now, is there?' Kenvin said.

'Just shut up!' Dan shouted, pressing all the buttons he could think of to reboot the system. A clean boot, that's what was needed: shut the whole thing down and start again. He pressed a few commands, a few of the ones he'd safeguarded himself against. Suddenly one of the alternative Dans sped up at random and was to be seen rushing around the main exhibition hall at great speed.

'See, this is why you can't just employ criminals and hope for the best,' Kenvin said behind him.

Dan froze every screen. Each and every shot in this particular section was taken from a few weeks ago, a place he longed to return to. He was on seven screens now, gesturing differently in each one. All alone, doing his rounds. Apart from one screen, which showed a silhouette. A librarian, possibly, following a few steps behind. He zoomed in. He saw, to his surprise, who it was. It was her. Before they'd even met. The same cold eyes, hard with intent.

'That's Nan Oodig,' Kenvin said. 'Looks like she's obsessed with you.'

Nan? Was that her name? He spun the footage on. Everywhere he went, she seemed to follow. Observing his every move. In particular she observed what he locked and how he locked it. Then it came, suddenly, the moment of their meeting. He saw himself walking down the dark basement corridor that hosted the closed-stack collection, reaching out to wind shut one of the narrow shelves he assumed had been left open overnight by a careless librarian. A squeal from inside had alerted him to the fact that there was someone in there and he'd hastily unwound them again, finding her clutching some old manuscripts and laughing at the fact that he'd nearly crushed her to death.

But looking at this scene again now in slow motion, and whizzing back and forth along the footage, he could see that she'd not been working there at all that morning; in fact she'd been sitting there in the dark since the early hours, waiting for him to come, so that she could spring out at him.

It was only now that the penny was dropping; that everything that had happened between them – every look, every gesture, every strange shag – had been carefully curated by her, plotted out in order to fall into place just as she wanted it. And he'd been completely oblivious to it, genuinely thinking that those decisions were his own, that he'd sought her out after finding her in the darkness that one time, that he was the one who'd guided that rather shy creature of those shadows and brought her upwards towards the light. He'd prided himself that he'd spurred on a willingness in her to be seen, by him, by others. To dare to do things she'd never done; to risk having a secret part of herself exposed. But it was all bullshit. There was no such thing happening between them; it was all a narrative written by her.

He shut the screens down, trying to think his way through it, which was still proving difficult with the spice pulverising his brain cells, shooting them down like lemmings in a video game, hindering his ability to make connections between one thing and the next. He remembered all the promises she had made for the day ahead. How they would have all the sex they wanted, wherever they wanted. It had obviously been a ruse in order to rig the cameras. But for what? He thought of the way she blew hot and cold, and how, when she was cold, there was something positively arctic in those eyes of hers.

'Is she . . . all right, I mean . . . has she got problems?' he said, turning to Kenvin.

'No more than anyone else in this fucking place,' he chirped, reaching across to see if he could control the images himself. 'Does it get any steamier? You and her? I bet it does, you filthy pig.'

Dan pushed Kenvin's hands away and shut down the whole system. He realised that no matter what he did now, he was fucked. He'd spun the tape on. The arch-porter could be in the middle of his presentation right now, demonstrating the sophistication of the live porter-cam, hearing Dan's voice welcoming a visitor while the corresponding CCTV image would actually show him speeding up through the next three hours, carrying out his duties in double time the way every porter dreamed of doing. Everyone in that government building would know, and the arch-porter would surely alert the authorities then and there. Dan hurriedly checked the tracker on the monitor to see exactly where they were. The pin on the map showed they were all in the large function room at the Government Office. The arch-porter ight be stuffing his face, Dan thought hopefully. Even better, he might already be helping himself to the free wine, with the CCTV footage being the furthest thing from his mind.

'Well?' Kenvin asked. Dan had almost forgotten he was there; that he was answerable to these two figures by his side. 'Are you going to tell us what the hell is going on, or what?'

'I . . . I don't know,' he said. 'I just can't work it out . . .'

'What kind of fucking amateur security guard are you?' Kenvin screamed in his ear.

'It's quiet around here, isn't it? Are you sure nobody died?' asked Dora.

Dan was bordering on a whitey now, feeling all his energy draining away from him. Damn that spice, he thought to himself. Usually he had to lie on the floor and breathe when this happened, concentrate on the tiniest scraps of carpet, until the feeling had passed, until his insides had solidified again. He imagined the horror that could be unfolding right now in other parts of the building, how his virginal nun was being manipulated by her, for God knows what purpose. Perhaps she intended to kill herself in a very public way, in front of the visitors, and needed to lock him out before she could be stopped? Or worse, she was planning on taking people with her. The thought hadn't actually occurred to him before now. The schools, the shopping malls, the other places in the neighbouring country where terrorists had started to act out, in imitation of worse massacres in the bigger countries. Was that it? He thought of those vulnerable lives that were meant to be his sole concern. Him turning his back on them, choosing to go for a spliff instead.

'Oh God, oh God . . .' he muttered to himself, looking down to see the redness of the carpet that resembled blood now, congealing around his shoes. 'I've fucked up big time, haven't I?'

'Yes,' Kenvin said. 'You have.'

'There, there,' said Dora, reaching into her apron pocket and taking three little drop scones out of it, wrapped in cellophane. 'No need to overreact, lovely. It's just your blood sugar dropping. Do you want a little something to eat? Can't make you tea unfortunately until the electric's back on . . .'

'Jesus,' he heard Kenvin say. 'Look at the state of him!'

Kenvin and Dora were becoming more and more distant in his eyeline, as if he were now looking at them through a peephole. He turned away from their tiny, distorted silhouettes, before staring back down at the carpet, which was no longer a bloody path, but now looked luscious and inviting, like a soft mattress. He glanced up to see if he might get away with a nap, but he caught Kenvin's eye. *Don't you dare, Matthews,* he seemed to be saying to him. *Don't. You. Fucking. Dare.*

If sleep wasn't an option, then he would need to think of other ways of getting himself over the whitey. It always helped him to see his own body as mechanical somehow, an insignificant, functioning thing; just an assembly of body parts. But then the notion of *body parts* sent his mind spiralling in another horrific direction.

You need to override the programme, he told himself. *It's all in the configurations. Feet,* he thought to himself, remembering another tactic of his. As long as his feet were still attached to his body – and looking down at them now, he was pretty sure they were – then all he had to do was program them to keep moving onwards until the rest of his body, and his brain, somehow moved automatically in the same direction.

'I'll have to go around the building to see for myself what's happening,' he said, lifting his feet up and rotating them until he felt the rush of blood going back up into his body, awakening his brain from its spice-slumber. 'It might just be a glitch on the system. You two best stay here.'

'Fuck that,' Kenvin said, 'we're coming with you.'

'Fine, but we'll have to move slowly, OK?' he said.

'Well lucky for you, I don't have any other speed,' said Dora, munching on a drop scone. 'Now concentrate on the task at hand – that's a good boy.'

He could open his eyes a little wider now, each step solidifying his intent. As long as he kept moving forward – like it wasn't any kind of big deal, he told himself – he'd be fine. He continued along the red carpet with Dora and Kenvin trailing behind him. As he'd been taught (but had never put into practice), he spread out his arms to become a kind of protective shield for them both, for in the event of an actual emergency or threat rule 556 in the handbook did state that he needed to prioritise their lives over his. The whole thing still felt distinctly unreal to him, like a kind of performance. A circus ringmaster, entering a spotlight.

One foot in front of the other, Matthews. No big deal.

'What is it?' Kenvin asked, whispering. 'Can you see anything?'

They were inches away from the North Reading Room. Something was going on in there. He paused, turned, and before he could tell them to make a run for it the automatic doors opened with a click and out she came – the woman he'd been shagging in the basement – Nan, Kenvin had called her – leading a crowd of people with a large copy of a Bible in her hand. He ushered Dora and Kenvin into a small gap between some white pillars and stood in front of them, willing himself to disappear into the shadows. But they needn't have worried, for Nan paid no attention to them. Her focus was firmly on her book, which she waved around at the crowd following her, and it wasn't until she raised her hand right into the air that Dan saw that the book was obscuring a weapon.

A fucking hand gun, of all things.

The crowd filtered past them as they stood there, invisible, frozen to the spot. Then strangely, it was as if Nan appeared a second time, at the end of the crowd, having somehow run back to usher them onwards, looking a little more unsure of herself this time. He rubbed his eyes when he saw Nan again, wondering if the myriad versions of himself he'd just seen on the screen were still messing with his head. It gave rise to a vision of all the potential Dans he'd seen on the screen rushing into the scene all at once, the best selves he could imagine, restraining her, taking her gun from her, ushering the rest of them to safety. But then, almost instantly, they grew small again, a flurry of video-game lemming-Dans trampled underfoot, until he could see no trace of them on the carpet.

Fuck. He realised he was still, really really stoned. Which was also a strange kind of comfort. Because this couldn't really be as bad as he thought it was. Surely?

He heard the lock being activated to open the private quarters of the library, and into the corridor that led to the emergency exit. Click, click, click. His fingers ached with the absence of his nun-device.

Once the door had been shut, he released himself slowly, letting Dora and Kenvin breathe. He was now starting to wonder whether this was an elaborate safety drill of some kind, something designed to make him do some actual *work*. Was the arch-porter watching him from somewhere, to see how he'd respond to it all? There was no telling, after all, if that gun was a real one or a replica, or if it was empty or loaded.

Until, that is, until a shot rang out further down the corridor.

Ana and Nan

12.15PM

They had been so close to getting them out. After realising that some (though not all) of the hostages thought this was an elaborate security drill, Ana had taken advantage of the situation and had started hurrying them all out of the reading room and down towards the emergency exit by the car park. Their responses to this were varied. Colleen still wasn't buying any of it, the middle-aged academics seemed unsure, and yet Pale seemed positively jubilant, waddling along merrily as though she thought she were engaged in some kind of promenade performance. The young couple were harder to read; they seemed catatonic, stoned perhaps, as they followed suit. As long as everyone followed protocol, Ana kept telling them, trying to sound as calm as possible – as though she were not brandishing a gun that threatened to kill them – they would be absolutely fine.

Nan trailed quietly behind them, eyes flickering strangely from side to side.

Ana reassured herself that the very act of leaving the reading room seemed to have calmed them all – even Colleen who, apart from the odd sniffle, seemed relatively composed as they worked their way through the side doors, through stacks and archives, and towards the stairwell that led down to the ground level. Colleen, more so than the others, at least knew they were moving in the direction they had promised, towards the emergency exit at the back, and that soon the car park would come into view below them. When it did, she saw Summer and Lily – who she surmised were not as convinced as Pale that this was all an elaborate drill – gaze longingly through the long, tall windows to freedom of the wide-open space that lay beyond them. The freedom she and her sister would lose forever, once they went back into the library.

She wondered what would happen if she blundered along into that fresh air with them all; if she hurled her gun into a nearby hedge, pretended that none of it had ever happened. Ana felt the feeling creeping up on her, that it wasn't too late. That she could, like when they were kids, convince Nan that this wasn't the game she wanted to play after all, and trick her into doing what she wanted to do instead.

Three more steps and one more level. That might have been the end of it, if she'd been allowed to get there.

But then everything had changed. A gunshot rang out, and she turned to witness the peculiar phenomenon of a crowd hurling themselves down at her feet in some kind of desperate worship. Ana was almost impressed that they had all paid attention to the safety drill that the library ran every Tuesday morning, where a government official came to remind everyone that if you – God forbid! – ever heard a gunshot, you should drop immediately to the floor, face down, either to show you were not a threat, or to make the gunman think he had already shot you. 'Playing dead,' he'd said chirpily, 'is actually the best way to stay alive!' Any other action was a risk, a danger to oneself and others. 'People who make a run for it,' the government official had added, 'rarely survive.'

It had surely been a mistake, a mishap, Ana told herself. An accidental shot ricocheting off the wall. Until she saw Professor Nicholas groaning in a corner, the blood surging out from beneath his leg, with Nan pacing restlessly at his side.

'He was trying to escape,' Nan said, to no one in particular, with an odd, blank look in her eyes.

'I wasn't!' he said. 'I just saw something on one of the shelves. It was a title I'd been looking for everywhere . . . I reached over and . . . What does it matter? Help me, please!' Nicholas shouted out, holding on to his leg with his shaky hands, as if willing it to stay attached. 'I think she severed an artery . . . I'm going to bleed to death.'

Ana turned back to look at the hostages, as their heads began to rise up tentatively to see what was going on. Pale's eyes met hers, bulbous with the realisation that this was no performance. Summer and Lily shifted closer to one another. A classic Colleen caterwaul shot up as Nicholas's blood began seeping into the fabric of her pink knitted cardigan.

Ana looked up at Nan, searching for some kind of explanation. And perhaps for something else, too – remorse perhaps, or fear – something in those eyes identical to her own to show her she hadn't meant to do this, that she was *sorry*. But Nan still wouldn't look at her. She was encircling the crowd on the floor, pointing the gun at them, as if looking for reasons to shoot someone else. One by one those heads planted themselves firmly back on the linoleum floor, the only sign of life in them being the tremor in each pair of shoulders as Nan paced past.

As she hurried over to Professor Nicholas, Ana wondered if Nan had merely been humouring her all these months as they'd been orchestrating their plan, practising their steps, building the library in the bathtub. This latest manoeuvre – the bullet, the blood – it was more than shooting a person, it was an actual shooting down of their intentions. They had told themselves over and over that they were not like ordinary terrorists, because they didn't plan to harm civilians. They only intended to kill Eben. Revenge, yes, for the loss they had endured at his hands, but also a symbolic death; the end of the hateful woman-bashing critic with an agenda, a clear signal to others that there was no place for their literary hate crimes. And she couldn't remember now, looking down at him, whether Professor Nicholas had been part of the so-called Smotherhood, but she couldn't imagine there had been any real reason to shoot such a frail-looking man. She hoisted his leg into the air, leaning it against her, an exclamation mark to denote the situation they now found themselves in.

'Is there a doctor here?' she shouted out. She could no longer hide the panic in her voice. 'Raise your hands if you're a doctor.' There was still a chance, she thought, if she could palm the professor off on someone remotely responsible, that they could get to Eben. Three minutes to the archive if they went back the way they came and then hurtled down the spiral stairs into the basement. Then again, the way your entire life flashed in front of your eyes while you beeped and waited for those doors to open when you reached every new level, as though they enjoyed making you wait, enjoying their power over you; perhaps she was better off heading for the older part of the building, towards the rickety old attic with its unlocked doors and battered wooden staircase which may get them there in half the time.

Four trembling pairs of hands went up, while the faces remained down. She reached out to pull up the person closest to her – a young man in his twenties. She hadn't been prepared for the shock of the feeling of his hand in hers, a real, corporeal reminder that they were messing with other people's lives now, pulling them into their own chaos. So many of them. Complete strangers who had nothing whatsoever to do with this. A young, blonde woman at his side held on to his leg and tried to tug him back.

'Please don't kill him,' she pleaded. 'He's not much but he's all I've got.'

Before Ana could answer Nan waved the gun in the direction of the girl's head, until she had no choice but to let go of his leg.

'Just tell me what I need to do, OK?' Ana said, as the boy knelt next to the professor's body. 'I'm elevating the leg – is that right?'

'Erm, well yes,' the young doctor said, rather unconvincingly. He gently removed the leg from Ana's shoulder and placed it on his own. Nicholas by now was only half-conscious, hands spread over his face in pain. 'Then we need to create a tourniquet to stop the bleeding. We need a cloth of some kind, a garment . . .'

He gestured towards Ana's scarf. Ana shook her head. Without it, they'd have something to differentiate her from her sister, and it had been important to them that as they carried out this plan, they remained in unison, as unidentifiable from each other as possible.

'Colleen,' Ana said, kneeling down next to Colleen's rigid body. 'Colleen, your cardigan, and your blouse . . . they're already soaked so . . .'

'No, please, no . . .' Colleen whimpered. 'Please no. I have a scar. No, please.' Ana remembered that Colleen had been off work recently for some kind of operation. What had it been? Why hadn't she ever asked her?

'Someone else, please?' She turned around wildly now, gesturing towards the desperate girlfriend. 'You.'

Reluctantly, and spurred on by Nan's gun hovering inches from her face, the girl got up on her knees, undid her shirt and hurled it across towards Ana. She had nothing underneath but a purple-laced bra, and a butterfly tattoo on her left breast. Those shivering breasts seemed to Ana a grotesque reminder of the indignity of it all, a ghostly flickering of flesh in a place where such a thing never needed to be seen, a place where everything should have remained comfortingly plain and ordinary.

The young doctor took his girlfriend's shirt and wrapped it around the wound. He seemed strangely self-composed, under the circumstances; Ana thought she noticed a little of what they had noticed in Dan when he'd been smoking, a detachment from the task at hand. But stoned or not, his tourniquet did the trick; and within minutes Nicholas's breath was steady again, his hand firmly in hers.

'Urrrr,' he ventured.

'Don't you worry now, Professor Nicholas,' Ana said, as if she were his carer and not the one holding him at gunpoint. 'There's a lovely young doctor here to look after you. You're going to be just fine.'

Nicholas opened his eyes hesitantly. He saw the young doctor smiling back at him.

'He's not a doctor!' Nicholas shouted, suddenly finding strength from somewhere. 'He's an English student, a bloody joke of a one at that!'

'I am, actually, a doctor now,' he replied. 'No thanks to you. He failed me, you see, in the viva . . . the first time around . . .'

'Because that thesis was a load of nonsense!' Nicholas said.

Ana realised he meant an academic doctor, and recalled a joke her mother always made about these kinds of credentials – 'don't they know that the term "it's all academic" means to be utterly useless?' – but she was still soothed by the thought that if the professor was well enough to argue with him, he'd probably be OK. She moved towards Nan, realising she would need to extract her from whatever reverie was now claiming her mind.

'Nan,' she ventured. 'Nan, we need to go, or else we won't . . .'

Nan wouldn't budge, curiously transfixed on the conversation happening next to her.

'He wrote this stupid thesis about the pitfalls of digitisation,' the professor continued. 'It was just the ramblings of a stoner – arguing that the national memory was being eroded, poet by poet, that the library was effectively trying to change and manipulate our identity!'

But Ana wasn't listening to him as she moved towards her sister and placed her hand on her shoulder. 'Nan!' Ana was shaking her now, but to no avail.

'It's not that I couldn't see the worth of it, Professor,' she heard the so-called doctor say. 'It's been crucial for our survival. It's just like, in the case of most things in this country that start out pretending to help us, it could become damaging in the wrong hands, become positively evil.'

'Evil, honestly! We're stronger than we've ever been as a nation and some lad like this tries to argue we're going backwards.'

'You want to talk about evil, how about these two?' It was Colleen, back to her former glory. Boldly sitting upright now on her knees, having managed to nullify whatever panic had claimed her earlier. 'I haven't survived cancer only to come here and be killed by you two. I don't know about anyone else, but I'm leaving.'

Colleen started to gather her bloodied cardigan around her, the blood splattering across Summer and Lily as she did so. She rose from the floor. No one around her moved. Now it was Ana's turn to be impressed by her.

'Colleen, just stay where you are for now, please,' Ana started. 'Nan, come with me, please, and we can leave them.'

'It's not so much that we're going backwards,' she could hear the lad still wittering on to Professor Nicholas. 'More like we're moving sideways. Into oblivion. That's the thing about moving sideways. One hardly notices that there's any movement at all.'

'Will you two shut up, please!' Ana screamed at them, with one eye on Colleen, who looked like she was ready to make a run for it. Nan picked up her gun and casually pointed it at Colleen, whilst fixing her attention on the young man.

'Do you know how much work goes into digitising books, lad?' Nan said, without taking her eye off Colleen. 'We're not just glorified scanners you know. We repair, we keep the character of books, we restore, we maintain—'

'Nan, no!' Ana screamed as she saw Colleen make a dash for it, around the corner of a bookshelf. Nan fired the gun again, but narrowly missed this time, a bullet lodging itself into a cast-iron box that stored some of the country's ancient nautical charts.

'Nan, stop, OK, I'll get Colleen,' Ana said, walking towards the shelf into which Colleen appeared to have vanished. She, too, was shaking now, having no idea what was going on with her sister, or why things were spiralling out of control so chaotically. Whatever had tipped Nan over the edge enough to shoot Professor Nicholas, she couldn't let it happen again. She rounded the corner to see Colleen desperately piling books on top of a library stool in the far corner, her tights snagging on the sharp edges of lever arch files as she tried to climb the shelves like a ladder, aiming to make her way to a clerestory window at the top, for all the good it would do her. Ana moved slowly towards her.

'Colleen, get down, before you hurt yourself,' she said, trying to sound as reassuring as possible. She put her gun down on a shelf, as if to show she had no intention of shooting. Colleen turned to look back down, clinging to the shelves like her life depended on it, eyes puffed from crying. Ana had never known Colleen to show any emotion whatsoever. It had even been a bit of a joke around here, how brusque she was with everyone; how every researcher, every visitor was terrified to ask her anything, even though it was her job to answer those queries. And yet Ana could see it was just a protective layer. And though they had not stripped her garments from her, they had stripped everything else.

Suddenly, Ana saw that Colleen's manoeuvring was more purposeful than she thought. Right at the top, hidden at the back of one of the shelves, was another trigger point for the terrorist alarm. The red button which, when pressed, would release the sleeping gases. Seeing Colleen's five foot two frame elongating itself, become curiously malleable as she reached for the button inches away from her fingers, Ana knew that even if she made a run for it now, the gases would get them all while she was waiting for that electronic door to make up its mind about letting her out. It would all be over. She had no choice now but to press the gun right up into Colleen's back, grab hold of her waist, and pull her back down with force.

'Colleen, please . . . don't . . . there's no need, OK, we'll get you out safely I promise . . . ' Ana whispered into her ear.

'Ana, I don't understand what this is,' Colleen said, turning to face Ana, her face utterly grief stricken. 'Did she make you do this? This isn't you, is it, eh? Please just stop.'

'I can't . . .' Ana started, as the unstoppability of what they had put in motion suddenly struck her. 'But I can get you all out safely, OK? Away from us.'

A conversation was still going on, on the other side of the shelf. She could hear the young man still blathering on about his thesis. Another academic arguing that the boy had a point, that the library's records didn't seem all that up to date if you looked carefully. And that there seemed to be some inconsistency behind the library's reasoning for documenting some works and not others.

'My sister's job is to make sure nothing is lost,' Ana heard Nan screaming at him. 'You don't know what you're talking about! Ana, Colleen? Can you come back out here please!'

Ana looked apologetically at Colleen, grabbed her gun again, and as gently as possible, used it to nudge Colleen back out into the crowd. When she rounded the corner, she felt she saw the situation as Colleen saw it. An image of destruction and terror. Nan standing there with her usual expressionless stare, a smear of Nicholas's blood having appeared on her face, while a crowd of innocent, petrified civilians tried to control their whimperings, and the professor's voice and breathing becoming more and more laboured. Each word taking him further and further away from his life, as the stoner-doctor kept arguing with him about how corrupt the library's systems were, calling Ana and Nan's occupation into question, as if that were the most pertinent thing to be discussing about them right now.

As she moved towards Nan, trying to find some way of getting her on her own, the words reverberated in her mind: *My sister's job is to make sure nothing is lost.* Ana felt a surge of shame, then, thinking of how she had never shared the specifics of her job with her sister. How she had convinced her sister that everything Nan scanned and handed over to her, all the precious texts, would then be carefully prepared by her, restored, saved, kept for posterity forever more. How not only her sister, but the whole of the small country, depended on her to complete this task, for their own sake. And how she had let them all down. She knew full well what the young man meant by moving sideways, out of view, because hadn't she facilitated that very move?

'Nan, we really need to get them out now. And to keep them calm,' she said.

Nan finally turned to her, her eyes seeming to make sense of everything once more.

'Yes, you're right,' she said. 'We do. Sorry. I don't know . . . what I was . . . sorry, Ana . . . I . . .'

Nan looked lost again now. It was almost as disconcerting for Ana to see Nan switch back to this. She stood in front of her slightly as she addressed the crowd, so that they could not see that Nan had lost her steely resolve.

'OK, OK, let's all calm down here!' Ana said, her voice cracking.

'Yeah, this is a very calming situation,' someone said, followed by a nervous laugh.

'Who's laughing?' Nan said, pushing her out of her way. She was back to normal again, more determined than before. The next person her sister shot at, Ana realised with terrible clarity, was going to die.

'Nan, it's all right. Keep calm, OK?'

'Stop fucking saying that! And I swear if she laughs one more time . . .' Nan's eyes turned to look at someone in the crowd.

Ana swung around to see who the perpetrator was. It was the blonde girl, still shivering in her bra; shoulders heaving with laughter as she held her palm to her mouth. It was another thing she remembered the government official saying: 'At times of great stress or anxiety, sometimes one can be consumed by uncontrollable fits of laughter. But try to control it, or you might get a bullet in your head, and that won't be funny for anyone.'

'Nan,' Ana said quietly now, trying to mouth the words across the crowd of bodies. 'We need to forget this, let someone get them out while we . . . you know . . . Colleen can do it, she has a pass. We need to go.'

Ana looked at her watch. Twenty past twelve. Those in their locked offices would be incandescent, but their phones would all be dead. There would be nothing they could do until help arrived. Dan would have been outside for an hour; long enough to get hold of someone. How had they ever thought this would work? That they would have completed everything within the hour? That they'd be ready, when the police came, to give themselves up? As usual, they had made things complicated when it should have been simple. And it was primarily, she realised, her feelings for Dan that had derailed them, and not Nan's earlier error. It was her urge to keep him safe, pure, to keep him out of all this that had led to where they were now. Despite all she had protested about protecting civilians, she had put Dan's reputation above her supposed desire to protect the library's visitors from the risk of those gases. But she had surely now increased the risk of those gases being triggered, for the fact that they were now static instead of moving forwards, it gave everyone more time to think and to focus on their surroundings, and who knew how many more trigger points there were down here, that Colleen may full well know of their location?

The whole debacle was now slowing everything down, and more importantly, was keeping them from Eben, who might, if they didn't get to him soon, find some way of raising the alarm. In which case they would have achieved nothing, and would be made to look like deranged idiots, acting out some fantasy of power.

'Eben,' Ana said, not caring who heard her now. 'We need to get to Eben.'

Eben would be sitting in a locked archive, wondering what on earth was going on. There, ready for the taking, and they were here.

'Eben?' Her sister looked up at her like the name meant nothing to her. 'What's Eben got to do with anything?'

Ana could not tell if Nan was acting or not now, perhaps trying to dissuade her from revealing too much in front of their hostages. But she was also frightened by the genuine confusion in Nan's voice; how it was happening again, how she was shifting from seeming threatening only a second ago and now seemed to become small and fragile, closing in on herself somehow.

'I don't think we need to worry about him,' Nan said. 'We'll work with what we've got. We've got enough bullets, I think, for them all.'

With that the air was somehow sucked out of the room. The crowd had heard what she said. Ana stared back at her sister in disbelief. The whole floor felt as though it may give way beneath her, send her plummeting into the bowels of the library. They were once again children, their mother in the room, scolding them, muttering again about one being so determined to go against the other, to be each other's polar opposite, acting out just for the sake of it.

'She doesn't mean it,' Ana said, hearing how shaky her voice sounded, clogged with dust particles. 'We're not here to harm you. We're not . . .'

'Yes we are!' Nan shouted out, shooting another bullet in no particular direction.

Ana realised it was futile trying to argue with her sister now. She had made a conscious choice to turn the whole thing topsy-turvy; perhaps it had been her intention all along. Ana felt like everything she had known had suddenly fallen away from her, and she was in this building with a complete stranger, one who looked so much like her, yes, but really didn't resemble or represent her in any way.

'Where are you going?' she heard Nan asking, a tinge of desperation in her voice. It wasn't until then that Ana realised she was actually doing it; she was actually walking away from her sister. Because it was her best hope, she thought, to achieve what they came here to do.

'I'm going to find Eben,' she said. 'That's why we're here! Come on!'

As Ana walked past the crowd, weaving herself between the bodies, she tried to focus on the task ahead of her and block out any thoughts of compassion for those who grappled with her ankles as she slid past; their sweaty palms a reminder of how desperate they now were, how she was their only real chance of salvation. She held fast, for she was fairly sure, as far as she could be, that this defiant little move of hers was all that was needed to get Nan to see sense and follow her away from this whole mess and down to the archives. That way, Colleen could take over, and they would all be so desperate to get out now they surely wouldn't even think to raise the alarm until they were outside.

Ana turned around and headed back the way they had come, opening the door at the end of the corridor with her staff pass, holding her gun out ahead of her, to make sure that no one in the crowd would make a run for it. Even as it closed, and Nan remained standing above the hostages, Ana still believed, until she heard the click, that Nan would come. Nan would realise that the game wasn't worth playing if she didn't have her sister at her side, and Ana, as always, would have tricked her with promises of a better time elsewhere.

But Nan didn't budge, and that windowless door closing between them felt like a particular kind of severing, one they had never experienced in the entirety of their intertwined lives.

*

In that split second when Professor Nicholas moved, he had seemed like a clay pigeon. That was the only way she could explain it to herself. Just the slightest movement and it was almost involuntary. She needed to shoot him like she'd been trained to do. Hit the target. It was an action driven by instinct; not by thought. And in a room like this, it made sense to aim for a human body – the very thing that could absorb a bullet like a secret and make it disappear. Whereas bullets could mercilessly travel through certain substances – glass, plaster, wood – and leave them behind, the human body could actually draw it deep within itself. And keep it, like a memento.

Bodies were the most complex things on earth, Nan thought, remembering the scan of her brain; the luminous white trails of her neural pathways against the black abyss of the screen. She'd never thought of herself before as a thing made up of components, whose very existence depended on one of those pathways connecting to another. But her brain, as the surgeon had put it, was starting to look like a series of dead ends. (He'd looked away as he said this; she thought he'd probably considered later it was an unfortunate turn of phrase.) 'See here, we have the disconnect,' he'd said, pointing to another part of her brain, which looked like a little clearing in a dense wood.

She wondered whether those lying on the floor in front of her now had given any real thought to what was happening inside their bodies. She thought it was unlikely. They were more interested in looking for connections and patterns in a book. Looking for theories that did not exist until they had sought them out. Not understanding that they themselves were the most interesting theories of all; that there were more unusual activities and connections in bodies than could ever be surmised between the pages of a (digitised) book. Nan thought maybe that's why she had shot Nicholas after all; to make him realise he was a body – nothing more, nothing less. That our bodies functioning properly was the only real thing that mattered. Health is wealth, her mother had always said, an adage that had now been manipulated into a political slogan, to try to get the inhabitants of the small country to accept their lot in life.

She was annoyed with the library goers too, now that she thought about it. Perhaps that had been the root of it. Annoyed by how easy she made their lives by digitising books. That lad taking it for granted that a book could appear in front of him with the click of a button, and then daring to criticise it, without considering for one moment the work that had gone into it; what had been expected of her and then Ana in order to make sure those books made it safely onto the system. Placing them lovingly under the light like newborns, checking for anomalies, fixing their imperfections with filmoplast, trying to make sure they went onwards in life as well preserved as they could be. Sometimes she saw someone uploading a text and then losing interest in it; wandering off for a smoke and then just leaving it there, staring back at no one, as if they had the divine right to click on any page of any book they wanted. They didn't spare a thought for how, after she had digitised the book, she was the last to hold it in her hand, before she handed it over to her sister to archive it behind the closed, prohibited doors of the preservations chambers.

Nan had been rushing jobs recently. Mainly because that clearing in her brain was starting to get bigger and bigger, and she was worried, with some texts, if she didn't digitise them as quick as she could, then she would be sure to lose the flow of the process. She was worried that those gaps in her mind might actually start becoming gaps in the texts she was sending out, that the page numbers wouldn't follow each other, that her own crumbling mind would somehow seep into the nation's consciousness, that her losses would be everyone's losses.

That was part of the reason she'd begun to feel as if it didn't really matter what happened in the next few hours. The sooner someone descended on the place and took her away, the better. Because she'd sooner be dragged out of here like some kind of terrorist than be remembered as someone who had *a brain disease*, as the doctor had called it.

Eben, her sister had said, *Eben. Don't you remember?*

She spun around the room now, looking for her sister. She saw fleetingly, in her mind's eye, the vision of her sister on the other side of the door as it closed behind her. Had that happened just now, today, or some other time? She could not recall. Again and again it came to her, the image of her sister walking out of the room, turning back to look at her pleadingly; waiting a few seconds as the door locked behind her, then the faint sound of her turning on her heel and walking away. Her mind had stored and recorded the image and sound of it, like her own personal CCTV, yet she could not remember feeling any emotion at the time. Now, however, it devastated her, the notion her sister had walked away from her, that she had willingly let her go, and that she had no intention of going after her.

Without Ana, she hardly remembered who she was or what she was meant to do. She could no longer remember the name for this object in her hand that seemed so potent whenever she pointed it at anyone. *Find a path back to the word,* her doctor crooned in the abyss of her rattling, decaying brain.

Eben

12.30PM

Eben's panic had taken on a different texture. It wasn't the kind of panic that made him feel worthless, but more the kind of panic that made him want to put his fist through the wall (if he were physically capable of doing such a thing). It wasn't his name in the original document. He'd seen it with his very own eyes. The quote that had appeared in every paper, in every periodical, in every crappy little online journal and forum, singling him out as the very reason for Elena's death, simply did not exist. The original document had been interfered with in a way that made it appear real. Skimming through the diaries leading up to her death, he could see clearly now what was bothering her, and what had been responsible for stopping her writing in its tracks.

He looked up the relevant dates that had been responsible for concocting the aptly called narrative verdict of her death. She had not, in fact, paid any attention to his article. There didn't seem to be any particular evidence that she had even read it. Yet during her inquest, her daughters had claimed it had been the start of her paranoia, her neurosis, and had fuelled feelings of self-loathing and suicidal fantasies.

He stood in the centre of his cell, trying to make sense of it all. It was quite obvious that he had nothing to do with Elena killing herself. That much was a relief. The words in front of him proved it; and he would be able to prove it to others.

'I am not responsible for the death of Elena Oodig,' he said to himself, with added vigour this time, finally letting himself believe it.

The name written down in her diary had been CJ, not Eben. *Creutzfeldt-Jakob disease*, or so the attached letter from the hospital revealed on the next page of the diary, and in true Elena fashion, she had made a character of her illness, almost imagining him as an embodiment of Eben himself, stalking her, loitering outside her house, following her everywhere. *When I read those words in black and white, they pulled me down. Down into the depths. There is nothing to do now but to admit that he has undone me. That I will never be whole again. CJ has come for me – I must give myself to him willingly.*

Eben has come for me, he recalled reading in the online paper that next morning, a quotation released by the family. He had almost choked to death on the hillock of cereal he had just pushed into his mouth. He remembered writhing on the floor, bits of brown cereal hurtling into the air as he tried desperately to cough away the obstruction in his windpipe while his cat looked down on him, enjoying the entertainment. Eventually he had mustered enough strength to get to his knees and shove his stomach against the side of the chair, which had finally dislodged the offending cereal chunk and left him gasping for air. Yet in the hours following the incident, having scoured all the online publications, journals and periodicals, and seen his name mentioned again, numerous times, he then wished he had not saved himself.

Now, however, everything was different. It was here – the evidence he finally needed in order to clear his name. CJ, Elena had written, would advance so rapidly that she would be dead within a year. Her doctor had said there were abnormal proteins in her brain, *prions*, which caused the brain to fold abnormally, to cave in on itself. *CJ has invited me to do the dance macabre with him*, it read, instead of *Eben has invited me to do the dance macabre*.

How had everyone accepted it so willingly? Taken the twins' word for it? The police had obviously not done their work properly and read the diaries for themselves; they had merely accepted the quotes given to them, which seemed to corroborate the claims of hate crimes. He still remembered the smugness of the female detective who had questioned him, who – he surmised – had been determined to find him guilty of all this from the outset.

Perhaps those opposed to the Smotherhood had been behind it. Frankton had told him that there were many people working in the library who were determined to bring the Smotherhood down. But it didn't necessarily matter, he thought. Everything would be different now. Frankton would welcome him back into the fold; his literary reputation would be restored.

Then again, what kind of reputation would this leave him with? After all, he'd had everyone in this town talking about him as though he were a murderer, attributing him with a kind of twisted glamour he'd never possessed at any other time in his life. He'd convinced himself that he, like the library's founder, Sir John, had been elevated to a state of attractive infamy. Those unfounded Jack-the-Ripper rumours had made Sir John far more interesting, with true-crime-obsessed teenage girls often to be seen draping themselves across his marble feet, taking selfies with him.

It was all too easy, Eben thought, for someone to come along at any time in the future, when you were long gone, and completely change the story.

Elena, of course, had foreseen this, and her portrait bust now seemed to be nodding in agreement in the darkness. She had more than likely been in on it; perhaps had even asked someone to change the digital version but leave the paper copy as it was, so that it allowed the potential for him to discover for himself that it had all been one big joke. And she knew, too, that in order for him to find out, he would have to be doing something as desperate as writing her biography as a public apology. Being here now did prove, in a way, what she'd once claimed, which was that he *was* obsessed with her. He saw that this much was true. He loved and hated her in equal measure, in a way that made him the least objective reviewer possible. He was only intent on ruining her. And it had led to this: she'd used her own death, her own illness, as a way of getting back at him.

He was angry now. Angry that he had fallen for it. Angry that this new evidence, and all that she had written about him, exonerated him but also deflated his ego considerably. When the whole literary community had turned against him in the way they had, he'd become visible in a way he'd never been before. He would return to being a nobody now, in the worst possible way. He would revert from being dangerous to being completely innocuous; he would fall from the pages of history, as though he, like his namesake, had never existed.

Then again, he wondered how on earth he would go about proving this. They did not allow phones in here, so he could not take a picture of the page. He certainly couldn't rip it out and take it with him. He would need to find another reference that would prove it. There had been another section of her donated paperwork labelled 'Miscellaneous', which he had caught a glimpse of earlier, in a box file bulging with rather boring official-looking documents – travel itineraries, invitations to festivals, insurance certificates, car tax reminders, that sort of thing – kept perhaps as a sign of the indulgent times in which Elena had lived, when society allowed her these paper-related privileges. Wasteful bits of paper to hoard as she wished, nothing more than mementoes that were never again looked at. But a printed document was something that could leave clues of that life you had lived; even something you hadn't written down explicitly in your diary. And if there was some evidence in here of the condition she was suffering from, something in there that would be relatively easy to sneak out past security (if security ever remembered he was in here) then perhaps he could have half a chance of being believed.

It had not been easy to leave the country in the past ten years or so without intense medical screenings; he was pretty sure there would be at least an appointment letter or something to indicate she was being assessed. The paper cut-off would not have happened until she was well into her illness, and if she had kept her car tax reminders perhaps she had also kept her hospital correspondence. Something that he could perhaps take to the police, so that they could check her medical records and issue him with a public apology for everything they had put him through.

He took down the box file and pulled the cover open. He began to take the documents out, one by one, and lay them face down on the table next to him, so that he could easily slip the whole lot back in, without drawing attention to the fact that he had been rummaging. A million thoughts raced through his mind as he quickly scanned every document before placing it down – the fact that his project was in tatters and could no longer be completed, the fact that the last few months had been a waste of energy and emotion and regret. On and on he sped, lifting up the more mundane reminders of the life Elena had lived – remittances from payments she had received, festival programmes – all felt like a complete extravagance of paper in his fingertips now. The dates at the top of the letters seemed to be getting further and further away the deeper he ventured into the box, and with that, the hope of finding anything even slightly relevant dwindled.

But then he reached the very final document in the box; an officious letter on headed notepaper, from a medical organisation of some kind. He lifted it up curiously. This could be it, he thought. As he read on, he discovered that it was a result, dated two years ago, issued in response to a recent sample that she had provided.

But it was nothing to do with her medical condition. And this time, it really was his name on the paper, halfway down the letter, in black and white; next to a statistic.

Such was his shock at what he was reading that the urine broke free from him in an instant; an involuntary gush as he felt his knees give way beneath him. He fell against the cabinet that held Elena's portrait bust, causing it to fall from its podium, and land on the floor with a loud crack.

Eben Prytherch, it had said. A 99.9998 per cent probability.

Dan

12.45PM

The hostages were now positioned at the top of the stairs above the emergency exit while Dora, Kenvin and Dan remained hunched another level above them. They'd had no option but to travel through some of the older doors without security strips, and when they found themselves emerging from a dark corridor in full view of the hostages below them, Dan engaged the security protocol and shoved them both on the floor, landing rather awkwardly on top of them. No one below stirred, and so he assumed they hadn't been seen.

He was surprised how much his training was ingrained in him, considering how stoned he'd been for most of it. Then again, his efforts to appear alert in those sessions had meant he was concentrating a little too hard on every manoeuvre they were taught, whereas the rest of the sober porters were probably zoning out. When Dora and Kenvin wriggled beneath him, he instinctively reached out his hands to cover their mouths, dredging up rule 47 in the handbook: *Where there is danger to human life and free civilians roaming the building, all measures must be taken to ensure their silence and co-operation.* Kenvin bit him, of course, but Dan held fast; telling himself he would deal with the twat later. Dora stared straight on, eyes frozen in panic, reminding him of a grandmother in a freezer in some godawful horror movie he'd watched late one night.

People seemed to be lying face down on the floor, from what he could gather from his quick glance, but it was impossible to tell why. He remembered the one, solitary leg he'd seen hoisted up into the air. The large patch of blood, that seemed to highlight how monumentally he had fucked up. Could they all be dead? Or had someone triggered the sleeping gases in this part of the building? He imagined, according to his exposed position, that it would be taking hold of them all now if that were the case and if anything, he was frighteningly alert now, more so than he'd been for hours. Perhaps the hostages were just lying there in resignation, having given up on the notion of being saved.

He remained lying down with Dora and Kenvin for a moment, and placed his arms around them both. Kenvin did not know what to do with such strange tenderness at a moment like this, and writhed against him. Dora did the opposite, patting his arm as it came to rest upon hers. He breathed in the scent of them – the unlikely trio that they were – and there was something comforting in the commingling of sweat, spice, potatoes, baking and ammonia. The odd perfume told him that, despite everything, three people who'd had no real relationship until today could sit together like this and their union would make a strange kind of sense.

Nan's voice came to trespass across his inebriated musings; everywhere and nowhere at once. He heard her talking to the hostages – demanding this, that, and the other – telling people to stop moving, to shut their mouths. He recognised all too well, from those disastrous shags they'd had, the coldness in the commands. *Stop talking. Make love to me.* But what was new to him now was the way she'd ask a question, and then seem to answer it herself. Like she was conversing with herself in front of everyone. Also talking about herself in the plural. *We've got enough bullets, I think, for them all.* Or was she working with someone? He had heard a door shutting somewhere, as if someone had left, but he hadn't heard any voice in the room but hers. He still couldn't actually believe that she'd been capable of harming people. He knew he had a track record for choosing unsuitable women – this much was true – but to have chosen someone so unhinged, someone he'd read so drastically differently, this was new.

Then he remembered: he had not chosen her. She had chosen him.

He listened awhile to the silence. It was the kind that would descend on the library often, a dense air that was so rich in its texture, it was almost suffocating. He'd never known silence like that; not in prison, anyway. In prison, there wasn't such a thing. The long days and nights were punctuated with beeps and buzzes and clicks; the man next to him in the other cell snoring, the sounds of something being dragged along the floor, the ominous footsteps of the screws. Prisoners, of course, did not deserve silence, whereas the library goers had earned it.

Bodies, however, would betray silence in the way a mind would not. Dan could tell that a sneeze was building somewhere in Kenvin's body, an involuntary expulsion ballooning in his nostrils; a storm gathering in his eyes. And all too soon it was gone, released, before he could do anything about it, and it had come out like it was meant to; a thing to be noticed and to be heard.

The silence that followed was a different kind altogether.

'Is there someone up there?' Nan shouted, her voice reaching up into the air, over the rim of the balcony.

Kenvin and Dora looked at each other. Then, they looked to Dan; and there was a split second where he felt a sense of achievement that they assumed he would know what to do next. But he had not thought any further than lying down in submission and hoping the whole situation would go away, which was not recommended anywhere in the safety manual.

He scrolled through the various options in his disintegrating brain.

Option 1: get on his feet, surrender. Walk towards Nan and leave Kenvin and Dora where they were. But then he'd be breaking rule 124 in the handbook: *If a terrorist attack occurs, do not, under any circumstances, leave civilians to fend for themselves.*

Option 2: give Kenvin up, and make a run for it with Dora. But he wasn't sure her heart would cope.

Option 3: give Dora up, and make a run for it with Kenvin. He still wasn't sure he liked him enough to do that.

It reminded him of the conundrum with the chicken, the fox, and the bag of corn.

'Is there anyone there? Answer me!' Nan's voice came at them again. Closer this time. As if she was moving towards them.

He had horrific images of the fox eating the chicken and the chicken eating the corn.

'Is there someone up there?' came her voice again.

Then he imagined Dora eating him, and Kenvin eating Dora; the inevitable carnivorous pecking order.

'We're up here!' Dan hollered suddenly.

Kenvin turned to glare at him.

'What the hell are you doing?' he said. 'She's going to kill us!'

'Stand up,' he whispered. 'Stand up and take Dora with you, OK? Pretend it was you who called out.'

'And what about you?'

Dan shook his head. Dora and Kenvin wouldn't appear any kind of threat to her whatsoever. If she saw him, however, she would panic, and there was no knowing what she'd do in retaliation. Kenvin was still staring at him, awaiting futher justification for this rash move of his, but Dan couldn't speak, not now, for fear of being heard. Kenvin got to his feet. He managed to pull Dora up with him. As Dan had suspected, their movements provided the necessary foil for a quick bum shuffle further up the corridor. He heard Nan insisting that Kenvin and Dora come down the corridor to meet her.

'There you are,' he heard her say, as nonchalant as if she was waiting to be served at the canteen. 'Lie down please. Both of you. And be quiet. As long as you all keep quiet, you'll be fine.'

They did as they were told. Words fell away and coagulated in the air around them. Dan couldn't move any further for fear of giving the game away. He listened to the breaths down below; some low, some erratic. Some easing into sleep; because sleep seemed easier at this point in time than consciousness. Stomachs rumbled too, in protest at being kept from their lunch.

Dora piped up. Dan knew what was coming next. The whole small-good-thing business.

'Maybe,' Dora started, 'I could give them something to eat. I mean, food . . . it's a small good thing, at a time like this.'

Nan didn't reply for a while. When she did, he was surprised by the softness in her voice.

'That's from a short story, isn't it?' she said.

'Yes, that's it! His name . . . I forget . . . something to do with food . . .'

'Their son dies, doesn't he . . . in the original version of the story, at least,' Nan said, 'and they're eating buns in a bakery,' Nan went on. 'They find that they're actually hungry, though they shouldn't really be . . . It's an oddly comforting moment. They eat one bun, and then another – and it makes you think they might be able to somehow function again . . . eventually. I suppose. It couldn't hurt, to give them something.'

Peering cautiously over the edge, he caught a glimpse of Dora rummaging around in her apron and bringing out a bag of something, making her way through the crowd. The crowd seemed to come to life, hesitantly, obviously not sure what they should talk about under such strange circumstances, even if they were now permitted to speak in this curious interval during hostage proceedings. They could not talk about their situation. It was out of the question. They could not talk about the pacing librarian with a gun.

He heard Dora urging a pregnant woman to eat two of the cakes rather than one. And talk with absolutely zero authority about how a spike in blood sugar could prevent a coma. People soon followed suit, and began making small talk in any leftover vocabulary they could dredge up from their traumatised selves.

'Yes, I've never been in this part of the building before! Interesting, isn't it? I didn't know it existed!' From here, if he didn't know better, it might sound to Dan like some dead boring book launch or reception.

All the while, she paced back and forth, back and forth with her gun. And every now and then, she threw her eyes upwards; which was when he ducked back down again from view.

Once the noise had reached an acceptable, safe level, he was able to move along and open the door with his shoulder, pushing himself into the corridor where the management team worked. He crawled his way across it, trying to be as silent as possible; ignoring the faces of the management team and the fists that squashed themselves against the soundproof glass as he went by, trying to get his attention; wanting to be saved.

He didn't have his nun-device to be able to do anything about it. And even if he did, he knew that by ignoring them he was saving them. He knew where the danger was now, and that the safety protocol was completely accurate.

They were safer in than out.

Ana

1PM

Ana was racing towards the archive now, moving expertly through the labyrinthine corridors in the way only an archivist could; left past the collection of rare books, onwards through the film and TV archive, cutting across the blue-velvet-seated auditorium where some film from long ago was always playing to no one, downwards through the restoration rooms and past the conservators' cubbyholes, navigating the maze with ease. Faces of long-gone eras peered back at her as she made her way past them; dark, dolorous eyes staring out at her from those paintings no one saw anymore, those she had to squeeze past, hoping she wasn't taking off a layer of their ancient faces with her blouse.

Flurries of marbled paper and chiffon-thin maps upended themselves as she climbed across some of the shelves to get to the exits quicker, paper taking flight in her wake like giant butterflies. So much stuff, she thought, cluttering up the darkness when it should be out there, being seen, being read. Being valued. But it couldn't all be exhibited at once; it had to go somewhere. And when it had started to overflow, the archivists had struggled to find a place for these things. Valuable items became hazards, death traps; they needed to be kept from view, because they were possibly rife with germs, but they needed to be kept for reference, all the same. The head librarian was adamant that the visitors shouldn't ever be privy to the kind of cluttered chaos that came with documenting your own history, the library needed to uphold the image of order and precision, keeping from them the secret that they were always a page's breadth away from being smothered by their own history.

It was only in a place like this that the architecture would be so strange and nonsensical that you needed sometimes to go upwards to find the best possible, fastest route down, and so up she went towards the attic – where a portrait bust of her mother's head had once been stored alongside the other heads that eagerly awaited their real owners' deaths. Her mother had disliked the portrait bust intensely, saying it wasn't a true representation of her, that the sculptor had deliberately added not one, but two extra chins. When she died, however, it had been a comfort to them both. The arch-porter had instructed Dan to take it down to the archive, and Ana had watched him on the CCTV, telling Nan that she just wanted to make sure it wasn't damaged in transit. But the real reason was because she wanted to see them together, as tenuous as their connection might be, even if Dan was completely oblivious to what that decapitated bronze head meant to her.

That evening, she and Nan had worked late and gone back down to the archive to look at where he had placed the bust. He had plonked it rather unceremoniously in the corner of the archive, next to a collection of her mother's notebooks, two eyes peering over the row of colourful leather spines. *Heathen,* Nan had called him, as she set about finding a more dignified location. They decided that placing it on the empty shelf overlooking the study desk in the archive would be best, so that when Eben came, he would have Elena literally looking over his shoulder, and would be rattled from the moment he sat down.

Ana remembered being stunned at the amount of material her mother had accumulated over the years. She had been donating regularly to the library throughout her career, always insisting that the other archivists should take care of her collections, to free Ana and Nan to keep doing their own important conservation work. She had been as diligent about this as she had been scatty about everything else. 'Maybe I'm not much of a house-keeper,' she had joked, 'but when I die, all my memorabilia will

be in order. You won't have to be sifting through everything, trying to make sense of it all.' And it was true that when she died,
apart from her vast personal library, there didn't seem to be anything hoarded under her bed or in her safe.

She had not written anything for weeks at that point. Her last
real book had come out almost two years before; right on the cusp
of the paper ban, one of the last books of the small country to
appear in print – something she prided herself on. The only thing
they had to hold on to was the open letter she had left on her laptop, which she'd already sent to the media, in which she blamed
Eben for her death. Although she had not explicitly stated that she
wanted them to take revenge on him, Nan had convinced Ana that
it was the only way of bringing him to justice. To write a better end
to the story; one that did not simply make Elena the victim.

It sometimes occurred to Ana that perhaps, in concocting this
plan, they were attempting to be creative in a way they had never
truly been before, as though trying to atone for the disappointment they felt they had been to their mother. She had encouraged
them, from the outset, to express themselves through writing, but
while they may have loved the books she read to them as children, they appreciated them almost in an aesthetic way, wanting
to possess them like treasures rather than be inspired by their content; they wanted to be involved in the journey they made into the
world and into the future that was beyond them all. And perhaps
some creativity might have flourished, Ana often thought, were
it not for the paper ban itself, which seemed to render the whole
exercise pointless to a large degree. You got rid of the paper, you
hampered the need for creativity. You created a nation of archivists and technicians, storing work for an uncertain future.

Ana entered a blue-coloured corridor reserved for the most
important collections. She felt weightless now, ready for anything,
and seemed almost to float across the river of linoleum leading
to the door at the far end of the corridor. She would have to do

this quickly, she thought to herself, before she had time to think about it too much. How long would it take for them to find her down there and arrest her? She wondered whether she would have enough time to sit there and read some of her mother's diaries. Would she be able to do so, with a body at her feet? There was a clause in Elena's will that stipulated that no one should read her diaries until she and her daughters had passed away. Even Ana and Nan themselves. It was something that had upset Ana greatly at the time, the thought that she was being denied this last insight into her mother's life, a connection with her when all other connections had been lost; but Nan had reasoned with her, told her they needed to remember her as their loving, gentle, surprising, funny mother, and not as a writer with thoughts and feelings and neuroses like any other person.

'There might be stuff about us we don't want to hear,' Nan had said. 'I mean, can you imagine how difficult it would have been for her raising twins as a single mother. She probably wished we'd never been born at times. Her diaries are a resource for a future, a future far from here. They are not resources for right now.'

Until they were, of course, Ana thought. Until they had realised that Eben's request being granted, when all the other requests were denied, would be a way of getting him exactly where they wanted him. What would he read or discover? He would soon be dead anyway, and Elena's secrets would go with him to wherever he was going. But she still couldn't help feeling indignant that in order to get him here, they had to allow him a kind of privilege that they themselves were denied. Even in death, he would have that over them: secret knowledge disintegrating along with his body, to become nothing, eventually, but dust.

Perhaps she'd read just one, Ana thought. Later. Before they came for her. Just a single entry, during a year when she knew they had all been happy and secure. Just to hear her mother's voice; to carry it with her in her mind when she was carted off to wherever they would take her in the aftermath. And to see her handwriting, something she'd been denied for those two years after the paper ban; that hurried, looping doodle that had been lovingly placed on all those wasteful birthday cards, shopping lists, and notes from the tooth fairy under their pillows.

Ana was outside the archive now. This was it. She pressed the security device up against the lock to see if she could first disable the fire suppression system, for she wasn't sure if the heat from a gunshot would perhaps set it off. This particular CO_2 agent was said to be able to kill a human within seconds. Staff always joked about this, the fact that if a fire broke out in one of those rooms then the books would be fine, but not the librarian. It hadn't however been able to stop the fire which had claimed the life of their rare book collection, as those books had not yet made it to the safety of the archives. They had been left out haplessly overnight, vulnerable and exposed on tables and chairs in one of the conservations rooms, with nothing to protect them. But Ana had heard rumours that some of the books that were said to have gone up in flames had never been in that room in the first place. She shuddered at the thought of this now, because she could guess where those books had gone, and knew that it was partly her fault.

She and her sister had briefly considered that one simple way to get rid of Eben would be to set off the fire suppression system while he was in there. It would be almost instantaneous; the room flooding silently with a deadly agent while he worked. He would perhaps start to wonder why the words in front of him were becoming harder and harder to read, why they lifted off the page of their own accord, but by the time he looked up and tried to grab hold of them, he would have only a fraction of a second to surmise that there would be no more words available to him, ever again. No more Eben. But this was almost too good for him. Too easy. He would never be held accountable for anything; simply drifting painlessly away, unlike their mother had done. No, they wanted him to know what he had taken from them and how he would be paying for it with his life.

Running the device across the strip again, she heard another click and beep, before the door declared itself unlocked. In she stepped.

Eben

1.30PM

The door that had seemed impossibly shut for hours had finally opened, and in its frame stood one of Elena's twins. Still reeling from what he'd read in Elena's diary, he found it hard to fathom if what he was seeing was real at all, or whether his fragmented mind had conjured her up out of thin air. She looked so much like her mother and yet also like a strange impersonation of her, her legs slightly longer, her chin of different proportions, her hair poker-straight, like a helmet on her head; so unlike Elena's unruly bohemian mop. She was Elena, and yet she was not; she was infused with something else.

That something else, he thought, his stomach lurching now, was the set of genes she'd inherited from her father. His donated sperm presumably *had* conjured her up out of thin air. Not just her, but her sister too.

She was hiding something; one hand angled slightly behind her back. Her face was curiously unreadable. He tried to calm himself. He knew she worked here. For all he knew, she had just been sent to let him out. Now was not the time for pleasantries, or to broach what he had discovered. He needed to look at the letter again; the letter he had so boldly shoved down the front of his piss-stained trousers, where no one in their right mind would want to rummage.

'I've been locked in here for hours,' he said, deciding that to act affronted was the best way to get her to keep her distance. He threw his gloves down angrily on the desk in front of him, and, as an afterthought he hurriedly took off his blazer and swung it

165

erratically in front of his trousers. She might catch a whiff of the urine, perhaps, but as long as she did not see the stain, he hoped he could leave with his reputation intact. 'If you'll excuse me, I'm late for an appointment.'

He slowed down as he went past her, pausing now to take another good look at her, haunted by versions of his grandmother, female cousins, his own sister, physical remnants of whom seemed to jump out from her eyes, her face, her curious indignant expression. Even her silence now seemed familiar to him; that, and the fact that she did not seem to be making way for him to pass.

She laughed. He assumed that for all his swinging around of his blazer, she had noticed the stain. He tried to reason with himself that it would be the least of the humiliations he'd endured in the last few hours. And yet it was painful, to think that this wasn't a complete stranger mocking him, but his own daughter, to whom, in another world, he should have been a role model, a confidant. He knew how small and puny, so un-father-like, he appeared as he ventured a 'Can I just get past . . .'

That's when he realised what was going on. She was the reason he was in here. Ever so slowly she retrieved what she was holding behind her back and held it up in the air. It was a gun. She strode towards him, pointing it directly at his forehead. For all his catastrophising, all the thoughts of bombs and terrorists, he had not imagined himself being the sole target of someone's anger, the only person by whom the terror was meant to be felt. He looked up desperately at the CCTV at the corner of the room. What on earth was she doing? Surely someone could see this happening? Shouldn't an alarm sound or something? Shouldn't there be someone coming to the rescue?

He froze, just as she did; the gun feeling painfully real now against his forehead, positioned a little above his glasses. The hopeful seconds ticked on, offering no kind of salvation whatsoever. There seemed to be no stirring, no sound, nothing but his own laboured breath leaving his body and struggling to re-enter.

As he finally met her gaze, he studied her face to look for a resemblance. Was that red hair of hers the colour that had once sprouted from his own head, before most of it fell away? Was that his mother's sharp, authoritative nose, recast above a less offensive jawline? Were those dark green eyes the eyes of Eben the Poet he'd read about in one of the works Nicholas had quoted, resurfacing in the gene pool after lying dormant in the abyss of non-existence for centuries? If she didn't know, he would tell her, right here, right now, and it might change everything. If it was the reason she was holding the gun to his head, he was done for.

'Is this . . . are you . . . angry with me because . . . Look there's something . . .' His breathing was uneven as he struggled to push the words into the gaps. He didn't know how he could possibly express it. What words were there for what Elena had done to him?

'Don't speak!' she shouted back at him, moving around so that she could move the barrel of the gun towards the back of his head. She kicked a chair underneath him and shoved him down into it. 'You've done enough talking. All we've heard is your voice, everywhere, all the time. Making itself heard. We all know you're not the neutral reviewer you claim to be, Eben, that you've got your own little agenda.'

Reviewer. Not father. She didn't know. Unless she was building up to it. Eben thought of the few times he'd seen the twins before. At readings. At literary events. Passing by him in the library. Utterly identical. He knew their names, and he wondered which one she was. Nan? Ana? *My daughters*, he suddenly thought to himself, the idea filling him both with excitement and revulsion. Flesh and blood. Without him, they could not exist. He had actually produced something; not just one, but two. He was responsible for other existences in the world, and therefore not completely redundant after all. *I have the power to change my life at any moment*, he thought, recalling another of the therapist's affirmations. It was now fundamentally changed for him, but – strange as it was – it was not entirely unwelcome either.

'Look, Nan . . . Ana . . . which one are you? If we could just . . . There are lots of things we need to discuss.'

'Why should it matter, which one I am?' Her voice came from behind him. She sounded genuinely curious, yet without seeing her face, he couldn't tell if this was some kind of trick question.

'We need to talk properly . . . Ana . . . It is Ana, isn't it . . . ?' he ventured. Eben worked out that he had a fifty-fifty chance of getting it right. When he heard her stop in her tracks, he knew it had been worth the gamble. 'Look, Ana,' he continued. 'Whatever you think I've done—'

'What I *think* you've done? You killed our mother! You took her away from us.'

'Listen, I didn't. I know what everyone thinks, but I've got something here that might prove it to you. Just let me show it to you—'

'No!' Ana screamed at him, her voice becoming thick with tears now. 'You don't get to convince us otherwise. You already convinced the police. You won't do the same here . . .'

'But please, there's so much more than that, if you—'

'One more word and I'm going to shoot you in the head,' she said. Emboldened. 'Just try me.'

She walked back around to the front of the chair, into his eyeline, her finger hovering perilously close to the trigger. Eben was starting to piece together the circumstances that had led him here. All those times his request had been denied. All the times he'd been told that no one was permitted to see Elena's diaries until she and her daughters had died, and yet, here he was. He couldn't believe he'd fallen for it, walked right into the trap. He had even dressed smartly for his own death.

'You don't realise how much your words hurt her,' she continued. 'She was a strong woman but when it came to her works, she was sensitive. They, too, were her babies. You attacked them. Every single one. You told the world they were worthless. You may not have convinced the masses but there were certain people who latched on to those words. People who liked you bringing her down. They didn't want her to be as powerful as she was. And it ground her down in the end. She decided she would give you what you so desperately wanted. She couldn't tolerate being attacked like that anymore!'

Floods of tears were pouring down the girl's face now, and Eben saw that she genuinely believed what she was saying. Either that or she had decided to ignore the real reason for her mother's demise, because it was too painful for her, and so much easier to blame him. Did she know about the other, bigger thing? Although he was still processing it, he still wondered whether it would be enough to save him. But then, her grip on the gun was solid, too solid, for him to risk revealing one potentially traumatic thing, let alone two. How could he venture to contradict her when she'd specifically told him a single word, a single utterance, would mean the end of everything?

He could do nothing but close his eyes and appear to be listening to her, agreeing with her; all the while spinning through the details in his head. He presumed Elena would have plucked the DNA from a scarf he remembered leaving behind at one of her readings. There had been a change in the legislation a few years back; meaning if mothers had an inkling who the father might be, you were able to present samples, and if you were correct, they confirmed it: a kind of genealogy lottery. Although they did not know each other personally, she knew him well enough to know he would not go back into the room after she'd publicly ridiculed him for whatever comment he'd dared make that day. He'd convinced himself he had not liked that scarf anyway; it had not suited him. He imagined her in an empty auditorium, approaching the scarf with trepidation, wondering what secrets it held. Why had she wanted to know? Surely it would have been easier to leave it alone, even if she had her suspicions?

He pressed his lips together and ventured a sound into the room; a sound unlike any he'd made before. It was a hum both of terror and of hopelessness; one that demonstrated his desire to speak, but did not break the code of silence.

'I guess everyone deserves their final little speech,' Ana said, in a mocking tone. 'Just make it brief.'

These words, he thought, the words he uttered now, would have to mean something. They were his only way out of this. He thought of all the days he had sat at his laptop and angrily bashed words out, then deleted them, before starting again. He rarely got things right the first draft; the tone was always wrong, his personal agenda glaringly obvious. But now, he had to try to formulate something perfect.

'I admired your mother,' he started. 'Really I did. I think that most of what I wrote didn't humiliate her in any way, not in the way you think.'

She didn't flinch, didn't move the gun away from his face, but at least she was still listening.

'It wasn't humiliating for her to be belittled by you?' Ana replied. 'No, of course not. It was a joke. But you know, if you repeat the joke too many times, it isn't funny anymore. And even though you pretended to be drawing attention to the weaknesses in her work, what you were trying to do was to create a weakness in her, and that weakness, ultimately, led to her death. So no matter how you did it. You still did it.'

'But there were other weaknesses, Ana, weren't there?' He looked up pleadingly at her then, and as she looked back down at him, he got a haunting glimpse of Aunt Nora, his mother's long-dead sister, resurrected in a single gesture.

'What do you mean?' Ana asked. It was obvious she didn't know about her mother's condition either. It was a risk, now, he thought, to just come out and say it. Far better to tell her to look for herself.

'There's a certain diary,' he began. 'Look, the blue one over there. There's a passage in that, a passage whose digital copy has been amended. It says in there that . . . something else caused her to be . . . upset, perhaps drove her to do what she did. And there's more, once you've read that. Something else I think you need to know. But you know . . . first things first.'

This was the best method, he thought. To talk her into seeing him as he really was first, seeing that he wasn't responsible for Elena's death, before revealing that he was probably her father. To do it the other way round ran the risk of freaking her out, and who knew what the devastating results of that could be for him?

Ana glanced at the diary. Her attention on Eben faltered just long enough for him to be able to consider grabbing the gun from her hand; except he did nothing but imagine himself doing it. As usual he was overthinking it. What if he tried and it went off? At least she seemed to be promising him a quick, sharp shot in the head. What if, in wrestling it from her, he ended up taking off half of his face? Or even worse, killing her and being made to look like a murderer for the second time?

'Whatever you think you can prove . . .' she began, now entirely focused on him again.

'I don't think I can prove it, I know I can! Please. Just read the diary. I won't move, I promise. Just read it.'

It would be better coming from Elena, was his reasoning. Ana was considering it – he could see as much now, in the way she lowered her gun ever so slightly, before inching hesitantly towards the blue diary. There would come a point, he realised, that she would have to turn to pick it up, and that would be his chance. The open door was behind her now; and beyond it lay his freedom, his exoneration, and the rest of his life.

She turned, and in that split second, he stopped thinking and let his body take over, getting up to make a dash for it. Except she was already one step ahead of him; she had pressed the button on her device to close the door the second she'd reached over for the diary, which meant that just as Eben was getting to it, it was closing; and because of his heavy frame, he was unable to squeeze through. As he felt the door crushing his arm, he pulled back, leaving him on the wrong side of the door, with Ana right up against his body now, the barrel thrust into his horrified, open mouth.

'Right, that's it!' she screamed at him. 'I'm doing it now.'

'But I wasn't lying about the diary. Please . . . you should still—'

'I'll read it afterwards.'

Afterwards. When he was gone. Eben felt suddenly the trickle of urine coming again; a vile steam rising up from his trousers. She looked at him with disgust. Although he had one trump card left, it still didn't seem like the time to use it.

'You'll be very sorry you've done this when you realise!' he protested. 'You'll go to prison. For years!'

'It'll be worth it. It will be my legacy,' she said, though he could tell from her voice that she didn't even believe her own words. Was that it? That this girl had been made to feel so redundant next to her own superstar mother, she thought there was no other way of gaining immortality?

'It's a pointless legacy, to kill someone . . .' he whimpered. 'Do something useful if you want to be remembered . . .'

'Oh they won't forget me, don't you worry about that. I won't just be killing anyone, will I? By getting rid of someone like you, think of all those writers I'm saving. All the new female writers you planned to silence. I'm giving the country the work they deserve, from writers who won't be crippled by self-doubt. All those sentences that would have been deleted, because they would have worried what you would have made of them. I'm their saviour!'

She seemed more composed now, as though thinking that this was a political act of some kind had given her purpose. Yet if you looked closely – which he had been doing, ever since he'd come across her, fascinated with every single expression that crossed the continent of that strangely familiar face – you could see how hollowed out she was somehow, by her own grief, how the words were removed from what she was feeling, how what she was spouting felt utterly removed from who she was, like she was pretending to be someone else.

Either way, there was no reasoning with her now. He was most certainly going to die. He closed his eyes and tried to connect back to the dark state he had been in a few years back, at the height of Elena's powers and influence. He had decided that he would never amount to anything, and so he had decided to take his own life. But he hadn't managed to do it properly; not like she had. Although he had stood on a chair and tied the noose around his neck, the noose had broken under his weight and he had knocked a tooth out in the fall, spending all evening in an emergency appointment with the dentist. Perhaps there was nothing for it now but to appreciate that someone had come along to do it properly this time.

'Say goodbye to the world, Eben. It'll be a better place without you.'

The gun was pressed further into his forehead. This time when it came into contact with his skin there was no disputing its potent reality. Or the intent in her eyes. She was going to kill him; there were no two ways about that. There was no other reading possible.

'She killed herself because she was . . . Look, you don't understand, or you don't want to . . . The truth about your mother is . . . The truth about me is that I'm . . .'

Eben could not make the words come. There was part of him that wondered whether he was wrong, after all. Or if those papers had been there to play yet another trick. Once he'd voiced those words there would be no getting them back. They huddled in his throat, getting tangled up in each other.

'Look, Ana, I'm your . . .'

The gun went off in his face. Accompanied by the sounds of things clattering down from above, as though the whole building had collapsed on top of him; everything, the whole world, coming apart at the seams. He was hurled onto the floor by the force of it, finding himself sprawled outwards under a large ceiling panel, plasterboard and dust in his eyes. He felt around his body for the bullet wound, waiting for the sharp pain to flood him, but was surprised when he couldn't find anything. He seemed still miraculously in one piece. Either that or he had already passed over into the next life, which looked suspiciously similar to the real one. Had he known it was this easy to die, he thought, maybe he should have done it a long time ago.

But no, now that his eyes were open, he saw a large, rectangular abyss in the ceiling above his head, where the air vent used to be, a ceiling panel having also come loose.

He rose to his feet. He saw what had happened. A porter, the one he'd met that morning, had kicked away a single panel and air vent, and entered through the ceiling. He now lay on top of Ana on the floor, restraining her. She was trying to push him off, screaming at him to let her go, but he would not budge. The porter wrenched the gun from her hands and threw it to one side. It clunked its way across the floor towards Eben, the porter shouting at him to take it. He stood there looking at it for a few minutes, this thing that had intended on ending his life. He wanted nothing to do with it, and yet, the way she was wrestling with the porter made him think she might break free from him any second, and so he swiftly deposited it into his blazer breast pocket. If nothing else, he told himself, it was the evidence he needed.

He didn't have much time now – Ana was reaching for a box file to bash against the porter's head, papers flying everywhere, and it looked as though she might start to take the upper hand in the battle. The thought of having to face her again sent him rushing to the door, only to find that it was still locked. There was no key to be seen anywhere in sight, just an odd-looking plastic contraption that looked a bit like an upside-down nun, split in two, rolling around on the floor next to Ana. Yet there was a strip of light flickering on and off under it. Could that activate an alarm, he wondered? He looked up again at the CO_2 warning signs all around him. What if he activated it? He wasn't going to take that risk, not when he was so close to freedom.

He ran back to the other side of the archive and looked up at the black hole in the ceiling. It seemed to smile back at him; like a gap-toothed child, wanting to play.

Dan

2PM

At last the nun was back in his possession. But there was a problem. In trying to stop his lover from whacking him unconscious with that box file he had rolled onto the nun's white plastic cranium and snapped the device in two. There was no putting sister back together again. He tried, in vain, to assemble her broken body in his hand and rub her up and down against the security strip, but she was totally defunct.

'Now look what you've done,' he turned around to shout at her, still feeling the impact of the box file against his cheek. She wasn't even looking at him; she was staring up at the air vent, into which the man she'd been threatening had just disappeared. He still couldn't quite believe what he'd stumbled upon, as he'd been making his way through the crawlspace towards the emergency exit; a shortcut only the porters would ever venture using, as it had been condemned in the last safety report a death trap. As he'd moved along on his front in the cramped tunnel, he'd heard voices coming up through the air vent and looked down to see her holding a gun up to a man's face. Not just any man, but the most unexceptional of men, the one he wound up daily.

'What the fuck were you doing?' he said, now, turning around to face her. He felt something wet on his cheek and saw the smear of blood on his hand from where the box had cut into him. She herself seemed to have fared rather well, apart from a paper cut on her ear where they'd fallen against the heavier papers, and she was scrabbling around in the rubble of plasterboard and paper, looking for her gun. He tried to resist the familiar urges when he saw the contours of her breasts through the red blouse. She was a psychopath, he reminded himself.

'Where is it?' she screamed at him in desperation. 'It was right here . . .'

'I think he took it with him,' Dan replied, vaguely recalling a flash of something black in the man's hands, right before he hauled himself into the opening, the one Dan had so readily made for him. Where the fuck would someone like her have gotten a gun from? And brought it to work? Dan couldn't believe that after all that effort to get him out of prison and working for a reputable institution he'd still managed to walk headfirst into disaster.

'You ruined everything!' she spat back at him. 'I had him just where I wanted him. And then you barge in, and . . . Have you any idea how long I've waited for a moment like that?'

'It's my fucking job to stop things like that from happening!' he shouted at her. 'Is this what everything's been about, following me around, seducing me, asking me how the CCTV works, getting me to fix it? Jesus, I've been so fucking stupid . . .'

She turned away from him like a petulant child.

'You shouldn't have interfered.'

'Oh sorry, you're right. I mean you obviously had something very important going on with that guy there, so I'm sorry for stopping you from fucking killing him and spending the rest of your life in prison.'

He'd been in enough situations to know the difference between someone who intended to shoot and someone who was only threatening to do so. Through the slits of the air vent he'd seen her finger curled around the trigger at precisely the right angle, poised to perfection, ready to act. There had been seconds in it, seconds where he decided to abort his escape mission and kick away that ceiling panel with all his might.

'How did you manage to get down here so quickly? You were by the emergency exit ten minutes ago?' he asked, trying to hoist himself up on his painful foot. 'Fuck I think I've broken my ankle.'

She was getting up onto the table now, trying to peer into the vent, to see if she could climb in after the other guy. Dan hobbled over and grabbed hold of her legs.

'Let me go,' she squealed, trying to kick her legs free. Dan held on.

'Just stop this, now, OK? You can't carry on like this. Taking those people hostage upstairs, then threatening that poor idiot . . . It's not right.'

What would be happening to those hostages now that she was down here? Hopefully some of them would have listened to the safety information and knew how to make their way to the emergency exits via the stairwells. Either way, there was no need to do anything now but wait for the authorities to arrive. As long as she, the threat, was in here with him, there was no longer a threat to the building, and rule 129 noted that if a lone terrorist was identified, and they were weaponless, the best method of defence was to keep them where they were and, if need be, engage them in some light conversation in order to distract them.

'Do you want to talk about it?' He tried to sound jovial as she thrashed around in his grasp. 'Let's just have a chat, yeah? I'm sure whatever it is we can sort it out. It can't be as bad as you think.'

Something finally buckled in her, and she allowed him to pull her down off the table. She slid down onto the floor and placed her head in her hands. Dan remembered the way he'd heard her talking to herself downstairs as she marched the hostages onward. Asking and answering. Perhaps she wasn't fully aware of what she'd done. Perhaps she genuinely thought it was someone else who had done those things.

'I know you probably need a minute to calm down, but look on the bright side: nothing major has happened here . . . I mean,

I know that someone's been injured upstairs but if that turns out to be OK, you won't have done much harm, eh . . .'

'Exactly! You've ruined it all,' she said quietly. 'It was all for nothing!'

There was no reasoning with her now. He winced as the pain travelled up his leg and began throbbing at the hip. He sat down next to her and began taking in the room. This was one of the archives he quite liked; it was weird to see so many real books, and real paper, filling the space. He hadn't been in here for a while, at least not in person. So few people visited these archives now there wasn't much call for it. He only had to check that the books were still here by viewing the CCTV footage every now and then. Dan didn't see the logic in that. Wasn't the stuff there – of which there was no other copy in the world – worth being guarded a little more closely?

The arch-porter had been very tetchy recently about some parcels that he insisted only he was qualified to deal with. More diaries, he assumed. He wondered whether the arch-porter had some fetish about real books, which kept him from sharing them with the rest of them. He could just see him now, down here at night, trousers around his ankles, sniffing the pages with a sordid lust, his fist thundering in his pants.

Fuck it, thought Dan, he isn't here now. He reached out to take one down from the shelf.

'Stop it!' came a voice from the corner of the room. 'Those are my mother's books! And if you must touch, please wear these.'

She threw a pair of gloves in his direction.

'Rule 778,' he said, laughing at her, putting the white gloves on.

'Don't laugh at me,' she said. 'Please.'

He studied the book in his hand. A pair of black-rimmed eyes stared back at him from the minimalist cover of *The Sperm Suicides*, a single sperm swimming in each pupil. He'd seen the film, in the days when he rented a flat with some film students. Lots of men had died in the first few scenes and their wives had been pretty nonplussed about it. He couldn't remember much else about the film really.

'I could still get to him,' she said, staring upwards into the black cavern in the ceiling. 'If you help me up, I could . . .'

'Jesus no, what the fuck is so bad about that guy that you'd want to kill him?' He grabbed her arm ever so slightly, pulling her towards him, like he'd done a million times before. 'I see him in here all the time. He's annoying, and a bit of a dick, but essentially a harmless one.'

'Harmless when he hasn't affected your life in any way,' she replied. 'But he took everything away from me. Everything. He killed my mother.'

The portrait bust came into his line of vision now, the one he'd moved down here all those weeks ago. It was now lying prostrate on the floor with a crack down its middle. Moving closer he thought he spotted a flash of something white inside, was there some paper hidden in there? He knelt down to investigate, trying to imagine the elegant figure captured by that sculpture having the life squeezed out of her by the chaotic mass of blubber that had just escaped.

'Don't touch her!' she screamed at him, pulling him back towards her. 'Just leave her, please. If he's broken her again, I can't bear to see it . . .'

'I still can't imagine him actually killing anyone,' Dan replied, recalling Eben awkwardly stuffing himself into the air vent. 'Surely a man like that couldn't even shove a finger up a fly's arse.'

'He'll never admit it. But it was! It was him!'

'How?' Dan was suddenly curious. If not a little impressed.

'It wasn't, you know, actual murder. Not in the conventional sense. I mean he didn't stab her or poison her or . . . He's not a psychopath or anything like that. Just, he made her depressed, and angry, with his reviews, which led to . . .'

'Reviews?' he said, rummaging around in his pocket for a spliff. He needed something now. To hell with rule 823: no illegal substances in the building, especially nowhere near any rare materials. The light on the door showed that the fire suppression alarm was now disabled, the nun having granted them that particular privilege as she martyred herself. He found a prerolled spliff and stuck it in his mouth, rummaging around for a lighter.

'You can't smoke in here,' she said, angrily, snatching the lighter from his grasp and hurling it half way across the room, where it disappeared into a pile of papers. He lowered the spliff and placed it on a shelf next to some of Elena's diaries. He'd have it later, when all this was done. Perhaps just before the police came for him. Something to take the edge off it.

'You can't kill someone with reviews,' he said, turning to look at her in earnest. 'That's just not a thing.'

Whether there was any logic to what he was saying, its impact on her was deep; as deep as the ink ingrained in all those diaries.

'I never thought it would have that kind of effect, either,' she said, her words faltering. He wanted to hold her. Tell her everything would be OK. This was the softest, most vulnerable he'd ever seen her. Which was ironic, really, considering it was in the aftermath of nearly blowing someone's head off.

'It spiralled into an insecurity so deep there was no coming back from it, I suppose. And so, yes, he didn't kill her, but what he did . . . it started the process of killing her. It was the beginning of the end, in one way or another, whether anyone would care to acknowledge it or not.'

'Couldn't there be other reasons?' he said.

'Like what?' she asked.

He was surprised by the look in her eyes then; the expectation that he, of all people, could come up with a better reason, there and then.

'Well I don't know,' he replied quickly, so as not to lose the attention she had now focused on him. 'I mean, there are loads of reasons why people top themselves, and it's not always for just one reason, even if they like to claim it is . . .'

Dan realised it wasn't what she wanted to hear. She wanted to hear that it was Eben: that it was all as clear-cut as she'd imagined. She wanted some confirmation that she was right to be standing here now, a sprinkling of ceiling dust on her red shirt, the back of her skirt in tatters, scratches on her face and a heavy absence in her hand where a gun had once been. All those things needed to appear absolutely rational.

She rose slowly to her feet.

'I haven't been in here since . . .' Her words escaped up the air vent. 'It was too painful to see all these diaries, but I'm glad they're here. Telling a story. Telling the truth. We didn't want anyone to access it until he had, so he could read for himself what he'd done. I can prove it to you,' she said, reaching for a diary. A blue cloth cover, with yellow birds scattered across it.

'Look, you don't need to prove anything to me, OK? If you say he did it, that's good enough for me. You understand?'

'She said he did it, at least,' she said, now looking slightly unconvinced with her own logic. 'Or that he was someone we could hold responsible. That's the whole reason this had to happen today. I think this is how she wanted the story to play out. She wanted someone to go after him. To challenge him. To make him eat his words, quite literally, to choke on them. It's something she always wanted to do in life – make these self-serving, arrogant, middle-aged men realise they were not the ones in control. Ironically, she could only do that by allowing them to think they had the power to end a writer's life. You see?'

He didn't. It seemed like a lot of bother when you could be getting on with your own suicide.

'We had to, OK? We had to!'

We? Did she mean him and her? Did she think he was part of this now? Again he thought of the way she had talked to herself in front of the hostages. He remembered a guy he'd shared a cell with: meek as a lamb one day, an absolute monster the next.

'You can get help, you know, for this kind of thing. There are medications . . .'

'There's nothing wrong with me. I was just fulfilling her wishes. I'll prove it to you.'

She started flicking hurriedly through the pages of the diary.

'Look, here it is. This is the one, this is the diary,' she said. 'It says here somewhere, I think it's here on the last page, it says his name. I mean, he tried to trick me into thinking that it said something else, but . . .'

'Don't do this to yourself,' he said quietly. He saw a vision of his own mother then, crying in a corridor the day his father hanged himself, telling him *not to go in*.

'I don't need to see it, OK?' he said. 'You don't either. Fine, you can blame him if you want, but people make decisions at the end of the day. He didn't actually kill her, did he? Not really. You must be able to see that. There's a part of you that sees that, at least.'

A shudder went through him as he said it. It was what he had told himself, repeatedly, in the wake of his own crimes; though he had not really believed it until he was saying it out loud to her. *People make decisions.* He prised the diary out of her hands and set it down on the table. Fear flickered in her eyes, along with something else he could not quite read; grief, perhaps, rising to the surface under her pale, translucent skin. He could see that no one had ever reasoned with her about her desire to take revenge on this poor guy. This discussion was something new, something vital, and he could see that it meant something to her, that this was coming from him. The awkwardness between them dissipated, and for once, she didn't seem like such a stranger.

And even though he was wary of the change in her, wary of the monster rearing its head again, another part of him said fuck it and moved forward to kiss her. Slowly, surely, she yielded. Not only that, but within five minutes she was kissing him back more eagerly than she ever had before; as if, for once, she was not just passing the time, but actively aware that time between them was soon to be lost, that she had to seize what little of it was left.

And that's how they remained, for five minutes or so. Breaking rule 654 – no intimacy between library employees on library property; kissing against the rare materials that were meant only to be seen from afar, never up close, with the blue diary left completely abandoned on the desk next to them.

Nan

2.15PM

Nan had adjusted to her sister's absence quicker than anticipated. This, she realised, was what she had been waiting for
– an opportunity to control things on her own. Their mother
always commented on the way the twins defined themselves in
opposition to the other. Nan knew she was much weaker without her sister to oppose, but also freer to be like her sister if
she chose, without anyone passing comment on it. She found it
easier now to make eye contact with the crowd, whereas it had
seemed impossible only minutes before. Some looked away,
resuming their gaze at the ceiling, but some did not.

Pale, Lily and Summer were trying their best to communi-
cate something to Nan. Summer seemed to be asking *what the
fuck are you doing?* with every blink, but there was some tenderness in Lily's eyes, in the way she seemed to be scanning
the room for an escape route – not so much for herself – but
for Nan. *Drop the gun, and get out of here, as soon as you
can, Nan. Run! We'll not tell a soul.* Lovely, selfless Lily. Nan
dared to meet their gaze, but did not flinch. She brought the
gun closer, as a reminder of who was in charge now. Summer
cried when she did this, curling into a ball on the floor as Lily
embraced her tightly. They slotted together like lovers, as if
they did this kind of thing every night.

And then suddenly it dawned on her, as Lily gently kissed
the top of Summer's head, that they did indeed do this every
night. That all those stories about their romantic trysts with
men had been a whitewash, a fiction. Why had she been unable

to see this? Was this really what it took, for the fiction to fall away? For her to be towering above them, a gun in her hand?

Pale wouldn't look at her at all. Nan could only guess at the kind of rage that would be building inside her, spiralling around the poor, locked-in baby. She would be furious that she had believed it to be a drill. And now, to be asked to lie down with the others, as though having another life inside her did not warrant any special consideration, would be driving her mad. And she *was* different – you only had to look at the crowd to see it. She couldn't lie face down for one thing, and the rounded dome of her stomach spoiled the uniformity of the row of slim, flat bodies. Pale was also the loudest of them all. She couldn't help but groan and moan and rub her belly incessantly to mark herself out as someone who was suffering more than everyone else.

Nan considered trying to talk her round in some way. But she didn't want an altercation that might push Pale into that early labour she kept going on about either. She couldn't bear that on top of everything; to bear witness to a new life coming into the room. A whole new being, fresh as anything, who had everything to play for and nothing in its life yet ruined.

The professor was fast asleep now, or dead: she dared not check. The non-doctor – Luke, she thought she heard someone call him – was stroking the remaining tufts of the professor's grey hair. Dora and Kenvin were still fussing around the rest, insisting on food and hydration, and on the mention of some cakes Nicholas opened one eye and looked up. Dora turned her back wilfully on the gun (the first one to do so) and began feeding the professor like he was a starved bird. Nan considered shooting her then and there – she had probably five years left in her if she was lucky – then shuddered at the thought. All these urges, these imaginings, were new. Something was changing. Or something was being lost;

she could not quite tell which. *The white patch*, she thought, *is spreading*.

'The filter between you and your deepest, darkest thoughts might fall away,' the doctor had said. 'You'll say and do things that other people will have a hard time understanding.'

All too soon things were quiet again. She had almost forgotten how this part of the library looked without bodies strewn all over the place. She remembered walking towards the balcony the morning her mother had died. Seeing it empty instead of seeing the familiar, comforting sight of her mother sitting there; a cushion with an indentation in it, a half-drunk cup of tea, one of the forbidden books she hid under her bed being reread for the hundredth time. Signs of absence where there had once been a presence. That's what had floored Nan. Not the death itself, but the emptiness where a person had stood, a vacuum where her mother had been, that she could now freely inhabit whenever she wanted to. The space her mother had left for her.

Ana, of course, had felt things differently. She'd been down on the pavement below when it happened, coming back from the shop, and had only seen the aftermath, the horrible, undeniable coupling of flesh and pavement. Life trickling away on tarmac. Ana had seen *something*, which she later claimed set her slightly above Nan, who had seen nothing at all.

Nan had not budged as her sister screamed for her help. 'Why didn't you come down, even if it was just to console me?' Ana had asked her. Nan had said she was too traumatised to move. Which wasn't untrue – it was just that Nan had not said what she was traumatised *about*. It wasn't so much the final, devastating act, as she knew that was coming somehow, but more because of what she'd read in the letter. The original handwritten letter that was left for her, only. Not the email that she'd read aloud to Ana later on that day, which had already been sent to all and sundry, claiming that Eben Prytherch had effectively reviewed their mother to death.

Elena's letter to Nan had revealed something else entirely. Several things, in fact, one of which was that she had a rare form of early onset dementia, *Creutzfeldt-Jakob disease*; that there was a small chance it could be inherited by both her and her sister. They would need to get themselves checked out when they reached her age. *There's every chance, of course,* she had written, *that you won't have inherited it, that you'll be lucky enough only to have inherited your donor's health.*

Elena had stipulated that fifty was the age they needed to get themselves checked out, and the age that Nan could finally disclose to Ana the real reason for her mother's sudden departure from life; but Nan knew, perhaps even before her mother had died, that something was wrong. She had noticed these strange jerking movements in her body when she least expected them; she had torn a very rare medieval manuscript one day as she was preparing to load it into the machine, ripped the page clean in half. She had stayed on that evening, repairing the damage with filmoplast in secret, scrubbing her hands clean, afraid to use the white gloves in case she transmitted any of the fibres onto it, which would betray her crime. Smoothing down the tape over the rip, she was so anxious that another twitch might happen, and dislodge pigments or inks as it came, creating even more destruction. Somehow, she managed it, and stood there waiting for the tape to disappear back into the brittle paper. Loading it then into the machine and seeing it on the screen, she was relieved to find it was something you would only notice once you knew it was there, but Nan returned to that page often, fascinated with how the fault lines running through her could become a fault line in a whole nation's history.

A month after her mother's death, she took herself to the doctor, where they had run brain scans and diagnostics that had finally confirmed it was the very same disease, one that had been incubating inside her own brain, the doctor said, since she'd been born. She'd felt a pang of closeness to her mother then, when it was far, far too late of course; that this was at least one thing that she and her mother had shared and could have gone through together. Then again, if her mother had still been alive when Nan got her own diagnosis, it would have been up to Ana to care for them both. 'Ana doesn't have the caring instinct,' her mother had always said, with a loving glint in her eye. 'Likes to be looked after, that one.'

When the doctor had asked Nan if she had any siblings who needed to get checked out, she'd said no. She was almost afraid to have it confirmed that Ana didn't have it, to see on black and white that she'd been the unfortunate one in the pairing, her sister having inherited all the goodness, though not from the source she imagined, either.

This insistence that Ana was somehow the baby, the best one to nestle with, had always riled Nan growing up. Despite being the eldest by twelve minutes, Ana had somehow managed to break free from the responsibility of being the eldest child and had turned the first-born narrative on its head, somehow perpetuating the notion that because she had lain claim to her mother first, they were the closest. This often left Nan out in the cold, leaving her to be the one fetching them their teas while they discussed her mother's stories, the one filing away their day's creativity and bookishness with her archivist's precision, stacking the novels, stashing away any forbidden scraps of paper. Nan, the runt of the litter, was made to feel as though she should simply feel honoured to be granted any kind of role within the confines of her mother and sister's own private universe.

It wasn't until she received the letter, however, that Nan realised that Elena considered her superior to her sister in all sorts of ways, trusting she would never tell anyone the truth. Elena may have thought that Ana, as loving as she was, or perhaps *because* she was that way, would need to share the information; to have it felt by others. Ana may well have gone running to someone, some man, perhaps, and disclosed to him that it was dementia that had taken her mother. She would make a song and dance about the fact that it could kill her too, one day, even if her tests proved negative. It was not the narrative Elena wanted, and in trusting Nan with that information, she was ensuring that at least one of her children understood the motivation for her death.

And I trust you will somehow make sense of it to your sister, she'd written. *That you will be able to find some comfort in it, in some small way for her, to make sure that she sees it as a good thing. Or that she at least understands that I was completely in acceptance of my passing. Not that it would hurt, of course, to make the Smotherhood feel a little guilty about it all. To have some fun with them.*

Even though her mother's instructions had been for her to destroy the letter immediately after reading, Nan had held on to it. She often wondered if she hadn't, whether they might not have hatched the plan they did, for by that time she may have forgotten what it said. But the more she read it, the notion of 'having some fun' with the Smotherhood seemed to inflate uncontrollably in her mind, so much so that when Ana started discussing with her the possibility of holding Eben hostage – of making him accountable – Nan had gone even further and said they should not only keep him captive, they should actually kill him. By then, the notion of 'having some fun' with Eben was so tangled up with her disgust at the other thing the letter had disclosed, that she could not see the wood for the trees. It still made her feel ill, that section she'd read time and time again with incredulity, coming to it every time as though it were the first time she'd read it:

You will know that it was always my intention to raise you without a father, Elena wrote, *and, in doing so, to change the odious narrative that befalls so many women and leaves them sleepwalking into unhappy marriages. I have always insisted, and still do insist, that it does not matter how you were created, only how I raised you both. But part of me could not leave this world without confirming your full parentage, and confirming the fears that I have had for a long time, which is that donor #512 is indeed Eben Prytherch. Although I do not wish either of you to seek a relationship with him, I do worry that my own condition means that I may reveal this to him, or the wider public, at some point, and I hope by dying in this way I will curtail the chances of this ever happening.*

It is in everyone's best interests, therefore, for me to leave this world before I undo the good I have done, before I lose my ability to write, or before I am humiliated for accepting the sperm of a man I despise. I leave this information in your wise hands, Nan, for I know you are the best person to decide, on behalf of both you and your sister, how this should now play out. I am confident that you, like me, will want to ensure that this information is never disclosed, and that Eben deserves to be humiliated by my final letter, in the way he has humiliated me and my works.

As you know, it is only if the child actively searches for the donor that the information can be revealed to them, and I trust you will not make this possible for Ana, however much she begs you. For I see something in Ana, which is perhaps not in you, a kind of impressionable nature that could so easily be swayed and manipulated by the Smotherhood. It would be devastating for me, if she were to end up in their fold, believing their theories. You must make sure this doesn't happen.

As Elena predicted, in the fractiousness of Ana's grief, she had started becoming obsessed with the notion of finding their father, needing desperately to replace one parent with another, even though Nan reminded her, time and time again, that it simply wasn't possible to fill the hole Elena had left. 'She was our mother and our father. More than one person. Just like us.' Ana pretended to listen but Nan sensed a defiance in her eyes.

Later, she found computer searches about donor tracing, and – on hacking into her sister's email – found a request sent to the town's sperm clinic. The reply had come that as theirs was a twin birth, she would need the consent of her sister to seek out her donor, and they would both need to visit the clinic together to prove that they were in agreement about disclosing the identity. Nan had smiled to herself when she'd read this, thinking of how their random doubleness, the zygotic splitting their mother had always talked about, the one Elena could not have foreseen, was now a safeguard against all that Elena did not want Ana to know.

Nan's attention was drawn back to the people lying scattered in front of her – those she had taken command of, while her sister had bottled it. She wondered what Elena would make of the scene in front of her, how Nan was 'having fun with them' in a way perhaps Elena had never anticipated. Almost feeling her mother's gaze on her now – for the light she had noticed coming down from the clerestory windows, she told herself, was surely her mother, making her presence felt in the room – Nan thought she needed to build on what she had started. To do something else that would set her further apart from her sister. *We are not the same,* she told herself. *Not the same.* Two people. Halving in the womb for a reason, so as not to stay entwined forever. Even the letters of their palindromic names could play out differently. Nan could easily become a Nins (although she took issue with a nickname that had more letters than her actual name), or N, if you were being ridiculous. Ana could morph into Ann, or Ani; though not comfortably, either.

'Nins!' someone shouted, as if reading her mind. It was Pale, who had never called her Nins in her life. 'You have to . . .'

'I don't have to do anything!' she screamed. She'd had enough of that, her whole life. Her mother, her sister: *don't tell her this; do that.*

Pale lay back down and became utterly silent for once. There was something odd in her eyes now; some kind of blackness, a strange trance taking hold. Nan walked over to take a closer look. That's when she saw it – a steady trickle working its way down her cotton leggings, out onto the linoleum floor, signalling that someone else was preparing to enter the room; to fill up the absence with its tiny presence. And she could do nothing to stop it, for it would not know she had a gun in her hand. It would not have the faintest idea of what kind of world it was entering.

She watched it all play out, utterly horrified with what she was seeing. More blood entering the room, a gush of purple and crimson as Pale groaned and grunted like an animal, writhing this way and that. Luke hurried over, after several prompts from his girlfriend, to do what he could, finding it hard to fix his eyes in the area he was meant to, before eventually catching the poor baby in his already blood-soaked arms. Then, the sigh of relief from Pale, and Luke, and the rest of the hostages daring to lift their heads, a birth somehow making it feel safer to do so, as though a child's presence had fundamentally changed everything.

Celebratory murmurings flitted hesitantly through the crowd as they kept an eye on the gun in Nan's hand. Dora offered Pale a small piece of fruitcake. Kenvin stood poised above the mess, mop and bucket at the ready. The girl in the purple bra insisted that Luke should take off his shirt and wrap the newborn in it; which he did, holding the baby to his bare chest like a proud father as the child squirmed in his arms, the umbilical cord still attached to it, a ghoulish white, pulsating tether that Luke seemed at a loss to know what to do with.

'Should I cut it?' Luke called out, struggling to keep a hold on the slippery baby that was covered in some awful, viscous substance. 'Does anyone know what to do here?'

Pale was still grunting. Nan lowered her gun and stared. She remembered her mother's words: 'It wasn't until one was out that I knew another one was on its way. I never went for my scans you see, point blank refused, because, well being over thirty-five, they considered me what they call an *elderly primigravida*, and they put all sorts of pressures on these mothers to make a decision when there isn't something quite right with the baby. But I knew instinctively somehow, it would all be OK. And this was the only child I would ever have, and I wasn't going to let anyone or anything stop me from having it. Imagine my surprise when I got not one, but two healthy babies! We never knew you were there, Nan.'

The grunting continued. It was grotesque to see it close-up, the awful, bestial quality of childbirth; what it did to a woman. Had Pale attended all her scans, Nan wondered? Or would a woman like Pale have the same indignance as her mother, thinking that she had enough *instinct,* to see this through herself? *This was it,* she thought. Nan's whole life had been building to the moment where she would witness the birth of twins. Surely, this was what the whole mission had been about in the first place; to position her in a place where she could get a better grasp of her own beginnings.

And out it came. A dark-brown, slimy stingray.

It was the placenta, not another baby. The afterbirth. The elation Nan had felt only minutes before transformed itself into anger as she recalled that term being hurled at her when they were younger: 'You were only the afterbirth, sis, the afterbirth!' And some of the school kids had latched on to that unfamiliar term themselves, hurling it around like a tennis ball above her head, back and forth. 'Afterbirth! Afterbirth!' Though the word was shorter in their native language, it sounded pricklier than the English, even more disgusting. She tried to recall what it had been. Something like *bree-och*, with a scraggly, screaming *ch*, the coupling of letters considered a single letter in their small country until it had been deemed unpronounceable by the neighbouring country. It was subsequently 'discontinued' by the government, like it was a face cream that hadn't quite delivered on its promise.

Hostages were walking around freely now, as if they had forgotten who was in charge, the happy chaos of a newborn making people bold. Luke's girlfriend ran over to an abandoned conservator workstation to retrieve a pair of scissors, bringing them over towards Pale and the baby.

'I don't want her touching that cord,' Pale screamed. 'She doesn't have any idea what she's doing. It isn't even sterilised; it'll be full of germs from books and maps and God knows what else. And if she does it wrong, she'll harm the baby . . . Someone please, help us.'

Nan stared intensely at the rest of the hostages, swinging her gun at her side.

'You heard her! Somebody help!'

It was Colleen, of all people, who suddenly stepped forward.

'I think I have some idea . . .' she said. 'I mean I'm not a medical professional, but I could try. I've got some antibacterial wipes here and . . .'

Pale burst into tears as Colleen moved forward to take the scissors from the girl and wipe them clean.

'It wasn't meant to be like this,' she cried. 'Colleen isn't meant to be my midwife! Nan, if anything happens to this baby, it's on you . . . It's . . .'

'There, there, Pale. Come on now. Look. Look, the cord's stopped pulsating hasn't it. That means baby's got all the nutrients it needs. Oh, it's a boy! A good healthy boy. We'll do something about this; now stay still, OK?' Colleen said, trying to pacify Pale.

'You don't know what you're doing,' Pale said again, her voice more of a whisper as she lay back, looking at the ceiling, utterly resigned to her fate. Pale put her hands over her eyes, fingers spread out hopelessly over her face, failing to block the tears that were coming thick and fast through the gaps.

'No, I don't,' Colleen replied, her voice trembling slightly. 'But let's just say, once, very long ago, I witnessed someone doing this . . . very wrong, so I think we'll get this as right as we can get it, yes? For the sake of that baby,' she tried to continue, voice faltering now, 'who didn't get the chance it deserved.'

It seemed that the whole room held their breath as Colleen pulled the cord towards her and placed the scissor blade over it. Just as she was ready to cut, she seemed to reconsider and move the blade back a few inches. Then, she finally cut it, a small shower of blood shooting up into the air as she retrieved a small book peg from the pocket of her cardigan to clamp it shut.

'All done,' she said, as Luke placed the baby in Pale's arms. 'All done.'

Someone, somewhere, dared start a round of applause. They had all totally forgotten themselves, it seemed, as Pale finally stopped crying and pushed her face into her newborn son's body, breathing him in. Nan wondered if she ever would have known about Colleen's dead baby had it not been for today, whether it would have been something she might have learned in the aftermath of her death. *Beloved Colleen, mother of the dearly departed.* There was something good, she reasoned with herself, in what she was doing; even though she was taking everything from them, she was giving them something too. The right, some-how, to be more themselves than they had been in years.

Yet she pushed the thought of goodness away as she began to sense her complete loss of control in the flurry of people around

Pale. As they congregated around the new mother, she began to suspect that it was a ruse, that they were frantically plotting against her, whispering instructions to each other as they did so.

And so she fired the gun again. Into the ceiling. Just to show that she, the afterbirth, was in control. She would not be trumped by a baby.

One by one, they resumed their face-down positions on the floor, while Pale tried to bring the baby to the breast. There was some liberation in feeling that these people around her now simply assumed that she had been like this her entire life. That she was hard, unfeeling, cold. Dangerous. She saw in Summer and Lily's eyes that they felt they had been duped. That all the while, while they shared oat cookies with her at coffee time, Nan had been waiting on the day she could kill them all, crush them to death like she did her biscuits. Nan continued to be fascinated by Summer and Lily's intimacy, the fact that they had not let go of one another for many hours, and that when one of them moved, even the slightest bit, the other would flinch in fear of losing her, even for a second.

'Nan,' Pale ventured. 'Do you want to hold him?'

'No,' Nan replied, without turning to look at her. 'And please don't speak.'

'If you just hold him, you'll see things differently. Please, Nan. Come here. Come meet him,' Pale pleaded, the baby starting to fuss in her arms, making strange, kitten-like noises as she pressed him to her.

'I said, don't speak!' Nan shouted, pacing towards her with the gun, so that it was a finger's breadth away from her face. But as she moved towards her, Nan's mind went blank again. Blank like a crisp, clean sheet.

In that moment, she understood nothing. She no longer recognised the woman in front of her; any more than she understood the purpose of the object in her own hand. The creature writhing in Pale's arms seemed alien and otherworldly, a thing she could not name. She felt faint; every muscle in her body suddenly heavy and limp. She wanted to resist but the darkness was enveloping her, seeping across her line of vision, and as she fell headlong into it, her only real understanding of what was happening was that she was becoming small and insignificant again, all her power drained from her. And as she lost consciousness, her hearing seemed to go with it, until she was only aware of dim, faraway echoes that seemed nothing to do with her.

A shot ringing out, then screams, and then further away again, a small, small cry rising up into the air.

Eben

2.30PM

Eben had no idea where he was. From the moment he'd ascended from light into darkness, he'd been feeling his way through a million tiny tunnels above the air vent, pulling himself along on his front, all the while trying to keep hold of the gun at his side, his fingers sticky with sweat. After feeling his way through the second, third, fourth cramped tube, he knew it was too late to turn back. The very notion of turning was impossible. He'd given himself over to this suffocating maze, which permitted him only the smallest lungfuls of air. Anxiety dreams came back to him in the swathes of darkness; dreams where he was drowning, fighting for breath, the darkness a deadly wave dragging him down.

Every morning when he awoke from such dreams, there would be the desperate gasp of air, and he'd realise that the reason for the dream was because he'd been trying to breathe through his nose. Which was simply useless; because it was always clogged, full of mucus. It wasn't unlike where he was now, sliding along in some horrible glutinous substance. It was like being inside his own nose.

Thoughts of light kept him going. The bright chandelier above his mother's kitchen table. The strip of lighting around Frankton's new kitchen island. The ghostly hue of whiteness that shrouded the library at night, when he sometimes gazed at it from his flat; the most beautiful vision in the world. Little flashes of brightness in his otherwise dull, grey world. He would appreciate such things when he saw them again, he told himself; he would. He had escaped death like a trouper, up through a ceiling. He imagined the look on Frankton's face when he told him the story, perhaps with a little flourish; he would claim he had wrestled the gun from a madwoman.

The gun. For such a small thing it seemed to take up all the space at his side. Potent like a living person. Yet it seemed to provide all kinds of hopeful possibilities. If all else failed, at least he'd be able to shoot anything, or anyone in his way. He might even be able to use it right now, to make a hole in the surfaces around him, to try to get out of here quicker. But perhaps that was an unnecessary risk. What if the bullet just ricocheted off the air vent metal and came hurtling back at him? What if he hit something electrical? What if the whole tunnel exploded, a fire hurtling up at him, swallowing him up from his feet?

Even when his anxiety was at its height he had never imagined the scenario of being burned alive in a tunnel. For now, the safest thing he could do was to keep slogging forward, through the sludge. At least the substance made it easier for him to move. What on earth was this stuff? The smell made him gag. Just as he thought he was going to be sick he was surprised to find that his pace suddenly quickened, and before he knew it he was yielding to the force of gravity, hurtling downwards, arms trailing above his head, like a child in a water park. The tunnel no longer wanted him. He landed with a thud in what felt, disappointingly, like yet another room.

Stretching his arms outward felt like a treat, a benediction. He embraced the cold space. He rose cautiously, fingers reaching out tentatively for any low ceilings, trying his best now to regain a steady pace of breathing; in, out, in, out, a little deeper each time. The gun, where was the gun? He felt around for it and found it dripping with the same substance that had gushed on top of him as he'd fallen.

This was a more generous darkness compared with the claustrophobic one of the tunnel. In the absence of vision, his other senses took over. Despite how alienated he felt there was a whiff of something familiar in this room; something that made him recall university corridors and that fresh excitement when one entered a library, the promise of all one could know. The waft of knowledge that came up at you when you opened large, long-forgotten trunks in attics. When you fingered the books of the dead. The short-lived buzz of finding these things in your possession before you inevitably had to hand them over to the authorities.

But pretty soon it was gone and he could not smell it anymore; something acrid and sharp took over, chemicals drowning the sensation, cleansing the memories.

Undoubtedly the aroma meant he couldn't be far from *real* books now. Within touching distance of the very thing that had become an impossibility. Only the scent of real books could carry that kind of wistful fug, and those kinds of dust particles somehow made it easier for him to breathe. Perhaps he had stumbled across the hidden underground bunker he'd heard whispered about at Frankton's dinner parties; one that wasn't open to the public, which had kept valuable artworks safe during the Second World War. No one seemed to know what the bunker now contained, although it was rumoured to be hiding forbidden works that the government thought would incite radical thinking.

He stumbled along, his hands in front of him like a blind man, his nostrils flaring like a dog's. In no time at all it seemed, his fingers had come into contact with what felt like real paper – thick, ridged matter, piled up against the wall. Vellum. Papyrus. Ancient, forgotten materials. He continued onwards a little further again, and he felt the unmistakable bulk of hardback spines, stacked in a small tower; the like of which hadn't been seen in any shop or library for years.

He was suddenly transported back to the time before all the nonsense had started, before the Great Sickness, when you could freely browse rows upon rows of books in shops, thumb them all you wanted, before deciding which one you wanted. How had he taken all that for granted? The idle perusal of all that was in front of him, sometimes choosing not to buy at all, as he had the luxury of returning later. He couldn't remember the actual moment it had happened, that those shelves had been replaced with those tiny screens, those slivers of plastic, made to look like a row of books. He supposed it had been happening for a while before the actual paper ban was made official – shelf by shelf, book by book – but he'd been so absorbed in his own life, and in his quest of ruining Elena's reputation, to even notice.

Elena's books kept appearing in lavish window displays, obscuring everything else, and he'd been known to upset the window display 'by accident' when the store manager was not looking, and rearrange them, placing Elena's books at the back. Now he could see the situation for what it was – and how, when he had turned back from that window to look at the shop, he was too late. All else inside was gone, just like that.

The books in this room hadn't been arranged with the usual precision of a library collection or bookstore, but rather they were scattered haphazardly all over the place, as if they'd been upturned from boxes, or hurled at someone in abuse. Spines breaking apart like cheesy string. Others had their yellow tongues out in protest. As everything came into a kind of monochrome focus, he started to make out embossed golden titles, which had letters peeling away from them, making it impossible for him to identify what they were. Further on again, he saw there were piles and piles of books in all four corners of the room, reaching up as far as the eye could see. There didn't seem to be a ceiling as such, either; he seemed to have landed at the very bottom of the library in a space that reached right up to the top of the colossal building, and the pile of books seemed to go with it. There was something strange about seeing books given so little care like this. Left to fend for themselves.

Something was seriously wrong here. He suddenly craved the intimacy of Elena's little archive, the order of it. The respect bestowed upon shelf after shelf of an author's memorabilia. This was a kind of disordered bookish hell, where books were not held in great esteem, but rather seen as a nuisance, cluttering up what would otherwise be a perfectly good space. It was the opposite of an archive, whatever that was. Somewhere where things were not documented, recorded, held there in place for all, but somehow extracted, pulled out of life, squashed down until they were no longer seen.

And that was the point, Eben realised. No one was meant to see this. No one was ever meant to discover that this kind of place existed at all.

Dan

2.45PM

The change in her was startling. She possessed none of the malice he'd heard in her voice on that balcony. And yet there were facts that he couldn't ignore. She'd duped him, made him change the CCTV footage for her own benefit; she'd stolen the nun-device from his pocket; she'd held all those people hostage, seemingly to settle some score with that idiot researcher guy. He knew that she had done all those things, and yet within this room, the information seemed to suddenly fall away again, as if inside Elena's archive the fiction of their relationship was intact.

The kiss had become one they could not tear themselves away from. She had undressed herself in a way she never had for him before, tugging at her own blouse until it slid to her waist, pushing her bra down on one side to release a breast for him to suck, while keeping her skirt on, legs closed. It was almost the complete opposite of how she usually operated; leaning back and staring at the ceiling as if waiting to be examined by a doctor. Her hands roamed across his face and his chest this time, rather than hovering aloofly at her side, and it was as if she were exploring him fully for the first time, taking him in, reading him differently, deeply.

As he lowered himself into her, there came a sound he'd heard before, the first time they'd done it. A gasp; a shock almost that this was really happening. He moved back to check if she was OK, but she grabbed hold of him as if she were worried he was leaving her, pulling him further in, into a softer, more accommodating place, and they rocked quietly, slowly, like this, tightly bound together, until her breathing became even again. She looked right at him this time, rather than looking away as she so often did, never once breaking eye contact with him as her lips gradually parted more and more with each exhalation.

He pushed her up against the bookcase in order to steady himself, and she began grabbing the books above her head and hurling them across the room with each thrust, the occasional one hitting his back as it descended, the sharp corner of each spine intensifying the pleasure. She talked too, in his ear, muttering breathlessly how she'd read about scenes like this in books, how she had always dreamt of doing this with him, in this way. She told him how it felt, as he moved inside her, where each ripple occurred and when; mapping out how those tremors travelled through her body so that he could follow them with his hands, his eyes, his mouth. The commentary was almost as arousing as the act itself, until he could hold out no longer.

'Not yet,' she said, 'please,' guiding his hand down under her skirt, where he gently moved his palm against her until her words fell away and the map was no longer necessary. It was electric, watching her body convulse and dance under the movement of his hand, entirely uninhibited, for the first time ever.

'I'm sorry I came so soon,' he said, once they were finished. 'It's just . . . I've never seen you like that.'

'Well hopefully it was worth the wait,' she said, smiling back at him.

Dan wasn't sure how to respond to this. What had been so different?

'I'll always remember it,' she continued. 'It's part of your life story, isn't it? Your first time. A real moment.'

He wasn't sure what she meant by that: her first time? Was that the first time she'd climaxed with him? He supposed that was possible, considering the cold, lifeless way she'd lain beneath him on previous attempts, simply enduring him. Even if that's what she meant, it didn't make him feel particularly good that he'd taken that long to please her, despite the way he'd felt it too; the way everything had been different. As though everything had suddenly clicked; the chemistry between them had righted itself. Was it because of what she had done? Had she been aroused, possibly, by threatening people? Thrilled by the situation, by her own power?

'Look . . . Nan,' he said, trying out her name for the first time in the darkness of the room. 'Do you mean . . . it was better that time? So that counts as the first time? I mean, it's OK if I've not been doing much for you all those other times, but I just think if I don't ask you what you mean, I'll only overthink it.'

She raised her eyes to meet his. There was no doubt that he had said something truly terrible. She suddenly stepped back from him as though he'd hit her, scrabbling for the remainder of her clothes, hurriedly assembling her bra with quivering fingers and doing up the buttons of her blouse in the wrong order.

'Nan,' he said. 'Nan, that is your name isn't it? Look at me, please.'

'I'm not her!' she screamed. 'Don't you understand? I'm not Nan. And she shouldn't have . . . She never told me . . . that she did this, with you.'

Dan stared at her. Before he knew what was happening, she had climbed up onto the desk and had disappeared through the air vent, leaving him standing alone, utterly bewildered, in a room that only minutes before had seemed like the safest place in the world to be, with Elena's portrait bust staring back at his limp penis with a mocking smile.

Ana

3PM

She had become one with the dark, her tears flowing freely into the blackness around her. When he had called her Nan, when she realised with devastating clarity that he thought she was her sister, the opening above her head had seemed like a blessing, a chance to fold herself away into nothingness again, to erase what had happened between them. She had made Dan think, of course, that she was going after Eben, but the truth was that she needed to get as far away from Dan as possible; for even looking at him now, knowing that her sister had looked at him that way, was painful. As the stench coming up from the basement flooded her nostrils, her mind was filled with images of what her sister and Dan might have done together, and the unfortunate combination meant that she retched sporadically, emitting a bestial sound that echoed all around her.

She felt her way forward across the crawlspace, and searched the ceiling above her with her fingers, looking for openings she knew were there somewhere. She was one of only a handful of people who had access to those rooms directly above the archive, those small box rooms recently elevated to the status of 'preservation chambers', though what exactly they preserved remained a mystery to the majority of the staff. Ana knew that their location was purposefully chosen exactly because of the crawlspace beneath them, a secret layer between them and the archives, into which materials could be deposited discreetly, without anyone having to know that they'd left the chamber.

She had never anticipated finding herself inside the crawlspace, either, travelling towards the chute like those books. Then again, considering what had just happened to her, it was strangely fitting for her to feel so rejected, so discarded, as though she didn't matter to anyone, despite having moments before felt like the most important person in the world in Dan's arms.

It was testament to the success of their plan, of course, that Dan still believed there was only one of them. Hadn't they tried so hard, after all, in the month or so since he'd arrived, to give him that very impression? And yet, the fact that he knew her sister's name, and not hers, riled her. Hadn't they also promised to keep names out of it, to become a sole, nameless entity for as long as that was possible?

'But he might ask someone about us,' Ana had said, to which Nan replied, 'He won't. He doesn't talk to anyone if he can help it.'

In all these weeks, Dan had not taken enough notice of either one of them to even attempt a computer search to find out who they were (they'd hacked into his search history on the system every evening; some porn sites, fishing equipment, and the random googling of what one could and couldn't do while on probation). Everything was very much surface level for him; the here and now. There was no delving deeper, no investigation, no research into anything that involved his daily working life; what you saw was what you got with Dan Matthews. Patrolling corridors, keeping his head down. Ana was almost jealous that someone could live like this; hour by hour, never looking back or ahead, just living in his own bland, uneventful reality. Then again, perhaps he was grateful for such a simple life, considering his past.

They had read the reports about his computer hacking and internet fraud, and knew about the dope-smoking habit that frayed the edges of his reality. They also knew that this made him unpopular with the other squeaky-clean, judgemental porters, so that he had no real friends to speak of, or anyone to confide in. Ana found it desperately sad, at times. Occasionally she'd go for an evening walk and glance up at that small window above the arcade, wondering what he was doing in there. The report said he was prohibited from going out after six pm, which was when they knew they were safe to roam the town together. Seagulls congregated at his window just like they did at theirs, and Ana almost envied them their closeness to him on nights like these, separated as they were by the dusk; a tide of longing for him gathering up in her chest.

Not that she confided to Nan that she harboured real feelings for him. Their daily flirtation was not meant to lead to anything serious and should have provided nothing more than a bit of a distraction for him. It thrilled the twins that playing this game allowed them to do something they never did in reality, which was to play out each day, each entrance, as a lone person, without having their own reflection trailing at their heels. 'Never the twain shall meet,' they whispered to each other in corridors, giggling helplessly sometimes, when there was a narrow miss, or when they happened upon one another in the staff toilets, where their doubleness once again converged and multiplied behind them in the mirror.

But there had been rules. About all this. About him.

'If we start to become too friendly with him,' Nan had said, 'he might try something. And we can't give in to that. We must leave him wanting more. Wanting us.'

Ana had listened. Followed the rules. No matter how desperately she wanted him to kiss her, and the rest. Ana realised now that Nan had convinced her to refuse Dan's advances so she herself could go on to experience something, for once, without her. And every time Ana had done so, had pushed his hand away, he had looked at her strangely. Because she was denying him something he had already had. And Ana shuddered thinking of those nights when she was alone in the flat, when she had taken off her clothes, lain on the bed, and imagined Dan on top of her, realising now they would have been the exact same nights that Dan was actually on top of her sister in the library. What Ana had considered a fantasy, brought to life by the rhythm of her own hand between her legs, was actually happening in real time, less than a mile away.

But yet, this time, it had not been pure fantasy. She had felt him inside her, and the memory of his touch was still racing around her body. It had not hurt as much as she'd thought it would, or at least the hurt had been tinged with so much pleasure that she had been willing to consider it a necessary precursor. She had discovered sensations she had not known she had access to, and there had been a release of all sorts of wonders deep inside herself. And she had felt loved, and wanted, in those moments too, as he gently held her to him, as she rested her head in a space that seemed designated for her, in his collarbone; although she knew now that this was nonsense, because Dan did not love her, any more than he loved Nan, and he probably had just seen an opportunity for one last dalliance before the whole world came crashing down on top of him.

But she had felt free in that moment, that one moment when she had allowed herself to break the rules and do what she was not meant to do, without realising that, as per usual, her act was a copy of another act that had already been performed by her sister. That her experience was just another take on the same old thing. A digitised version of a much-prized original.

And yet their conversation, she assumed, had not taken place before. He had listened to her. Rationalised with her. 'People make decisions at the end of the day,' he'd said. 'He didn't actually kill her, did he? Not really. You must be able to see that.' A thought that neither she nor her sister had allowed themselves to entertain. That Elena had chosen to do this, not only to herself, but to them.

Slivers of light appeared above her head. Eventually, she found one of the openings to the chambers and pushed upwards with her hand. The cover would not budge, having been locked firmly on the other side. She tried another tactic, manoeuvring herself around onto her back, and then kicking upwards with her foot. It cracked slightly, but not enough to be able to slip a hand through, and yet through that crack a noise escaped from the building above her, rebounding in the darkness around her. Another gunshot. Nan. She shuddered. Nan must have shot someone else. And if so, there was very little Ana could do but accept it. Accept the fact she'd let it happen. And for what? Only to find herself suspended here in this strange nowhere space, between one world and the other, having achieved nothing but to make herself smaller and more insignificant than she had ever been, lost in the dust and darkness?

Nan might be headed here now, Ana thought. She might arrive in the crawlspace at any moment, urge Ana to keep going, push her sister into a decision before she was ready. Or she might even decide to go into it alone once she knew where he was; although Ana knew her sister knew nothing of the preservation chambers, the basement, of the truth of what lay down there. It would perhaps be enough to stop her in her tracks, when she realised that the library had made worse decisions recently, than even their mother had.

She was tired, now, so tired, her limbs aching with the effort of it all. Even though she had a vague idea of where Eben was – assuming he'd travelled the length of the crawlspace until he slid down into the chute – she wasn't sure if she had the energy to go after him. There was something soothing about not having to make decisions or plans anymore. Perhaps she could just lie here, in the darkness that asked nothing of her. Disappear completely into the foundations of the building. It brought to mind the first suicide attempt of her favourite poet from one of the bigger countries, the poet who, as a young girl, had taken an overdose and nestled into the crawlspace underneath her mother's home to die.

For two whole days everyone had searched and searched for her without being aware that she was right in front of them; or rather beneath them. Ana thought of how the poet's mother must have walked across her, over her, as she paced, as those out looking expanded their search into rivers and woodland and vast, open spaces. All the while the young poet was crammed into the smallest space there was, vomiting her overdose all over herself, too weak to call out; until she was eventually found and rescued. But there must have been some solace in it, Ana thought; that time lying there suspended between two surfaces, to make yourself part of a building, to feel like nothing more than a construction, to let blood and bile and water and mortar and bricks and plasterboard and cables and veins all become one indistinguishable thing.

The poet had managed to kill herself eventually, of course, much later in life, a head-in-the-oven job, which always made Ana think that she was just toying with death when she hid in that building the first time around; playing an elaborate game of hide-and-seek with it, wondering whether life or death would find her first.

Then Ana thought of her mum and the ledge; the opposite kind of suicide. Elena wanted it to be direct. To be seen. She wanted witnesses. To make a show of it. Although Nan had rationalised it to her, had said that it made sense for her mother – who, throughout her career, had come up with endless dramatic deaths for her characters – to die in the most memorable way she could, Ana still couldn't forgive her for it. Her life, after all, had not been a fiction. And she and Nan had not asked to be part of a story, they had just wanted to be her children. It comforted her, that although others talked about their mother the writer, this great persona, someone almost untouchable, that for them she was the opposite, a physical entity, a person whose presence and touch was essential. Their twin, scarlet heads had once sunk comfortably into her warm bosom; their small hands had searched for hers at night when they were afraid; their arms had tied themselves in ribbons around her neck.

Even when they were older; the closeness remained. Their mother never seemed to feel the need for a partner, and neither did they. It seemed as though there would never be anyone who would threaten the bond or come between them. It was too much of a risk, after all, to sever the holy trinity they had formed. They had accompanied her to festivals, to award ceremonies, flying to various destinations across the world with her, their hands latticed across each other with each bumpy landing; always relieved to have made it to the other side alive, always terrified that the life they were living was too good, that it was always in danger of ending. They had done everything together, and yet, right at the end, Elena had decided to go it alone, to break them up, timing it so that they were all in completely different places, as if emphasising that the union ended along with her.

Ana had been the only witness. She had seen the fall, without being able to do anything about it. And it was perhaps this powerlessness of hers, which she saw now as something Elena had foisted upon her; not being able to do anything to stop that fall, which had led her here. With no gun and no dead body as she'd planned. Stuck in darkness. And it was this, more than anything, recalling her powerlessness in that moment, which made her shake herself awake and tell herself that if she stayed here any longer, she wouldn't end up disappearing into the building or dying a dignified death at all. No, it was more than likely that she was going to be found and arrested, with nothing to show for it but a deranged sister who'd left a trail of dead bodies in her wake. Ana would be sent down for something she hadn't even been part of.

And even though she accepted now, in some small way, that Dan was right, that Eben hadn't *actually* killed her mother – he hadn't made her climb out of the bathroom window and hurl herself off that ledge – it still seemed imperative now to find him, and at least have it out with him, as they'd intended. Whatever the reality of it was, it was clear that Elena had desperately wanted someone to be responsible and she still needed to honour that, and at least make him think he might die, otherwise what would she have achieved? She couldn't be known as the sister who'd bottled it halfway through a siege and gone into hiding. Her only real legacy being the awful things she had done in her work. Even if she couldn't actually pull the trigger in the end, at least her intent would be clear, and she would have made him face up to the hurt he'd caused.

Ana heard a noise. Some shuffling at the far end of the darkness. The sound of someone moving about in the bowels of the library. Then, above her head, the sound of someone running. Let loose in the building.

Eben was down there somewhere. And she needed to get to him. Before Nan did.

Eben

3.10PM

The thicket of books threatened to engulf him. Every time he tried to pull at something, to find an opening, he only succeeded in making himself further incarcerated, dismembering half-rotten books in his hands. It seemed impossible to pull one book away intact from the pile, and there was a strange surgical smell wafting from the yellow substance at his feet. It was the same odour as the substance that had eased his movement along the tunnel, and now it was easing his transition across the floor, or at least it was until it sent him flying into a small clearing at the far corner of the paper forest.

This is it, he thought, seeing the pile wobbling unsteadily upon impact, *I will be known as the man who avoided being shot only to be crushed to death by books.* He closed his eyes and waited for the books to fall. But nothing happened. After the initial tremor, the pine tree of books that looked so haphazard had righted itself. It now stood firm above him, perfectly still as though the whole thing had congealed back into place.

Eben rose and kicked it. The seemingly soft books were as dense as lead. Studying them closer, he saw that they were not stacked on top of each other, as he'd first thought, but rather melded into one another, merging into the building itself, simply part of the wall. An ingredient, a meaningless component. And the process seemed to be ongoing, for everywhere around him the books were at a different stage of disintegration; fizzing away their words, narratives, subplots and subtexts to become meaningless gloop.

What were they, these chosen ones, these unfortunate books? Where had they come from? How could a library of all places justify such a thing? Shouldn't the library be archiving them? The library was meant to keep every single printed copy of everything published in this country; even if it had been digitised. It was its duty to store the original copies, and a special privilege they were granted above others, for the common reader could not be trusted to handle them in the correct, disease-proof way. If a National Library wouldn't keep them safe, who would? He tried to make out the titles from the mashed-up letters. The names on the spines seemed unfamiliar to him; though he prided himself on knowing the literary history of the country better than most. And he could see from the faded publication stamp that they had all been published here; there wasn't a single book that belonged to the neighbouring country anywhere. Pulling away a tag from the bottom of the pile he saw the title RARE BOOK COLLECTION hastily crossed out with black pen.

He shuddered as it dawned on him what he was seeing. The supposedly missing antiquarian book collection was still here. It had not, as the library claimed, been razed to the ground in a mystery fire that had been caused by a member of staff being careless with some flammable chemicals a few years ago. He remembered how the head of government had robotically announced that 'lessons had been learned' from the debacle, and that this showed that real books were always in danger of being snatched or destroyed, something the country couldn't allow to happen when paper was such a rare commodity. They had already been cutting down on them, because of the role they had played in the Great Sickness, and the only way to truly safeguard a nation's identity now, she claimed, was to digitise and print books on demand only, and to cut down any books anywhere in the public spaces, for fear of those spaces becoming contaminated. Though rest assured, she had continued, they would all still be housed safely, behind the scenes.

'Let me be absolutely clear,' she'd said, in a voice as clear as mud, 'we are not ridding the country of books, but dramatically reducing our carbon footprint and safeguarding ourselves against disease in this radical move, and we are the first country in the world to show such a progressive attitude.'

Now Eben saw for himself what had happened. 'Let *me* be absolutely clear,' he muttered to himself, 'this is not really happening. Our books never went up in flames! We just threw them away.' And yet he still couldn't see the logic in it. They hadn't actually removed *all* books: that much had been proved to him in Elena's archive. Her books were still there. You could thumb the pages; not just an illusion of pages. And he thought he recalled seeing some rare books in her personal collection, too, which had remained intact. How did they decide which ones to get rid of? Was there a pecking order? He scanned some of the names again; he'd never heard of some of these writers. Perhaps those considered less visible, less popular, were condemned to death. But how was their oblivion decided upon; were they simply the not-read, or the unreadable? Was this what Frankton and his cronies had been going on about all this time?

He spared a thought for the authors of these books, dead in their graves, decomposing underground while their books did the same here. Had they not written in order to be immortal? And could they not have foreseen that it would come to this, in such a stupid country, a country that would wilfully rid itself of its own history? And where were they headed, these book-corpses, those that had not yet solidified? For they all seemed to be moving in the same direction, towards the far wall, where he could hear a distant whirring of some sort.

He backed away from the sound, into the final tower of books in the corner of the room. This one felt softer than the others. There was a freshness to the pile, as though they'd only recently been placed here. And a pale green triangle caught his eye, the corner of a book not-yet-dead. He grabbed it firmly with both hands and tugged ever so gently. Seeing it come away from the pile, more or less intact, felt like a miracle. He had managed to save one, he imagined himself telling Frankton later. He had not only saved himself, he had brought a book back from the brink of death, a heroic act his friend might congratulate him for. As his eyes searched for the title of the book in the dimness, he felt something go through him. He had not just plucked out any book at random. The book was part of a series, *The Series of the Round Table*, it read, *the treasures of a small country*. And then, below those words, in bold print, the title, as though the book had chosen him and not the other way around:

EBEN THE POET: an anthology.

Dan

3.20PM

It was the first time it dawned on him that, of course, there were two of them. The way she'd looked at him when he'd called her Nan would have been realisation enough for anyone – it wasn't just a matter of him having misheard Kenvin when he'd said her name – the name was simply wrong because it wasn't hers. He could see that he had wounded her by calling her that. And he didn't have to scour the archive far to confirm his suspicions, for there were pictures poking out of several diaries that showed Elena with two babies in her arms, two little girls, virtually impossible to tell from one another.

Dan sat down on the floor of the archive amidst the clutter of paper and books and tried to get his head around it all. They had deliberately misled him, making him think there was only one of them. It had been a different woman he realised, lying beneath him passively all those other times; that much was evident now. Nan. It was her twin, the one for whom he didn't yet have a name, who had felt so different in his arms just now, so hungry, so willing. He wanted to go after her and demand some answers, but his ankle was still throbbing from the fall from the ceiling and he wasn't sure it would bear his weight. Something in the way she had looked at him had also deterred him. The sheer, deflating disappointment in her eyes. He'd seen that look so many times over the years, fading from view behind closed doors; his mother, his grandmother – people who had once believed in him having to make a choice not to see him again. Each door a reminder of a life that was now closed off to him. Even Elena's portrait bust seemed to have expected more from him.

And although she – not-Nan, whoever she was – had seemed closed off to him in that moment, didn't he also have a reason to be disappointed in her? She'd used him after all, tricked him into thinking she wasn't quite who he thought she was, and they'd both gained his trust just enough to make him return to a life of crime, and fix those CCTV screens for them so that they could go ahead and kill someone. He shuddered thinking about what he'd seen through the slits of the air vent, a gun pushed right up to that poor guy's neck. After they'd spoken, however, he had sensed more uncertainty in her, and relief, too, that someone like him had come along to tell her how irrational it all was. Even though he hadn't been able to stop her from going, he hoped that he may at least have weakened her resolve enough for her to think twice before pulling the gun on poor Eben again.

The room was a mess, diaries and discarded sheets of paper strewn everywhere; a real delight for a paper criminal, he thought, trying to push the temptation away. It had been one of the arch-porter's main concerns, according to his probation officer, that to place someone like Dan in an institution full of what was now considered 'contraband' was indeed a risky thing. 'He'll be filling his pockets with paper every day,' the arch-porter had said, not realising that Dan's interest did not lie in paper but in the very opposite, the paperless cyber world, the world in which he felt most at home, as he could achieve the feat of becoming faceless, invisible, as he went in search of a host of unsuspecting victims. He'd been born with an inherent talent for this, reading codes and pixels like notes of music. Data compression, programming, line coding; all those things came easy to him. Hacking was a breeze. He knew almost instinctively how to override systems, create fake entities, find himself right inside the brains of the computer, becoming one with the machine.

When she/they had asked him to rig the CCTV, he'd actually felt purposeful again, and it had felt good, flexing those muscles, doing what he was best at. The CCTV rig was easy compared to some of the other stuff he'd done before. And it was thrilling, the knowledge that he could go even further again, if he chose to go back to it all. He hadn't reached the heights of what he could do, by far. He had the ability to bring entire systems down, governments, military operations, if he chose. As yet, he had only really bumbled along committing internet fraud from his bedroom, ripping off thousands of pounds from various large companies and gambling it all away in the casino. He always felt that if he went back to it, it would be about more than money and taking the piss out of large companies, it would be about proving he could mess with the whole world, bring it to its knees, if he wanted to.

And yet, he'd messed with enough lives, he thought guiltily. It had all been fine, until the incident with the account manager of one of those large companies. Thinking that the sudden emptying of the company's bank account was somehow a result of some anomaly on his part, and teetering as he was on the verge of a nervous breakdown, the account manager had walked out in front of a car on a busy highway. Unfortunately, both he and the woman driving the car had died. It was the husband of the woman driving the car who had eventually tracked Dan down, becoming obsessed with finding the person responsible for this terrible chain of events, and there had been a host of other charges brought against him as a result. All of a sudden, his faceless endeavour had faces, and they were frighteningly real. Especially those of the man and woman he had killed, both smiling out at him from the press photos, hands draped around their loving families.

He wondered how not-Nan – the other one – would feel about him if she knew that he too, indirectly, had ended someone's life in the way she considered that man had ended her mother's. Would she understand that it had not been his fault, considering the way she saw things? Then again, he wondered whether he would have tried to argue for Eben's innocence at all had he not once been at the receiving end of the same kind of vitriol and felt a little sorry for him. Not that any of it mattered now, as she probably wouldn't ever want to see him again. And it was likely neither one of them would ever be coming back here again. Or anywhere else, probably, for that matter.

He pulled himself up and staggered across to the table, dragging his injured ankle apologetically across Elena's diaries. He hopped onto the desk, using his knee to draw himself up. Wincing with pain, he just about managed to bring himself to a standing position on his swollen ankle and stuck his head into the opening. There was no trace of her. A smell wafted towards him from the direction of the opening. A smell that wasn't altogether unfamiliar. It often came to greet him when he was doing his rounds at night, rising only from certain, hidden parts of the library. 'Specialist antiquarian antibacterial,' he recalled the arch-porter calling it. 'Another delivery on its way tonight. Sure you and Johnno wouldn't mind working a few extra hours to help us get it up on the roof? Plenty of storage space up there. We'll provide you with the necessary protective equipment of course.' He and Johnno had signed a non-disclosure agreement once they'd transported the hefty barrels to the rooftop in their masks. 'It's potent stuff you see, boys,' said the arch-porter. 'Can't have everyone knowing that we have it.'

Both Dan and Johnno suspected that the confidentiality agreement was nothing to do with preserving books; but Johnno had advised Dan to keep his mouth shut, sign the form, and keep it to himself. Dan wondered whether the agreement was there because the stuff was toxic; whether he and Johnno would end up dying of some inexplicable illness in years to come like so many in his country had over the centuries, finding they'd waived their rights to sue their employers for chemical exposure. And again now he wondered what would happen to her if she was directly exposed to it, without a mask to protect her. What if she died, and it was considered his fault, because he had failed to protect her? He could not let that happen. And so he hoisted himself up into the darkness, pulling his frame across the same narrow space that she and Eben had inhabited minutes before, pulling himself along on his front, his redundant ankle like a dead weight behind him.

As he did so, he heard a commotion beneath him. A door being battered repeatedly, before what sounded like a large heavy object was used to bash the lock. He hauled himself into the opening and started to scurry like a rat down the crawlspace. Behind him he heard the door finally giving way and swinging open. Was it her, Nan, down there? He wondered whether she was likely to kill him, as he was no longer useful to her. He lay perfectly still and was surprised to hear several voices all at once. Perhaps the hostages had managed to overturn things, he thought, perhaps he could turn back and tell them he was here; but now that he was committed to the darkness, turning didn't seem an option. There was only onwards, further into the blackness, enveloped with the stench of those chemicals.

He suddenly recognised the rhythm of movement, the boom of the voices. And then the plod and scuffle of what he assumed must be the arch-porter and his minions. They were finally back, then, the flawed CCTV having alerted them to what he was doing and sent them flying back here at the speed of light. Far off, he thought he heard gunshots too – were the militia in the building? He supposed the arch-porter would have asked for backup, if he'd managed to switch the screens back and seen what was really going on.

'Where's that good-for-nothing Dan Matthews?' he heard him shout at the other porters. 'I want him located now!'

The best policy, Dan surmised, was to stay perfectly still, as any movement across those rather flimsy ceiling panels would be sure to attract attention. The only thing that could save him would be the varying degrees of darkness all around him, and Dan tried to stretch out as best he could, so that if anyone popped their head in the opening, he could fool them into thinking he was part of the fabric of the ceiling, a dislodged puff of insulation or fallen plasterboard. If all else failed, Dan thought, he would just have to call out and pretend he needed their help. Perhaps at this precise moment in time, it was still possible for him to play victim, for he had done nothing much wrong, apart from being as ineffectual as they had always considered him to be.

Then he recalled the CCTV footage and the fact that his past double was still seemingly roaming the building unfettered, playing his part perfectly for all to see.

No, he should press on now. If nothing else, he would much prefer to align himself with not-Nan than with a bunch of inept, good-for-nothing porters.

He decided to place his trust in silence for the time being and wait to see how it would play out.

The porters spent five minutes walking aimlessly around the archive, clucking like chicks around their boss, looking for answers.

'He's got to be in here somewhere!' he heard the arch-porter squeal. 'Find him, and the other one!'

Never mind the body-sized hole in the ceiling, Dan thought, wondering how he'd managed to end up working for such an inept bunch of muppets.

Dan planted his face on the thin veil of ceiling and listened to the racket of the porters turning the archive upside down; the archive that could not realistically be hiding a person, even if it tried. He heard the porters emptying box files, opening stacks, even pulling books down from shelves as though he could be hiding in between them. Then, Dan heard the predictable slap of the arch-porter's silver stick hitting the roof.

'Oh no,' he heard him say. 'Don't tell me that they've . . . not up there. Boys! One of you go and take a look. Johnno – you go.'

Johnno was one of the very few porters who actually liked Dan. He had to pretend that he didn't, of course, when they were at work, because he had worked hard, he'd said, to achieve the kind of ranking he had within the arch-porter's system, but Johnno often called round for a smoke, and to laugh at the absurdity of the system. Dan almost admired the way Johnno ganged up on him with the other porters when they were at work; because Johnno, unlike him, knew what games you needed to play in order to survive. And that sublime performance of Johnno's, day after day, was the very reason he was being trusted to do the right thing right now – because the arch-porter believed that if anyone would betray Dan, and insist on him being punished, it would be Johnno.

Dan could hear Johnno breathing, quietly, steadily a few yards from him as he looked left and right into the opening. There was no way that Johnno would consider a face-down porter in front of him to be a piece of plasterboard or insulation, and sure enough, he felt Johnno's hands manhandling his leg, to make entirely sure of what he'd seen.

'Well?' he heard the arch-porter shout. 'Has anyone gone through the opening?'

'It looks like it's been entered, yes,' Johnno said coldly, in his best civil-servant tone. Dan recalled the many nights they'd had where they mimicked this, stoned out of their brains, the downbeat, identical voices that had been gradually acquired by all the porters in the building, their automaton drones.

'Dammit!' the arch-porter replied. 'No one is meant to enter that opening. No one! It's a hazard. We'll have to get this ceiling patched up as soon as, and we'll have to let the police know it's been tampered with. Johnno, is there anything else up there?'

Johnno paused. Dan recalled their stoned conversations. *Do only the bare minimum. Maintain the status quo. Answer only the question being asked. Never do anything above your pay grade.*

'I can't see anything,' Johnno droned on, retreating. Dan kept still. Johnno was not lying. It was far too dark for Johnno to make out what exactly the shape at the far end of that crawlspace was. It could be anything. He was technically not lying, and not breaking any code of conduct. He was merely *answering the question being asked*.

And with that Johnno retreated, replacing the panel, safely pressing against anything above his pay grade, anything that threatened the status quo, back into the muggy place where it belonged.

Dan lay there for a few minutes before hearing them leave the room one by one; being tasked with other, more pressing orders. He heard the arch-porter mumbling something about a lighter and an unlit spliff, and he kicked himself for leaving that particular piece of evidence behind. Obviously they would have bigger fish to fry now than reprimanding Dan for smoking around some of the rare materials, but still – it wouldn't help his case.

It was obvious to Dan that there was no going back now. No way of resuming his duties or positioning himself back at the porter station as though nothing had happened. He had heard them mention the police. The building had been unlocked again; the security team were no doubt freeing the captives and arresting Nan. It was only a matter of time before other people arrived at the building too; this incident was possibly even a cause for alerting the newly founded militia of the country, made up of many of the town's citizens who had nothing better to do, and simply liked a good crisis and the thought of being able to possess a weapon. Wherever he went from here, Dan knew he would no longer have a job. It was likely he would end up back in prison; or be given yet more community service elsewhere for the duration of his probation. He would possibly never see Nan or not-Nan again. This new opportunity of his, this new chapter, would be well and truly over, and yet again, he would have learned nothing from it.

He looked down into the opening, as the scent grew stronger and stronger ahead of him, and he decided that there was only one direction of travel now: onwards into the darkness that had already congealed around him, towards that unnamed twin and her intentions, and whatever disaster, stench and chaos lay ahead of them both.

Nan

3.25PM

When Nan opened her eyes, she found herself in a chair with many of the hostages congregated around her in a semi-circle, looking at her curiously. Her neck felt strange, and she slowly realised that it was because someone had taken her scarf from her, leaving her skin cold and exposed. Somewhere, a baby cried and cried. Pale, wherever she was in the room, was completely silent, and Nan had the terrible niggling feeling that she was responsible for this. She remembered thinking as she fell that she must not shoot the baby – *do not shoot the baby, do not shoot the baby* – but it had not occurred to her to let the gun go. She had clung on to it for dear life, as though it were the last remaining thing that made sense; her last claim to consciousness. Had she shot someone else? Was that what the mark on her hand was? Had it not been caused by her awkward landing, but by the vibration of the gun in her hand? Then she recalled those jerking movements that sometimes happened. Was that it? Had it decided this time to end a life, not just a manuscript?

The gun was now in Lily's possession, and she was standing directly in front of her holding it out with shaking hands, seemingly needing those other hostages around her in order to appear bigger than she was, more threatening. Like a lion, Nan suddenly thought, remembering their earlier conversation. But Nan knew that Lily wasn't used to taking the lead in any kind of situation, and as she inched closer to her, those on both sides moved with her, perfectly synchronised, like a chorus in a musical, every single one of them anxiously watching Lily's trembling fingers, as she switched the gun uneasily from palm to palm. Each one awaiting the moment when it would be dropped, and when they would be forced to take over.

Nan felt perfectly calm for once. Any tremors of nervousness she had felt before had vanished. She wasn't afraid of anything now. Certainly not of Lily, who she knew full well wouldn't be able to bring herself to shoot her. Then again, a few hours before, perhaps Lily would have considered the same thing to be true of her.

'She's still alive,' she heard Summer say at the other end of the room.

Of course I'm still alive, she thought. *And no one's going to have the guts to change that.*

'Luke, get over here now!' Summer shouted, her voice breathless with panic. Nan realised they hadn't been talking about her. As the chorus around her parted like a curtain, she suddenly saw Pale outstretched on the floor, bleeding from her side, as well as from between her legs.

'You shot her!' Lily was sobbing through her words, her initial bravado gone. 'She's just become a mum . . . You're an animal, Nan!'

The room was in disarray, the chorus scarpered, most of them running back up the stairwell, banging on the locked doors of the corridors from which they'd just come, finding them resolutely shut, throwing whatever they could find – bins, tables, chairs – against the steadfast bomb-proof glass. Nan could do nothing but watch; this crowd that she'd so carefully guided, assembled, controlled, were now completely fragmented, scattering this way and that, with no concept of the fact that they only needed to go down one stairwell in order to let themselves out.

Where was Colleen? Surely she had her staff pass on her and would be able to get them out of the emergency exit. But she was nowhere to be seen. Had she made a run for it alone, Nan wondered, deciding that was the best option rather than risking having to worry about other people, other tragedies, slowing her down?

In some misguided attempt at heroism, Summer and Lily had stayed where they were, as had poor Professor Nicholas, who, pallid and unmoving, didn't seem to have a choice in the matter.

'She's losing a lot of blood here,' Summer shouted. 'Luke! For fuck's sake do something!'

It all seemed distinctly unreal to her now, like a game, a mere imagining. She visualised Pale boasting that she'd experienced life and death within thirty minutes of each other, without, it seemed, any particular feeling or emotion attached to this notion that if Pale died, she would be responsible.

Luke had stayed. Nan couldn't help but admire his loyalty. He was kneeling above Pale, a few pitiful sighs emanating from beneath his shaking shoulders, his hair flopping this way and that. His girlfriend was long gone; having abandoned the scene the first chance she got, placing the poor baby on the bottom of a disused book trolley where the little creature continued to writhe and squeal in Nan's scarf, making the rusted trolley screech with every kick.

'I'm not a fucking doctor. Jesus. I'm just . . . so tired.' Luke started to walk away from Pale now, resigned. 'There isn't anything I can do. Anything any of us can do. We're fucked.'

Nan saw him take out a small plastic pouch with some green, craggy substance inside it. The kind of stuff they saw Dan smoking.

'Jesus – Luke!' Summer's voice rose into the air. 'What are you doing? Help me, now! Or someone, Jesus, anyone, help us, please. She's going to bleed to death . . .'

'I'm allowed one last smoke,' he said calmly, taking out a rizla paper and placing some of the green clumps on the paper, 'before I die. She's obviously going to come back, isn't she – the other one – and finish us off. If we were going to be saved, it would have happened by now. No one gives a shit about us.'

The other one, Nan thought. *Of course there's another one.* Not that she had forgotten her twin, but her consciousness was only just returning to her, and it had, momentarily, removed Ana from the whole scenario. She had the feeling, upon waking, that this was very much something she had done alone, had brought on herself, and it took her a few minutes to remember that they had been in agreement about it all, before her vision and her sister's vision had separated, and that Ana had removed herself from the situation, evaporating it seemed into thin air. Either way, Nan knew instinctively somehow that there was no question of Ana emerging from anywhere and finishing anything. Since they were children, that had always been up to Nan; as though the last one to enter the world would forever be lumbered with tying everything up, sorting everything out.

Professor Nicholas's limp body in the corner of the room was surely testament to this, she thought. An attempt, on her behalf, to stop someone from escaping when her sister would have been willing to stand by and let it happen. Not that she could justify Pale's injury in the same way.

Summer began to cry, pressing her head onto Pale's body, taking off her skirt now to use as a tourniquet, pushing it down to try to stem the blood flow from Pale's hip, as it spurted up defiantly towards her, staining her face, her fingers, her hair. There was a sudden halt in the baby's wails, and in those few seconds Nan imagined that everyone appreciated the return to silence. If a baby was content, surely it meant all was well in the world. It could even be confirmation enough that nothing bad would happen to its mother. But suddenly the quiet revealed itself to be a horrifying absence – for it was simply a gap, she later realised, the gap that babies sometimes allow in their wails, to gather momentum and strength for the next huge wave of sound; to make their discomfort even more audible to the world. A gap that was not so much an admission of peace, but of the opposite.

Out the second wail came, bigger and better than before, the baby having learned, in its first few minutes of life, how to make a room a terrible place to be.

Slowly, surely, the crowd responded to the baby's call to arms, in a way they had not responded to the call of their fellow hostages. Nan caught a glimpse of the girl in the purple bra balancing on one of the banisters, being pushed up towards a ceiling panel by some of the other hostages, trying to batter it open with a fire extinguisher. Dora and Kenvin, who had also been on the verge of escaping, ran back down towards Pale and removed their food hygiene coats to soak up what was left of Pale's life, with Dora then lying down next to her to keep her warm, leaving a sobbing Summer in Kenvin's awkward embrace.

And because of all this movement, Lily lost her concentration and turned her head. Lowered the gun for a few seconds. Nan again felt that indignance rise in her, the fact her sister had left her to deal with all this on her own. The fact she would have to take action again, she thought, would be her sister's fault. As the haze in her mind finally cleared she stood up, and looked directly at Lily. Such was Lily's shock that she had dared do such a thing, it took very little force for Nan to prise the gun from her and push her back down onto the floor.

'It was an accident!' Nan shouted at them, her mind clear again now that the gun was back in her grasp, the simplicity of that power giving her strength. 'OK? I want it to be known that I had no intention to harm Pale in any way. Sometimes, my hands, they don't work . . . like they should. They're unpredictable.'

Lily looked at her with pity. *I don't want your pity,* Nan thought. *I want you simply to understand what I'm telling you. I did not intend to hurt, or even worse, to kill my colleague.*

'I want you to promise,' she said, moving closer towards Lily. 'That you will tell them that. Even if no one else will. That you saw with your own eyes; it was an accident.'

'And the rest of it, Nan?' Lily shouted back at her. 'All this? How can this be an accident, what you're doing right now? What the hell is wrong with you? Why would you do this to us?'

Lily it seemed, had suddenly blossomed into her name; she had become big and bold, had opened right up. Suddenly Nan felt a very real urge to kill her, cut her at the root. But she steadied herself, remembering something her mother had said. 'Beware of the first sin; for there is a legion hard on its heels.' She understood this proverb now in a way she never had before. Once she had made that decision to pull the trigger and shoot the prof in his leg, it had paved the way for her to shoot Pale. Despite the fact that it had been an accident and not her choice, the sequence of events – when discussed in court – would suggest otherwise. She had placed herself in a position where shooting someone else was always a possibility. It wouldn't matter that she couldn't even recall making the decision to shoot anyone at all.

It was happening again, Nan realised. She was starting to come undone at a time when she needed to be most together. There had been a plan, a sequence. Or had there? A building made of foam, its white bold peaks, their soapy hands so sure of their intentions. Again, that feeling of emptiness struck her. The collusion, the camaraderie in the build-up to it all; what happened when it all fell away? Where the fuck was Ana? Why didn't she come running back from wherever she was hiding and object to all this, stopping those on the loose from making such a racket, banging those doors, smashing those ceiling panels?

She turned, expecting to see her sister standing behind her somewhere, urging her on. How long had it been since Ana left?

Some recollection of Ana's movements, the sight of her defiant, turned back, her bouncing mop of hair flickered somewhere at the edges of her consciousness, but kept escaping her. She must know where her sister was, deep down, but at the same time, she seemed to know nothing at all.

Until she heard a voice. It was an unfamiliar voice. So unfamiliar that it sent shock waves through her body; making her lift her gun, now fully aware of who and where she was, and what her intentions were. A high-pitched, mock-authoritative greeting, which didn't seem to belong to the room at all. It seemed to be coming from some other world almost; from above their heads, from an unreachable place. From inside her own head, possibly.

'Put the gun down. I repeat: put the gun down,' came the voice again. It was coming from the tannoy system. 'We have surrounded the building. We want you to trust us. Please put the gun down, and release the doors using the security device.'

Nan's first instinct was to laugh. It was a funny little voice, thin and persistent. She imagined a face behind the voice, made an instant judgement about what a bore this man was, how this would be the most exciting thing that had happened to him his entire life. How he would relay the tale over dinner to his family this evening; and keep relaying it for years to come to anyone who would listen. How he'd be brought out of insignificance to finally be given a footnote in someone else's history.

Nan scanned the room to see how the others were responding. Surely they wouldn't take him seriously? Surely it was more appealing to stay with her than listen to that stupid little whine? Dora looked at Kenvin, and Kenvin looked at Dora. Luke, an unlit spliff now in his mouth, searched the room for his girlfriend, only to find a glimpse of her shoe heel dangling from an open ceiling above them. Then, slowly, they all turned their gaze back on Nan.

'We have a witness here who tells us you are armed, have injured two people and are in danger of injuring more. Please give up your weapon and wait for us to enter the building.'

Fucking Colleen, she thought. Back to being her bullish self, with no sympathy for anyone.

Nan knew full well that what she should do now was to give up her weapon, accept that it was over now. She was tired, too. Tired and confused, her mind glitching like a burnt-out computer. It would be nice to be free from all that. To sit in a cell that expected nothing from her; surrounded by those who thought only the very worst of her, so that they could never be disappointed.

Away from Ana, for the first time in her life.

'We can see that you still have your gun. Put the gun down,' came the insignificant little plea again. 'This is your last chance to surrender peacefully. If you do not, then we will take measures to incapacitate you.'

The gas, Nan thought. The thing her sister had feared more than anything. She looked up and identified the air vents through which the gas would come – four above her and around three or four others dotted around above the skirting board. The militia must already be in the building, she thought, just beyond, poised, ready to trigger those alarms. After all, if Colleen had gotten out, they had almost certainly gotten in. Would they really risk setting off those gases with a newborn baby in the room? If Ana was here, she imagined she'd be more than ready to surrender now. *No more Nan,* she'd say. *Enough is enough.* Perhaps it was enough, Nan thought, feeling her hand relaxing somewhat around the gun, already imagining what a relief it would be not to have to carry it anymore, to hand it over to someone who would put it away for good. But what on earth would she say to them? She could hardly tell them she couldn't remember how she got here, although that was partly the truth. That they had only to look at her scans and medical reports to know that her brain was forever altered by her condition; and one thing she could remember, in the jumble of half-remembered things, was the doctor making one particular joke: 'Well, Miss Oodig, look on the bright side. If you ever did decide to commit a crime, you wouldn't be able to stand trial.'

Diminished responsibility he'd called it. Had it been in the back of her mind when she'd presented this idea to her sister, the notion that she could never be held accountable? Ana would have no such case to argue, of course, when she stood trial. She had made her decisions with all her faculties intact. And if she had believed in the word of a diminished person, what did that make her?

The entire room held its breath to see what she would do. She had never felt more keenly watched, more visible. And she suddenly felt sad that she would have to give up this room, and those people in it – for Pale, Lily, Summer, for all their foibles, had been her colleagues. Her daily life. She featured as a crucial component in their existence. She wanted nothing more in that moment than to be able to go to them, to embrace them, tell them she was sorry; and to ask them to speak kindly of her when they were interviewed, though she knew how unlikely that was. They owed her nothing now.

It was the sound of the baby that finally compelled her to make her move. He sent one final almighty wail up into the sky, which seemed to be her cue. She fired the gun, up towards the ceiling to show her intent, and the second she did this, she heard an alarm sound. Although she couldn't see it or smell it, she was pretty sure the gas was now flooding into the room, wrapping itself around its unsuspecting victims. She hastily unwrapped the blood-stained scarf from the baby's body as he continued to scream in her face, and held her breath as she pushed it up against her nose and mouth. The hostages who had gone wild following the gunshot were now visibly slowing down, as though trudging through sludge, and the purple stiletto of the blonde girl dropped from the air, leaving a bare foot hanging limply over the side of the ceiling panel. Summer and Lily slumped to the floor, a strange, catatonic look in their eyes. Luke was already unconscious. Nan fought with all her might against the heaviness pressing down on her lids, and, shoving her gun down the back of her skirt, slipped through a side door with her staff pass into the clean air of the corridor beyond, while behind her the baby's wails seemed to become laborious for him, until he finally gave up, and succumbed to the silence.

Eben

3.30PM

A series of treasured literary works from a small country, it had said on the front cover of the tiny pale green book by Eben the Poet. But if this literary work was so treasured, then what was it doing dissolving down here? It was now starting to become obvious to Eben that someone, somewhere, had the authority to decide who was worthy of a place in the national consciousness and who was not. And it was clear that Eben the Poet had not been deemed suitable as part of the nation's literary history. Reading the foreword of the treasured works he had discovered that *Eben the Poet stood out as one of the most unique poets of the last century.* Maybe this was Eben the Poet's problem. This 'standing out' of his, this uniqueness that set him apart. It was a tendency of the small country to like those who did not make too much of a spectacle of themselves. *Should have pulled your head in,* he thought.

The series editor had written that Eben the Poet's *reputation was partly saved by the literary tradition. His instincts were not too solid; and he wrote a number of extremely substandard poems.* Eben had almost laughed. To see such frankness, such sincerity, in a foreword! He thought the whole purpose of a foreword was to lie and flatter. Eben imagined how he'd feel if Frankton wrote something similar about him. He'd be incandescent of course, and never agree to it being published. He mused that he himself could have written a foreword like this for some of Elena Oodig's novels. Weren't many of her earlier novels 'extremely substandard' in his opinion? Had he not said as much in his reviews? And yet no one would permit him to say so, especially not to stamp his assertion on the pages of the very same text.

It was evident that Eben the Poet had paid a high price for the series editor's honesty. That one sentence had cost him his literary legacy. It didn't matter that the following sentence went on to state that he was *without a doubt one of the country's finest poets,* the fact that those earlier weaknesses had been acknowledged and committed to print had sealed his fate. His words had survived almost a century only to become pulp on a whim. Eben's heart sank at remembering another little detail about Eben the Poet's life – that he bound books, in order to increase his salary as a schoolmaster. How many of these old books now surrounding Eben had been bound, potentially, by him? Not only was his literary reputation becoming undone, but the very craft he'd laboured over was being pulled apart. Those bound books had survived, against all odds, across the decades, and such was the skill of the binding that they were almost the last in the dissolving pile to break down. Eben the Poet had safeguarded himself well against destruction.

But it still hadn't been enough, somehow. All along his fate had awaited him; someone pasting his name into a database to make him disappear. The meaning of those names in the *ebb-end* was suddenly clear to Eben. Those poets being swept away by the unforgiving tide of time.

He moved towards the whirring sound at the end of the room and discovered that the books, once they seemed to have reached a certain level of ruin, were being tugged along towards a small exit at the end of a conveyor belt. The books then seemed to be tipped into a huge silver cylinder, becoming further pulped in the process, and at the bottom of the cylinder a long steel tube was spouting something angular and white out at speed, which looked from a distance like huge teeth. He took off his glasses, wiped them, and tried to focus again on what was coming out of the tube. He saw suddenly what those white rectangular flashes were – they were sheets of paper. Once the paper had reached a certain height, accumulating a hundred sheets or so, another machine then carefully lifted them and packaged them in bright red and green paper, and they were then deposited into boxes and the boxes then stacked in a corner.

Moving slowly into another section of the basement, side-stepping round the teetering books, Eben saw another cavernous space filled to the brim with boxes that boasted a government logo. A completely unmanned operation was going on there, too; boxes being moved across the floor on tracks, eyeless machines stacking them into a symmetrical and triumphant tower, so different to the mass of amorphous books he'd just left behind him.

He moved quietly and cautiously towards the boxes. On top of one box he saw an address located in the neighbouring country. The same address on another box. It wasn't an address he recognised, but it was somewhere in the capital. Somewhere, he presumed, not far from the neighbouring country's own national library.

Suddenly Eben could see exactly what was happening. The entire history of this small country was being crushed to bits to provide paper for the neighbouring country. All the confiscated, so-called disease-riddled books and errant bits of paper were not being destroyed, but they were coming here to end their days, along with whatever other collections the library claimed had already gone up in flames. In the melange of pulp, thousands of the small country's thoughts and impressions and dreams were being obliterated in order to provide clean, neutral, amnesiac sheets for their ungrateful neighbours to scribble all over in any way they wished. Children could happily scrawl over their antiquities. Blank diaries could be served up that had once been fine poetry collections. A notebook in a hallway would be filled with innocuous grocery lists as though it had never been a sacred antiphonal.

Eben started to claw at the pile to see what other titles he could find, and to see if there was anything else he could save. As the titles moved past him he realised he hadn't seen a single work by a woman yet. Not one. And as titles by male author after male author passed by him, he realised what the truth of the matter was. The ones considered disposable were all by men. It was as if Elena's novel, *The Sperm Suicides*, had come to life, or rather death, in paper form. And it could be rationalised perfectly, he thought, when it came to the inevitable inquiry. The head of government had once been a statistician. It was all in the numbers, she would say. The men had had a head start in publishing history, and there were simply too many of them compared to women.

And so if it was a matter of choosing who to eradicate, then it would be a clear-cut decision, and there was nothing more clear cut than deciding to discriminate against fifty per cent of the population. The *ebb-ends* were the men ebbing away in order to make way for the flow of women into literary history. But why throw them away unnecessarily, when they could be recycled to make paper for a neighbouring country?

The realisation stopped him in his tracks. Whatever they were doing here, it was already in motion and already working. Possibly had been going on for years. Eben the Poet had ebbed away out of existence on a tide of clean white paper, and he survived only in the ramblings of people like Nicholas Griffiths. And even Nicholas, being of a certain age, would soon ebb away himself, leaving no one to vouch for the fact that Eben the Poet, Eben's namesake, had ever existed. How many other scholars had already passed away, taking the names of their dearly beloved thesis subjects with them? Were there perhaps other men, already half-ebbed themselves, sitting in old people's homes across the country, being lifted on and off toilets, muttering names in the hope that someone, somewhere, would listen and take note of those names before they were flushed down the toilet by a carer who couldn't care less?

Thinking about himself becoming one of those old codgers, taking all his memories with him, he suddenly imagined the twins, standing there, in the doorframe of some dismal little room, the place where he would no doubt end his days. Would there be a time, he wondered, in the far-flung future, when they could come back from all this, when he would perhaps welcome those faces at the door? Where a carer would tell him his *daughters* were visiting today, and wouldn't that be a treat for him? Not just one, but two, two whole beings who would carry his legacy far on into the future and would be able to keep him alive for a little bit longer. And who knows, if they had children themselves, then particles of himself, of Eben the Poet, could continue forever.

Then he realised how ridiculous it was, considering they wanted him dead. Not even in a far-flung future, but right now.

He touched the fragile spines of those books again, realising that whether these forgotten men had descendants or not, they had all relied on their books for immortality, assuming their texts safeguarded their names from obscurity. His fingers tightened around Eben the Poet's little green book. It was paramount that if nothing else, this title survived intact. It proved something; he was sure of it. And if he could save Eben the Poet from extinction, maybe he could save others. Who knew what generations of lost poets lay under the viscous drool of that stinking liquid?

Dan

3.40PM

Dan had found a quicker route down to the basement, up through the crawlspace into one of the preservation chambers. It helped that one of the openings had already been damaged, so that it only took a few further thrusts to break it open and propel himself into the room. From there, he knew there was another unlocked door behind a cabinet that led on to a secret thoroughfare, where he and Johnno usually wheeled the crates of antibacterial liquid through and from there, he could get to a rusty escape ladder that would take him down to the basement, a ladder that was strictly prohibited from use, because it was so shaky and dangerous, but Dan felt that it was worth a try now. He might even be able to get to her before she got to Eben, if his ankle held out. And if he died trying, well, at least they would know, when they found his crushed remains under the rust and the books, that he'd been actively trying to do something to change the situation, which was more than he could say for those porters who'd gone off in the completely wrong direction.

But just as he was about to cross the thoroughfare, a bullet had shot past him, tearing right through the thin plasterboard, inches from his right foot, and lodging itself in the ceiling above him, where he stood frozen now, staring incredulously at the hole in the floor. Had he not paused for a few seconds to give his throbbing ankle a rest then he could easily have been shot in his heart or his stomach. And that would have been it. The end. And for Dan, it was not so much a case of his whole life flashing in front of him, but rather the grim reality of his end. Who, really, would care about the demise of the ex-con porter who had died burrowing around in a library's crawlspaces like a rat?

He imagined the very minimal crowd in attendance at his funeral. His mum, a mere biological fact in a black dress, relishing the kind of attention that would be lavished upon her; the quiches and lasagnes that well-meaning neighbours would bring. His brother, on day release from prison, plotting his escape as the hymns were sung, thankful to his little brother for providing him with such a golden opportunity.

There probably wouldn't even be an obituary. It was more likely that his death would go unnoticed, and that he would be left here to rot, gradually becoming one with the building he so despised; only to be dug up by archaeologists in centuries to come and tagged or displayed. *Skeleton of staff member from twenty-first-century National Library*, like that song that his mother always used to listen to about some unfortunate soul who was found a hundred years after he became lost on some arctic expedition. He had been perfectly preserved in ice, and hadn't aged a day.

It seemed more pressing than ever now – with the thought that another bullet could strike at any moment – to prevail, to survive. To tell his story and not let himself die misunderstood. And yet he was also aware that if he moved an inch further, more bullets might come. His best option was to kneel and look into the hole, to see what was going on beneath him. His heart palpitations increased as he knelt down cautiously, the image of a bullet in the eye or face recurring in his mind, envisaging himself thrown against the wall, a splatter of blood covering the thoroughfare. Yet when he finally did muster the strength to look down into the hole left by the bullet, he saw the library goers he'd let in that morning dispersing in a mad panic before becoming strangely heavy-limbed and soporific, until eventually they just stopped moving. In their midst, he saw Nan – or who he assumed to be her, as the other twin had travelled in a different direction – shoving her gun into the back of her skirt, holding a scarf up to her face, and slipping quietly from view.

The militia now stormed the room. They were dressed in protective gear which made him realise the sleeping gas had been triggered, and he saw them rush to the side of the bewildered hostages, trying to rouse them before they took in any more gas, with paramedics frantically trying to stretch someone out on the floor in order to resuscitate them. As a tide of blonde hair swept over the floor he was shocked to see that, out of everyone, it was the prima donna who was in most in need of assistance, while a bleeding woman in the corner seemed to be faring rather well, finding strength, no doubt, in the new life she seemed to have delivered into the room. With the assistance of another paramedic, the baby had been placed on her breast, and seemed to be sucking ferociously, happily, completely unaware of the chaos that surrounded it. He saw Nan for who she was now. A woman who was willing to turn her back on all this, caring very little about what happened to these people she'd terrorised. She did not hesitate as the other twin had done, before making her exit. She had foreseen the gas, and knew how to escape its effects. She made quick, snap decisions, and carried them out with precision. She was the opposite of the woman he had held so tenderly in his arms only moments before, who had scurried through a gap in the ceiling without considering that it led nowhere and could potentially make her problems even worse.

Dan cringed at the fact he had considered himself so clever in his own doubleness. That he thought that presenting the world with another Dan, the one who was still walking the corridors of that CCTV tape right now, was such a novel thing to do. It seemed truly pathetic in comparison with the very real, physical doubling of the twins. And in his own silly imitation of doubleness, he'd made everything easier for them. They knew that his fake CCTV tape would make everything they did untraceable.

And Nan and not-Nan would surely have ridiculed his attempts to create his own twin, when they were living that very reality, a reality they had been so careful to keep from him. Did they plan all along for him to look guilty, when it came down to it – to the library, to the authorities, to everyone? To look as if he'd been in on it? Doubling himself up to protect his real-life double-lovers?

And if so, why was he still pursuing her? Not-Nan knew what she was doing, as much as her sister did. But he still couldn't help but feel that there had been a vulnerability there, a single moment of honesty and originality in an otherwise duplicitous day, when she had let him make love to her. And despite the fact that he'd vowed himself a few hours ago to help those innocent visitors get to safety, it seemed rather crucial now to save the woman who had wanted to bring the whole place down in the first place, perhaps even to save her from herself.

He paused before moving on, moving to the side of the thorough-fare in case any more bullets, or remaining gas wafts, came his way. It would be disastrous, he thought, if the militia heard the noise above their heads and thought it was Nan.

He waited for the noise to die down, thinking about how he had never before been in any kind of trouble with the law without having been fully responsible for it himself. He tried to work out which charges could be brought against him. The manipulation of the CCTV tape would certainly be considered a crime, first and foremost. The arch-porter would undoubt-edly argue for some kind of negligence case to be built against him, for allowing such a thing to happen in the first place. He had allowed himself to be locked out of a building of which he was in charge, and he had also allowed the security device to be stolen from him, without reporting it, though it was con-sidered government property. Was that considered treason of some kind these days? There was no evidence, however, that it had been stolen and not wilfully handed over. And it was not a simple device to use; the prosecution would find it easy to argue that he had shown her how it could be used to disconnect the internal phones, disable the fire suppression system and lock the offices. Could his own re-entry into the building also look like trespass, as he had done so without alerting the authorities, causing criminal damage to the canteen entrance downstairs?

Had he not interfered with the CCTV, he would have been free to call the authorities. That was the fact. But because he had already been bound up in wrongdoing, so much of it, he had continued on a path of wrongdoing that had played completely into their hands. He was pre-conditioned to follow the wrong path; because it felt like his rightful place, and had always felt to him as though it would eventually lead somewhere good. The arch-porter had not left him in charge because he thought he could handle the responsibility, he had left him in charge to give him enough rope to hang himself with. What worried him most was that these two women had taken his criminality to another level; and he realised for the first time now that on top of the other charges, he would also be looking at perverting the course of justice and being an accessory to murder.

Was it too late to salvage everything? There was still commotion beneath him. Murmurings. Peering back down below he saw that the prof was conscious, being attended by paramedics, and that a screaming baby was also being comforted and wrapped in foil, as was the woman he assumed to be its unconscious, bleeding mother in the corner of the room. But their survival was nothing to do with him; in fact, they had managed full well without his interference.

And yet, it wasn't beyond him to perform some of his duties. If he could stop them – Nan, and not-Nan – from killing Eben, then potentially he could still exercise his authority as security guard. To do the job he had come here to do. No one else, after all, had eyes on the perpetrators in the way he did; no one else was stupid enough to be heading towards them as he was doing; and possibly there was a chance, if he could somehow disarm them both, perhaps his sentence would be shortened? It was worth a try.

He saw the rest of the militia storm into the building now; the red and green of their uniforms sporting the trademark governmental logo. Under those shirts were just the ordinary people of the country; those people like his thug-uncles who wanted to play soldier.

He could give himself up, right now. Tell them the twins had forced him into the crawlspace, that he was just escaping from them by being up here in the thoroughfare; that they wanted him dead, too. But then he thought of the traces of himself that would tell them otherwise, not least the remnants of his semen that were no doubt on the floor of the archive somewhere; dying a tiny death, a stain of complicity that would be almost impossible to argue against.

Ana

3.45PM

The mossy landing pad that had broken her fall was entirely constituted of books she'd specially selected for annihilation. This was the first time she'd come face to face with the decisions she had made on the library's behalf. All those titles were included in her confidential report, one that had been personally commissioned by the chief librarian.

The library's management board, without her knowledge, had been secretly assessing her for a new role. Six months before her mother died she was pulled into the head librarian's office to meet three serious-looking women who told her they had been searching for years for the right kind of person to fill a new position, a knowledgeable, well-read member of staff to make crucial judgements about which works should remain in the catalogue. Ana remembered being overjoyed that someone had singled her out like this, and couldn't wait to go home and tell her mother. But there had been a catch. A non-disclosure agreement would have to be signed, and she would not be able to share the details of this new position with anyone, even family members. Still, she got a buzz out of knowing she'd excelled at something. That she stood out. There had been no mention of anyone else having come close to achieving her kind of excellence – certainly not her sister, her supposed double. She had hoped that this new position might mean getting her own office, but she was instructed to stay where she was, and to appear to her colleagues as if nothing had changed, as if she were just carrying out her usual archivist's duties of updating the catalogue.

As she slid down now from that pile in the dungeon, the fading yellow sides of a fourteenth-century antiphonal had become stuck to her tights. Peeling it off, she recalled how it had come into the library's possession after being purchased at auction from the neighbouring country around a decade ago. A valuable item, undoubtedly, considering its references to an earlier patron saint of the country; but Ana had decided that the liturgical history of her country was of little use to most people. The chief librarian had been particularly impressed with her ruthlessness. 'To be fair, it's not the kind of nation we're building now,' she'd said, approving its immediate removal from the glass cabinet at the heart of the North Reading Room with only her fingerprint, authorising its instant erasure from all electronic databases, and making sure that if the digital copy was sought out online that it would trigger a fatal exception error and shut any computer down. The logic being that if people lost their work in the process of searching for it, and if repeated searches caused damage to their computer's hard drive, they would eventually forgo (and subsequently forget) the troublesome text.

From then on, it gradually became addictive, the notion of ridding a nation of its excesses. Once she'd started, she couldn't stop. Her nation was bursting at the seams with stuff she assumed no one would ever read. There were reports of sheep dog trials, which dated back to the Seventies of the last century; witness statements from historical court cases; minutes from meetings in the Eighties she doubted anyone had even cared about at the time let alone now; parish magazines whose readership were long dead and local community newspapers whose communities had been either flooded or built over. It seemed almost embarrassing to hang on to them, for all they seemed to indicate were the many losses the nation had suffered; the ways in which the neighbouring country had made it impossible for them to sustain their way of life. Keeping such records of their small triumphs in their small communities somehow prevented them from ever becoming the big nation they always sought to be. The fact that these people hoarded, and took pride in, the minutiae of their lives, that they were content to be satisfied with it, depressed her, and in order to rid herself of that feeling she condemned the whole sorry, tiny lot to her database of doom.

There was so much poetry and fiction that was not worth reading either. Flimsy little pamphlets by long-forgotten poets, terrible novels written under pseudonyms, boring biographies of farmers, local councillors and politicians. The biographies of men far outweighed the biographies of women, of course, as though no one had thought a woman's life worth documenting. Although she had known that her own biases and proclivities were driving these decisions, the chief librarian had put her mind at ease.

'Someone has to make the judgement call,' she'd said. 'We need to rid ourselves of thirty per cent of our material. It will be somebody else's bias, if not yours.'

The triangular corners of discarded photographs also poked out from the pile of diminishing books. Lily's territory. Once a person had been erased from the catalogue, it was Lily's job to scour through all photographic evidence of the erased author. You could not murder a book and not its author, after all. She had assumed Lily had signed a similar non-disclosure agreement, but they never discussed the fact that their jobs were dependent on one another. Yet Lily often threw her a strange look when a box file arrived on her desk following a certain decision she had made, seeming shocked to discover the latest writer Ana had condemned to obscurity. It was this detail in particular that haunted Ana, perhaps more so than making the decision itself, seeing the last photographic evidence arrive in those little box-file coffins, yet another death for an already long-dead writer.

She pulled at the edges of one of the photographs and out it came, so potently coated with the liquid that it made Ana retch.

Ana remembered this one, which the head librarian had told her about. Lily had tried to remove a prominent poet from a photograph taken at a protest against the investiture of the prince of the neighbouring country, who was being invested with control over their country. The two figures on either side of the poet in question, a protest singer and a politician, had been allowed to remain because their families had donated a large amount of money to the library. But sadly, having no descendants, there was no one left to vouch for the poor poet in the mix, who – though being the centrepiece of the photograph – now needed to be erased, to be blended somehow into the placard he was holding.

Lily had failed to notice the faint contours of his fist, still on the placard between the two figures. It had been processed all the way through the system before it was spotted by one of the executives. A hand without a body attached to it, floating in the middle of the photograph. Giving the whole game away, right there and then. Ana still remembered Lily's puffed red eyes when she returned to her desk after a rollicking from the chief librarian, who thought that she'd done it on purpose. That it was some kind of protest in itself; the remaining errant fist. Lily had pleaded her case and had been allowed to complete the work. One by one, each finger disappeared. The poet was no more. But still the picture was not perfectly doctored, because you could tell that the other two figures were looking at someone; and somehow, the poet's presence seemed to remain in the photograph. As if his fist had always been clenched in objection to that particular moment, as if the now invisible figure had always known that his identity would one day be carried off and destroyed along with the placard.

Seeing these books and photographs turning into sludge in front of her, the chemicals waiting to dissolve the poet's hand forever, made her feel sick. What on earth had they all done? Perhaps she had been naive in thinking that all the discarded materials would still be kept somewhere safe, in their original form, for posterity, rather than discarded like rubbish. Where were they going, those little pieces of history that were no longer deemed necessary in order to build a nation? Did they just meld together like this, becoming part of the foundations of the building? She noticed that the pile seemed to be moving, as though a gravitational force were pulling it forward. That's when she saw that the books were actually on a conveyor belt of some kind, chugging along towards a small opening obscured by rubber flaps. Nineteenth-century novels descending into some unknown darkness, their physical end worse than their fictional ones.

That's when Eben emerged from the pile of books as though he were an apparition of one of the male writers she was trying to erase. He held the gun out towards her.

'Eben,' she said. 'Eben, let's just talk. Please . . .'

He swung around wildly, the gun in his hand.

'Did you know about all this?' he hollered back at her. 'About what they're doing down here?'

The gun did not rest easy in Eben's trembling, sweating hands. Ana remembered the farmer telling them there was nothing more dangerous than someone who had never used a gun before. They were the most likely to kill, entirely through incompetence.

'Eben, put the gun down, please . . . before it goes off.'

'It's ridiculous,' he continued, his voice breathless and raspy, 'that men are expected just to make their . . . donation, to you lot, but that you're still intent on destroying the legacy of men through doing what you're doing down here. I mean . . . you do know that people like Eben the Poet – you came from people like that, the people you're trying to destroy. You're destroying your own roots. You couldn't even exist without him, or me . . . and now you're trying to erase me, too. Because I'm no use to you anymore!'

Ana couldn't make sense of anything he was saying. He had a wild, feverish look about him and saturated as his face now was with sweat, his glasses slid right off his nose and into the structure of darkness, blending with the sludge and the shadows. Eben flailed around for them desperately, and although Ana could see full well where they had landed, inches away from his feet, it soon became obvious that without them he could make sense of nothing around him, let alone direct a gun at her. She saw the realisation dawning slowly on him, that he was the one in danger yet again, as he fumbled to grasp the old escape ladder behind him, and placed his foot on the bottom rung, not seeing the clear hazard signs all around it.

'It's not safe, Eben, please ... That's an old ladder ... Don't ...'

He wasn't willing to listen. He tucked the gun away in his blazer and began to climb. With every rung the wall fixings groaned perilously in objection. But still he went.

She considered picking up his glasses, using them as leverage to get him back down, but she realised it was doubtful it would work. She wasn't sure herself what the best course of action was now. She no longer had a weapon to terrorise him with. Then again, he could easily fall to his death from that ladder, break his neck. Should she just stand back and let it happen, let him experience a fall like their mother had, an eye for an eye? Surely he would have to die now, either way, it would be in the library's best interests if nothing else, considering he had witnessed the pulping of the books in the basement. But she couldn't get his nonsensical little rant out of her head. What had he meant, she could not exist without him? She tried to remember who Eben the Poet was. A quick-fire decision, if she recalled correctly, because the only remaining little green pamphlet of his had a foreword that declared him to have written a number of substandard things. She'd been happy to take the editor's word for it and hadn't thought twice about placing the pamphlet on the trolley. Had he been a long-lost relative of theirs? Perhaps he had discovered something in her mother's diary that suggested as much.

Although her mother never admitted to being influenced by any male writers, Ana suddenly shuddered to think that she might have erased someone her mother may have been a closet fan of, or someone to whom she was indebted for her own great genius.

'You're destroying your own roots,' he had said.

Eben

4PM

He was partially blind now, and did what he usually did when he found himself in a pickle like this; he followed the light, which seemed like the most sensible direction of travel for a short-sighted man. The ladder did not feel particularly stable, but it seemed the best route out of here, towards a shining rectangle in the distance that was, he hoped, some kind of opening. As he drew closer to it, he felt the warmth of daylight seep over his skin. Such luminosity was an unusual and surprising thing after all those hours in the darkness. It flowed down towards him like some golden elixir, full of promise. He couldn't believe that it was still daylight out there; for his world seemed to have entirely turned to night since he entered the library.

He reflected back on the chaotic wreck he'd been that morning, compared to the one who was now climbing that ladder with renewed vigour, powered by sheer will and determination, a gun weighing down his blazer. It was hard to believe that it had only taken a few hours, not even a whole day, for such a transformation.

He had seen from the look in her face that she'd had no idea what he was talking about. Her desire to hurt him had nothing to do with him being her father. She considered him the complete opposite, as having no significance whatsoever in her life, a person who could be snuffed out as easily as those authors whose work was being turned to sludge. She obviously didn't even know about her mother's illness either. Eben the Poet's green pamphlet was now tucked firmly under his armpit, the DNA letter still rustling down the front of his trousers. All he needed now was to get the evidence into the right hands. Rise like a phoenix from the papier mâché, the pages he had saved from death clinging to his wings.

The rusty ladder was now vibrating with movement; not just his and hers, but others, too. Two other figures had come from somewhere and had started to climb. Looking down he could roughly make out some tiny locust shapes crawling towards him – were they police? Coming to sort all this out? The heavier the ladder got, the more it murmured its deathly intent to come apart. Eben slowed down slightly, trying to push away the vision in his mind of himself falling to his death, catapulting into the vat of pulp, becoming a clean white sheet in a box, the fibres of his being melding with the paper. Suddenly, a wall fixing detached itself and flew into his face. The ladder jolted suddenly to the left, a chorus of gasps echoing his own.

'Slow down, you two!' a man's voice rose up towards him. 'We need to distribute the weight evenly or it's going to collapse. You need to wait for him to get higher . . . just wait, yeah, for him to get out. He's the main bulk of the weight. Once he gets out, we'll be OK.'

Eben sensed Ana stopping behind him. Taking a breath. He, too, stopped for a moment. Caught between light and shadow. He had never before been so conscious of himself as a body. Every single ounce of flesh needing to be aware of its rhythm, its positioning in space and gravity. The main bulk of the weight, the main burden for everyone, at the apex of the library, for all to see. Eben Prytherch. Author killer. Failed writer. Sperm donor. He breathed in through his nose, out through his mouth.

'I am enough,' he whispered to himself, trying to rectify the abuse he'd just hurled at himself. 'I am a critic. Biographer. Father.'

'Eben, you can move, now, OK? Keep going. That way we all get out alive,' a man's voice said from below. He recognised it now; it was the porter from earlier, the one who took the piss out of him every single time he came here. Was he trying to save him now? He hadn't done much to help him earlier.

Eben breathed in and out, in and out. He tried to remember that behind him there were only problems and darkness. Ahead there was light and immortality. Slowly, he manoeuvred his heavy, unwilling legs up the final few rungs, through a safety cage, and up towards the rectangular opening.

Like the door in the archive, it didn't seem to have a handle of any kind, and was sealed tight. Panic shot up his body, as those beneath him seemed to look up, willing him to do something. He visualised himself with his face pressed to the glass, screaming in terror as the twins pulled him to his death, his face moving further and further away, an indistinguishable full stop, fading from the page of his own life.

'He has the gun!' someone shouted below him. 'Eben, shoot the window open!'

Turning towards the voice, he nearly lost his footing, his hands slipping on a sodden piece of paper that had clung stubbornly to the final rung. When he steadied himself again, the thought struck him that there was no way a page like that would have floated up here of its own accord. It could only happen on the way down. Was that how they avoided detection? Coming up to the roof and pouring books into the blackness without giving them a second thought?

He heard another ping; another wall fixing gone, then another. He had to do something. Fleetingly he remembered that those on the ladder were his daughters, and though he resented this fact with all his being, it also somehow spurred him on to show some kind of example, to be effective in some way, in a way perhaps a father would. He reached into his pocket for the gun and held it up towards the glass. He held tight on to the ladder with his other hand, and pulled the trigger.

The impact of the shot somehow powered him through the shower of glass and out into the open air on the other side. Glass shards littered the space around him, and he felt the sharp prick of some of them in his face and his side, deciding not to meddle with them, for fear of causing himself more damage. It would be just like him to tug at something and sever an artery, bleeding to death on the library roof when he was a mere stone's throw away from pre-eminence.

The winter sun enveloped him. He rose to his feet unsteadily and took a few steps forward. He couldn't see much, but could make out the contours of the ordinary world that he knew was still there, the smudge of a seaside town flickering in the distance, the green clump of fields on either side of it, and a blur of blue sky and clouds. A fluttering around him grew louder with every passing second, and finally he was able to make out what the sound was: seagulls were congregating, landing left, right and centre, as if they had been waiting for him to arrive, so that they could cover the roof for him, a down fit for a king. He tried to forget how he felt about these creatures as they flocked and cackled around him. How they had brought him to his knees more than once, fearful that they were going to attack him, devour him. He told himself that now he was a different kind of man; a man who had been through something, a man who had travelled too far to be floored by a common bird. A seagull was just a seagull – that's what the therapist had told him – and so he breathed deeply and repeated the mantra.

'A seagull is just a seagull.'

He hadn't expected to find himself alone on the roof with only a flock of seagulls for company. Where on earth was everyone? He turned to look at the opening. Should he go back, check that they were OK? Take them to safety, like a father would do? Then again, he might drop them, or make things worse. They still no doubt hated him, and one of them, at least, still had a gun. What if he tried to help and they still shot him? He would have looked his own death in the face, willingly, and that's how he would be remembered by everyone.

Why wasn't there anyone here to help him? He'd just shown an uncharacteristic display of bravery without anyone there to witness it. Shouldn't the authorities be here, ready to whisk him away to safety, so he wouldn't have to be pondering all these things on his own, or be forced to make any more decisions?

It wasn't until Eben took a few steps forwards towards the edge of the building that he realised that he had misread the situation. Or rather the situation had misread him.

Below him, spreading out across the library car park, were concentric circles of red, white and green. Gradually, it dawned on him what those shapes were. The country's militia were precisely, evenly positioned, much in the same way as the birds around him were. This was no huge surprise, given the reduced police presence in the town, but he hadn't expected to see quite so many of them, or for them to be pointing their weapons directly at him. He froze, worried that any movement on his part could cause them to shoot. He tried to remain perfectly still. He found comfort in thinking of all the accolades and honours that were sure to come as a result of his actions; the meteoric rise to fame that could ensue if he could only survive this final misunderstanding. All he had to do now was to ensure that his heart continued to beat, that the oxygen kept flowing freely through his lungs, so that his story could be told by him, and no one else.

But he also needed to do something that would somehow let the militia know that he had information, sensitive and confidential information, that could overturn everything. The thought that they even risked pointing a gun at him, let alone a hundred, was scandalous. He wanted to scream at them, tell them how ridiculous they were being, but he couldn't risk doing so either. And for once in his life, the presence of the seagulls – the sense of their close proximity beyond his tightly closed eyes – offered him some kind of solace.

He heard shards of glass being crunched underfoot. Someone was approaching, slowly, until her presence made itself felt behind him. His daughter, he thought, again unsure about how that word felt to him. A burden, yet somehow, as much as he tried to fight it, there was something hopeful in it. He tightened his armpit around the book; felt around for that piece of paper in his trousers. He would tell them, now, that he was their father. It was the only way. But as he moved towards her, he heard the militia beneath him changing position, to point in a different direction.

Then, came Ana's voice: 'Eben. Eben, please, put the gun down. They think it's you. They think you're behind it all.'

The panic returned, a sudden explosion in his veins and across his chest. Until that moment he hadn't realised or remembered that he was, in fact, still holding a gun. The shock of the reverberation against the glass had made it feel surgically attached to him somehow, as though being separated from it was not an option. As he had taken in the scene below, he had been pointing in the direction of the crowd.

'Put it down, Eben, or give it to me,' she said again. 'Before it goes off, or you do something you regret.'

'Stand back,' he hissed, through his teeth, putting on his best act of ventriloquism so as not to alarm the crowd. 'They don't need to see you. They only need to see me, OK? Not you. Do you understand?'

Surprisingly, she did as she was told. He felt a surge of pride that he was someone who could make commands, a person someone else listened to. An authority figure. *Listen to your father, that's a good girl*. Yet daughter or not – provider, protector, whatever role a person like that was meant to play – he knew he would still need to tell the authorities everything: how he'd been held hostage in that room by them both, how he'd been mocked and threatened and psychologically abused, even though it almost certainly meant a heavy prison sentence for them both. A thought struck him then that this perhaps was the best place to tell them about their parentage, rather than right now. Perhaps he had been imagining this new future all wrong – it would not be him in the old people's home waiting for them to visit, but them waiting for him in prison, safely ensconced behind bars, where their reaction would not be a danger to him.

Their incarceration would put everything in perspective. As shocked as they may be, perhaps if he kept visiting, they would eventually be able to accept it, and be grateful to see him, for who else in their right mind would visit them, after all this? He'd have the perfect opportunity to grind them down over the years until their release, and when they finally did come out, they would all be ready to move forward with this new relationship.

I make the plans, he remembered the therapist encouraging him to say. *I don't let others make plans for me.*

Eben stared back at the blur of the unmoving militia below him. It helped not to be able to see them clearly, not to have a full realisation of the risk they posed to his life. He was surprised that no effort had been made to fire at him, when there seemed to be so many of them and only one of him. And they were all far more able, he would have thought, to use a gun than him. But then he remembered the policies of the militia that he'd read about in the online papers recently. A militia like this, made up of volunteers, was not permitted to shoot unless it was shot at. No one wanted a group of untrained civilians going gung-ho; or wanted unnecessary lawsuits on their hands. And it increased Eben's pride of being the only one with any real free will in this moment, to do as he wished with the power that had been suddenly thrust upon him.

For a moment, it seemed that the whole world was still and quiet, even though he knew that couldn't be the case. He saw the shape of a fire engine snaking its way up the hill towards the library, the blue light flashing. He saw some distant silhouettes with foil blankets around them, their eyes red from crying.

Someone the same shape as the professor was being wheeled out on a stretcher, puffing on gas and air, one arm waving animatedly in the air as though clutching at something no one else could see. Far off, he imagined he also saw a man with a build similar to Frankton's, shaking his head. Even from this distance, through the haze, he imagined seeing the condemnation in his eyes. And there were lights, hundreds of them, clicking and flashing below, cameras he assumed, oppressing him with their gaze. All the people and things and sounds that he had somehow summoned here through no fault of his own.

It felt almost as though he were always destined to do this, to stand on this rooftop, with this gun in his hand, as if a meaty chapter from the long-lost book of his life had come to light. And he imagined that even when he told the authorities everything he knew, even when his name was cleared, even when he would be considered some kind of hero, an iconic figure in history, some would never ever forget the image of him standing on this rooftop now, pointing a gun at them, like a senseless criminal. Some would forever cling to the notion of his criminality, no matter what.

'I am no longer a weakling,' he whispered to himself.

And this thought made him grab hold of his gun with a new determination. He took ownership of what they thought they were seeing: a dangerous man in possession of a weapon.

A man with power.

Dan

4.05PM

Not-Nan was talking quietly with Eben now, trying to reason with him. The gun was still in Eben's possession, and he was waving it around like a madman, mainly in the direction of the crowd below.

Hoisting himself up the ladder with a swollen ankle had been a painful endeavour, and terrifying too, considering how unstable it felt, like it could give way at any given moment. Although he'd intended to use it to haul himself down, by the time he'd manoeuvred himself onto it, he realised that Eben and not-Nan were already on it and that they were above him. He'd had no choice but to follow them, up a ladder he knew would almost certainly not withstand the weight of three people, let alone the fourth one he sensed getting on it right at the bottom. When he felt that they were all putting too much pressure on the top half of the ladder, he had asked them to stop. Everyone seemed to listen to him when he told them to pace themselves, allowing Eben, the heaviest climber, the greatest threat to all their lives, to exit first.

Dan was almost impressed how swiftly Eben had extracted and fired the gun under the girl's instruction – it confirmed to him something else he recalled from his safety training, that they were likely to be surprised by those under their charge during an attack, how the meekest of people would find a strength within them they never knew they had while the outwardly brave people cowered. It was not until he was nearly at the top of the ladder that Nan, who was below him, started to disobey him, almost clambering over him at one point, and then clutching on to his back like a monkey as he attempted the final rungs, as if trying to pull him down with her. It took every ounce of strength in him to get them both safely out through the roof, and as his leg had left the final rung, and they fell to safety on the rooftop floor, they heard the ultimate wrench of that ladder giving up on itself, falling back into the abyss.

Trying to extricate himself from Nan was almost impossible.

'Get off me,' he said, trying to prise her fingers from his torso. She still had her gun, and he could feel it pushing into his abdomen. He calculated quickly that all he needed to do now was stay here, stop Nan from getting to her sister and Eben, then at least someone, somewhere, would be able to testify that when it came down to it, he'd actually done something worthwhile. It would surely go in his favour that he had placed himself between her and her target.

He rolled on top of her and managed to push all his weight against her arm and the gun. Her eyes widened in surprise when she realised she couldn't move, almost impressed that he was taking action.

'If this goes off now, it'll shoot your dick off,' she said. 'And you're very fond of it, from what I remember.'

'I'll take my chances,' he said. 'Just stop it now yeah, Nan? It's all over – you know that. There's no point to any of this anymore.'

Dan threw a quick glance towards the other one and Eben. Eben was still restless, and the girl who wasn't Nan was trying her best to reason with him. A few more minutes and surely someone was going to come and stop all this.

'God, it was so easy with you. All it took was a bit of sex. I didn't even enjoy it, you know. I mean, you can't say I didn't give it a good try but I think you really confirmed it for me, Dan, that men . . . well, they aren't really my thing.'

'You don't say,' he said. She was writhing against him now, kicking against his sore ankle, going for the weak spots. She'd identified a glass shard sticking out of his torso and she was manipulating it slowly with her one free hand, twisting it until it hurt like hell.

'But she wanted it, you see, Ana . . . I could tell she did. And whatever we experience, well we have to do it together, you see? I thought I'd try it out first. Break her in.'

Ana, he thought to himself with fondness, remembering her body against his in the archive. So that was her name. It made total sense to him that it had two syllables, rather than Nan's cold, single-syllable bullet.

Nan was having some success with the glass shard now, and it felt perilously close to puncturing something vital inside him. He pulled her hand away and turned her onto his front, but in doing so lost control of her other arm, which instantly raised the gun right up to his neck. As she did so, he heard a shift somewhere, a flutter of weapons, moving, repositioning. The murmurs of a militia. Hidden from view, but watching, all the same, as he struggled. Waiting for the right moment, trying to decipher who was the aggressor. Dan saw that it wasn't exactly an easy thing to work out, even when you were right in the middle of it.

'Nan!' came a voice. 'What are you doing?' Footsteps came clattering across the roof as Ana hurtled back towards them both.

'We don't need him anymore,' Nan said flatly. 'What do you think? Should I kill him?' The question sounded entirely innocuous on her lips, like she was musing on a grocery list. *Do we really need this?*

'Nan, don't be ridiculous. Stop it! We don't need to do anything to him, just leave him be. It's Dan. He's on our side.'

'Oh come on, Ana, don't be stupid. He's going to testify against us,' Nan continued. 'And it's one less story to contradict ours.' Dan closed his eyes as Nan pushed the gun further in towards his throbbing neck.

Closing his eyes, he waited for the shot. Was ready for it, even. Had he not escaped many bullets, real and metaphorical, his whole life? Someone had tried to take a shot at him outside court that one time, only it had ricocheted off his Bluetooth headphones, tearing a hole in the leather but leaving his brain intact. A miracle, some had said. A travesty, wailed others. Either way, he realised his mother had been right when she said that a bullet like that would somehow come back at him sooner or later. You could only dodge it for so long.

He prepared himself for the shot, hoping that Nan would aim well enough to take him out in one go. But then he felt the weight of the gun lift from his neck. He didn't dare open his eyes, for he imagined that Nan probably had some twisted notion of wanting to look at him as she executed him; but much to his surprise, when he eventually prised his eyelids open, she was gone. The sisters were now a few feet away from him, discussing something heatedly, arms flapping. Nan pacing with her gun; Ana pointing anxiously towards Eben.

Dan turned to look at the lonely figure on the precipice. Eben somehow looked as if he were part of another story altogether. Fending for himself for once, gun in hand, so unlike the meek library goer Dan had wound up that morning. Dan imagined it as one of the photographs you would see hanging in the gallery at night, as if Eben were some violent rebel taking direct action against the establishment, ready to martyr himself from the top of one of its most iconic buildings.

The seagulls gathered around him, as though knowing something was coming. As though they too, wanted to be captured in a moment in time, to rise above their reputation as the town's scavengers, and have their dirty feathers elevated forever in the library's hall of fame. The impaled seagull from the night before still hovered there rigidly on the flagstaff, a sure sign of the awfulness that was to come, had anyone been paying attention.

The cameras were ready to capture Eben's fall from grace. The guns were ready to fire when it happened. But no one would capture the view he had now, Dan thought, watching helplessly as those sisters moved silently away from him and into the dull, afternoon sun, their shadows merging into one as they moved closer and closer together, their hands linking and heads bowing towards one another. Uniting once more; instead of following different pathways, as he'd hoped.

It would be imprinted only on memory, he thought, that moment when they had seemed uncertain; when Ana, at least, had turned backwards to look at him, as though considering giving herself up. A split second before she had stepped into full view of the crowd below and of the militia all around them, crossing the boundary between who she could have been and who she and her sister would now forever be.

A moment, a split second, a hair's breadth, Dan thought. That's all it was, between obscurity and history.

Ana and Nan

4.10PM

Standing on the rooftop, looking down at the crowd, Ana allowed herself for a moment to imagine a world in which she had never been a twin, never had a sister, never been a double. There had been a time, after all, when the potential had hovered there inside their mother's body. A million possibilities swirling around in that zygote, those cells dividing and subdividing, assuming they were on their way to creating an individual. But then at some point, it had split. Had the zygote considered it a success, a clever move on its behalf, a way of getting more than it bargained for in life? Or a failure, halving its potential like that, weakening its intent?

As her sister's fingers curled around hers, Ana couldn't help but wonder which one of them that single zygote would have developed into. Perhaps it would have been neither one of them, for without the doubling, without living their lives in conjunction with, and in opposition to each other, they would not be who they now were. It was what had paved the way for two sets of everything, two ways of looking at the world, two notions of how to exact revenge and bring a man to justice, which had converged into a single pathway leading up to this moment.

'Ana,' her sister whispered in her ear, strengthening her grip now. 'Shall we do it? Shall we jump?'

Death had always been an alarming prospect for them, even since they were young girls. Knowing they had been born together, within twelve minutes of each other, it frightened them to think that death would not have the same predictability. Their synchronised entry into the world didn't automatically mean that

269

their exits would be the same; that at some point, one of them would be forced to live life without the other. Unless, Ana thought. Unless they planned to go out of this world exactly as they had come into it: completely united.

She moved forward with Nan towards the precipice, placing her feet next to her sister's, the gun at Nan's side between them. The crowd was restless now, the militia impatient. Raising her head slightly, Ana caught sight of the management team of the library staring up at them in disbelief, still trying to process, she imagined, how these two archivists had never even been on their radar. Lily and Summer clung on to each other openly now, glittering in their foil coverings, and behind them, Ana could see that Pale was being carried into an ambulance, eyes wide open in shock, an oxygen mask on her face, a baby splayed like a starfish on her chest. Professor Nicholas was being wheeled closely behind in the direction of another ambulance, talking animatedly to the paramedic as if reeling off some quote or other.

No harm done, she thought, hopefully. *Not really.*

'Get back!' Eben shouted at them as she and Nan drew closer towards him. Ana saw the same strange look in her sister's eyes that had been there in the reading room; struggling to make sense of what was in front of her. Eben was still within reach, she seemed to be saying, as she tugged her sister along. They could take him with them.

'Nan,' Ana said, standing her ground firmly now, refusing to budge an inch further. Eben had his back turned to them and seemed dangerously near the edge, a horrific reminder of her mother's suicide. It would only take the slightest movement. 'Nan, let's just wait a bit.'

Nan didn't seem to be listening. There was nothing to stop her from shooting Eben in his back now, or even just to push him clean off the ledge. Pull him down with them as they went. As armed and ready as the militia were, they weren't going to do anything until someone else had fired the first shot. But something was stopping her. She turned to look at her sister, something dolorous in her eyes. Ana had seen that look before on her face; usually when she had to confess to doing something wrong.

'I don't think you should die without knowing,' she said, almost breathless. 'To make the decision, with that knowledge, is one thing, but to make the decision without . . .'

Nan was rambling, and Ana couldn't quite follow her train of thought. Nan turned slightly away from her, and stepped even closer to the ledge.

'I don't understand what you're saying,' Ana said. 'What don't I know?'

'He was our sperm donor,' Nan replied. 'But it doesn't change anything, OK? He doesn't deserve a title. It doesn't mean anything. He's not a father because he made a donation. Gave them a sample. He didn't even have a choice in the matter . . . It doesn't change how we see him.'

Ana felt the shock flood her body. Eben, her mother's sperm donor? Upon hearing this, he turned to look at them both, his expression difficult to read. With the sunlight behind him, she could identify the hues of redness in what she had taken as a uniform grey mop of hair. The remnants of who he had once been were still there, clinging stubbornly to his scalp – a truthful, inherent part of him that would not go gently; an unusual auburn shade so similar to the colour of her own hair.

Eben, her father.

'Oh, of course it doesn't change how you see me!' Eben turned to face them both, incandescent; his rage making him fearless. She saw that this was not news to him, either, and that seemingly, she was the last to know.

'Have you always known, Eben?' Nan shouted at him. 'Is that why you were so obsessed with her? So much so that you were intent on killing her?'

'Oh it's so easy to think I killed her, isn't it? So much easier than accepting she was all over the place on that day. She didn't even know what she wanted. All I did was write some bloody reviews! Look, I never particularly wanted kids, OK? But I didn't have a choice in the matter, did I? Surely we're all just victims of the system, and not to put too fine a point on it but – it's your bloody mother's book that influenced that decision in the first place. If that book hadn't been so influential, if more men had been in charge, that policy would never have passed. But it did, and here we are, OK? We've got to make the most of the mess we find ourselves in, not bring it all to an end, please – can we just see where it's possible to go from here . . .'

Nan raised her gun to mirror his. The militia did nothing but watch. Ana again saw traces of those family traits they shared with Eben. The faint hint of freckles on his cheeks, the like of which had started to develop across the bridge of their noses when they were around nine years old, a curious sprinkling that their mother had joked was the sunshine seasoning them, making them even more delicious. But then Ana remembered how her mother had studied this new feature of theirs curiously as she coated their noses with sun cream, a strange look in her eyes, as though something had just occurred to her. Something awful.

Eben was her father. Their father. The missing piece she had longed for secretly, the fourth member of the family who would give everything a perfect symmetry; or at least, it would have done, if only her mother was still alive. And now they were trying to eradicate him, trying to rid the odd number to ensure their evenness again.

'Tell your sister to put that gun away,' Eben said, appealing to her directly, as if sensing some shift in her as she absorbed the news. 'Then we can talk. Properly, yes? Like a family.'

Family. Again, another word she had longed for when she was younger, when she saw other children skipping off with two parents by their side. Yes, they'd had Elena, who was larger than two people in some ways, and yet less than one whole person in others, in the way she kept part of herself hidden from them.

'Nan . . .' she said, aware of the tears coming thick and fast. 'Nan, please . . . we need to process this before we do anything . . . If he's who you say he is . . .'

'It's why she didn't want you to know. She knew you'd be like this. Why can't you see that it doesn't mean anything? It's just a fact of biology. It doesn't change any of the things he did,' Nan said. 'We either jump or I kill him. Which one is it, Ana?'

Nan turned to her sister, her eyes mirroring Ana's, filled to the brim with tears. Ana recalled a day when they were about seven years old, when they had been swinging each other around on the kitchen floor, laughing uncontrollably as their mother made dinner. Nan had gone flying into the side of a cabinet and started crying, and when Ana had run to her with a cold compress she'd pushed it away, saying she wasn't crying because she was hurt, she was crying because she'd realised that one day Ana would be dead and there would be no more laughter to share with anyone. It had then escalated into an argument, and subsequently a fight that their mother had to break up, by unhelpfully saying, 'But, Nan, you might die first – you never know.'

'So, what, you need to kill me now, because I'm redundant, I've done my job?' Eben shouted. 'Well what's to stop me from killing you both, eh?'

'If you shoot Eben, the militia will shoot you,' Dan said. Ana turned to look at him. She recalled his hands on her, the way he'd made her feel in that archive; how visible, desired, complete. Like she herself was enough. She gestured for him to come closer, to stand next to her. Perhaps he would pull her back, when it came to it, she thought. If it was his decision, rather than hers, for her to stay, then perhaps she would be able to live with it.

'And what if she shoots me?' Eben croaked, gesturing towards Nan.

'The militia will shoot her,' Dan continued. 'And then maybe all of us. The only way out of this now is that no one shoots anyone. We drop those guns down, over the side of the building. And then, well, at least we all stand a chance of getting out of this alive.'

Ana saw that her sister was floating away from her, like a balloon, her mind visibly detaching from the situation, like it so often did. But her body remained in place, determined and rigid, and Nan still would not let go of her hand. It was just as imperative to keep hold of that as the gun. Ana was five years old again, standing at the side of the road, Elena leaning into Nan's ear, saying, 'Don't let go of your sister's hand, OK? You know what she's like.'

Eben, she saw, was weighing up his options. Dropping his own gun could mean freedom, and it could mean death; keeping hold of it had similarly contrasting prospects. Carrying on as he was provided the only certainty.

'It wasn't my fault; none of this was my fault,' he whimpered, shoulders shaking as he began to lose his composure, sobs threatening to burst their way out through his windpipe.

'Nan, I think we need to sit down with him and talk,' Ana ventured, desperate to buy herself some time, so that she could let this new information sink in, to work out what to do with it. 'I don't know how you know all this, but you should have told me before now, maybe we wouldn't even be here if you'd been honest with me . . .'

'Yes and maybe Elena would still be here if it wasn't for him,' Nan replied curtly, her voice hardening again, the emotion somehow slipping away.

'Don't give me that shit; you knew full well it wasn't me. One of you must have changed those diary entries before you gave them to the papers! Don't you dare try to drag me into this business any longer. I won't have it, you hear me! Your mother was ill.'

The diary entries. Those few little nuggets they had fed to the press. Nan had argued that as the experienced restorer of manuscripts, she would fish them out and offer them up like bait. Although their mother didn't want anyone reading her diaries cover to cover, Nan reasoned with Ana that she would have been more than willing to release some choice quotations that proved how much Eben's words had destroyed her. 'Let me find the quotes,' Nan had said. 'It'll just be like work for me. It'll be too upsetting for you. I'll skim through. Then I'll put them away.'

'Nan,' Ana ventured now, turning to face her sister. 'What's he talking about? She wasn't ill, was she?'

'She had a disease!' Eben said. 'Jakob . . . something . . .'

'Creutzfeldt-Jakob,' Nan echoed, turning to face her sister. 'Ana, I'm sorry, I should have told you that too. But she didn't want me to.'

'What the hell are you talking about?' Ana's head was spinning. She was dizzy with it all, in danger of losing her footing at any moment and plummeting down. Perhaps it would be easier, in some ways, to just do it, she thought. Get away from all these new facts that were being pelted at her one after the other, with no time to process what they meant, or how it complicated what they had done.

'She left me a letter, Ana. She trusted me with it. She wanted me to destroy it but I couldn't – it was the last thing she ever wrote, so I hid it, inside her portrait bust in the archive. She had a form of dementia. It was getting worse. She wanted out. She wanted to go while she could still make the decision to leave . . . She couldn't have asked us to do it. She knew we never would.'

Ana was floored. Her mother. Her close friend. Her ally. Trusting Nan, not her, with the most important information of all. *Hold on to her, Nan, you know what she's like.* Ana knew she had always played the baby, despite being the eldest. Thinking that being the first to meet their mother, her existence took priority somehow. But this attitude had also made her seem like she needed protecting. From everything.

'No, she wouldn't have told you and not me . . .'

'She knew she wouldn't write another book. That was already a death for her. And it's what they all wanted, the Smotherhood, wasn't it? For her to stop writing. She wasn't going to give them the satisfaction of watching her deteriorate. If she could make a big drama out of it, make them feel guilty, she might have been able to change something, to stop them from doing it to someone else.'

'But we weren't doing anything. We were just . . .' Eben let the sentence hang there limply in the air, as if he didn't quite believe his own assertion anymore.

The crowd below them seemed small and insignificant now. And she and Nan grown huge, too big for their own skin, towering above them all. How would they look as they fell? Like their mother had, no doubt, just like a hopeless sack of skin and bone whom gravity was content to let drop. Dissolving back into the nothingness from which they had come, the zygote's quest at an end. Dan crept into her eyeline, moving towards her. Broken though he was, he presented the possibility of another life.

'Ana,' he said quietly. 'Don't. Please.'

Perhaps their mother had been wrong to emphasise their unshakeable bond. Had it not been the experience of so many of their school friends that, as much as they loved their parents, they had known they would eventually leave home? That it was a way of preparing for the eventual loss that would befall them? She, Nan and Elena had all been three very different people from the outset, but they had told themselves otherwise. As if there was no real division, no filter between them; their thoughts, dreams, desires all indistinguishable from one another. And yet, they had hoarded their own secrets all the same, and it was somewhere in that chasm of misunderstanding that the mad ideas had formed, ideas that led them to a library roof, without quite knowing how it had all happened.

And yet Ana didn't want to jump. As much as Nan's hand tightened around hers, curtailing the blood flow and making her feel dizzy, and as easy as she knew it was, to do what their mother had done, just step out and let the air do the rest, she simply wouldn't let her sister make the decision for her this time.

'Let go of my hand,' she said, in a tone she knew her sister could not misunderstand. 'Let me go.'

'I can't,' Nan replied. 'Can't you see? This is the best chance we've got to end it together. It won't . . . be so simple if we don't take the chance now, will it?'

Nan lifted her eyes to meet her sister's. Ana saw that there was something disturbing in them, something so deep and hidden that it could only come to the fore in a situation like this, when all else was lost, the entire world falling away behind them.

*

She had stopped short of telling Ana the real reason she wanted to die; which was simply so that they could do it together, and relieve Ana of the pain that surely was to follow when the old CJ took her, like it had taken their mother. It seemed like one more unbearable truth for her to bear, when Nan had worked so hard, these last few months, and their mother before her, to keep everything from her.

The truth about Eben had slipped out to a degree, as she'd forgotten, momentarily, that her mother didn't want Ana to know.

But once it was out, it became a kind of test. She wanted to prove perhaps that their mother's instincts had been wrong, that Ana surely would not be as flimsy to be on Eben's side just because of a little fact of biology, but Elena had been quite right about this. Ana's determination had simply fallen away, that very second. *We need to sit down with him and talk.* Hours earlier she had been heading towards him with a gun. As though this one little fact, coupled with their mother's illness, suddenly absolved him from all he had done.

'Him or us,' she shouted towards Ana, a desperate attempt to position these two things as the only options. 'Him or us, Ana. Make your decision.'

'Are you listening to this?' she heard Eben holler towards Dan. 'I'm going to need someone to corroborate this madness. You'll tell them, won't you? That it wasn't me. That she was ill! That letter in the portrait bust . . . it'll prove that they knew full well she was . . .'

'One of us knew,' Ana said, bitterly. She seemed resentful, Nan thought, not of the illness but of the fact Nan had kept it from her. What would Elena have done, she wondered, if she'd known her youngest daughter was about to receive the same diagnosis? Would she still have gone ahead with it all? Or would she have tried to take Nan with her, perhaps? *Let us free your sister from all this,* she could imagine her mother saying, reaching out her hand and guiding her towards the bathroom window.

However things had worked out, Elena – and the life they had lived and loved – was gone. And not only was Ana inching away from it, on that roof, but she was moving closer to Dan, and it was him now who had his hand outstretched waiting to take hers, waiting to pull her into another life altogether.

Nan would simply not allow them the indulgence of being together, right at the end like this. It was not an option. No one had come close to occupying that space between them their whole lives, and she certainly wasn't going to permit it now.

'Ana, don't walk away from me,' she shouted at them, feeling the painful absence of her sister's hand. 'Or I'll jump. I swear to God I will.' Ana halted. Even with Ana's obvious refusal, it wouldn't take much, Nan thought, just to pull her from him, pull her away from this roof and descend into a place where they would always be together.

'Just stay still, all of you! Why isn't anyone doing anything?' Eben had grown frantic. 'Why aren't they coming to save me? Can't they see I'm the victim here?'

'I told you – if you're holding a weapon, they can't approach until it's been fired. If you want to be saved, then you need to let it go,' Dan reminded them.

'Nan,' her sister said. 'Just drop it, then Eben will drop his.'

'And you?' she pleaded with her sister. 'What will you do? Will you come with me?'

Nan's vision blurred suddenly, her mind malfunctioning again. Where were they? Why were they up here? Three confusing seconds passed, and then, suddenly, she once again knew. How much time did she have left, she wondered, before three seconds became three minutes, then three days? Her separation from her sister, from the life she knew, would be coming for her, no matter what. Had it been like this for Elena, she wondered, her mind changing direction as she teetered? Had it happened mid-fall, this blacking out, this sudden confusion about why she was airborne, and what on earth could have caused her fall?

'Nan, just drop the gun please.' Her sister's voice again, pleading. 'And step away from the ledge. This isn't what Elena wanted.'

Her mind flickered again. Wasn't it? Perhaps Elena hadn't wanted them to die, too. But she had wanted something crucial, she recalled. Something big. She had wanted the truth to die with her.

'How can I let him live now?' she said. 'He'll tell people he's our father. Elena didn't want anyone to know.'

Fflur Dafydd

Eben rummaged around in his trousers for something, retrieving a piece of paper, pulling it out towards them.

'You think I'm going to want people knowing about this? After everything? Oh, you'll happily destroy entire books down there, entire careers, but this horrid little document? Oh no, that gets to live. Well maybe not anymore, eh? Look, we can destroy it right now. Take it!'

'I wouldn't go waving that around if I were you, Eben,' Dan said. 'It's contraband; they might still shoot you if they think you've taken library property.'

Dan moved forward slightly to snatch the paper from him, but as he did so, nearly lost his footing on the precipice. Ana lurched forward to grab him back, pulling him back just in the nick of time. The paper slipped from his grasp, floating away in front of their eyes, beginning its slow, topsy-turvy journey towards the expectant crowd. The people below seemed entirely transfixed by it, this thing they no longer saw anymore, a loose leaf of paper hovering like a rare bird in the air. Even the militia seemed to lose focus for a moment. Nan watched helplessly as the story of their life, their genesis, fell away from her, waiting to descend into the hands of others, so that their story could become gossip, idle chatter, told and retold and remoulded and changed on people's lips. The thing Elena had died for, the very thing she was so desperate to keep from being known, and yet a detail Elena, in her fragile state, had willingly handed to the library with all her paraphernalia, just waiting there to be discovered one day. Just at the last moment, before the piece of paper reached the eager, outstretched hands of the crowd below, a seagull flew in from somewhere and grabbed it, and flew off without giving it a second thought.

'We might be the way we are because of you,' Nan said, watching Eben's look of horror turn to relief. 'Have you thought about that? That we got this,' she said, waving the gun around in the air,

280

'from you, not from her. This desire to punish people. Isn't this just your own weakness coming back to bite you?'

Eben was still staring at the seagull, who had now flown up towards them in case they had better titbits in their possession, making loops around them in the air as it began to gag on the urine-soaked offering, the paper falling in tatters from its mouth.

'Having taken no role in your upbringing I absolutely refuse to accept that I should take any responsibility at all for this! Elena couldn't just accept her lot and die like a normal person could she?' Eben screamed back at her. 'Look what she's done to you both, dying like that? Fuelling all your rage at me, because it's easier than blaming her. Even knowing I'm your father means nothing to you, does it? Because that's what she had you believe: that I was less than nothing. Just a scientific fact. You must know that this is only the story you've created to make sense of what happened to you . . .'

Although she couldn't bring herself to say it, Nan knew that he was right, in some ways. All the trouble her mother had gone to throughout her life, hiding things from them. Elena's life had always been hers somehow, and although she had made the decision to have a child, she had not expected two of them. Everything in her life had been written out, plotted like a story. She had been making all the decisions, until life had thrown her a curveball, in the form of a second baby. Nan. The one she probably could have done without.

Elena thought that she was regaining control when she threw herself from that ledge, when in actual fact, she'd lost control of the narrative of her life completely; for it would keep sharing and reshaping itself without her. Nan knew that she too, would lose control once her mind came apart. Eben would go from being her father to being a stranger again; he would revert back to having the same insignificance he had always had. But Ana, though, maybe Ana would have a chance without her. Without the burden.

Maybe even in the aftermath of all this she could make sense of it to the authorities.

It was my sister, Ana could claim. *My sister who was driving it.* Pleading her own diminished responsibility, her own grief and helplessness. Her father at her side. Nan saw it all clearly. Elena may not have intended it to work out this way, but her mother had made space, not just for her but for Eben and Ana. Nan could provide them with even more space to move on from here. Ana need never know about Nan's illness. About the burden of care that could have lain ahead of her.

'I'm not putting down my weapon,' Eben said. 'Until she drops hers.'

Fine by me, Nan thought. She wondered how long it was possible to keep doing nothing, to keep themselves suspended here, their guns warding off the rest of the world.

'Look, Eben, how do you want to be remembered?' Dan said, changing tack. 'Do you want to be that crazy guy waving his gun around for no reason or do you want to be seen as the hero? You haven't actually committed any kind of crime, here. If you drop that gun, it'll be the most freeing thing you'll ever do . . .'

Eben raised the gun. Nan saw his hand go limp. He was spent, utterly exhausted with the whole thing. The gun clattered against the concrete roof. Eben, slowly but surely, raised his hands in surrender. Far off, he heard an applause, and looking down, saw a chorus of tiny hands, fluttering like wings below. Eben turned and walked to the ledge so that the militia could see he was giving himself up entirely, and was no longer a threat. And Nan did not go after him.

'Now you, Nan,' Ana muttered quietly, hopefully. 'This is nearly over. Come on.'

Ana was right. It was nearly over.

Nan lifted the gun. Moved it ever so slowly towards her forehead; and then, just at the last moment, wanting to make sure it would do its job, manoeuvred the barrel into her mouth. Ana screamed, but Nan closed her eyes and started to press the trigger. Ana would be grateful in time, she thought, that it had ended like this. With Elena and Nan gone, she would be free to be herself.

A bang sounded, the force of which knocked Nan backwards onto the floor, landing next to Eben who had thrown himself down instantly, his hands covering his head. She felt around for blood, for a wound, expecting her head to be hanging off her shoulders, but it wasn't. It was perfectly intact. Next to her feet lay a dead seagull, with a piece of paper chewed to within an inch of life in its mouth. A bullet wound in its chest; feathers splattered with blood.

Dan now stood on the precipice alone, ashen-faced, holding the gun he had wrenched out of her mouth and from her hand as it went off. He dropped the gun and raised his arms but Nan could see that he knew it was too late. The shot was the cue the militia had been waiting impatiently for all afternoon; rousing them into action, giving rise to the firing squad. Ana rushed instinctively towards him, and Nan could do nothing to stop her. And it seemed to Nan that she saw the whole thing, almost in slow motion, the bullet that was headed straight for him, the one he'd probably been dodging his whole life, lodging itself into him as another lodged itself into her sister, leaving them stumbling towards the precipice, fumbling for one another's hands as they plummeted like seagulls over the side of the building.

Eben

5PM

They used a crane to bring him down, and though he had been terrified of heights throughout his life, compared to everything else he had been through in the last few hours, the anxiety of it barely registered. He even tried to smile down at the crowd, supposing that the press would need plenty of photos and angles to choose from, hoping that no one would notice his knuckles turning white as they clung to the metal gate. The mood was slightly more sombre than he'd anticipated as he was lowered onto the concrete; no applause, just a look of utter shock on everyone's face, as far as he could make out through his grainy vision. Heat was coming from somewhere, too, and, turning back, he saw that a black plume of smoke seemed to be coming from the bottom half of the library, with a fire engine positioned right in front of the building. What on earth had happened there? Had the twins set the place on fire, too, before coming after him? In the far distance he also recognised the bulbous outline of Frankton bounding through the crowd, trying to get to the front. Frankton would already be riddled with jealousy, Eben thought, a feeling that would no doubt increase when he realised what an incredible discovery Eben had made. *My name,* Eben thought smugly to himself, *will live on. Yours will be forgotten.*

He wasn't quite sure what had happened when those shots had rung out. There had been a dead bird next to him when he finally opened his eyes but seemingly no other injured bodies. The twins and the porter were nowhere to be seen, but he had kept his eyes closed for so long that he imagined, or hoped rather, that they had been disarmed, to remove the most dangerous individuals first, and that the twins would already be facing an interrogation for their role in proceedings. And although he didn't wish to feel anything for either one of them at this moment but contempt, there was something else gnawing at his insides when he thought about them now, something, that felt annoyingly like concern. What would happen to them? His girls?

Once he was on the ground, he was unceremoniously dragged away by a member of the militia in the direction of a police vehicle, the crowd thronging around him, voices vying for his attention.

A familiar gruff growl cut through them all like a knife.

'Can you tell us what happened?' It was Frankton, having used his paunchy frame to part the crowd. 'Look he's a friend of mine . . . Eben . . . Eben . . . what happened? Are you OK?'

Friend, Eben thought. A friend now, when it meant being part of something, taking possession of a story. He remained silent. He would share the story, in his own time, and not let the press or Frankton gather up the titbits and scatter them like confetti, making the whole story seem less of a thing than it was. He would find the right journalist, he thought, who would tell the story in exactly the right way. And possibly that person would go on to write *his* biography, he thought excitedly.

'I'm afraid Mr Prytherch is not at liberty to say anything until he has been questioned,' said a female detective to whom he was now being handed over by the soldier. 'Now if you'll just let us pass please . . .' He recognised the detective as the one who'd investigated him for his so-called hate crime, for being responsible for Elena's death. Now she would be sorry, he thought, that she had treated him so badly the first time around.

'Frankton Emlyn,' said Frankton loudly, as if the sheer volume could make it mean something. 'I'm a colleague, critic and author. He needs support at a time like this. Can I accompany him?'

'I'm afraid those connections are of no consequence, Mr . . . Emlyn. Now if you'll let Mr Prytherch pass . . .'

Eben saw Frankton's shock at being told, by a woman, that he was *of no consequence*. That those self-proclaimed titles amounted to very little. That his name meant nothing to her. The name Eben Prytherch, he thought, would soon be imprinted on everyone's consciousness.

The detective directed him into the car, pushing back the journalists who tried to edge towards him. Once the door was shut, Eben was finally able to breathe. He had made it, he thought to himself. He was free. Alive. Frankton moved around to the other side of the car and pressed his face right up to the window. Eben took advantage of the fact that Frankton could no longer see him through the darkened windows, and stuck his middle finger up so that it lay right across his face, splitting the last of Frankton's pathetic, conjured-up identity in two.

*

It wasn't until they were at the station that he realised he was a suspect. The detective, it turned out, had not been watching him with concern in her side mirror, but rather assessing him for signs of criminality.

'You looked very smug getting into the car,' she said. 'As though everything had worked out just as you planned.'

Eben choked on his lukewarm coffee. 'Just as I planned? It wasn't anything to do with me,' he spat back at her. 'I'm the victim here! I was kept in a room for hours, threatened with a gun, chased up the fire escape, and very nearly fell to my death in front of you all. None of this is my fault. I want a lawyer, do you hear me?'

'We'll arrange a lawyer for you in due course,' she replied, 'but it really would be in your best interests to help us with our enquiries at this point. We just need to establish, if what you're saying is true, then why you were holding the gun, when you first appeared on the roof?'

Eben had almost forgotten about this. What had he been thinking? It wasn't something that was easy to explain; that surge of rage in his veins towards Elena for making him spend all those months feeling guilty about her death. The way she'd used his sperm to create new life and then had the audacity to resent him for it. All those ill feelings had been directed downwards towards the expectant crowd. But, despite those private thoughts he'd entertained of punishing those below him, the establishment who'd ignored him for so long, he'd also assumed naively that they all knew he was only in possession of a gun for self-defence reasons, and never intended to harm anyone.

'Look,' he said, trying to sound a little less rattled. 'I'm sure you can appreciate that I've been through quite an ordeal today, and I think that anyone in my position would have found themselves a little . . . disorientated, don't you think? I was just trying to defend myself. They'd threatened to kill me for God's sake!'

'But you weren't pointing the gun at them,' the detective said flatly. 'But at everyone else.'

'As I said, I was disorientated. I thought everyone was out to get me . . .'

'Our records show that you made several requests to visit the Elena Oodig archive. Is that true? And kept requesting even when the request was repeatedly denied?'

'That isn't really the issue, anymore. I've got something more important I need to discuss with you . . .' he said, feeling around his torso for the little green book. Where was it? He shot his hand into the inside pocket of his blazer, only to recall that he was no longer wearing his blazer. They'd placed all his possessions in a clear plastic bag before zipping him up in some blue cotton bodysuit.

'I'm afraid what we discuss isn't up to you, Mr Prytherch,' the detective replied. 'Now then, if we could just get a clear indication of what happened today . . .'

'Well why don't you just look at the CCTV? Won't it all be there?'

'The CCTV seems to contradict the eyewitness accounts, I'm afraid.'

The detective moved to the other side of the room, turning on a screen embedded into the wall. As the screen lit up, it showed the porter moving along the red carpet, towards the large mahogany doors. The date was correct, and the time code in the right-hand corner of the screen showed it to be nine twenty-nine. Any second now, the door would open. And in he would come.

'I'm there,' Eben said, seeing himself clearly walking in. 'You can see me . . .' But even as he said it, he noticed something strange. He wasn't wearing the same outfit.

'Yes, you are there. But you don't go anywhere near the archive, do you?'

Eben looked up at her, confused.

'I wasn't wearing those clothes when I came in, I don't . . . I don't understand . . .'

'So you were hiding another outfit somewhere, then, yes? What was the idea, dressing up a bit smarter to carry out your plans?'

'No, no, you don't understand. That footage you're showing me . . . that didn't happen today, it happened some other time . . .'

'I'm afraid we can't argue with those time codes,' she said dryly. 'But yes, it doesn't quite match up with what we've been told, so we will be looking into it. And unfortunately the CCTV cameras in the archive haven't worked for some time . . .'

'Listen . . . there are witnesses, who were there, they'll tell you what happened,' he said. 'There was a woman, who took me down to the archive. She'll tell you. That footage . . . it wasn't on the same day.'

'A few have mentioned the twins being a bit threatening in the reading room,' said the detective. 'Maybe a gun or two. But unfortunately, there's no footage of it. We've managed to trace the guns to a farmer who has links to an underground organisation, who is also part of this so-called Smotherhood. Is that where you sourced your weapon?'

Eben was stunned. He had a vague recollection of once meeting a farmer-poet at one of Frankton's soirees. A man who hated his wife with a passion, joked about killing her. He had found it funny; had laughed, even.

'No, no, no. The guns were theirs, the twins' – you do understand that?'

'Apparently, one of the twins left the reading room and transferred the gun to you. That's our deduction anyway. That the three of you were working together on this.'

'What? No, no, you've got this all wrong. This was nothing to do with me. She came down to the archive and she threatened to kill me with it. You can ask the porter – he was there.'

'If you're referring to Dan Matthews, I'm afraid he's deceased.'

Eben took a moment to process this. The gunshots that had rung out on the roof. So someone had been hit.

'Yes, but even then, I'm sure those hostages will tell you that it was the sisters who started all this. You just need to ask them.'

'The spoken word, an eyewitness account aren't what we like to rely on unduly these days. Neuroscience shows us that trauma can make memory fallible.'

'Fallible?' Waves of nausea started to rise in him, his breathing becoming erratic. One of the therapist's affirmations haunted him: *I surrender to the universe*. It was meant to put him at ease, but she had never specified what kind of universe he would be expected to surrender to. What kind of awful reality he would be powerless against.

'Variations or absences can occur. Substitutions of what actually happened. A traumatised brain might, for example, posit a different person in the memory as opposed to the one who was actually there. It may have been, say, yourself and one of the twins holding the guns in the reading room, just like we saw on that roof, only that the traumatised mind had taken you out of the picture because, well, the twins are identical, and they are perhaps less threatening figures, and so—'

'Less threatening? Than me? Who has done nothing? I can't actually believe you would . . .' Eben stopped in his tracks. He needed to think now, to word everything as carefully as he could. Was she really saying an eyewitness account couldn't be relied upon?

'I don't really see where you're going with this,' Eben said, truly exasperated. 'If people say they saw the twins come in with guns, why wouldn't you believe them?'

She was drinking an espresso, now, with great satisfaction, out of a demitasse, and looking mockingly at the ochre-coloured liquid he had to endure from his paper cup.

'Well because a memory is a memory. An experience is shaded, coloured. Without the actual footage to back it up, we can't provide the physical evidence. And that's what we need in terms of corroboration these days. Since they did away with the juries, we need to present a judge with hard facts. Witness statements, yes, of course. But actual video footage that confirms it. Two versions, that make up the whole.'

'But I can tell you exactly what happened,' Eben said. 'I've got a good track record with this sort of thing; I was writing a biography. I know it's not always easy to get at the truth of who a person was but there are enough clues to—'

'Ah yes, this biography,' she scoffed. 'Weren't you investigated for a hate crime against the very writer you're writing about?'

'That was a misunderstanding.'

'Really? I seem to recall that some of your reviews were read at her inquest?'

'Yes, but, look, that isn't relevant now, because—'

'I'd say an accusation of murder is relevant, wouldn't you?'

'It was a narrative verdict, for God's sake. I was just one tiny little piece of—and as it happens actually now, I wasn't even *that*—Look, you've got to listen to me, there are things going on in that library that people know nothing about . . . There are rare books in the basement being turned to pulp as we speak. You've got to do something!'

'Rare books?' The detective raised an eyebrow. 'There are no rare books anymore, Mr Prytherch. Hardly any. The antiquarian collection was destroyed in that fire. It's what inspired the library to complete their extensive digital collection in the first place. It's just a shame that they hadn't gotten around to digitising Ms Oodig's archive, because I'm afraid that, too, has been lost now . . .'

'What?' Eben couldn't process this. The archive had been fine when he'd left it. Covered in plasterboard and dust, perhaps, but intact all the same. *The plume of smoke*, he thought. Had that been Elena's private thoughts going up in flames?

'There was a fire . . . in the archive,' the detective continued. 'You must have been aware . . .'

'Well it wasn't anything to do with me,' he asserted quickly, in case that's where she was going with it.

'Oh no, we know that,' she said. 'The deceased porter had rather unwisely left a spliff burning on a manuscript before he came after you,' she continued. 'Another case of human error, just like in the case of those antiquarian books. In all honesty, I think the library really need to re-evaluate some of their recruitment schemes – the porter had come to them from prison, you see, so it was perhaps to be expected that he'd mess up in some way.'

It took a moment for this to sink in. Another fire. Another set of important documents gone; and a ready scapegoat who was conveniently dead. The letter in the portrait bust Nan had mentioned – he assumed that would be gone too, the flames having snaked their way into it to take away the last of the evidence that could exonerate him.

'They set fire to it themselves! The library!' Eben whispered, almost breathless with the realisation. 'It's how they did it before, too! It's how they explain away the losses. But nothing ever got burnt! It just got pulped and remade. And that missing panel in the archive would have exposed everything they were up to, so they had to cover it all up. And while they were at it – why not erase all of Elena's stuff, too? I mean, if anyone hoarded paper, she did. There would be more than enough there to ship off to the country next door. I can only imagine what a killing they're making out of selling all this paper. And – what luck – the porter's dead, so he can't even tell his side of the story! It's just too easy for them . . . '

'Are you finished now, Mr Prytherch?'

'No, I bloody well am not! Look, if your officers are there now, combing the place, they're going to find it . . .'

'Find what, Mr Prytherch?'

'The place where books go to die. The place where they are murdered at the hands of our own people.'

'They kill books?' the detective said, suppressing a smile. 'All books, or just some books?'

'Books by men, mainly,' Eben continued. 'Although I think Elena might have become a casualty in this particular instance.' A strange feeling of elation rose in him then, in spite of himself. Elena's works destroyed. She had not trumped him after all.

The detective burst out laughing, sat back in her chair.

'OK, well, I'm listening, Mr Prytherch. We've got plenty of time. So go on, tell me about this so-called cover-up of fire. The slaughter of books. The murder of manuscripts.'

'I won't need to, because you're going to find the evidence soon enough, and you won't be laughing then; you mark my words. And besides, I have my own evidence, or at least I did . . . a book of poetry, Eben the Poet's poetry . . . It was in my jacket . . . if you could just check . . .'

'Eben the Poet?' The detective rose another eyebrow. 'Who's he, your alter ego?'

'No, he's one of the poets they killed,' Eben replied, still feeling all around himself for his non-existent jacket and his invisible book.

'Oh so they don't only kill books, they kill people,' she said.

'No, not literally killing him – he's been dead for over a century! But they are killing the memory of him,' Eben said. 'There's more than one way of killing a person isn't there?'

'You see what I mean about the spoken word. It can be confusing, can't it?'

Eben looked up. 'Where are my things? My possessions?'

'If you mean the things that were in your jacket, they are perfectly safe, don't you worry. They're being analysed for evidence.'

'Well once you've done that, I would ask kindly for you to retrieve the small green book in question and bring it to me.'

'I don't take orders from you, Mr Prytherch,' she continued. 'And I have an inventory of your possessions here: shirt; trousers, heavily soiled, I'm told.' She paused, looking up at him, with a wry smile. 'Vest, reading glasses, tissues, some tablets, a nasal spray . . .' She wrinkled her nose. 'Nothing else. All those things have been shown to have vital evidence on them.'

Eben shuddered at the thought of the urine stain being tested, magnified for all to see. But what would they find evidence of, apart from his weak bladder? He supposed he must have certainly touched Ana, in the archive, as she pressed up against him with that gun; would his DNA be on her? The gun undisputedly had his prints all over it. All Elena's possessions would have marks on them too, despite the gloves; bits of his dandruff and eczema covering the floor like confetti. What kind of horrible narrative had he left behind without knowing it? Surely the Eben the Poet collection would exonerate him?

'There was a book! A small green book.'

'I'm afraid not.'

'Well then it must have fallen out of my pocket. It'll be in the police car or the car park. You have to—'

'I think I've indulged you enough, Mr Prytherch. We really ought to get back to discussing the crime you committed here today, don't you think? I'm afraid it's all a little too transparent, this attempt of yours at casting the blame elsewhere, making the library staff out to be schemers and arsonists.'

The detective's screen suddenly pinged with a notification. Seeing her lean in towards the blue light made him suddenly leap to his feet in excitement. He'd forgotten that there were records to back up his story; that someone had recorded the ebb and flow of books.

'The ebb-end!' he said suddenly. 'It's on their files, on the library's system . . .'

'Mr Prytherch, please sit down.'

'That's what they call them. The ebb-end, the male writers they're eradicating from history! And those files are encrypted; you can only get to them with a password, but I'm sure, you know, the police could get access . . .'

'If these files are encrypted, how on earth did you gain access?'

'Oh well it was by accident, really,' he said, feeling like an idiot for getting ahead of himself. 'I was looking for something else . . .'

'It's a very serious crime, gaining access to classified information, encrypted files and the like,' said the detective. 'It could lead to separate prosecution.' The screen in front of her lit up her face again in a deathly glow. 'If you'll excuse me, we have some new information coming through.'

Yet again, Eben felt like he was on the outside, like he was insignificant, like he, too, could be erased whenever they felt like it; made to feel like he wasn't even in the room. It had been this kind of dismissal, he thought, that had led to him swinging that gun around. If only he had it now, to command their attention; though he realised that nothing ended well for a man who brandished a gun; certainly not one who made such a spectacle of it on top of one of the nation's institutions.

The detective typed away on her phone and two other policewomen entered the room. Eben hadn't seen a single male officer since he'd arrived here. He wondered whether it was deliberate, or whether another one of Frankton's theories was actually true: that they were phasing out men in the force.

'Can you let the press know?' the detective said to the policewomen. 'Someone will have to make a statement.'

They nodded their heads and scurried out of the room, leaving Eben alone with the detective. Something about the change in her mood made him think that perhaps she had lost whatever battle she was fighting against him, perhaps some truth had finally come to light; which meant that what she was trying to prove here was fruitless.

'Am I free to go?' he said hopefully, rising to his feet.

'Absolutely not,' she replied, suddenly moving towards him so threateningly that he had no choice but to sit back down immediately. 'We've just had confirmation that a second individual has died from their injuries. One of the twins.'

'What?' Eben took a moment to register this. He transported himself back to the moment he'd been lying on that roof, eyes closed, as the chaos ensued all around him. They'd already been taken away, had they not, by the forces? Could she really be dead, or was it a trick? The detective waiting to see how he'd react?

'Which one,' he asked, 'which one of them is dead?' He thought of the way one of them had softened slightly, on the roof, learning that he was her father. The other one still wanting him dead.

'I don't think it's . . . been confirmed yet . . .' she replied, though it seemed as though she did know, and simply wasn't telling him, for some reason.

'She's . . . she was . . . my daughter,' he whispered to himself, trying to work out how he felt about it all. Now that she was gone, it suddenly floored him. His daughter. Dead. Without him ever having been her father.

'Your daughter?' the detective said, with an incredulous snort. 'The twins are yours?'

'Only on paper really,' he replied, thinking of the letter that was halfway down a dead seagull's oesophagus. That shift from present to past tense had pained him. The twins had been there in front of him all along, in the town, passing him on the street, staring at him at events. Now one of them was gone. All that time wasted. The completely different history he could have had, the person he could have become.

'You're upset, then, I take it,' the detective continued, eyeing him up. 'If what you're saying is true, it's going to affect you a great deal . . .'

Eben's mind was whirring now. Was he upset? He wasn't sure. A few hours ago he would have relished the thought of one of them lying dead at his feet. A day ago, it would have been nothing but a cold fact to digest over breakfast. Now, though, perhaps it was something useful. Something that could get him out of this.

'I was Elena's sperm donor. I wasn't going to tell anyone, but . . . I think it's important that someone knows that this is going to be a bereavement for me. I had a document that confirmed it; I took from the archive, but it's lost now . . .'

'Wait, so you're admitting to taking another document from the archive?'

'It was just a document,' he said. 'A seagull . . . a seagull took it.'

'Oh how convenient,' she said. 'So you took a document that was not yours, an important historical document, and then discarded it like a piece of rubbish.' She paused for thought then as she made her calculations. 'So, this new information, about you being their father, it helps us to make sense of things, doesn't it?'

'Does it?' Eben looked up at her hopefully.

'It's just a shame that we've lost our most valuable witnesses in this case,' she continued. 'The porter and the twin, who might have been able to corroborate all this.'

'Yes, but what about the other twin? Isn't she able to answer your questions? I mean, with all due respect, I think she should have been questioned way ahead of me.'

'She needs to be assessed by our psychiatric team first,' said the detective. 'So, Eben, I can only guess you weren't too pleased to find out that you were their father. Was that what spurred you on? Did you blackmail them both with the information that you were their father, to get them to do things for you . . .'

'No, that isn't right . . .' he protested. 'I didn't make them do anything . . . they . . .'

'They didn't want anyone to know either, did they, and so this is how you eventually got them to agree to let you into the archive. You sourced those guns for them from your farmer friend. You were possessed with the notion that the institution had shunned you, held you responsible for Elena's death, and you thought that if they pretended to hold you hostage, then people would feel sorry for you, and you'd somehow be absolved. You preyed on two innocent girls who had already been driven mad by grief and pushed them into something even more traumatic . . .'

Eben couldn't believe what he was hearing. He thought of the image that could never be eroded now, an image of him standing on top of a roof, waving a gun around like a lunatic. Confirming to everyone, it seemed, that he was responsible for all that had befallen the library that day.

'Look, this isn't what happened at all. And you're ignoring the real issue here, which is those books that they're trying to—'

'You think this will get you out of it, do you?' she asked. 'This notion that somehow this siege was a political act? It's nonsense, this claim of yours. We sent someone to search the building thoroughly, the second we got you out of there, all the places that you and the porter and the twins moved through – the reading rooms, corridors, tunnels, basement. The underground bunker. We have combed them for DNA, for blood, for any sign of wrongdoing. And I'm afraid that what you've suggested, this notion of some kind of literary pulping place, it just doesn't exist, Mr Prytherch. The whole thing was a fantasy on your part. Perhaps as a distraction for what's really going on here. Perhaps it was easier to justify your attack on the library if you thought that they, too, were somehow guilty of something. But when it comes down to it, this was a cold and calculated siege, which has resulted in several injuries and two deaths. Which means it could be deciphered as a murder plot . . .'

'Well yes, there was a murder plot – no one's denying that!' He realised he was shouting, but he didn't care. It seemed the only way to get the message across.

'So you confess?' she said flatly, as though it was of no more interest to her than her next espresso.

'No! The murder plot was to murder *me*!'

'I'm afraid there's no evidence of that, Mr Prytherch.'

Eben was stumped. How could there be no evidence of everything he'd been through, when he felt it, still, along all his veins?

And no sign of those books, the ones he'd seen with his own eyes, the ones that had felt so fragile on his fingertips?

'Look,' he said, his voice no more than a whisper. 'I know what I experienced. I know what I saw. I own my own truth.'

I have the freedom and power to create the life I desire, he thought to himself, rather hopelessly, already feeling as though he would never experience freedom and power ever again.

'Yes, we all own our own truths, which is part of the problem of subjectivity,' the detective continued, yawning disinterestedly as if she had bigger fish to fry. 'The mind makes us see things not as they are, but as we are. Especially when we are trying to deflect from other things. No doubt you were disturbed by your actions today, and it may well be that focusing on those books, finding criminality elsewhere, was one way of dealing with it all . . . Have you considered that maybe what you were seeing in those books was your own wrongdoing, reflected back?'

Eben considered what a troubling, distressing couple of months it had been. And yes, no doubt it would all be used in the case against him. His panic attacks, the way he'd been vilified by the public, put under pressure to do something to prove his worth. He had been in a dark place; no doubt about that. But today, for the first time in months, he'd been happy. Excited, even. He'd had a purpose. His anxiety had been under control; impressively so, considering all that had been thrown at him.

And yet, when he thought about it, wasn't it true that people got better, just before they got worse, that people appeared contented in the days before they killed themselves, or seemed to exude a deathly calm before they killed someone else? Was he, in fact, unbeknown to himself, careering towards disaster from the very moment he woke up that morning, dressing himself up like someone else entirely, about to do everything the wrong way? Had he perhaps threatened Ana when she came in, rather than the other way around? Could he maybe have procured a gun without knowing it, said something stupid to that poet-farmer as a joke which materialised into a terrifying reality? He could barely recall now what he had done in the last couple of days. In fact, nothing came to mind; it seemed that the whole week was a blank. How could he account for his time? He lived alone, with only a cat to testify to his whereabouts. Would it be brought up in court: the fact he couldn't remember the things he had done, that he had no alibi for anything?

He took a deep breath. No, no, this wasn't right. He had seen those books. It wasn't some strange vision of his; or some trick of the light. He had seen them. They existed. Or at least they had, in those moments before they were destroyed. And they must still be there. Because how else could they all be moved, just like that, in front of such large crowds, undetected?

Then he remembered the ambulances. So many of them, too many, a blur of blue, slinking away, one after the other. Carrying more than a dead Dan Matthews and Eben's own dying daughter.

I am not responsible for the death of Dan Matthews, he thought to himself. He tried to utter the same affirmation in his mind about his own daughter, but somehow it would not come, especially as he did not even know which one it was. As a father, should he somehow hold himself responsible, even if he was not? Was there truth in what Nan had said on that roof, that perhaps they were genetically predisposed to doing some of the things they had done, because of some inherent nature foisted upon them from his own corrupted gene pool?

The silence seemed to congeal around him; a whole library's worth. Eben realised it would be the last real silence he would ever experience. He could barely breathe, knowing what was coming. He saw it all in her cold eyes: the fact that it was the country's government who ran everything: the library, the police, the heritage sector. They all owned whatever truth was convenient in the moment; and he would never be able to tell his story.

'I am not responsible for the death of Elena Oodig,' he whispered to himself, one last time, knowing full well he would be held responsible for the death of Elena Oodig and every terrible thing that had come in its wake.

Nan

24 HOURS LATER

The last time she'd been at the morgue, she'd been with her sister. It had been simply a matter of routine procedure back then; for there was no real question whether it would be their mother lying there on the cold slab, any more than there was any doubt in her mind that it would be her sister who would be rolled out in front of her today. But things needed to be done properly; the forms had to be filled in and, more importantly, the police needed to tick their boxes. They pretended, of course, to be allowing her a sense of closure. 'It does help one to cope,' the policewoman had said, as she guided her to the door.

The cleanliness of the morgue was a blessing. The precision of its angles, the mercurial sheen of its disinfected corners. The purity of its emptiness, all unpleasantness stowed away, hidden from view, so unlike the place she and her sister had worked all these months, the corridors and stacks and archives that were bursting at the seams with decaying cadavers of old manuscripts, disembowelled maps, forgotten pamphlets. Half-deaths scrunched up in corners, haunting them, calling out to be revived. At least here, you knew salvation was out of the question.

She was allowed the standard ten minutes on her own with the body. This was the first time she'd been left alone; properly alone, since the siege had come to an end, without doctors or police or liaison officers assessing her, interrogating her, manhandling her. This was the greatest freedom she had felt in days. It still felt like a miracle that there was no one by her side.

Co-operation was key, the detective had said, and would play out so much better for her in court. It had been so much simpler than she'd anticipated; she only had to nod her head in acquiescence at the police station, before signing a witness statement to confirm what they told her had happened. The real sequence of events would not play well for the police, the militia, or the government, and certainly not for the neighbouring country. The fact that they had shot two civilians without questioning them would result in a damning report of government operations. They had also failed to identify an attack as soon as it happened, which had resulted in another woman, a new mother, suffering life-changing injuries, and an elderly academic having to have his leg amputated.

Even worse, one of the hostages, a twenty-four-year-old research student, had suffered a fatal allergic reaction to the sleeping gases released by the militia and had died shortly after in hospital. Someone needed to be accountable for those deaths, the detective told Nan, and – as the psychiatrist had already advised them that it would be fruitless trying to prosecute the surviving twin because of her condition – the detective seemed determined to find another way to bring the case to court. If she co-operated fully, the detective said, and signed the witness statement they had provided for her, then she would be free. The only price to pay was that they wanted her to adapt her story to suit theirs, and certain concessions had to be made.

Reading through the witness statement, Nan tried her best to view it as an attempt at some kind of truth, just that the truth was not arrived at in the usual fashion. It mentioned that Eben was their father, but it also stated that he had used this fact against them, in order to blackmail them into doing certain things. Like those words she so often forgot, the police, too, had *found a path around the story*, and the way she saw it, it fitted their own story perfectly, in the end; for hadn't the main objective been to hold Eben accountable, to have him admit his guilt? Did it necessarily have to be for the exact thing they believed him to be guilty of, providing the long-awaited punishment was finally doled out?

Eben. No matter how else he would be remembered, for all their mother's efforts he would now forever go down in history as their father, because it fitted the story best. The very fact that this was now known by all somehow weakened her hatred for him; for once the very thing she'd worked so hard to keep at bay was out, it seemed to lose all its potency. Everyone had origins, she had begun to tell herself. Beginnings. Not all of them good, or desirable. If Ana had survived, rather than her, Nan knew full well that she would have risen above the embarrassment of being related to him, and found a way to forge a relationship with him, visit him in prison perhaps. Making plans for when he came out, when they could develop a proper father-daughter relationship. She wondered whether she should consider doing the same, before the illness really took hold and her mind completely derailed.

There was still time, she thought, to explore those similarities and differences between them, to see if anything about him helped her to make sense of her own existence. Perhaps he would remind her of Ana, even. His presence filling the gap, for the short time she remembered the loss. It wouldn't matter, ultimately, whether their relationship flourished or not, and if it did, then surely she would be honouring her mother's wishes by punishing him further when she started to drift away. Yes, surely Elena would have loved that, she thought, the final turn of the screw – to think she could still, even in death, snatch his daughters away from him, one by one.

Nan had been happy to comply with their version of events in the end. She even agreed to say she had witnessed Dan taking tobacco and a lighter into her mother's archive, that he was responsible for the fire which had destroyed all her mother's works, although she doubted he had been responsible for anything of the sort. Although she knew how much it would have pained her mother that her work, her memory, had been erased in this way, Nan felt that at least it had swept away all trace of the Creutzfeldt-Jakob disease, and that everything was cleaner this way – for she herself would not be distressed in future by reading about life events she could not remember.

Signing the witness statement felt like letting go of everything that had plagued her these last few months. Choosing a different narrative. For once it was a relief to have someone else decide what should happen next, to simply obey orders. She made one tiny little alteration, however, to the story they seemed so intent on telling themselves. One final little flourish to make it more interesting, without anyone noticing.

The morgue workers did not try to comfort her, or to reel out platitudes. Nan appreciated their clinical way of dealing with things; they were here to show her a body and nothing else. Lifeless skin and bones that needed to be identified in the name of bureaucracy. Ana was dead; that was the fact. And it was, sadly, at the end of it all, an entirely factual, non-literary document that would be the final chapter of someone's life, which showed nothing of their variation, their difference. Nan always thought people made too much of a fuss about their individuality, when really, they were not as different to others as they wanted to believe. Had she not stared into her sister's face on countless occasions and seen nothing but her own face staring back at her, which was both comforting and terrifying? *I am both alone and yet not,* she thought, *not myself and yet wholly myself.* It reminded her of something her mother had said about becoming three people when they were born; never being able to consider herself an individual once she had bred people from her own body. 'I contain multitudes,' she'd said on the days before the illness took her multitude away and began dismantling her into tiny little segments, no longer even one whole thing; just a jumble of parts.

Nan was worried about seeing Ana's face now she was dead. Would it still feel like it belonged to her, had something to do with her? Or would death be the very thing that would split them apart?

A small bald man approached the body bag and undid the zip. She hesitated. What if the bullet had destroyed the face; the thing she knew best? What if seeing her like this took away years of staring into her perfect, unblemished eyes?

Peering cautiously in, she saw that it had not. A cry escaped her; something primal, awful, from deep within herself. She steadied herself. Ana looked beautiful. Perfectly calm. As though death suited her. But with her eyes closed and with the scarf gone from her neck, it was no longer her. The very thing she'd been debating the existence of earlier – individuality – seemed to have been infinitely lost. It had been there all along, right there right under the skin, all those tiny configurations that made a gesture what it was, that made you look at people in a certain way. Perhaps Ana had always been herself, just as Nan had.

'I'm sorry to rush you,' the little man said. 'But I've got another family coming at three. Are you happy to confirm . . . ?'

Nan looked down once more; a final time. She smoothed down one of Ana's eyebrows. Her skin was cold like marble. Nan knew that she would never be compared to anyone ever again.

'Yes, that's her. That's my sister.'

She paused, remembering what the story was; how she had decided not to contradict the assumption they had made.

'That's Nan. Nan Oodig.'

The man seemed satisfied as he pressed his fingerprint to his screen and passed it to her to sign. Nan used her own finger to scrawl the signature: *Ana Oodig*. A palindrome with a different emphasis. Strangely enough, it felt completely natural to her, as if she'd been waiting for this moment her whole life. She was no longer a reflection; she was the only copy. The only surviving thing. And it was a way of keeping Ana alive for herself, hoarding her like a secret inside her, letting Nan, the person she no longer was, take the blame for those things they could not pin on Eben. Nan had shot Dan, they said, before killing herself, hurling herself off the building with him. Isn't that what happened? Nan had nodded away at their assumption; looking up at them helplessly, meekly, like Ana would have done, the way she always looked up at their mother when she wanted to wriggle out of something.

This was the best way to frame it for everyone, Nan thought. Despite Eben's cries to the contrary, the sister on the table in front of her had also been nothing but an accomplice the whole time – impressionable, guileless, psychologically manipulated by those around her.

This was it, she thought, looking down one last time while the morgue attendant glanced anxiously at his watch. The moment of separation they had dreaded all their lives, her very last opportunity to see her sister. They had always prided themselves on never feeling lonely, even when they were alone, knowing that the other one existed in the world. Would that change now that she was really gone, she wondered? Or would that feeling remain, because it was a feeling only twins or multiples could possess, regardless of whether their siblings were alive or not – that notion that they were always part of something bigger?

'Goodbye, Ana,' she whispered, making sure the attendant wouldn't hear her utter her real name. She kissed her sister's cold forehead. 'I'll see you soon. We'll be together again, at some point, I'm sure.'

As Nan walked out of the morgue she felt a surge of relief in having erased herself, once and for all. She had wiped her own record clean. She had become Ana, the way she might have been able to do from the outset, had that zygote held fast in the womb, and allowed only one of them to be born. The baby their mother had planned for.

Stepping into Ana's skin now, she could become that one, whole person that their mother had always expected them to be. She could huddle in Ana's warm skin like an impostor, and keep her alive, for the brief time she had left. Perhaps her own death wouldn't be an actual, physical death, like her sister's, but in a few years, or so the doctor had said, it was possible she wouldn't remember who she was, what she had done, or what kind of life she had led.

She certainly wouldn't remember any of this.

She wouldn't even remember that her name wasn't her own.

Acknowledgements

Many people have helped me, directly and indirectly, to get this novel finished and to find its way out into the world. I am greatly indebted to the National Library of Wales for providing such wonderful inspiration, and also for being a world away from the nightmarish institution depicted in this book. I am also very grateful to Y Lolfa, my publisher in Wales, and especially to Garmon and Lefi Gruffudd for supporting me as I decided to take this English version in a new direction. Thanks also to director and collaborator Euros Lyn for bringing these characters to life on the big screen in such an unforgettable way.

I started writing this book in 2009 while at Iowa University's International Writing Program, and I owe much to the writers I met there, and to program director Christopher Merrill, for making me feel so welcome, and a true part of an international collective. As I eventually gave up on the novel after many failed attempts, I will be forever grateful for the intervention of Wales Literature Exchange, who, in asking me to contribute a chapter to the 'Words Without Borders' Wales issue ten years later, brought this project back to life and made me think in earnest about giving it another go.

Thank you to my agent at AM Heath, Euan Thorneycroft, for finding such a wonderful home for my books, and for being incredibly patient with me as I made my way back from screenwriting to fiction over the course of a decade. Thanks also to my fantastic trio of screenwriting agents Tanya Tillett, Sophie Kelleher and Emily Smith at The Agency who have championed me endlessly and transformed my career. I am also incredibly lucky to have found such a wonderful, collaborative editor in Bethany Wickington, whose astute observations and creative suggestions have improved this book on every level, steering the narrative in new and exciting directions. Thanks also to Hodder and Stoughton for taking me on and seeing the potential in my work.

Thanks to my writing confidantes near and far – Sarah Reynolds, Lowri Hughes and Gunnhild Øyehaug who let me blather on about all things writerly, and especially to Jane Fraser, who read the first version of this manuscript. I am also grateful to Eurig Roberts who allowed me to pick his brains about cyber crime. Thanks also to my mother Menna Elfyn, for allowing me to use her translation of the poem 'Cofio' by Waldo Williams, and for her excellent proofreading services. I am also grateful to my father, Wynfford James, for driving me to so many airports, train stations, and literary events over the years, and I am equally appreciative of the support of my brother Meilyr Ceredig and my surrogate sisters Mari Siôn and Nerys Evans, who set the gold standard for sisters-in-law everywhere.

And last, but not least, a heartfelt *diolch o galon*, to Iwan, Beca and Luned, my beloved crew, who make everything fun, interesting, and worth writing about.